BLOOD
FLOWERS

Published in the UK by Scholastic, 2024
1 London Bridge, London, SE1 9BG
Scholastic Ireland, 89E Lagan Road, Dublin
Industrial Estate, Glasnevin, Dublin, D11 HP5F

ISBN 978 0702 32877 0

A CIP catalogue record for this book is available from the British Library.

Printed and bound in Great Britain by Clays Ltd, Elcograf S.p.A
Paper made from wood grown in sustainable
forests and other controlled sources.

MIX
Paper | Supporting
responsible forestry
FSC® C018072

3 5 7 9 10 8 6 4 2

This is a work of fiction.
Names, characters, places, incidents and dialogues are products
of the author's imagination or are used fictitiously. Any resemblance
to actual people, living or dead, events or locales is entirely coincidental.

www.scholastic.co.uk

JAY McGUINESS

SCHOLASTIC

For my little one. Thank you.
Every single second, silly and sacred.

On the distant town of Calleston, the Cup of the Free City

The wind that moves through endless fields,
From black earth blooms the scarlet yields,
Blue waters, and the yellow sun, flow endlessly in Calleston.

Their rule endured in ages past
and surely thought their rule would last,
But they were razed and then undone
For battling the Feyatung.

Their line was dashed, their war was lost,
Our mighty city named the cost.
And though they came from noble birth,
They bow their heads and turn the earth.

Each night concealed behind their wall,
Enveloped in our mighty thrall,
And far beyond the broken mountain,
Calleston, the ruby fountain.

The town that toils in endless fields,
The scorched earth and the scarlet yields,
Blood flowers flourish, one by one.
They drown the land of Calleston.

Calleston

Tower
Garden

Grub Dock

Overlord

Treat St

Trine Street

The Keep

Corcass Court

Main
Market

Rusty Compass

Main Gate

N

PROLOGUE

He was clearly uncomfortable, she thought. Townspeople were always uncomfortable touching strangers. It wasn't cold, but it was windy, and so she stood close to him at the edge of the town wall. They looked out over the endless, empty fields.

She stood close, but not close enough that their bodies touched. Her arm simply encircled his. She was keen that the man see himself as her protector, and not her guard. However, this one mustn't fall in love with her. That always made things tricky.

The crowd around them was in high spirits. It was a celebration of some sort. The rather dishevelled-looking people packed tightly down below the wall were clearly having a good time. Banging drums, dancing and singing raucously.

Up on the wall, men and women jostled politely for a better view. He stood stiffly. Good. The awkward ones were more easily manoeuvred. He cleared his throat.

"I didn't introduce myself. My name is Aber." He turned to her expectantly.

Here we go, she thought, preparing her lie.

"Elsbeth," she said. *May the name grant me protection.*

"Well, Elsbeth, it looks like we're right on time."

He looks sad, she thought, but maybe that was just his eyes.

She followed where the dark eyes were looking. High above where they stood, among glinting rooftops of the town behind them, a golden flagpole extended up into a clear blue sky. Below the pole, dotted along the marble parapet of a long rooftop balcony, stood a smattering of important-looking figures. They were dressed in a dazzling array of brightly coloured suits and gowns and furs. Though she and Aber seemed shabby in comparison, they were almost invisible amid the opulent surroundings.

She preferred that. They were in the middle of the pack. Discreet. Contained.

At the base of the flagpole, behind a gleaming balustrade, a young man in watchman garb began hoisting a large white flag into the air. The crowd below began chattering excitedly.

She frowned. "Surrender?"

He frowned right back at her, then realizing her meaning, he huffed out a short laugh. "You haven't seen the flag before? Keep your eyes on it."

The material flapped loudly in the wind as it was drawn to the top of the pole. The crowd hushed as crisp white cloth rose up into deep blue.

She glanced at Aber. He was still studying her face. He

2

gestured for her to continue looking upwards. Snapping back and forth in the wind, the large flag was the only sound for a long moment. Then, without warning, and in the blink of an eye, the cloth flooded a deep and unmistakable red.

She gasped. Aber's dark eyes crinkled as a wide smile spread over his face. The people around them erupted into loud cheers, and from somewhere below, the various drums began beating fast, in unison.

"Was that…?"

"Just a trick." He said it almost defensively. It told her everything she needed to know. "Nothing *unnatural*. They dip the material in something just before they hoist it up. It reacts to the air. Or the light maybe. I forget."

He was still looking at her. *He's easy to read*, she thought.

She decided not to look back, to keep looking at the flag. The rapid drumming below was building. He cleared his throat again and continued.

"Just a trick. But I love watching it through new eyes, so thank you."

She turned to look back out over the empty fields. She'd better stop all this talk of eyes and love.

He cocked his head to one side, the way a dog might.

"You're not from this town at all, are you?"

She kept her face as blank as she could.

She needed to tread carefully. The drums continued. He sensed her unease.

"It's OK. Whatever it is you're running from, I don't need to know."

She unclenched her jaw. He carried on.

"Field Day is a day of new beginnings. You … You look like you could use a fresh start, Elsbeth."

She let out her breath. Even in death, sweet Elsbeth was still protecting her.

"So Field Day, the flag turning red… What does it mean?"

"Well, the red flag is supposed to signify a good harvest." He paused a moment. "Truthfully, it does turn red every year, good harvest or not. But really it's the signal for the new bloomers to start the first bloom." He nodded to the fields. "If you liked the flag, you'll love this."

She followed his gaze. Dotted across the field below, spaced around fifty paces apart, were several rows of people, all dressed in white. They stood quietly now. Some wore wide-brimmed hats. Their eyes were closed. Many appeared to be muttering to themselves.

The racing drums stopped.

The crowd hushed.

As one, the people in the field raised their hands and lifted their faces to the sky.

She saw now that they were all young, newly adult. Some held their hands on their chests. Others let their arms drop to their sides.

The drums began again. A slow, steady beat that throbbed out over the fields. The closest in the field was a young, plump girl with glowing skin, freckled by the sun. Her brown hair was very fine, and very long. It flowed around her like silk as she began to turn elegantly on the spot. Her arms opened delicately outwards, like a bird stretching its wings. Behind her, others began going through their own set of motions. Some strong, and others tender, even tentative.

As she watched, she sensed that this moment, these actions, were something personal to each soul. It was like watching someone undress. This was beginning to feel … What was the word Aber used? *Unnatural.*

She felt her heartbeat quicken.

She placed her hand on his forearm. They watched together.

The girl with the fine hair smiled a sweet, closed smile. Her whole body leaned to one side like a sapling in the wind. Her hair wafted like a sheer curtain. The drum was a heartbeat. The girl extended her arms outwards and to one side. Her fingers seemed to play an instrument that nobody could see.

And then, as unnerving and as quiet as bleeding, neat rows of shoots surfaced from the ground beneath her twirling fingertips. As one, they bloomed into deep red flowers, an unrelenting scarlet eruption that continued to extend as the young girl let her hands drift in front of her. More red petals blossomed where her arms flowed, twisting and unfurling into the light. The girl sighed. Her closed smile opened wide. As did her arms.

Like blood in water, the red blooms spread far and wide. Each person in the field began to cultivate their own pools. A red tide.

She couldn't believe her eyes. Elsbeth had been right. After all this time. She had found it. Magic.

Springing up in a corner of the land thought long dead. As simple and as clear as morning.

She felt a tear roll down her cheek.

She looked up at Aber.

He was so very stupid not to see it for what it was.

He couldn't see because he didn't want to.

He was easy to read.

He looked at her as if he had discovered a magic of his own.

Oh dear. *He's clearly falling in love*, she thought.

CHAPTER

Bear looked back across the field at the town rising crookedly beyond the town wall.

"Did you hear that?"

"What?" said Felix, glancing over his shoulder as he worked.

"I thought I heard a scream."

"Not unusual, for this town."

That was true. Wandering the streets at night had never been a good idea in Calleston, and wandering outside the walls was even worse. But these days the screams had become more frequent than ever before. The people were hungrier and more desperate. And when darkness fell, it felt more and more like there was something sinister in the air, something—

"We still on for the plan?" said Felix, interrupting Bear's thoughts.

Bear hesitated. Right now, things didn't look so bad. The sun was getting low, the deep blue of the sky slowly making way for orange. Dotted around them, the workers of Calleston weeded the fields. It was still warm, it was still light and they were still comfortably close to the town wall. Yet Bear couldn't help but shiver as the day shifted into something else. Suddenly, what he and Felix had planned didn't seem like such a good idea.

Felix turned and frowned at him. "You wimp!"

"It's getting late already."

"You're scared, Bear. Admit it." Felix put his hands on his hips and raised an eyebrow. "We need to practise, right? Field Day could be announced any day now. This might be our last chance."

Bear nodded. A good harvest this year was not just desirable – it could be the only thing that saved the people of Calleston. The sinsenn blooms that were the town's prize export had been poor for years now, even with more and more land being allotted to the growers. Calleston was starving, and the Queen would not send aid until the harvest improved, for the Queendom had an insatiable taste for sinsenn.

"Well, then," said Felix. "Stop whining."

"I'm not whining," he said, shooting an anxious look at the dark forest that edged the fields. I'm just … keeping track of time. And so should you."

Felix lugged his field sack down the ploughed lines of Top Field, away from Calleston's thick stone walls, to where a large pile of dark, thorny vines was being burned. A billowing column of black smoke curled up into the sky, where it hung, twisted, like an old tree root.

Bear turned and plodded after Felix. The bronze skin

of his friend's back shone in the light of the setting sun. Speedweeding was strenuous work and Felix had long ago removed his scratchy cotton work shirt, baring the golden skin that, along with his pointed ears, revealed his Fennex blood.

Bear unbuttoned his shirt as the sun faded behind the town. He never took it off during the day – he had skin that burned easily. He gazed down at the top of Felix's head. Bear was a good foot taller than his friend, but as Felix was quick to remind people, Fennex were notoriously strong, and renowned fighters, despite their diminutive size.

It had been a hard winter; people were hungrier than ever, and Felix and Bear were no exception, though Felix was proud that his athletic form didn't show the same signs of the shortages as his human neighbours. The load weighed more heavily on Bear than usual as they stomped across the field, matching field sacks on their shoulders, matching wide-brimmed field hats on their heads.

He was grateful for the straw hat's protection from the sun, but today he was more grateful that it hid him from the scrutiny of the watchmen up on the wall, and especially from the rather sour-looking watchman who patrolled the field.

Today, the field workers were tasked with pulling up speedweed: a dark, thorny plant that could grow by an arm's length in a day. It had really taken hold in the last few weeks, streaking across Top Field in record time, choking out the sinsenn seeds the workers had so diligently planted. Field workers, who were already exhausted, were sent back in their droves to pull up the speedweed before it had a chance to destroy the entire harvest.

Bear's father, Aber, complained that it was the worst year for the blight in living memory. Each year more speedweed, and less sinsenn to be exported throughout the Queendom.

Thankfully, it looked like most of the thorny disease had been removed. Just a bit remained, encroaching from the outer edge, where the field met the dark forest beyond. The boys walked towards the gloomy forest. Bear stopped dutifully here and there to pull tendrils of the creeping speedweed from the earth. His shoulders ached, but he preferred being out in the fields, away from Calleston, away from the dark, dingy streets of Cobbleside where the workers lived, and away from the unsettling, judgemental gaze of the Roofsiders that lived above them.

Roofside was where the highborn and the successful mingled. If a Cobblesider showed a talent for growing, they might one day be moved to live in (or at the very least retire to) the roof – the wish of every young field worker. For years, though, no one had been invited Roofside. The harvests had been too poor. The Overlord did what he could for the Cobblesiders – they knew he was a hardworking man who cared about the townsfolk – but the town was in need of aid from the Queen, even to feed itself. The fields around Calleston were now used exclusively for the growing of sinsenn, by the Queen's orders. The people grew and caught what food they could inside the town's wall, and the Overlord distributed food from his stores and fish from his lakes as generously as he could, but rumour was that even the lake was nearing exhaustion.

A lot was riding on this Field Day.

Bear dabbed at the sweat on his forehead with a grimy sleeve and looked back towards the town walls. He could see his father and his uncles were heading inside now along with the others, leaving the pile to burn. They filed along the wall and in through the gates, one by one.

"Someone's bound to see us," Bear mumbled.

Felix's amber eyes shone with a mischievous glint. "I knew you were going to chicken out! Come on, Bear! We aren't gonna get many more chances like this."

"We'll be lashed if they catch us, and then my father will finish the job."

Felix nodded. "True, but look on the bright side: they won't whip us before Field Day. They need us on good form."

Bear considered Felix's point. It was a good one. Having the new generation of growers arrive with bloody welts on their hands might dampen the festive spirit a bit. He stooped to pull a particularly vicious-looking weed from the earth. He placed it, dark roots and all, into his field sack.

Bear jumped as a watchman shouted, waving his arms wildly at them.

"Finish up, then get inside! I'm not waiting on anyone!"

His lips were stained dark.

"Why's he so angry if he's already drunk a ruby brew?" Felix muttered under his breath.

They waved their understanding, and the watchman headed for the gates.

Felix grinned. "Once he's through the gate, let's settle in that bushy area by the trees. No one will be able to see us there."

Bear peered anxiously over to where Felix was pointing. Admittedly, it was perfect: an overgrown patch of speedweed spreading from the forest into the field, grown high enough and far enough away from the town for it to be hard for anyone watching to see them.

But it wasn't just the eyes in the town that worried Bear. It was the eyes beyond those trees...

He shivered as he peered into the dark forest. Felix saw where he was looking and bristled.

"Don't start, Bear! It's way too early for blots! The sun isn't even behind the town yet!"

Bear knew Felix was right. Blots came out once the sun was down. They couldn't tolerate sunlight, but recently there had been worrying sightings of blots in the fields earlier and earlier in the night, and Bear didn't want to take any chances.

When the blot sightings had been much rarer, people had lived in homesteads in the fields as well as in the town. Now that the forests crawled with them, the town stayed safe within their walls, venturing outside only in the daylight hours.

The sight of a blot was chilling, and something you never forgot. In the dark, they almost looked human. They could be any hunched figure. In the dark, it was hard to see their mottled, decaying skin, their large, coal-black eyes or the rows of needle-like teeth that jutted out of their rancid mouths.

In the dark, you might think them a man. But the way they moved … that was unmistakable.

"Don't even put that thought in my head!" said Felix. "I struggle to concentrate as it is."

Bear turned from the trees and looked back at the gate. Only Megg still stood there, facing out towards the field. Bear watched her as she tucked a few loose curls back into her field hat and looked for them, a frown on her face. When she spotted Bear, she smiled and waved. Bear smiled. He had wondered if she would wait for him, for the both of them.

She wiped her dirty hands on her breeches, dabbed the sweat from her brow with the back of her hand, before signing in Field-Speak, *Are you coming?*

The boys responded simultaneously, rubbing a finger and thumb together. *Soon.*

Megg frowned.

One last patch. Near the trees, said Bear.

Megg nodded, but she kept standing there, her large brown eyes troubled.

"She's so thin," said Bear to Felix in a low voice.

"She is," Felix agreed. "So let's do this and make sure this harvest is a good one."

Bear grunted.

"She's definitely on to us," Felix said through his teeth.

Before Bear could respond, Megg's arms flailed wildly and she fell backwards.

Behind her, Cassius grinned widely. He'd yanked Megg to the ground by the hat strap round her neck. She didn't even cry out – the watchmen's responses to such things were often brutal, and usually indiscriminate.

Bear fumed. *Get off her!*

Felix, as usual, fumed harder.

I hope you choke! Do one, Cassius, you blotson!

Cassius laughed. *Says a Fennex and the son of a* Feyatung! he signed.

The word hit Bear like a punch to the stomach.

Felix began marching towards them as Cassius sauntered towards the gate with the rest of his gang.

Megg stood quickly and crossed her hands open a few times. *Don't bother, Felix! Ignore him. He's not worth it.*

Are you all right? Bear signed.

I'm fine. Just … come soon?

They agreed.

She slung her field sack over her shoulder and headed towards the gate as if nothing had happened. Megg would do anything to avoid the watchmen's notice. Bear watched her sadly as she went. She walked slowly to let the others pull ahead. Cassius lived directly above Megg's home, and the pride of it had settled in his bones. Bear was tempted to go after her.

"Don't you worry, Bear," said Felix. "He'll get what's coming to him."

Bear sighed. "The weird thing is that I think he likes her."

Felix pulled his wild hair up into a knot. "Well, he hasn't got a chance," he said, shooting Bear a sidelong look. "Clearly she's in love with you."

Bear felt his face burn. "Shut up," he said, kicking at the ground. "We're just friends. Like you two are. Like you and me. It's the three of us."

Felix's amber eyes regarded Bear's a moment, then he shrugged. "If you say so."

The field was empty now; it was only them left.

"Right," Bear sighed, turning towards the trees. "Let's get this over with."

The Overlord's daughter looked out over the town, towards the fields beyond.

She people-watched every day, and as of recently the boy was her favourite person to watch. Him and his friends. They were usually together, the boy, the Fennex and the girl.

Meya wondered what it would be like to be down there with them. The floorborn seemed so busy all the time, every day some project to work on together. She was annoyed to find herself wishing she were among them, even dreaming of them.

The sun was getting lower now, so it was harder to see. She needed to get up higher. Next time she should try to watch from the top of Snakewood Tower.

She leaned further forward, squinting into the half-light.

What were the two boys doing out there? They were going in the wrong direction. Surely a watchman should be calling them in by now? It wouldn't be too long until night would fall and—

Percy barked loudly.

She jumped and knew immediately she had lost her balance. Tumbling dizzyingly from the wall, she felt her skirts rip before she fell heavily into the bushes below.

Percy growled low in his throat. She looked across the gardens from where she lay. Lord Noka was snooping about in the distance.

"Yes. Thank you, Percy. I see him," she panted.

Meya lay still. Noka wouldn't like the sight of her torn dress. He had only just lectured her on being wasteful during Calleston's continuing misfortunes. She frowned when Noka slipped into Snakewood Tower, not that he shouldn't, only that he did it so carefully.

"I see him," she repeated, scratching Percy's head.

CHAPTER

2

"How is it growing so fast?" Bear muttered.

They were at the edge of the field now, hiding behind the tall patch of speedweed that they hoped would shield them from view.

"Clue's in the name," said Felix.

"I know ... but there's so much of it."

Speedweed was relentless. In the forest, the dark vines choked the underbrush; it was the second-best reason to never venture into the trees. Field workers constantly pulled, cut and burned the nasty vines that sped across the fields. Still, it had never been quite this bad before.

"Ow," said Felix as a tiny barb scratched at his ankle.

The larger thorns, near the base of the stem, were the size of owl's claws and easier to avoid when pulling them up, but the barbs that edged the new growth were no bigger than an eyelash, and acutely painful if they broke the skin.

Bear took in the position of the sun. It was almost behind the top spire of the Overlord's quarters now.

"Come on," he said. "Fifteen minutes – then we should go inside."

"You said that five minutes ago."

"All right, then – ten minutes. Let's go."

Bear and Felix dropped their field sacks on the ground, found some clear earth among the speedweed and sat down opposite each other. Bear looked over at the burning pile of speedweed by East Gate, the tendril of black smoke and the town beyond.

From here, Calleston looked deceptively beautiful, like a dark, glinting castle. A few lights blinked on in the lower levels of Cobbleside as darkness began to fall. The market, and the base of the Keep would be in shadow soon too. But the upper Keep, Roofside – all the houses of the highborn – were still soaking in the golden sunset, thrust into the light by the crooked mishmash of Cobbleside houses below.

"Ready?" Bear asked.

Felix grinned, then closed his yellow eyes. He began drumming out a beat in his lap.

The plan this evening was to connect with the seeds, to enlace with them, but not grow them into flowers. Enlacing a human mind with the curious red flowers was the way sinsenn bloomed. It was something that the people of Calleston had done for generations, and it enabled those who were gifted growers to turn the dormant seeds into seedlings, then a bloom, in an instant.

Usually, for youngsters hoping to become growers, there were months of practice, led by Rose, who was the most prolific grower in Calleston. But this year, thanks to the infected fields, the workers had had to dedicate most of their time to weeding, leaving them little time to practise and prepare for the big day, Field Day. And so Felix had convinced Bear to practise out of hours.

Bear breathed in the smell of the earth.

He closed his eyes and joined Felix, thudding the palms of his hands on to his thighs in a simple rhythm. He tried to let his mind relax.

DUM dum, DUM dum, DUM dum…

Megg would be home with her sisters by now.

DUM dum, DUM dum, DUM dum.

She did look a bit unwell… He shook his head… Focus!

DUM dum, DUM dum, DUM dum,

DUM dum, DUM dum, DUM dum…

Ah … there it was.

A quiet rushing.

The pounding of his palms on his thighs was suddenly deeper, more muffled.

DUM dum, DUM dum, DUM dum…

He relaxed into his mind's eye.

DUM dum, DUM dum, DUM dum…

He felt an endless folding into himself.

DUM dum, DUM dum, DUM dum…

The rhythm was a wave that carried him outwards and inwards. He was connected. He had begun to enlace.

Bear could feel and extend beyond his fingertips into the earth around him. Clusters of red sinsenn seeds vibrated happily as they felt the gaze of his mind's eye wash

19

over them. He let the surge of an all-encompassing pulse pull him back and forth, and he introduced himself to each seed. He had forgotten how joyful it felt to be connected to the red spirits in the ground.

When enlaced, Bear could taste and smell in unfamiliar ways. It gave new perspective to the plant life around him. He felt the soil, the water and the very air carrying information that was undetectable otherwise.

Bear tried to grasp the full picture of what he was connected to.

First, a happy gang of sinsenn seeds was clustered to his left.

Here, a lone seed to his right was overwhelmed with excitement. Through Bear, it sensed its neighbours nearby.

Ah! Here was a group of five seedlings, all in a line. The regimented group waited patiently for instructions.

Bear let his mind expand through the earth like an underground cloud. As he did, he felt the beginnings of roots forming within the seeds.

Then he felt something else. Something sickening on the edge of his territory. The nasty grip of speedweed overwhelming a patch of young sinsenn seeds. When enlaced, he could smell the invader, taste it in his mouth. The sinsenn seeds were deformed by the malignant tendrils that encircled them, stunting their growth, corrupting their development. Bear couldn't stand it. He felt wretched. He needed to protect the seeds. He had to help them.

Bear drove his mind deeper into the soil, like toes

sinking into sand, submerging himself till all other thoughts disappeared. He made a mental note of the tarnished seeds and turned his attention to the rest. He guided the newly growing sinsenn roots to avoid the rotten stench of speedweed in the earth. Then, stretching out his hands, he created a pulse that flowed through the seedlings below, focusing on extending their root tips. A buzz of action began. Vibrations, like a cluster of shooting stars in the dark, growing keener, and stronger and—

"Bear!"

It took a moment for Bear to realize the whisper was coming from above ground, from somewhere in front of him, from Felix. He felt familiar shapes reform around himself as he came out of his trance and his eyes snapped open.

Felix's eyes were wide with fear. But they weren't looking at Bear. They were looking past him, towards the trees.

"Bear," Felix whispered, panicked.

Bear grunted his quiet acknowledgement. The smell of rot was in the air.

Bear's blood ran cold.

"It's behind you," Felix whispered, trembling. "Bear, don't!"

Bear turned his head, squinting in the direction in which Felix was gazing. A cluster of pine trees: thick, tall trunks, darkness between. That was all. Except…

His vision refocused, acclimatizing to the shadows, until … goosebumps ran up his arms. There it was.

It looked like an old man, a shadow, hunched among the tree trunks. It was motionless, facing almost in their direction, but not quite. The smell emitting from the dark entity made Bear want to gag. Festering flesh and rot.

His voice came out low and hoarse. "Felix. We have. To. Run."

Felix nodded, and they pushed themselves slowly to their feet. Neither pair of eyes left the blot, who still stood motionless in the shadows.

They took one measured step, and waited.

Another step.

The blot snapped its head in their direction.

It made a wet noise with its mouth as its jaws fell open.

They froze.

The smell worsened.

Felix dared to whisper. "We need to—"

The blot jolted into action, hurtling from the trees towards them, its feet snapping through bracken and broken twigs.

"Run!" cried Felix.

The boys fled for their lives. Silence being useless now, Felix screamed, "Help! Blot!" as they raced towards the town wall.

There was yelling from somewhere in the town. Lights appeared above the walls and calls of "Blot!" began echoing along the walkways.

His heart pounding in his ears, Bear tried desperately to gauge how close the blot was. Maybe five, ten metres behind him? They had the whole field still to cross. Bear was not a fast runner, and the blot was gaining... A dreadful realization settled in his chest: he couldn't make it.

There was a thudding sound from behind, then a furious screech. The blot had fallen. Bear glanced back and saw that it had sprinted straight into the boys' field sacks. It tumbled with the bags as they spilled their thorny vines. Thank the Overlord. That had bought them a little time.

Felix was halfway down the field now and still screaming for help. Bear feared they would shut the East Gate. It was dark enough now, and if they saw an advancing blot, there would be no hesitation even if Felix and Bear were stuck outside. It had happened before.

Still, those relentless feet behind him were getting louder. He was so slow compared to Felix. He tried focusing on the open gate as he pumped his legs, faster and faster, his heart pounding, his leg muscles threatening to cramp... Then suddenly his hairs prickled; he heard more footfall from behind him. Two blots? He didn't dare look back.

Ahead of him, Felix crashed into the shallow waters of the moat that surrounded the walls. Bear focused on Felix and the straw hat that bounced at his neck, a dancing disc, a rabbit's tail, bobbing and weaving.

The hat gave Bear an idea. He ripped his own hat from round his neck and spun it out into the field to his left. The sound of the blot's footfalls faltered, and swung to the left... He'd gained another few precious seconds. Bear pumped his legs as hard as he could, knowing the blot would be back on his tail in no time.

Then bile rose in his throat as he saw his worst fear come to life – the gate was closing.

"No! Please!" Felix shrieked as the gate chain whirred, and the East Gate came crashing down, sealing the town wall shut. Arrows started whizzing over his shoulders. As Bear splashed through the moat after Felix, he heard shouts from the wall.

"There's two!" and, "It's the Fennex lad! And Aber's boy!"

They skidded to a halt at the locked gates.

"Open the gates!" they both screamed.

No one had even thrown a rope.

"Bear!" Felix shouted, pointing at the beams jutting out above the gate.

Bear looked behind him. The blots, ever cautious of water, slowed as they crossed the moat. They screeched but didn't stop as they began to wade their way across. The water wasn't deep enough to deter them.

Bear slammed his shoulder against the wall for support as Felix inserted his foot into Bear's cupped hands. Bear catapulted Felix upwards. His hands stretched upwards, grasping on to the beam above the gate. Faces peered over the walls, but still no rope.

Bear turned to see how long he had left. A stark realization crossed his mind. He was about to become a bedtime story, a warning to children about the dangers of staying out after dark. So strange to be so close to safety, and so far. He was glad Felix had made it – there was that, at least.

And there they were. The blots slipped out of the shallow water, gliding quietly towards him like dancers, sensing they had him trapped. It was the first time he had ever seen them so close. Like shadows of men. Like walking corpses, driving straight for him. Dark, shiny eyes. Gaping wet mouths filled with red, bloody tongues that they worked tirelessly around, making awful sucking sounds. And the smell. Bear gagged.

"Bear, jump!" Felix called as he swung towards Bear, hanging upside down from the beam, his hand outstretched for Bear's. Bear jumped and reached upwards. He felt Felix's strong hands grasp his wrist, grunting heavily as he swung Bear up and up, out of the reach of the creatures below, until he crashed against the town walls. Bear's stomach flipped as he felt himself begin to slip.

"Grab the wall!" screamed Felix.

And then, as he began to fall, Bear's fingertips found the rough, jutting edge of the stonework. He gripped fingers around a protruding stone with all his might. His bare feet slipped against stone until he found the slimmest of footholds, then another. Felix had pulled himself up to stand on the beam and was already picking his way higher above the gate.

"Climb, Bear!" he barked.

Bear found a better handhold and heaved himself higher against the wall. His hands felt strong, but his knees were shaking. His breath came in hard grunts. He didn't dare to look down. He just kept pulling himself up, his heartbeat deafening in his ears. Arrows whizzed past him, and below the blots screeched at their escaping prey.

"Keep going, lad," came a clear voice.

He saw hands reach out and pull Felix over the lip of the wall. Bear's mouth was dry. His arms burned, but his hands grasped each crack and protrusion with an iron grip. He turned to look down.

The blots clawed at the gate, but couldn't do much more than leap for the beam, collect arrows and work their wet mouths. Bear felt his wrist grabbed strongly by a rough hand. He looked up. A man with a shaved head and a moustache. It was Uncle Jim.

"Well, I never," said Uncle Jim quietly.

Bear let himself go limp as he was pulled up over the wall into flickering firelight. Into safety.

Bear gasped as the bucket of cold water hit him.

He and Felix had been stripped to their underclothes, placed side by side on wooden chairs and doused with water. Old Fern was checking them for scratches or marks on their skin. Bear's feet hadn't touched the cobbled ground since he and Felix were hauled over the wall and bustled by the crowd into the light of the closest tavern, the Rusty Compass.

"We weren't bitten," Bear heard himself saying repeatedly, as if from a distance. The shock and the exhaustion were a haze hanging in his head.

He heard the voice of Old Fern in his ear: "I'll be the judge of that."

Old Fern had seen many of the rare few who survived an attack lose their lives to the rot. Even inconspicuous cuts had ended young lives far too soon.

Felix opened his arms wide. He compliantly turned his face left and right as he was inspected. He caught Bear's eye, and grinned, rolling his eyes.

"Not a scratch so far," said Old Fern with a nod.

She reached for a quick swig of her drink. Ruby brew was made from the red flowers of the sinsenn plant, and there was one effect: a wonderful calming feeling that brought smiles and loosened tongues, without any of the intoxication or headaches that came with fruitwines or ale.

Bear coughed as Cusht walked over to them and blew a big cloud of red smoke in his face. Like ruby brew, a puff on a sinsenn pipe was enough to slow the heart, calm hysteria, even lessen grief. Unfortunately, the effects were temporary. So most of the town, especially down in Cobbleside, steadily puffed on their pipes throughout the day.

"You just stumble from one misfortune to the next, don't ya, lad?" said Cusht. He had known Bear since he was born.

Bear didn't respond. He let the warm lights and the chatter in the tavern wash over him.

"Two full-grown blots clingin' on to the gate with claws like an old crone!" Cusht boomed to the crowded rooms. "Never seen 'em get so high in my life. Scares me thinkin' about it..."

Bear heard much of the response, though he didn't react.

"He was this close to gettin' chomped. Just imagine."

"The wee Fennex one?"

"Not 'im," said a voice. "That other one. It's Aber's lad, the one whose mum—"

"Enough!"

Uncle Jim's voice stilled much of the nearby chatter of the

tavern. Bear snapped out of his daze. The onlookers were baulking at the look on Jim's face as much as his outstretched hook. Only the wizened hands of Old Fern remained on Bear's skin. She calmly continued her inspection.

The crowd dispersed and rejoined the bustling bar, most likely to spread details. It was quite a story; not only had the boys survived, but they'd scaled the outer wall without a rope.

Bear let Old Fern lift his foot and rub the dirt away, examining his skin for the slightest scratch. He could still see the gaping mouths of the blots as they stepped from the shallow waters, studying him with their shiny black eyes…

"They're all right, Jim," said Old Fern as she completed her inspection. "As far as I can see." She tossed the boys their outer clothes and they began getting dressed.

"What have you let this little fe—" She caught herself – "Fennex boy drag you into, ey? I hope you're both counting your lucky stars…" She looked at them kindly. "I'll get you a ruby brew."

Felix grinned as he pulled on his trousers. Bear shook his head.

"No thanks, Fern," he said, sitting back down. Even with his heart hammering in his chest, Bear refused to drink ruby brew, or anything made with sinsenn. His father would never forgive him for that.

Uncle Jim crouched down in front of them. His moustache twitched.

"Bear, lad, one ruby brew will settle you."

Bear shook his head. "Father wouldn't like it."

Jim's face was impassive. Bear couldn't tell if he were furious at the pair of them or concerned, so he remained quiet.

"You shouldn't have been out this late. What were you thinking?"

"Where were the watchmen?" Felix asked. "They should have been on the wall."

"I asked you what you were doing out there."

"Weeding. We were weeding," Felix said quickly. "We found a giant patch of speedweed and we wanted to pull it before we came back inside. Field Day's coming up! We know how important this year's harvest is... Sorry, Jim. We lost track of time."

Uncle Jim rubbed his moustache in thought, then reached over and discreetly patted Bear's pockets. He was looking for sinsenn seeds.

"We aren't thieves!" Felix protested. "And we're not stupid enough to try anything that'd leave us out there with the blots."

Jim looked at them both, then pressed the point of the hook on the end of his arm into the wood above Felix's head. "I'll remind you I lost this hand to a blot, Fennex. And a lot more than the hand... If you were playing the fool out there, I don't mind giving you another haircut."

Felix's yellow eyes widened. Uncle Jim had once cut off Felix's top knot upon discovering a missing dagger concealed in his field sack.

"Honestly, we weren't stealing." Bear glanced quickly around the room. "We were practising enlacing."

Felix's jaw dropped open at Bear's admission. Bear didn't stop.

"Sorry, Jim. I know we shouldn't have, but we need to practise. We aren't ready for Field Day. All we do is tear out speedweed."

Uncle Jim looked furious. Bear lowered his voice. "We left the sinsenn seeds where they were, and we only enlaced with a tiny patch…"

"Here we are, lads!" came the voice of Old Fern. She was carrying two cups.

"Now these are on the house, but if your uncle fancies one he'll have to add it to his tab." She raised her eyebrows frostily as her gaze settled on Jim's hook hand, firmly stuck in the wooden beam behind Felix's ear. "Don't let my walls go blunting that point, Jim Garrason."

Uncle Jim pulled the hook from the timber beam and attempted to buff out the mark with his elbow sheepishly.

"My apologies, Fern. It's been a night. Yes, I'll take a ruby brew for when I'm back. I'm going to fetch the boy's father."

"No need."

Bear jumped to his feet at the sound of his father's voice. Aber emerged from behind Old Fern. She turned to look up at him, then placed her hands on either side of his face.

"Now, not to worry, Aber. Not a scratch on them, and

31

you heard they scaled the walls?"

"I heard." Aber's eyes were fixed on his son.

"It was a close one, by the sounds of it, but no harm done. They'll not be staying out past twilight again any time soon. We're out of food, but since I never see you, can I get you a ruby brew on the house?"

Aber frowned and shook his head.

"Suit yourself," said Old Fern as she disappeared through the arched door.

Bear felt people in the tavern stealing glances at their corner. Aber never came to the Rusty Compass. Bear remembered his parents sharing a drink there when he was a child, when his mother was still around, but his father hadn't drunk a ruby brew or smoked a pipe since.

Now, Aber's gaze rested on the cup in Bear's hand. "What's that, boy?"

"Fern got it for me. I wasn't going to drink it."

Uncle Jim held out his hand.

Bear passed it to him obligingly.

Aber eyed him. "I'm sure you weren't. Now, what were you doing beyond the walls?"

"Weeding." Bear glanced briefly at Jim, whose face remained impassive. He wouldn't give them away.

Aber shook his head in disbelief.

"You risked your life to pull black vines?" He held Bear's gaze and sneered when Bear didn't respond. "Idiocy."

"It was my fault, Aber! I convinced him to stay." Felix's voice was polite but firm.

"Quick to name yourself a fool there, Fennex. Why would you convince my son to do something so stupid?"

Felix's nostrils flared with indignation, but he kept his mouth shut.

"Brother, they couldn't have known the blots would be roaming at half-light. More confident now even than last summer. We're getting pinched beyond reason, Aber, all of us."

Bear was surprised to hear Uncle Jim defend them. As he watched the two men, Jim fixed Aber with a look that carried some meaning Bear couldn't decipher. Aber looked distressed. He ran his hands through his slate-grey hair, then shook his head.

"Where was the watchman?"

"No watchman on East Gate, and no rope neither," said Uncle Jim. "It was Burna saw the boys, had the good sense to send young Dorloc. Dorloc had the whole tavern out and running for the gates. The boys were already scaling the walls when we got there. You should've seen them climb, Aber, and without a rope – Bear launched Felix clear on the top of the gate like it was nothing. And this one." He waved his hook at Felix. "He pulled Bear up easy as an eagle pulling fish from the water. I wouldn't believe it if my eyes hadn't seen it. The way they climbed … why, they could make it from East Gate to the boatyard and never touch the floor."

Felix looked proud, but Aber was unmoved.

"They need to focus on getting prepared for Field Day,

not tempting blots out of the forest." Anger sizzled under his calm exterior as he spoke to Bear. "You're lucky no one died because of your stupidity. This time."

Bear looked down at the floor.

"From now on, you're to come inside the gates soon as the sun dips behind the rooftops. Is that clear enough for you? Since you don't have the sense to judge for yourself."

Then he turned and headed out again.

"Aber! Not seen you in 'ere in an age!" Cusht called from across the room. "Not since all that horrible business with the wife…"

Bear winced, but thankfully Aber was already out the door. The whole tavern was awash with sinsenn and unable to stop themselves blurting whatever came to mind.

Uncle Jim spoke quietly. "Your father was worried, lad. I'll go speak to him. But don't you two leave – I need to talk to you about something. Meet you up top in two shakes," he said, motioning towards the upper floor of the Rusty Compass.

He strode off after Aber. Bear exhaled a sigh of relief.

"No need to look so glum," said Felix with a nudge. "Could've gone a lot worse."

"Do I look glum?"

"You look like a bulldog licking piss off a nettle."

Bear smiled. "I'm all right – just feel a bit weak."

"Me too. My knees are still going, look."

They looked down at Felix's knees. They were jiggling like mice in a sock.

Softly, Felix added, "I really thought they were going to kill us."

The boys shared a look. There weren't really words to describe the feeling. Calleston people knew danger, and they knew death intimately, through destitution, sickness or misfortune. The undertakers were never short of work. But narrowly escaping the horrifying death by blot brought the danger of their world more sharply into focus.

"Thanks for the hand," said Bear.

"Thanks for the leg up."

"Maybe me."

"Maybe me."

Felix nodded and took a long drink of ruby brew. They sat together in silence for a while.

"They're bigger than I thought."

Bear didn't like thinking about the blots. He changed the subject. "How did enlacing go? I could *feel* the blight spreading in the sinsenn seeds. All soft and rotted. Did you notice?"

Felix's face dropped. "I ... I couldn't connect to anything."

Bear had half suspected it. He knocked Felix's knee. "There was too much speedweed around us – that's why. Next time—"

"You think there'll be a next time?" Felix scoffed. "After what your dad said? We'll not get another practice in now. I'm officially doomed."

Felix looked miserable. Last year, he'd only been able to sprout a tiny red flower (though Bear wasn't entirely convinced that it hadn't already been there before). He'd had no more luck since then, and Field Day would be announced at the Overlord's pleasure, usually with only a couple of days' notice.

"You're not doomed, Felix. Everyone's going to struggle to grow anything this year. Dad said the harvest used to surround the entire town in red flowers on Field Day. The most we've seen is half of Top Field, and that was when we were waist-high." He sighed. "Who knows, we might actually have to abandon the town. I mean, the blots are one thing, but if we can't grow sinsenn, what are we even here for?"

"Brilliant, thanks, Bear." Felix rolled his eyes. "Who needs reassurance when we have despair?"

He hopped off his chair and downed his ruby brew. "Come on. I need another one."

Bear followed Felix through the tavern. Immediately, the townspeople surrounded them and the questions began.

"We were sure you'd been bitten," said a short woman with cropped white hair and black designs inked over the skin on her arms. "Would have been awful. After everything with your poor mum, don't know what your dad would've done."

"Don't mind Burna," a large, muscular woman called Petal interjected. "She's full of ruby brew and her tongue is loose."

"You like my tongue!" shouted Burna angrily, and everyone laughed.

Felix grabbed Bear and pulled him further into the room. They hadn't made it two paces when Cusht grabbed Felix round the neck and pulled him roughly into his corner. Bear followed, looking into a circle of excitable, and rather wrinkled faces. They all looked as if they hadn't eaten properly in a long time.

"Guess why there wasn't a watchman at the East Gate."

In the dim light, Cusht's black beard and dark eyebrows made him seem almost as intimidating as Uncle Jim.

"They got bored?" said Felix.

"Witchwork," said Cusht with a flourish.

Bear froze. Cusht held the gaze of his audience and looked from face to face.

"And how did you figure that out, Cusht?" asked Felix obligingly.

"That's the word on the streets, Fennex. The watchmen are hunting a witch."

The group nodded agreeably, as one.

Felix rolled his eyes. "The watchman wasn't on East Gate because he got cold and bored and scurried back up to the roof."

Cusht looked annoyed. "That's as may be. Doesn't mean there *wasn't* witchwork at play, though…" He waved his cup. "Now, I'm not saying anyone in town is involved. But we've had a lot of strangers arriving recently. And those spell-casting *Feyatung* can do all sorts. They fly. They communicate with animals. Transform into them even! They can even communicate with blots, lad! All sorts of perversions against the natural order."

Cusht sat back, satisfied, as the audience resumed their agreeable nodding. Witchwork was the root of a problem that seemed to be spreading through the land from shore to shore. The current Queen had exposed her own mother – who had reigned as Queen at the time – as a witch, and had her executed. Since then, Queen Meléna had strived to eradicate any trace of magic from the Queendom.

"Cusht is right," one woman said. "Only last year I heard that the *Feyatung* who got into the Free City palace transformed 'emself into … a flock of ducks."

"Wow… Terrifying," said Felix dryly.

"Queen Meléna might think she's stamped out all the unnatural goings on, but she can't even keep the Free City safe! Is town not feelin' more dangerous by the day? You youngsters keep your eyes open. You can't be too careful."

The group muttered their ums and ahs of agreement.

Felix wriggled out of the circle and grabbed Bear's arm. "You old trouts worry about yourselves – don't worry about us. C'mon, Bear. We'd better go and find Jim."

Felix pulled Bear back into the centre of the tavern. The main room of the Rusty Compass held long wooden tables and benches, but there were also ladders leading up to private rooms, twisting corridors and countless nooks and crannies.

"Glad you made it, lads!" said a sing-song voice from behind them.

Bear turned. It was Dorloc Odittany. He tipped his raggedy flat cap at them as he approached.

"That was thanks to you, no, Dorloc?" said Bear. "It was you that raised the alarm?"

"That was me, yes. And friends call me Doc."

"You aren't our friend, Dorloc," said Felix with a dark look.

"Oi! I ran as fast as I could to get help. We have to stick together, us lot."

"Thanks, Doc," said Bear apologetically.

Dorloc shrugged.

"Maybe me."

"Maybe me."

They shook hands, and Doc gave him a friendly pat.

"He doesn't have anything on him, Dorloc. Move on," Felix growled.

Dorloc was gracious enough to look embarrassed as he pulled his hand out of Bear's pocket. "Sorry. Worth a try," he muttered.

"Boys, over here!" Uncle Jim waved to them from a smoke-filled doorway.

"Erm, we'd better find out what he wants," said Bear awkwardly.

"Yeah, sorry to interrupt your thieving, Dorloc," said Felix. "We'll be off."

Bear smiled at Dorloc and followed Felix into the red haze.

CHAPTER 4

Uncle Jim led Bear and Felix up a small curving set of stairs and into one of the private rooms on the upper floor. It was one of the smallest and seemingly smokiest rooms in the building. Bear coughed as they opened the door and a thick cloud of sinsenn smoke billowed out.

"We'll be needing this room," said Uncle Jim to a man with long black hair who was sitting in the corner. The man packed up his pipe and dried sinsenn leaves into a tin slowly. He looked unbothered until he saw Felix, when his lip curled in blatant disgust. Rising from his seat, and staring at Felix with contempt the entire time, he slunk out of the room.

"Ignore him," Bear muttered to Felix as they filed in.

"Sit down, lads," said Uncle Jim, and they did so.

"Now, listen. It feels like something is afoot in the town. Actually, it seems like multiple feet are a-feeting. I'm not going to pretend to know what all of them are, but the things I hear, boys … I don't like 'em."

"You don't like feet?" said Felix.

Uncle Jim sighed.

"Or are we talking about ... witchwork?" Felix whispered, an eager smile spread over his face.

Bear eyeballed Felix and the smile dropped.

"Don't speak that foul rot," said Jim. "We have enough trouble without inviting that sort of talk into town."

"But—"

"We don't sow seeds if we don't recognize the flower, Fennex. Don't encourage rumours, no matter how small. In towns like Calleston, talk takes up a lot of room."

"They're already talking out there." Felix had dropped the games; his expression was sombre. "Cusht and all that lot."

"Leave that to them. We have problems that go deeper than idle chat."

Bear looked curiously at his uncle. He'd never spoken to them like this before. Uncle Jim was intimidating, and, when he wanted, could seem downright murderous. Even before he'd gained the hook on his arm, he'd commanded the utmost respect. But tonight there was an unusual vulnerability in his voice.

"Things are tough. They've been tough for a long time, but it's got worse. People are starving, it's as simple as that."

Bear thought about Megg, about the gaunt faces in the Rusty Compass.

"Now listen. I know you boys are focusing on Field Day, and so you should. But the bloom could be even worse than last year, and with all that speedweed I don't know that we can wait to find out. We need food. Someone has to do something – *now*."

Uncle Jim rubbed his shaved head and glanced behind him. He moved to block the doorway with his back. Bear felt the hairs on his arms raise.

"So, how did you boys find that climbing?"

"Hard…" said Bear truthfully, waiting to see where this was going.

"But if it came down to it, you could do it again?"

"Course," said Felix proudly.

Bear nodded.

"I know you two have already had a rough night, but I have a request. Now, first, you swear not to discuss this with a soul but me. Not your father." He looked fixedly at Bear. "Not anyone." He glared at Felix.

They agreed.

"I need you both … to climb … to Roofside."

Felix's mouth dropped open. Bear didn't know what he'd expected, but it wasn't that.

"I know it's dangerous. But it's possible, given your talents. I know a route, and I need you to –" he crouched, lowered his voice, and came so close that Bear could feel his moustache against his cheek – "sneak up the Keep and collect something. It's important, or else I wouldn't ask this of you. But it's more important that you aren't discovered."

Bear looked at Felix's face, lit up like a candle. His eyes shone like pools of amber.

"What are we stealing?" asked Felix.

"Hush your voice."

Felix nodded obligingly, almost eagerly.

"You aren't stealing … exactly. I need an imprint, of a key."

"A key for what?"

"The less you know the better. If you agree, you cannot tell a soul about this conversation. No one. It has to remain a secret. Agreed?"

His dark eyes flicked from Bear's face to Felix's, waiting for an answer.

Bear didn't have to think. He already knew what he'd decided. And, from Felix's shining eyes, so had he.

"What's the plan?" said Bear.

Uncle Jim smiled and pulled out his pipe.

Meya crouched in the shadows. She concealed herself behind a long holly bush and watched.

Combat practice would begin soon. The watchmen stood around the Snakewood Tower, sipping their morning ruby brew.

Meya wrinkled her nose as a young watchman gulped from his cup and smiled with stained lips. She never drank sinsenn in the morning. Meya lied as required throughout the day and ruby brew made her careless with her secrets.

Percy growled from within his satchel. She scratched his head to settle him.

Noka was approaching. He was with her father. They mustn't see her here.

They were in the middle of a conversation, heads bent together.

Meya squeezed Percy close and crouched lower.

"… their strength is improving," Noka was saying.

"Yes, the watchmen have strength," her father replied. "But where is the obedience? I am told some have been leaving their posts at night. Is that not a cause for concern? I fear I must speak with them."

"My lord, all is in hand. Remember, we decided you shouldn't be giving the watchmen direct orders. You must remain a figurehead. You have much to contend with, the negotiations with the Queen most of all. Leave these more trivial matters to me."

Yuck. Noka was adept at getting in her father's ear, and her father was a good listener. Too good sometimes.

"Yes, Noka, forgive me. We did agree as much."

There was a furious clash of swords as the watchmen began combat practice. Meya took the opportunity to begin edging along the bush towards the gate.

"But, Lord Noka?"

"Yes, my lord?"

"Don't forget I am the Overlord, and I will have my men under control."

Meya grinned. Her father was nobody's fool, though neither was Noka. She would come back later when the coast was clear.

CHAPTER
5

Dawn Bell seemed muted as it rang out across the vast expanse of the empty market square. First light had barely broken, and a thick fog hovered over the wet cobblestones. Only the warm lights of the worker's cookhouse and the distant clatter of pots and pans revealed that some people had already left their beds.

On street level, the square remained unlit. Once upon a time, the bakery and the greengrocer's would have already started their morning's work, but since there was little food to speak of beyond the watery stew that the cookhouse provided, the square was still dark and quiet. The potters and the weavers and the many others that did still open wouldn't arrive until the labourers had come to eat in the cookhouse and left for a day's work.

Above the square, there were tiers of businesses and homes. Wooden balconies circled the entire market and acted as pathways for people to visit each other's quarters, or as a viewing platform above the hustle and bustle of the marketplace. Those who lived on the higher floors considered themselves lucky, though the Roofsiders above regarded everyone below the golden gates as the floorborn.

A rickety stairwell on the west side of the square led to the entrance of the roof level. The entrance was sealed by a pair of heavy gates, intricately cast in gold. Beyond the golden gates was the Roofside. There were several entrances to Roofside dotted around Calleston: each one marked by a similar set of golden gates, and each of those guarded by a watchman. No Cobblesiders were permitted entry through the gates, and these days few Roofsiders bothered (or dared) coming down.

On the third floor, beneath the staircase to the golden gates, was an oak balcony. It had a painted sign on it featuring a white square with wings. Above the sign, a window slid open and Olenta, the postie, looked out.

Olenta loved this hour. When Calleston's streets were empty, she could go fast.

She held one hand on the wooden frame of her bed, and the other grasped the sill of her window. She swung herself nimbly outside, on to the bench in front of her window, and began to put her feet on. As she pulled the leather cuffs up over her calves, she kept her eyes on the misty marketplace. This year marked her twentieth year living in the west corner of Main Market, almost half her life. For many of them, they'd been good years, but recently the hardships had left her feeling ill-tempered much of the time.

Still, she loved Calleston town, and she loved her job.

She fastened straps tightly round her muscular thighs. It was brisk at this time of the morning. She was looking forward to getting on the track.

The pretty voice of Rose sang from the window next door. "Morning there, Olenta. Can I pass you this, my love? For Jim Garrason, Ship Street. But best take a look first."

Rose gave her a meaningful look as she passed her the note. Olenta flipped the readers on her headband over her eyes and read the note. She almost smiled.

So the old gang was getting back together, the very old gang. She winked her understanding at Rose.

"Morning, Olenta!"

It was the sweet chirp of Rose's youngest child, Poppy. Olenta waggled her fingers at the tiny face that poked out of the window. Poppy's fine brown hair was stuck up at truly impossible angles, and the bags under her eyes gave her the wild look of a street urchin. Olenta's heart swelled. She always had time for children, and something about the way Poppy always looked as if she'd been hit by a frying pan Olenta simply adored, though she blanched at the sight of Poppy's ribs through her nightdress.

"You're up early, Poppy."

"I know," she squeaked.

"Did you have fun watching Mummy in the fields yesterday?"

A vigorous nod from an exhausted face.

"Did you hear about last night?" Rose asked as she wrapped her blanket around Poppy.

"What was last night?"

Olenta frowned as she stepped out on to the balcony and began strapping herself into her harness. She overheard a lot of gossip in town, but Rose's version of events was usually more truth-adjacent than most.

"Bear and that Fennex boy were nearly caught by…" Rose covered Poppy's ears and mouthed, "Blots."

Olenta's eyebrows shot up.

"They were pulling the last of the speedweed. Apparently, it was two or three blots that chased them to the East Gate. Now, someone shut the gate once the blots were close, but get this – there was no watchman and no rope."

Olenta was stunned.

Watchmen had spent less time down in Cobbleside lately, but guarding the perimeter wall was critical. The closing of the gates was a harsh but necessary part of defending the town, but the watchmen's ropes had saved countless people from death, including her own. The Overlord should know about this, she thought. He wouldn't want his men shirking their duty.

Unless he knew and didn't care.

Olenta felt her blood beginning to boil. She grabbed her cup and gulped her morning ruby brew. The distance between Cobbleside and the roof had never been greater. That distance bred a clear contempt between the two – but abandoning field boys to be slaughtered by blots, with no one to throw a rope, was a new low.

She recalled the moment she'd grasped the rope that

had been thrown to her, over twenty years ago. She remembered the rot crawling up her legs. She shuddered.

"How did the boys survive? Did someone fetch a rope in the end?"

"Olenta, *they climbed*."

Ruby brew sprayed everywhere. Poppy exploded into giggles that rang across the misty market like silver bells. Rose laughed heartily too, before shushing her daughter and squeezing her tight. They watched Olenta regain her composure.

"Impossible!" said Olenta. She tossed her empty cup through the window on to her bed and tugged each of her straps twice, hard. "You had me for a minute there, Rose, but that's nonsense. This town can't tell a story without adding a few embellishments, but that is pure fiction."

Fully strapped in, Olenta swung herself from the balcony into mid-air and grasped the rope that held her counterweight. She dangled in her harness for a moment and wiggled until she was sitting comfortably. When she let go, the pulley on the postal track high above her would release and she'd glide down to the ground. She twisted and planted her metal feet on the wooden rail on which she'd been sitting.

"It's true, my love. Poppy was there. Her and her dad were up on the wall. Saw them pulled over the edge with their own eyes."

"Hmm, and what were you doing up at that hour, young lady?"

51

"Me and Daddy were catching bats!" Poppy exclaimed proudly.

Rose shifted the blanket around her shoulders uncomfortably, drawing the red embroidered flowers around her and her daughter. She avoided Olenta's eyes.

"We were just thickening up a stew. Haven't had any lentils in for a while."

"Nowt wrong with bat, Rose; it fills tummies. In fact, if there's a mouthful left, I'll try some when I'm off work later today."

"Course," replied Rose a little tightly.

Poppy leaned eagerly out of the window to see Olenta off. Olenta braced her feet on the railing and flipped the readers from her eyes back up on to her headband. She pushed herself out into the air. Letting go of the counterweight line, the pulley whirred above them, the ropes released and she glided effortlessly down to the ground. It was perfect weather for a fast day. Her metal feet made a dull clink as she softly landed. She squatted deeply, then propelled herself upwards and onwards.

The wheel on the track high above began rolling, and Olenta was on the move. The pulleys turned and, as the counterweight began descending, she rose up and up. The breeze whistled past her as she began travelling speedily and quietly around the marketplace in giant, rolling leaps. It was effortless. And this time in the morning, she didn't have to worry about people stepping out from a doorway or sticking their heads out of the balconies either.

She headed to the postal column on the opposite side of the market to collect any letters sent down from Roofside.

She knew that Poppy would be watching her in awe, so Olenta made sure to sail to the highest tier before gliding slowly back down to the ground, lightly touching down in front of the marble postal column.

She pulled out her keys. Checking to see if Poppy was still watching her out of the corner of her eye, she found the key that she needed. The little face was still there at the window. Olenta smiled as she unlocked the column.

There was no mail.

That couldn't be right. Roofsiders were always sending messages down to the cobbles. The chute must be blocked. Olenta pushed softly up one level to the first balcony, where she dropped a pebble from her leather pouch into the chute. It clattered down the post column to the floor. Level one was clear.

She pushed upwards a floor, where she dropped a second pebble down the chute. This time, the pebble made a faint, muffled sound as it struck a cluster of letters somewhere in the inner tube.

There it was.

Olenta sighed and took out a heavy wooden tile which hung from her waist like a beaver's tail. She slotted it into the postal column. It plummeted down, driving the letters to the bottom.

Olenta glided back down and began gathering them up. As expected, a few envelopes to the shipyard, brown ones to the storehouses and – she whistled. One from the Overlord himself, addressed to the Free City Palace. She flipped it over and saw that it had a giant tear in it. She tutted. That was no good, someone going through the Overlord's mail; she would have to report it to Noka.

Olenta put the letters in her sack and reached down into the column for the last few. Her hands felt the touch of something silky. She frowned, drawing out a white piece of material.

She studied it. A simple white dress, but it could only have belonged to someone from Roofside. The quality was unlike anything Cobblesiders could afford. The translucent material was breathtaking, and completely impractical for working life. The bottom of the skirts were shredded and muddied beyond repair. A shame, the material was still valuable beyond imagining. Olenta grimaced at the waste. There was so much wealth up there; they didn't understand the value of anything.

She peeked over her shoulder to where Poppy's little face was still watching. Her brothers had joined her at the window.

Olenta discreetly stuffed the dress into her mailbag.

Now to give these kids a show.

She unhooked her line and pushed herself off towards Main Street. The wheel above her rolled into action, the counterwight sank, and she ascended quickly, loving the rush of cold air over her skin. Landing back down firmly on the ground, she gave an almighty push that carried her up and up, directly to the children's eye level, then she pulled in her feet and leaned smoothly back. In the middle of an effortless backflip, she whipped an envelope through the air. Spinning like a top, the letter whizzed straight into an open window. Olenta laughed with glee at the gasps and cheers from Rose's children.

The sun was just beginning to break over the town's walls. Today was going to be a fast day. She pushed out on to Main Street, her wheel whirring on the track above her, free as a bird.

CHAPTER

6

As the Dawn Bell rang, Bear rolled on to his back and stretched his muscles until his legs shook. He yawned, letting the rumble in his ears drown out the bells for a moment, and then lay listening quietly, eyes pressed closed. It had been a late night in the Rusty Compass, and his sleep had been fitful.

He'd slipped between waking and dreaming all night long. He dreamed of bloodcurdling screams out beyond the tree line. And blots. But the dream-blots didn't lurk among the densely overgrown forests; they stood hiding in the corners of his home, creeping slowly closer, clambering up and over the bed towards Bear, their teeth snapping and wet pools of red dripping from their mouths…

He would jerk awake and lie there in the dark, catching his breath, listening to the muted sounds of Calleston at night. Then, the cycle would begin again, and he'd slip softly back into a new chain of dreadful night visions.

As the last chimes of the Dawn Bell fell quiet, Bear realized he had begun to dream again – someone running their fingers through his hair, resting a soft hand on his brow. His mother.

He sighed deeply. There was the pitter-patter of tiny footsteps above and he peeled open his eyes; the mouse was awake too. The sight cheered him up. He smiled as it crept along the ironwood beam above Father's bed, twitching its little whiskers at him.

"Still surviving, then, mousey," he whispered.

His Uncle Caber slept in the large bed by the door, under the window that faced the street. He was much older than Bear's father, and Bear heard him chatting happily to himself in bed. The fire crackled softly. Bear smiled wider and shook his head; Uncle Caber had already had a ruby brew and the sun was barely up. Bear wished he could sink back into a warm slumber, but Father was stirring in his bunk now too. The mouse scurried through a crack in the wall.

Bear sat up and rubbed his eyes, recalling the night before. It seemed like a nightmare, the blot's mouths glistening as they chomped at the air furiously, like a monstrous pair of grotesque baby birds… He could hardly believe it was real.

Bear rolled out of bed on to the floor and folded his bunk up against the wall. Hearing Bear's cot squeak up into position, Uncle Caber hopped out of bed too. He trotted over to him in just his britches, revealing a once muscular torso that in his old age was now skin and bones, his ribs jutting out.

Uncle Jim's words rang in Bear's ears – *people are starving.*

"You're daft, you are. Nearly killed yer dad, you did last night! Nearly killed yourself! You're too smart for that, Bear lad."

Uncle Caber spoke in unbroken sentences, often, contradicting ones. This morning, Bear was glad of the cheerful chatter.

"We made it, though," said Bear, grinning.

"You did. And I'm glad you did. Clever sod!" Caber whacked Bear on the back before pulling his bushy white hair into a braid.

"Very clever boy," he said as his fingers worked fastidiously "More to you than meets the eye! Keep workin' hard you'll be livin' up in Roofside before long."

Roofside. Bear remembered Uncle Jim's plan. A wave of excitement and anxiety swept over him.

"He'll be dead and buried if he doesn't buck his ideas up."

Aber was awake.

"No more prattle until I've woke up," he said groggily.

Bear's father rose, folded up his bunk and slammed it heavily against the wall.

Caber's white eyebrows flickered up and down. "Prattle, he says! You'll miss it one day."

"Come on," said Aber. "Let's get to the cookhouse before there's nothing left."

After putting on their work shirts, field hats and vests, they headed out into the quiet courtyard.

"Your hat," said Aber to Bear.

"I tossed it in the field to throw off the blots," explained Bear. "I'll fetch it today."

"Make sure you do."

It was still gloomy when they emerged outside, and there was a cool drizzle in the air.

They lived in Corcass Court: a dark, dilapidated and rather damp square with families piled on top of one another. Bear didn't much like living down on the street level, but at least interesting artefacts sometimes dropped down from the houses above. Bear checked the small court for treasures daily: scraps of paper, bones, coins. Once there was a red apple with only the smallest bite out of it. Today, there was nothing but mud.

They headed out of Corcass Court into a long avenue. The workers exited doors along the street and joined the procession towards Main Market. There, they'd get a hot bowl of stew at the cookhouse and be given the day's tasks.

Bear looked up towards Roofside. High above, a watchman unlocked a golden gate and began his patrol. The gates were a visible divide that few crossed, going in either direction.

They passed alleyways and crossed bridges and the conversation was a low murmur, a few laughs here and there. Red smoke billowed from the pipes of men and women as they walked, or sheltered in doorways from the rain. A boy cried out from a window, and his father came back, gave him a kiss and then headed off again down wooden stairs that carried him to street level. The head postie whizzed above the workers on her track, carrying her mail sack.

"Mornin', all!" she called softly as she hurtled overhead.

She was especially fast today, thought Bear.

He stared upwards as they entered the square, enjoying the feeling of space and the morning sky above. Throughout Cobbleside, where the houses were all built on top of each other, you could catch a sliver of sun or a glimpse of the rooftops if you peered up between gaps in the houses or along the main streets. But in Main Market, and out in the fields, Cobblesiders got to really enjoy the wide-open sky.

The procession of workers crossed the cobbled square, heading for the comforting glow of the cookhouse. The long benches and tables had wax cloth covers over them today, but everyone was already sopping wet, and likely would be all day.

Uncle Jim walked past them, giving only the smallest of nods. It was like the conversation in the Rusty Compass had never happened. Bear gazed up at the Keep, a large stone building in the corner of the square that rose from the cobbles all the way up to Roofside. Inside, the watchmen and their families lived. The canal water separated the Keep from the square, but Bear saw now that there were other ways to enter the imposing building.

"Bear." Uncle Jim snapped Bear out of his thoughts.

He joined the queue with the others, waiting for a bowl of stew. He tried to smell what would be served today, but there was a distinct lack of any smell at all. The stew had admittedly become thinner, and more watery. But it would be hot, and it would fill their bellies before they got to work.

Bear spotted Felix and Megg. They strode over to him, arm in arm. Megg had pulled her long, dark hair back into a ponytail, which made her face look even thinner.

"My sisters are telling everyone you fought off twenty blots yesterday," Megg said, a worried smile playing across her face. She raised her eyebrows and poked him in the chest.

Bear flinched and grinned at her. "Sorry. Not quite twenty. But it was a bit close for comfort."

He didn't want to worry her, but he was glad that she worried.

"Tell the girls we were stupid to be out so late. Won't happen again, Megg. Promise."

He held her gaze with a smile until she overtly sighed her disappointment and shook her head. He saw the smile she tried to keep from her lips.

Felix gave him a subtle elbow.

Cusht's voice interrupted their conversation. "Long day today! Joy o' joys, we're re-cobbling Main Market!"

The crowd groaned. Cusht was used to being the bearer of bad news, so he smiled in a good-natured way. Calleston was in a perpetual state of repair. The minute they'd finished re-cobbling, re-pointing or resealing one area, they were called upon to start somewhere else.

"But we won't be joined by our younglings today. We

have a bit o' news. To everyone preparing for their first Field Day … you've got a practice."

Bear's heart pounded as a lukewarm clap rippled through the labourers. Bear, Felix and Megg stared at each other, stunned. Cusht took a deep puff of his pipe, and blew red smoke into the air.

"I know, I know. You young'uns are long overdue a practice day. Our Rose will walk you to the training field when you've finished your stew."

"Stew? Soup more like!" a disgruntled woman shouted.

"Oh, have a brew and shurrup, Sue!" Cusht laughed.

A sardonic laughter rippled across the square.

"Gather round me, new-bloomers!" shouted Rose from a first-floor balcony.

Rose was one of the few remaining field workers who created healthy blooms, not that she had ever been rewarded for her efforts. She stood up on the balcony and peered across the square at the new-bloomers. Her hair was longer than the last time she had taught them. It was tied in a dark braid, like a thick black vine, adorned with five red metal flowers. As she planted her bare feet on the wall, she flicked the braid over her shoulder and pulled the strap on her sack tight, so that it rested on her hip.

Bear recognized the bag. It was made of red leather, and embossed all over with leaves, vines and the scarlet petals of the sinsenn plant. Inside the bag would be hundreds of ruby red seeds, donated by the Overlord.

Rose's voice called out, strong and sweet. "Hello, my

loves. I'm grateful to share some time with you all. Finally. Today's about helping each of you rediscover your personal connection to that plant. Conditions are perfect for a fantastic day of training; I can feel it in the air."

Bear looked around the square at the gaunt faces, dripping wet. The air didn't seem fantastic. Everybody looked tired, and they looked worried.

"And there's something else you should know. Today is the last practice before Field Day. I'm pleased to say that Overlord Goodman has shared the date for Field Day with me this morning."

Everyone craned their necks, eyes on Rose. She shook her head and a glittering spray of water droplets flew from her. There was pity in her face as she said, "Field Day is confirmed at week's end."

Felix groaned.

This was their first practice in months. And it would be their last.

Week's end was in three days' time.

CHAPTER 7

Practice was about to begin. Everyone was standing in a long line across Top Field. Bear stood between Megg and Felix. He studied the soil beneath him. It looked devoid of life. But underneath the dark soil he knew the sinsenn seeds were waiting, waiting to be activated.

In the foggy morning, everything looked unusually colourless: black soil, grey sky. Training was being observed by two watchmen whom Bear knew by face, but not name. He looked down, avoiding their eyes.

Instead, he scrutinized Grace and Lutch, the two drummers who would be guiding the enlacement. Lutch had sleek grey hair and a coal-black beard. Grace had reddish curls that had given way to silver. They talked quietly, their drums resting at their hips, and discreetly kept tabs on the pair of watchmen. The Overlord's men looked more like they'd been tasked with overseeing a bunch of particularly despicable criminals than a young group of new-bloomers.

Rose walked from one trainee to the next, emptying a handful of the contents of the red leather bag into their outstretched palms. She delivered Megg's seeds under the watchmen's sharp scrutiny. Megg thanked Rose and buried her seeds into the soil around her, fussing with their positioning. She paused and rubbed at her temples briefly.

Bear wondered if she was feeling all right. Megg turned as if she'd heard his thoughts, and gave him a little encouraging smile. Then she exhaled, tucked her hair behind her ears and closed her eyes.

Bear tried to appear confident as Rose approached. He was thankful for the cover of his hastily retrieved field hat. The watchman shadowed Rose on each side, eyeballing him.

"Exactly twenty seeds, my love. You can count, can't you?"

"Yes," Bear replied stiffly, hiding his embarrassment.

He added up the seeds in his head, suddenly worried that he would mess up.

One, two, three… Bear could easily count up to one hundred.

Four, five, six… He knew that after the first hundred, you count to another hundred, again and again.

Seven… Uncle Caber could count into the thousands, maybe more, but some of the numbers started sounding suspiciously made up to Bear.

Eight… The watchmen bristled as the seeds shifted in Bear's hand.

"Pay attention now, Mister Aberson," said Rose. "I'm to return anything that doesn't grow, so take exactly twenty."

He looked down at his hand and swallowed. The watchmen were scowling, and Rose could tell he was nervous. Where had he got to?

He chewed his lip and began again.

One, two…

He wished he could disappear.

"Bear, I hear you had quite a long night," Rose said kindly. "Why don't we place out the hope-star formation, and then we'll go from there?"

He felt his cheeks burning, but she took the seeds from his hand and plopped them back into the bag.

"How many seeds do you need for a hope-star formation, my love?"

"Eight."

"Hurry up, then. Show me."

Bear took one seed at a time. He placed one in front of him, one behind, one on either side, and another four diagonally.

He liked the feeling of pushing them into the earth. Rose once said Bear was neat and it was something he'd remembered ever since. Once he was crouched close to the ground in his wide-brimmed hat, he could focus on making things neat. He almost forgot anyone was watching.

With the hope-star around him complete, he looked up.

"Very nice. Now how many more?"

"Twelve," he said with no hesitation.

"That's exactly right."

Rose crouched down to Bear's level.

"Your father's a clever man, Bear, and confident with it. But do you know something he never was?"

Bear focused on her hands. She rolled the seeds expertly between her fingers.

"He was never much of grower. And you can tell him I said so."

She placed six more seeds in his hand. Followed by another six. That was all of them.

"But you know how to enlace, Bear, and you know how to grow."

Rose lowered her tone to a barely voiced whisper.

"And I hear you're a good climber too."

Bear looked up into Rose's face and was surprised to see a mischievous smile.

"Hurry it up," a watchman barked, and with a final encouraging nod Rose walked on.

Bear couldn't help but smile.

He buried what seeds were left in a second circle around himself and then rubbed his hands together to break up the earth that clung to them. He looked over at Felix, who still held his pile in his hands. He looked petrified. Bear caught his eye and signed to him, *I'm with you*.

His friend flashed him a grateful smile and quickly began pressing his seeds into the earth.

Bear straightened and planted his feet firmly in the soil. Rose had made her way all along the line now. He watched her walking back with the watchmen, the metal flowers clipped into her braid swinging like a pendulum. Grace and Lutch separated, allowing Rose to stand between them. The skins of their drums were painted, Lutch's with a snarling face emerging from black vines. Grace's drum was adorned with luscious red petals, and a face so serene as to be almost smiling.

Rose faced the group. "All set, everyone? This is a thrilling day, my loves. It's lovely and wet in the soil and in the air. And it looks like we'll get some sun by the time we're done. So—"

"Get on with it," one of the watchmen muttered, and he yawned audibly, cutting Rose off. He was slimmer and taller than the other, with a regal face and a bored arrogance that was unmistakably Roofside. His hands rested on his hips and he cracked his neck loudly.

Bear glanced at his weapons. All watchmen carried a standard-issue sword, but this man had a set of daggers too and a long, looped whip attached at his waist. It was the whip that scared Bear most of all. He'd seen what it could do more than once and of late he'd seen it more frequently than ever.

Rose smiled a humourless smile before continuing. "Let your minds go blank. Make peace with any … external distractions, and quiet your mind before you enlace."

Bear felt as if she were talking directly to him, though she looked up and down the line as she spoke.

"You've all connected to a seed or two before. But connecting to one seed is like holding a friend's hand. You hold them, and they hold you. Enlacing your mind with multiple seeds is ... different. You must cast a net with your mind, and judge for yourself how far you can extend outwards, without collapsing or spreading yourself too thin. Do you understand me?"

"Yes, Rose," they responded.

Rose closed her eyes and opened her arms wide.

"You must wash over the sinsenn seeds like water ... like air." Her hands moved through the air as she spoke, drawing shapes with her fingertips. "You are the vessel that carries their power. When you hold them, you'll find that they are holding you. Do you understand me?"

"Yes, Rose," Bear murmured along with the rest.

The watchman with the whip sighed a bored, petulant sigh. Beside him stood the shorter, more muscular watchman. His face was unmoving and unhappy. He looked like a stone, his expression as cold and as hard as rock.

The Stone and the Whip. *Both should be avoided*, thought Bear, before forcing himself to concentrate.

"If you do discover speedweed, keep moving," went on Rose. "Avoid it. After our hard efforts this season, there should be little of the blight left at all, but be prepared." She shot the briefest glance at the watchmen. "We will never be free of it ... so we must *tolerate* it."

The line of trainees nodded in understanding.

"And remember, my loves, you can't force an enlacement. It's not a fight. You don't have the power here.

We simply direct the power of the plant—"

"All right, woman, get on with it."

The flat bark of the Stone was jarring. The man with the black drum took an angry step forward.

"No matter, Lutch!" called Rose, stopping him in his tracks. "Now, is everyone ready to begin?"

Lutch scowled, then nodded along with the rest. The other drummer, Grace, blew a grey lock of hair out of her face, spun her tipper in her hand, and hit her red drum. Rose faced the nervous line-up standing silently before her.

"Let's begin."

She looked directly at Bear.

"No distractions. Clear your minds."

Lutch and Grace began striking their drums as one. Grace beat her red skin slowly and steadily. The black drum matched the red at first, then Lutch began adding strident accents here and there.

Bear watched Felix spread his feet wide in the earth, place his hands on his hips, and raise his face to the sky. His yellow eyes snapped shut.

Megg crouched and placed her chin in her hands. With her head to one side, she looked almost as if she were asleep.

Bear looked down the line, each grower settled into a different pose. Cassius stood behind Megg. He covered his eyes with one hand and raised his free hand into the sky as if he were about to pick an apple.

"Find the stillness."

Bear heard a flapping noise and was surprised to see a large raven flying overhead. It landed on the town wall before hopping around to face him. Bear hadn't seen a bird that large for a long time. If it wasn't careful, it would end the day on a Calleston dinner plate…

"No distractions!"

Rose always knew when Bear's mind was somewhere else. He closed his eyes, and began breathing in time with the beat of Grace's drum.

DUM dum, DUM dum, DUM dum.

He kicked off his boots and buried his pale feet into the black earth. The black drum weaved in and out of the even pace. Bear heard flapping up on the wall.

DUM dum, DUM dum, DUM dum.

The red drum was low and steady. It helped focus Bear. He let his mind clear. Everything began to sound warped, slower, somehow more muffled.

DUM dum, DUM dum, DUM dum.

The red drum was a heartbeat, drowning out the black.

Bear swayed in tiny circles. His breath sounded like a river. From somewhere quiet, a rushing began, that familiar rushing that signalled a change. He had felt it only last night. Once more, the folding into himself. He felt himself smile.

He had begun to enlace.

He extended a pool of energy outwards, in a ring. Twenty seeds in perfect formation around him vibrated happily as his mind's eye washed over them. He'd never worked with so many seeds in his life. It was exhilarating. Each seed carried the endless potential to grow. They just needed encouragement.

"Good work, everyone! Keep the focus!"

Bear had a firm grasp of his seed circle. He dug his feet into the wet earth and pictured roots reaching out into the soil. They followed his lead, the ruby-red seeds sending taproots extending downwards. There was excitement in the connection.

He opened his arms out slowly and felt the roots spreading wider, absorbing life from the earth. He crossed his feet and turned slowly, cocking his head to the side as he studied hair-like connections, testing them, encouraging them to grow stronger.

The drums quickened and the wind picked up. He thought he heard a raven caw in the distance. The root network pumped like the blood in his veins.

"Lovely, Cassius! Keep at it, Megg," Rose called.

No distractions. Bear lifted his chin. His hat fell to hang at his back, and he felt the sun hit his face.

He clenched his fists and brought them together, drawing them upwards slowly; he felt twenty young shoots emerge from the earth and rise towards the sun.

The raven cawed loudly.

Bear held his position. The caress of light on the tiny, newly formed leaves was electrifying. He'd never imagined how much power lay in the ruby-red seeds when in larger numbers. He felt waves of energy pour into him. He let the energy wash through his body and released it back into the rapidly growing shrubbery.

And then he felt something wrong. Something sickening. Something that felt like…

"Despair," Bear heard himself whisper.

He opened his eyes. He blinked. To his amazement, he was surrounded by waist-high plants. He crouched down within them and placed his hands into the earth. He looked for speedweed emerging from the ground, but didn't see any.

Bear shook his head and held a barrier of strength around his plants. Whatever feeling had been there subsided. He would not let speedweed or anything else break his focus. The drums were unrelenting.

Bear drew circles around the bushes with his hands and their small leaves expanded, gaining strength as they unfurled.

"Keep going, Bear." Rose's voice was close and quiet.

Bear focused his attention on the tips of the plant. The red drum roared in his ears. He drove the energy upwards and tiny, waxy buds began swelling rapidly. He held his palms out towards the sun, soaking in light, waiting for a surge of power.

As he felt a new wave start to fizz through his body, he squeezed his thumbs and fingers into two points. The buds pulsated; they were ready to be released. He clenched his jaw and kept his arms wide apart. He held his thumbs and fingertips tightly together, and held on as long as he could, while the flowers begged to be released.

The red drum drummed faster.

When he couldn't hold it in any longer, Bear simply opened his hands. He opened his eyes and a ring of sinsenn blooms unfolded around him in an alarming red eruption. Bear gasped.

His bushes were teeming with scarlet flowers, healthy and vibrant. They burned brightly in the sun, fluttering proudly in the light wind.

Sweat dripped down Bear's face and back. In a daze, he blinked at the bright sunlight.

"Bear, it's beautiful!" cried Rose. "You see those larger leaves? The brownish-red tinge to them? The sign of a very potent bloom. Strong ruby brew from these, I daresay."

Her voice rang with pride.

"And, Megg … my dear, they are just gorgeous! Just perfectly formed, Megg! Well done! A lot like my early work. And you were the quickest of the bunch…"

Bear looked over at Megg's blooms. She'd grown an arch of sinsenn in front of herself, and from the arch hung vines, each one carrying multiple flowers. It was stunning. As for Megg, she was glowing. She turned to him and smiled.

Bear couldn't speak just yet. So he closed his fingers and thumb and touched his chin, then extended his hand to Megg, opening it like a flower.

Beautiful.

She tapped two fingers together twice.

And the same to you.

Bear felt his cheeks flush. A restrained excitement

rippled down the line as Rose appraised each bloom, giving pointers here and there.

"Briar! Nice and bushy! Oh, sweet, Cicely. Flowers are a bit small … but wow, your leaves! They're like ferns!"

Cassius looked up at his bloom of maybe ten flowers. Not a bad bloom by any means, and they were extremely large. But they were on the pink side … and they had bloomed on the end of one giant stalk, ten feet in the air. He looked rather upset. The raven cawed again; it almost sounded like a laugh.

Then Cassius's eyes narrowed and he gave a cold laugh. "At least I did better than *that*!"

Everyone turned to look where he was pointing.

Felix was standing completely still, looking at the ground.

At his feet was a perfectly red, perfectly formed flower. Just one.

"Worse than I thought," he whispered.

Everyone was silent. There wasn't much to say.

"Well," said Rose at last, "at least everyone has a bloom to take home."

"We'll be taking the blooms," said the Stone. He unfolded his muscular arms and placed one hand on his sword. "Direct orders. Everyone may keep one flower as a token."

There was a ripple of disappointment. The Overlord always permitted them to keep the results of their practices. It was a small kindness, though he made it clear that if the

Queen were made aware of such things she would not be pleased with him.

Rose flushed. "Trainees have always kept their practice blooms."

"Those days are gone, woman. The harvest dwindles. Don't make me repeat myself."

After a moment, Rose nodded and bowed her head. "Gather any remaining seeds," she said quietly. "You may keep one bloom."

A grim-faced Felix headed for the wall, leaving his flower where it was. Megg gave Bear a dark look before picking one of her own and hurrying after him. Bear was about to do the same when the Whip stopped in front of Bear.

"One hundred and fifty-nine," he almost purred.

"Pardon me?" Bear's voice sounded more confident than it felt.

"After you have taken your token, there should be one hundred and fifty-nine flowers left for the Overlord. We're counting. So don't try anything," the Whip snapped, before striding off towards Felix's patch.

Bear pinched the most obvious flower from its stem – a hand-sized flower with thick petals. The others were heading for the gate.

"Wait!" cried the Whip. He stared at Felix's empty plot. "The Fennex boy's plant. He left it. But it's not there." He swung to face Rose, "Where did it go?"

"I don't know," she said defensively. She continued walking towards the town wall, braid swinging behind her.

There was a sound like a thunder crack and Rose cried out as she hit the floor. The raven cawed loudly at the shocking noise. Everyone stopped in their tracks and gasped in silent horror as they realized what had happened.

The Whip stood holding the leather handle of his namesake in hand, and a cruel smile on his face. "And where do you think you're going?" he said.

Rose rolled on the floor in silent agony, holding her back where the whip had lashed her.

Lutch cried out angrily and charged towards the watchmen. Grace grabbed his arm, but too late, as a lightning crack dropped Lutch to the floor too. He cried out and clutched at his eye in pain.

"You've blinded me, you madman!" he cried.

The Whip ignored him, speaking softly to Rose. "Get. Up. And. Come. Here."

She stood up, grunting in pain, and hobbled towards the Whip. Bear saw a long, bloody gash flooding the material at her back.

The Whip licked his lips and cracked his whip again. Rose screamed and pressed her hand to her cheek, blood seeping from between her fingers.

"Empty the bag."

Still holding her face, Rose tipped it out and seeds tumbled into the dirt – but no flower.

"I – I didn't take it." Rose sounded like a frightened animal.

"Check their drum bags, Ashka," offered the Stone, pointing at the drummers.

"It's not in the drum bags," the Whip snapped. They hadn't got close to Felix's side. He squinted over at Bear.

"You…" The Whip pointed his whip at Bear and had just taken a menacing step towards him when the raven dived rapidly down from above, swooping between them, causing the Whip to jerk back in fear.

Lutch called out from the ground, holding his bloody eye.

"What's got you fellas wound so tight?" he asked. "You need to double your ruby brew tomorrow, boys. You'll have somebody's eye out." Lutch laughed bitterly as Grace poured water from her water skin over his eye.

The Whip stared menacingly at Bear as the Stone slammed his sword back into its sheath.

"The bird might've had it, Ashka," he said. He nodded at Rose. "You, gather the seeds and get out."

Rose nodded, scooping the seeds into the bag, her face drained of colour under the livid cut.

"Come," she said quietly. Everybody hurried through the iron gate after her in a rigid silence.

Only the raven called out, crying mournfully as it swooped back up towards the gleaming rooftops.

Tonight, thought Bear, *I will join it.*

Meya rattled the giant door handle. The Snakewood Tower was locked?

"Can I help you, Lady Meya?"

She let go and spun to face Noka.

"Meya Omega, unless you plan on becoming a watchman, you cannot enter the tower. It's for your own safety."

"I can't go safely anywhere, Noka."

He didn't look moved at all; he looked displeased. Oh, rats. This probably called for tears. She let them well up, but looked down, as if she were ashamed. Noka lifted her chin and a tear rolled down her cheek. Perfect.

"My dear child." His voice was softer now. "We each carry our burdens, and each have our restrictions, the Cobbleside far more so than us. Learning to live with them, that's the key."

That's not the key at all, thought Meya. But she knew a good place to find one.

CHAPTER

8

"Keep up, boys."

Uncle Jim led Bear and Felix through Calleston's winding streets, lit by the full moon. They passed through a wide alleyway, then under a three-tiered bridge that joined the upper levels of the towering buildings on either side of the alley.

They were following some distance behind a horse and cart as it clattered over the cobbles. The sound echoed down the street, past the timber-framed houses that lined it, their towering facades extending up into the midnight sky. Jim gestured with his hook as the cart disappeared from view.

"We're getting closer. If anyone approaches, let me do the talking."

The horse and cart wasn't the only noise any more; there was a gathering of people up ahead. The muffled hubbub of their voices carried down the curve of the street towards them. Felix pulled his hood up, covering his pointed ears. From somewhere above, Bear heard the soft hoot of a bird.

They edged through the shadows. Uncle Jim waved for the boys to stop when they reached the corner. The cart had halted just ahead. Dim figures began to surround it.

"What's happening?" asked Felix.

"Not sure yet," said Uncle Jim, peering through the drizzle. "But best we're not seen." He drew them into the shadow of a balcony, and they perched on a stoop.

"They're collecting the body."

Bear almost jumped out of his skin at the disembodied voice. A glowing orange light appeared next to him as the chamber of a sinsenn pipe spluttered into life.

"Them next door. Their little boy has been sick with fever for weeks … couldn't seem to shake it… Well, anyway, he died this afternoon."

The elderly man trailed off into silence. He sat and puffed his pipe as his sunken eyes looked at nothing. Uncle Jim nodded for Bear and Felix to get off the old man's stoop and come back into the street.

"May he rest. Pardon our intrusion."

Up ahead, a small, wrapped bundle was carried out of one of the houses. The man who held the youngling was slim, with a shaven head. He placed it tenderly on the cart. The people gathering around the carriage were quiet now as the cart began slowly moving away, clattering off down the cobbles again.

Jim, Bear and Felix resumed their march towards the quiet group standing up ahead. They were sharing cups of ruby brew, and a tall boy with matted hair sucked deeply on a sinsenn pipe, blowing red smoke out into the moonlight.

A woman sat on the front step of the warmly lit entryway, her hair wild, her eyes circled in black, and a cup in her hand. She had a glassy smile on her face as she watched the carriage disappear.

The mother, thought Bear.

"May he rest," Uncle Jim said softly as they passed.

"May he rest," came the subdued reply from the small gathering.

The man with the shaved head continued staring after the cart, ignoring the cloaked trio that slipped through what remained of his family.

The next few of Calleston's streets were mostly empty. High above them, passing over their heads, a watchman patrolled an upper-level walkway. A winding staircase led up to him from street level, ending at a set of golden gates. The watchman glanced down, but paid them no mind. None ventured down in to Cobbleside at this time of night unless they had to.

Here and there, they heard a baby crying, or saw someone leaning over their handrail, red pipe smoke twisting into the night air.

"Bear, look," said Felix, smiling.

They were passing a window mostly obstructed by a curtain. Bear knew the window very well. It was where Megg lived. They peeked inside. Her mother's back was to the window and she held a candle while gesticulating wildly. Her muffled voice was wildly exaggerated; she was recounting a story to Megg and her sisters. Bear and Felix ducked down.

The girls were piled on the bed, wrapped in blankets. Megg had her back pressed against the wall, her legs outstretched, smiling at her mother's theatrical movements.

The next oldest after her, twins Amber and Summer, leaned against the wall too, arm in arm. Freya, the loudest, lay on her stomach over Megg's ankles. She laughed hysterically at their mother, her face flushed and her eyes wild. The other girls giggled at their mother's performance, or perhaps at Freya's laugh. Bear chuckled too.

"Look at Andy," he murmured to Felix.

Andy had fallen asleep on Megg's shoulder. Her enormous hair blended with Megg's tumble of dark curls and her little mouth was wide open. The youngest, Ophelia, lazed in Megg's arms. Her chubby cheeks were rosy in the warm, and her big eyes never left her mum. Megg stroked her hair.

There was a sudden terrified scream from the window above Megg's. Felix and Bear sprang away and raced off down the street.

"What was that?" Felix hissed.

"None of our business, boys. Get moving. Now!" Uncle Jim hurried them along.

Bear stole a glance over his shoulder and saw Megg and her mother peeking discreetly from their window.

As they walked further on, fewer windows shone

with candlelight, and the streets became darker as the gaps between the towering buildings narrowed. The sky was just a sliver of silver clouds and moonlight between the dark rooftops. Bear saw the flash of something flying silently above. A bat maybe.

"Hold on. Need to use the light," Uncle Jim whispered.

He uncovered his lantern, holding it out on his hook as they passed doorways and alleys.

"Here."

It was a wooden door with a faded engraving on it. A red beaver smoking a comically large pipe. Jim swung the door open revealing a long tunnel with walls painted red. They entered and Bear closed the door behind them. Felix pulled down his hood and tucked his hair behind his ears.

Uncle Jim spoke quietly as he walked. "On the other side of this tunnel is Treat Street. There'll be people there, and everyone knows everyone. Hoods up. Heads down. We don't want any eyes on us tonight, please."

Bear's heartbeat sped up.

"Once we get to the Baby Gate, you're on your own. That's when you need to start worrying about watchmen." The boys nodded. Uncle Jim pulled a ruby-brew skin from his waist.

"Bear?" Bear shook his head. Felix grabbed the skin and took a swallow.

As they carried on down the red passageway, Bear heard mice fleeing the light. They passed unlit stairwells and a handful of archways until they reached the end of the tunnel.

"Watch your pockets," said Jim, "and hide your faces. If no one knows we are here, all the better."

They stepped out on to Treat Street into a light rain.

"Jim! How lovely to see you. You haven't visited in a while."

Jim cursed quietly. The woman's voice was so friendly that Bear was half tempted to look up.

"Good health, Olivia. Though I lack the time to talk tonight. Come, boys."

"Oh! You already have company. Well, goodnight, then, boys!" Olivia purred, and stood back for them to pass.

"Blotson," muttered Jim.

Bear had never visited Treat Street before. He stole a peek from under his hood when he thought it was safe. On the other side of the street was the usual mix of stone or timber-framed buildings, stacked on top of one another, with people meandering up and down the balconies. They passed a man wearing a strange veil in a style Bear hadn't seen before, and the streets seemed unnaturally busy for this hour. People called from upper decks raucously, and the windows were all aglow. Behind them, laughter and music sounded.

They headed towards a large group of women who blew great clouds of pink smoke from their pipes.

"Keep walking," Jim urged them as they entered the thick haze. "Be inconspicuous."

Bear and Felix emerged from the smoke spluttering on the other side. The women laughed bawdily.

"Nice hook, darlin'," said a heavily perfumed woman. "You much of an 'ooker?"

The circle of women screamed with laughter.

"Blotson!" Jim said again, and he tucked his hook inside his cloak as he sped away. "So much for being inconspicuous. Almost there, boys. Heads down."

The boys followed him below a row of rickety balconies. The streets grew busier. More and more people jostled Bear the further on they walked. He felt a huge temptation to lift his head discreetly and take in the crowds. He smelled some sort of spiced food that made his stomach gurgle loudly. He hoped the cookhouse was open tomorrow.

As the rain started falling harder, Uncle Jim raised his voice: "Here we are." He ducked under a red-tiled roof and into a little stone room. "Nobody should bother us now."

In the middle of the dark chamber was a statue of a naked woman, kneeling in the centre of a giant flower. Water flowed from the heart of the flower, over the woman's legs and poured from the tips of the petals into a circular stone basin.

"Where are we?" whispered Felix.

"They call it the Daisy Beds Well. The water comes from an offshoot of the Goodwater Spring. The residents of Treat Street have protected her for years."

She was stunning. Bear couldn't believe she existed down here in Cobbleside.

The Daisy Beds Well was lit only by a scattering of candles. They spluttered in the night air. The dark stone room opened directly on to the street with no partition wall. But the boisterous people passing by seemed to be deliberately avoiding the well, both with the way they walked and with the direction of their eyes.

"Is it sacred?" Felix asked.

"Not exactly, but nobody will bother us. The gate is back here."

Uncle Jim walked round the fountain to the back wall of the room. There was a waist-high archway in the stone wall, and set within it was a polished golden gate.

"Baby Gate," said Bear, reading the words that were inscribed above.

"Why is it called that?" asked Felix.

"In times past, Cobbleside babies without hope of care could be left here. They'd be taken up to Roofside, to find a new home. Those days have long passed, but the gate remains."

"Lucky babies."

Uncle Jim snorted. "I wouldn't be so sure."

He pulled at the little gate – it was stiff, but it opened.

"Is it real gold?"

"Task at hand, Felix."

"Does it lead to Roofside?"

"Not exactly," replied Jim, "but it leads to Trine

88

Street. Trine Street faces right on the Keep, the back side of it with no entry and where the watchmen seldom patrol. The old postal track crosses over that side of the Keep. You'll need to climb up a few levels, then you have to find a good spot to jump on to the track. I'm not going to sugar-coat it – the track's in bad repair. It's crumbling, and at a certain point it falls away completely. But the track gets you halfway round the Keep and towards that door we talked about. Look for what seems like chimneys leading up the wall. You'll have to climb up between them till you find a stone balcony and the door. It won't grab your eye, but it shouldn't grab the watchmen's either if you're careful.

Bear stared at his uncle. It was a crazy plan. But he knew what was at the end of it – Roofside.

"And what do we do when we get over the balcony wall?" asked Felix.

"That door to the Keep is left open. They don't lock it 'cause the balcony's so high they don't see how anyone could reach it. But I know you can do it. Inside, lots of keys, all hanging off the wall. You're looking for the key to culvert five – it will be labelled. Should be a small, metal key, nothing fancy. When you find it, press it gently into the clay mould inside this –" Uncle Jim passed Bear a silver case, like a small book, which he fastened to his waist – "then put the key back exactly where it was and get down again as fast as you can. Understood?"

Bear and Felix nodded.

"Now Trine Street has a strict curfew at Evening Bell. So if you're caught on that side... Well. Don't get caught."

They nodded. Jim put his hand and hook on their shoulders.

"Be slow when you need to be. Be still when you need to be. Be smart, unless you get caught, in which case – play dumb. And remember – anyone on the streets after curfew is bad news."

Bear crouched down and peered through the little entrance. They'd have to proceed on their hands and knees.

"We're ready," said Felix. "We'll be careful."

"You'd better be. No reckless moves, Fennex."

Felix rolled his eyes dramatically before darting into the tunnel. Bear checked the fastening on the pouch at his waist one last time. "We'll go carefully. Don't worry."

He ducked in after Felix. The golden hinge of the Baby Gate squeaked as Uncle Jim closed it behind them.

"Whatever it takes, Bear, don't get caught..."

Jim's words echoed down the tunnel, and then it was quiet.

Meya's mother gasped as rough hands pushed her towards the ledge. They were high above the market square. Stone cobbles below. And then she was falling.

Her stomach flipped as she fell, and her heart wailed in sorrow. Meya would grow up without her. She braced for the impact—

Meya screamed as she woke, heart hammering madly in her chest. Percy whined from under the covers and licked her fingers.

"Shh, Percy, it was just a bad dream," whispered Meya. "Go back to sleep."

Then she rolled over and looked at the key in her door.

"Although … we are awake now."

CHAPTER

9

The floor was remarkably smooth, which was lucky, given they needed to half crawl and half slide through the tunnel. It was also completely unlit. By the time they'd crawled twenty paces, Bear could see nothing but black. He was guided by the sounds of Felix crawling ahead and the uniform touch of the smooth stone on his hands. He felt somehow comforted by the calm, quiet task at hand.

An ear-splitting crack and a blinding flash of white light made Bear yelp. The light dazzled him, leaving him reeling in the dark.

"Did you see that?' croaked Felix. Bear's pulse raced and his ears rang.

"Yes! Where did it come from?"

"I can't tell, but it lit up the whole tunnel."

Felix shot forward and Bear followed, no longer experiencing calm in the darkness. Bear felt like a mouse in a trap. He couldn't tell if his eyes were playing tricks on him, but ghosts of the light flashed before him. Bear squeezed them shut, though it made little difference. He could still see the disorientating flash of light, as if his eyes had been burned.

"We're here." Felix grunted as he slid open the door on the other side and slipped through. "It's all clear. Get out of there quick."

As soon as Bear's feet thunked on to the ground, Felix thrust a large oar into his hand. "Take this. Not much of a weapon, but it's better than nothing."

Bear took it and looked around. They were standing on the banks of a canal. Trine Street stretched away in both directions. The street was completely deserted – not a soul in sight. Just rubbish and clutter, empty boxes and abandoned wares from the market, in piles along the street.

On the other side of the canal was the dark shadow of the Keep, rising up into the night sky. The backside of the stone building had no doors and no windows, and the canal circled the building back towards the town square. After Evening Bell, the route to Main Street was closed off by thick iron gates. The boys were alone in the dark, shadowy market.

During the day, Trine Market was filled with people up and down the multiple levels that faced the back of the Keep. Small punts and larger merchant's boats pulled up and haggled with traders. The market traded in the kind of shadowy things that you couldn't find in Main Market – the black-market medicines, unusual weaponry, superstitious talismans – and worse, no doubt. But as soon as night fell, patrons were kicked out, the market closed, and when the bell rang for curfew it was locked down completely. The rather curious residents sheltered in their homes till the Morning Bell, from the watchmen, from each other, from something else? Bear tried not to think about it.

They made their way down the dark canal, looking for somewhere to access the level above.

"What do you think that light was?" asked Felix.

"I've never seen anything like it," replied Bear. He stole a glance at Felix. "Do you think it was … witchwork?"

"No," Felix said quickly. "Definitely not. It could have been anything. No witches in Cobbleside, even if the Rusty Compass lot think different."

Bear felt the same: better not to entertain the thought.

They came upon a wooden ladder leading up to the first-floor balcony, and they climbed it quietly, if a little awkwardly, with their oars.

At the top, they peeked along the timber walkway. Signs from long-disused shops hung above the doors. All seemed quiet. Bear reminded himself to breathe as they began to make their way down the ramshackle shop fronts, oars in hand.

Behind an empty handcart, they discovered another set of crooked stairs and swept up to the second level. Bear thought they were making good time, the dark shape of the Keep looming on the other side of the water, when he heard a creak from above. Felix grabbed his arm. They stood perfectly still, listening to the drizzle of the rain.

Bear gestured in Field-Speak, *Let me look.*

Before Felix could stop him, Bear slipped past. Ahead, a sturdy-looking ladder led up to the next wooden deck. Bear climbed. As he stepped out on to the floorboards, he saw a wink of something move.

He froze. Though there was less clutter here than on the street level below, there were shadowy shapes everywhere: wheels, wooden crates, hanging baskets and barrels, all kinds of paraphernalia piled along the narrow market terrace. Bear's eyes passed over the shapes, studied each one for anything suspicious, until they settled on a figure leaning on the balcony rail.

The head turned towards him. Bear's heart flipped as a pair of eyes, glistening in the dark, fixed on him. It was hard to make out any other features, but there was something about them, something unsettling. They looked ... *unnatural.*

Bear held his wooden pole in front of him like a sword and spoke quietly. "We don't want any trouble."

They didn't reply. His chest told him something was very wrong with the person on the railing. If it was a person at all...

Those eyes. So large and shiny... He felt as if he'd seen them before...

Suddenly, a horrific thought rose in him. A blot.

A blot roaming Trine Market at night?

Before Bear could move, Felix launched himself up on to the deck with his oar in hand. Bear was baffled as the blot's head appeared to detach itself from its shoulders and it leaped over the railing and out into the rain.

Bear blinked. What had just happened? His eyes adjusted, and he found himself staring at a stack of barrels. He watched as an owl glided out over the canal on soundless wings. Bear let out a huge sigh of relief.

"It was just an owl," he said in shock. "I thought it was a blot."

"What?" Felix whispered loudly.

"That bloody owl on those barrels, I thought it was a blot."

The boys caught each other's eyes and bent over double, giggling in silent giddy laughter. They held the railing and gathered their composure. With the tension broken, they stood listening to the sound of the rain for a short while. The relief was heartening.

"I'll take the lead from here," Felix said. "My eyesight's better than yours at night."

Bear nodded and peered over the walkway railing. Here, the Keep still looked like an ominous cliff face, but high above lights twinkled from within its few arched windows. Felix placed a hand on Bear's shoulder.

"It's hard to make out in the rain, but I think I see the postal track," he whispered. "We need to go up another level. We shouldn't see anyone out here at this time—"

"Do you know, I had thought the very same thing."

Felix and Bear spun round to face the voice, holding their wooden oars up in front of them once again.

Walking towards them from the other end of the

walkway was a hooded figure, cloaked in the darkest black. Distant thunder rumbled, and the drizzle became a deluge.

"Wh-what are you doing, sneaking up on us like that?" Bear's voice faltered, but his oar held steady.

The figure's face was entirely concealed within the shadows of their plush, fur-lined hood. It was the sort of hood that only someone from the Rooftop could afford. Bear hadn't expected that, a Roofsider here in these shadowy upper tiers of Cobbleside.

"I was observing you."

The voice sounded female. Bear lowered his staff slightly.

"Well, we aren't doing anything worth observing," he said. "We were just rat-catching."

Bear hoped that she'd leave them to their business, if they left her to hers. The woman stopped walking and brought her hands together, interlocking her fingers. She wore black gloves, and circled her thumbs round each other slowly as she spoke,

"Your lie," she said, "insults me."

Her voice was low and carried an accent Bear had never heard before. It rumbled in his ears. His grip tightened on the oar.

"A lie is a defilement."

"Who says it's a lie?" Felix stepped forward from behind Bear's shoulder.

The woman flinched as if he'd struck her.

"Fennex!" she hissed. Her voice echoed impossibly through the air, ringing over itself again and again and

Bear was horrified to see plumes of smoke pouring out from within the sleeves of her cloak.

"Witch!" Felix gasped as the smoke massed and swirled around her body, engulfing her completely.

Bear swung his oar at her wildly, but connected with nothing.

There was an almighty *boom* and a blinding flash that lit up the wooden platform as if it were midday. Barrels rolled across the floor and hanging baskets swung in their brackets.

When the smoke cleared, the figure was gone.

A little way down the street, a door swung open. Someone held a bright lamp out into the night and yelled an indistinct threat.

A second door creaked open, closer and unlit.

"What have we here?" came a rough voice. A man slipped out of a narrow door, a blade in his hand.

"Run!" Felix yelped, and they raced down the walkway. The man sped after them. Bear pulled down piles of clutter behind them as they went. They hurtled up a set of stairs when Felix stopped suddenly and darted low among some crates.

There were new voices up ahead.

Felix sat with his back pressed against the wood, panting heavily, still grasping his oar. With his free hand, he signalled for Bear to stay hidden in the shadows. Bear swooped sideways into a narrow throughway between buildings.

More people up there, he signed, pointing to the floor above them.

He heard voices shouting from all directions, below them, behind and in front. Most worryingly, footfalls drummed on the floorboards above. The feet walked in rhythm with each other. Felix groaned and ran two fingertips over the back of his hand.

Watchmen.

Bear nodded and signed sharply: *What now? We need to find a way off this level.*

Felix nodded back. The heavy footsteps on the deck above them were getting louder.

Bear looked out over the railing into the rain, the Keep obscured in the shadows. Bear had an idea. He caught Felix's eyes.

Felix's eyes opened wide. *Are you thinking what I'm thinking?*

Bear nodded and held his oar like a vaulting pole.

Felix grinned and did the same.

"Where did you go? Quick now. Come with me…" It was the man with the blade.

As one, Bear and Felix sprang from their hiding spots and vaulted upwards and over the wooden rails. Bear gasped when the cold rain hit him as they launched themselves into the night air.

CHAPTER 10

They flew through the dark like bats. Then let go of their oars and reached out. As frantic as a pair of squirrels, they grasped at the walls of the Keep until their fingers found a crumbling ledge and held on tight.

Bear groaned with relief. They had made it as high as the postal track. Far below, Bear heard a deep *schlunk*, and then another, as their oars plunged into the inky water of the canal. Felix whooped quietly with delight.

Bear dangled a moment, his hands clutching the wood. He heard Felix grunt as he hopped up on to the ledge. Bear began pulling himself up.

"Hold still!" Felix whispered.

Bear froze.

"Come out quick and I'll hide you in my little guest room." The man with the blade crept along the walkway. "I know you're here somewhere…"

Suddenly another voice rang out, loud and authoritative. "You're out after the Evening Bell, Grundy."

The man stood up straight and carefully held his knife behind him.

"N-now, it's n-not a crime to walk in my own neighbourhood, is it?"

"That's exactly what the curfew means, Grundy, as you know full well."

Bear's ears pricked at the speaker's voice. He recognized that contemptuous tone. It was the Whip.

"Out after Evening Bell and, what's more, carrying a knife!"

The torchlight flickered all around Bear. If anyone looked over the balcony, they'd see Felix crouched on the ledge while Bear hung there in the rain. More footsteps. More watchmen.

"Anything?" asked the Whip.

"Nothing."

Bear knew who'd answered before he'd even turned his head; it was the Stone.

"Found this one creeping around with a knife," said the Whip. "What were you doing, Grundy?"

Bear watched as the Stone kicked Grundy to his knees.

"I was … I heard the noise. I came out my door and then… I-I-I-I was following someone."

"Good. You were following someone. And who were you following?"

"I didn't see their faces. Two of 'em, wearing cloaks. Up to no good."

Bear's forearm muscles were burning. He clung on to the railing with a vice grip – but he couldn't hold on for much longer. He breathed slowly. He was running out of time.

"Where did they go?" barked the Stone.

"They disappeared."

There was an almighty whip-crack and Grundy began whimpering. Bear's arms twitched. Felix slowly grasped Bear's wrist and held him where he was.

"I swear it, Ashka!" gasped Grundy. "I promise you! I followed 'em up here! They were right here, and they disappeared."

"Enough," spat the Whip Ashka. "Send Grundy up to Lord Noka. He can decide what to do with him—"

"I did hear a splash," said the Stone. "Maybe they jumped in."

"You'd have to be mad to jump that far down."

"Or scared," said Grundy.

Bear's heart hammered in his chest as footsteps walked towards the railing.

"Wait… What's that?" asked the Stone.

Bear saw a face leaning over the balcony and blinked as the blinding torchlight flared across his face. Fear churned in his stomach. They'd been spotted.

If he let go of the railing, there was a chance he'd hit the water and be able to escape. Their chances of survival were better than if they waited to see what the watchmen would do to them.

"Don't move," Felix whispered. His voice was quiet and insistent. But there was no use waiting. It was now or never. Either they jumped or…

The Stone laughed. "It's just an owl."

Bear scanned the shadows in confusion.

"Well, an owl didn't make that racket, did it?" snapped Ashka. "Something's going on here. Grundy, your night's about to get a lot worse."

The watchmen dragged a moaning Grundy away, and the torchlight faded.

Bear dangled, head spinning. How hadn't they seen him hanging there? Or Felix perched on the ledge? And where had the owl come from?

Felix hauled Bear up and on to the ledge. They crouched side by side in the dark, studying the snaking mass of stairs and bridges that the Keep overlooked. Finally, the watchmen's footsteps faded, and the golden gates clanged shut.

"How did they miss us?" asked Bear.

"Human eyes really aren't any good at night, ey?" Felix sounded as if he were convincing himself. "I could see the watchmen fine. But with the dark, the rain and that torchlight, it must've blinded them. I s'pose that raggedy cloak of yours did a good job of looking like a shadow."

Uncle Jim would be over the moon. Bear couldn't believe their luck.

"The owl, though…" murmured Felix. "That was something else."

Bear hadn't even seen the owl. He shivered, and it wasn't because of the rain out on the ledge. Something seemed to have got into the birds of Calleston.

"Witchwork," he croaked.

Instead of responding, Felix gazed at the water far below. He looked like a statue: huddled down on an elevated stone, his bare feet clinging on like a frog. His hair was scraped behind his pointed ears. He stared, expressionless, down into the dark chasm they'd leapt over. Bear looked down too; he didn't see anything, but then Fennex eyes could see better into the darkness.

"Let's get out of here quick."

Felix led the way. Two blurry figures on a rainy night tiptoeing along the track, if it could still be called such a thing. The long-abandoned track was in a terrible state of repair. It had been left to crumble. Years ago, there would have been a postie wheeling up and down along it, delivering to the inhabitants of Trine Street, but the posties had long ago stopped delivering here, leaving the old track to disintegrate into a cracked and crumbling bird-poo-covered mess.

Felix hopped along it, pointing out slippery or unstable sections as they went. In some parts, it had almost collapsed completely, and they edged along the fragmented ledge on their tiptoes, gripping gaps between the bricks with their fingers.

"It's brighter on this side," Felix whispered.

As they rounded the curved wall of the Keep, they left Trine Market behind. The rain had dwindled and the moon shone brightly. Below the postal track, the flat grey stone of the keep ran smoothly all the way down to the canal. Fortunately, the narrow track was better maintained here, with well-kept wood for hard wheels, and everything was safely secured to the wall.

Bear was grateful for the easier footway, though here they were more exposed to anyone who might be looking. They continued along the track until they approached a section of the wall with chimney-like protrusions that shot up several floors towards the very top of the Keep. In between the brick columns were shadowy recessions. Felix picked up the pace, springing along the track like a squirrel.

Suddenly he dived into one of the dark hollows. Bear followed suit just in time to watch an owl swoop silently by. He poked his head out and locked eyes with Felix. It was definitely following them. The owl perched somewhere on the roof high above and hooted softly.

Felix emerged from the shadows. "I'll be happy if I never see that thing again," he said.

"Careful," whispered Bear. "Look."

Down below, four watchmen were marching along the base of the Keep. They patrolled the canal silently. Bear held a finger to his lips. Felix nodded and ran a hand gradually across his forearm.

Slowly.

They navigated the rest of the brick projections more discreetly, watching the guards turn a corner and disappear, until Felix finally reached the very last crevice in the Keep's wall.

"This must be it," he said. "It's up there somewhere."

They began to climb. The towering brick flumes

rose up and up, high above their heads, all the way to Roofside. As they shimmied up the dark recess, Bear breathed in short bursts, and tried not to look down. At this height, they passed an ornate window set so deeply in its grand facade that it was invisible from down below. They climbed rapidly; chimneying up between the bricks of the Keep was much easier than scaling the town's outer wall, especially without blots in pursuit. After a short time, Felix called down.

"This is it! I'm going across. Be careful."

Felix secured his foot into a crack and swung out on to the breast of the moonlit chimney, then began edging his way round to the other side. He manoeuvred across the stone column and disappeared from view. Bear gathered his breath a moment. Climbing didn't come so easy for him. With his feet jammed in place, he massaged his cold hands before shoving them under his armpits.

"Come on, then!" Felix's hushed call came from the other side. Bear shunted out and round the brickwork. He didn't look down; he just focused on securing his hands and feet, one at a time, one after the other.

"Here you go, Bear, right here. I've got you."

Felix gripped Bear's hand and helped him hop over a little stone parapet. Bear let out a sigh of relief. The boys looked at each other, huge grins spreading across their faces.

"We did it!"

They were technically, for the first time in their lives, on Roofside, albeit the lowest level. They hugged and bounced up and down on the spot in silent celebration.

Bear peeked back over the edge. Down below, the streets of Cobbleside were small, dark and labyrinthine, with sad, crooked spires that failed to reach the sky, and only one or two pinpricks of light that denoted any life. Bear leaned further over the stone handrail and peered all the way down. The watchmen patrolled in the shadows below, and the canal that surrounded the Keep was pitch black.

"It all looks quite scary from up here."

They turned back to study the small covered entryway. The floor, walls and ceiling were made of the same flat grey stone that fortified the Keep. There were no stairs leading to or from this unassuming and out-of-the-way balcony. It was accessible only by the sturdy-looking door in front of them. On each side of the door was an identical stone bench below small identical windows, and nothing else. Behind the door was the room that they'd climbed all this way to access.

Felix tried the doorknob.

"It's locked."

That wasn't good.

"Let me try."

Bear turned the knob slowly, one way, then the other. Nothing. He pushed and pulled to no avail.

"Jim said they don't lock this door."

"Clearly things have changed."

"But why? You'd have to be able to fly to get up here."

"Or climb," Felix pointed out.

He stood on one of the stone benches and peeked through the window.

"I can fit through this."

"How do we open it?"

Felix tapped the window lightly, twice. His yellow eyes glinted in an unsettlingly mischievous way. He curled up his fist and smashed the glass.

"Felix!"

Felix shushed Bear. They listened in suspended tension. There were no sounds from within. Felix peeked his nose through the shattered glass and surveyed the interior.

"This is it! It's exactly how he described."

He withdrew his head and carefully punched through more of the broken glass. It tinkled faintly as it landed on the floor. He tugged off his shirt and folded it over the window sill.

"Wish me luck," he said as he disappeared inside. Bear stood on the stone bench outside and squinted through the window into the dark room. Felix was already on the other end of the room, by a closed door. There was a golden barrel positioned by the doorway, a cup resting on its lid.

"Ruby brew!" said Felix.

"Leave it," said Bear. "Don't touch anything."

Felix ignored him and fiddled with an oil lamp. It was alarmingly bright when lit.

"Should we really be burning that?"

Felix snorted. "How else are we going to see anything?"

In the lamplight, Bear looked around. The room was perfectly square, and there was no furniture in it at all save the golden barrel, which shone in the orange glow of the lamp. But it wasn't the only thing in the room that glittered. Felix groaned as he lifted the lamp higher. The four walls were covered with rows and rows of hooks, and from every single hook was hung a key.

There were hundreds and hundreds of keys, of all colours and shapes and sizes. Bear was mesmerized. In the flickering light they looked like fish scales.

Bear jumped at a metallic noise that clanged from behind. He jerked his head out of the window frame to see Felix opening the door to him.

"Wait... How—"

"The key was in the lock," he said with a shrug.

Bear smiled and followed him inside and they began their hunt through the key room.

Every hook was labelled with a placard. Silver keys with silver labels. Iron keys under rows of black iron placards.

"Pit one ... Pit two ... Pit three ... Pit fifty-three."

"Bear, take a look at this one."

A large golden key hung in the centre of the wall. The bow was moulded into a dragon's head, with the flame erupting from the dragon's mouth acting as the blade of the key. Bear read the sign above. "The lady's vault."

"Whoever she is, it looks like she has a very important vault," said Felix with a sly look.

"Well, it's probably not the one we're looking for," said Bear. "Uncle Jim said nothing fancy."

Felix stared at Bear for a moment, then shook his head and continued the search.

The variety of keys was endless: a brass key labelled *kitchen*; a wooden key labelled *den*; a glass key labelled *nest*. On and on. They read one row at a time, careful that none went overlooked.

"There's one missing up there." Bear pointed out a plaque made from a dark burnished metal.

"Just you watch it be the one key we came for." Felix held the lamp higher.

"Here, I'll give you a leg up," said Bear.

Felix stepped up into Bear's clasped hands and drew close to empty hook, holding the light to the inscription. "No. It says *Snakewood Tower*. But our key might be something similar. It's for a culvert." Felix hopped down. "So it'll sometimes be exposed to water. We need something strong-looking."

"Maybe we should look along the floor?" suggested Bear. "If the key to a tower is up high… All the canals are down in Cobbleside – maybe culvert keys will be down low?"

Felix, who'd been scratching behind a pointed ear in a very canine fashion, stopped and thought about it, then nodded. "Good idea."

They went back to their search quietly, focusing on the diverse array of keys in the lower half of the room. Felix crouched with the torch in hand, Bear crawled below him. They examined the most ordinary-looking ones they could find, ignoring the bejewelled, the ornate and the delicate.

"Culvert one!" said Felix. He looked a little further along the wall. "And here's five!" He held up a solid brass key with a celebratory flourish. The key was sturdy and unremarkable.

Bear squatted by Felix and examined the placards in the warm light. There were hordes of culvert keys, all in a long, identical row, many covered in cobwebs. Bear tried to imagine the vast network of passageways, chambers and tunnels that must be hidden away within the walls of Calleston.

He unfastened the leather pouch at his belt and slid out the silver book Jim had given him. He opened the metal casing, revealing the rectangular bed of clay inside. Bear pressed the key firmly into the clay, then repeated the same process on the other side, making a clean impression.

"Done."

Felix rested the lamp on the golden barrel and replaced the key on its hook as Bear slid the book back into the leather pouch. He tied it securely at his waist and felt a sudden wave of confidence. They'd done it. All that remained was to get back down to—

Without warning, the door swung open, and a fair-haired girl slipped into the room, a small white dog at her feet. Bear and Felix froze. She took the oil lamp and held it out to light the room…

Her eyes landed on Bear and Felix, huddled together in the corner.

She gasped. Bear thought she would scream. And then the horrified look on her face changed into something else.

"It's you!" She uttered the words in disbelief.

The dog at her feet barked and she blinked, snapping out of her trance. She dropped the lamp and sprinted from the room, her terrified screams ringing in the night.

Bear blew out the lamp and he and Felix scrambled out on to the little terrace.

"Bear! Lock that door!"

Bear hurtled back into the key room and grabbed the key from the lock. He slammed the outer door shut behind him and locked it from the outside.

He could already hear watchmen yelling as they raced through corridors towards the key room. Felix looked wildly over the edge at the drop below.

"No!" said Bear. "Even if we make it, there are patrols down there."

From inside the key room they heard watchmen yelling.

"Show yourselves!"

The door behind them rattled violently and torchlight flared at the windows.

"They've locked it!"

"Batter it down, man!"

"What do we do?" said Bear.

"Well, we can't climb down," said Felix rapidly. "We can't jump … and that door won't hold forever…"

Felix looked at Bear, a grin spreading across his face.

"There's only one way to go."

"Where?"

Felix's eyes flickered towards the turrets and lofty buttresses that loomed above them.

"Up."

Meya pushed the cup of ruby brew away.

"I said no, Luca! No is what I meant."

"Forgive me, Lady Meya. I thought it would help with the shock."

Luca stepped back. Her attendants gathered at her sides in their nightwear. Lord Noka stood at the foot of her bed with a look of deep concern.

"And then what happened, my dear?"

"Percy charged them! He stopped the intruders from attacking, and I ran for my life!"

Percy lay sprawled on his back. Lord Noka thought to give him a scratch. When he heard Percy's low growl, he thought again.

"It must have been a terrible fright," he said slowly. "I assure you, we will find them. The only thing I don't understand is … why you were in the Keep at all?"

"Percy was barking all evening," Meya lied smoothly. "He wouldn't sleep until I followed him. I think he must have realized…"

Noka nodded thoughtfully.

"Well, everybody should get some sleep. Long-laid plans are fruiting this week. Field Day approaches, and our visitors draw closer."

"I agree," said Meya.

In part, she was telling the truth. She had her own plans, after all.

CHAPTER

11

Bear winced as Felix gently raised his foot. "How badly does it hurt?"

Bear sucked in cool air and blew out hot, breathing through the pain in his ankle. It had twisted agonizingly when he'd jumped from a parapet down into the thick bushes where they hid now. Slowly, the throbbing lost some of its bite.

"It's getting better now." He unscrunched his face and looked around.

They were surrounded by a dense circle of leafy bushes dotted with white flowers. The sky was still black but carried some of the dark glowy blues that preceded the dawn. He had no idea how long it was until Morning Bell. He looked up at the wall they'd jumped down from. He was so very relieved to not be climbing any more.

Bear looked at Felix. "Thanks."

"For what?"

Bear kept his voice low.

"You kept us going. I couldn't have done that alone. That was incredible – the way you climb. You're amazing."

Felix grinned. "I could've told you that."

"Seriously. Everyone knows Fennex are stronger than humans, but I didn't see by how much before…"

Felix looked a mix of happy and embarrassed. "That's 'cause you don't have Fennex eyes either."

Bear laughed softly. "I suppose it is." He shook his leg and began twisting his foot in circles, one way, then the other.

"I'll be fine," he said at last. "Just need to rest for a bit."

Felix nodded and collapsed on to his back. "Me too. I could fall asleep right here, but *don't* let me."

They'd been evading watchmen all night. The search for the intruders had been exhaustive and the watchmen had scoured every nook and cranny they could find. By the time Bear and Felix had clambered to the roof, there were already watchmen combing the area, but the Keep's summit had become their gateway to the rest of Roofside. Bear and Felix had spent the night clambering along enormous window sills and ledges, bridges and balconies, scrambling up and over walls, through courtyards, desperately avoiding the attention of the guards. They'd huddled behind statues as watchman after watchman prowled by. Eventually, they'd ended up jumping from a towering wall into the bushes in which they now found themselves.

The bushes grew closely together, and well above Bear's height, so they were hidden from sight. Felix lay on his back, eyes closed. Bear stood gingerly and hobbled around their hideout.

"What's out there?" asked Felix.

"Looks like a forest to me."

"That's what I thought too."

Bear could never have imagined there would be so many trees up on Roofside. He'd never been inside a forest before, that was unnerving in itself, but there was something extra strange about knowing that right now there were untold numbers of people sleeping below them. It felt like having mice under the floorboards. Bear wasn't sure he liked it.

"Do you think Roofsiders think much about Cobblesiders? What we're up to?"

Felix took a second before responding. "Sometimes we see 'em looking down, don't we? They probably look down about the same amount we look up."

"Probably," Bear agreed. "It must be pretty easy to forget about us while they're walking through a real forest, though, ey? A forest without blots in it... Do you think it's safe to have a look?"

Felix rolled on to his stomach, and began shuffling through the bushes. Bear joined him.

They gawped around at the silent rooftop woodland. It was a huge walled space with an old, rusted gate at each end. Among the medley of trees, statues of various noble-looking people stood proudly, and in the centre of it all, in a circular clearing, was a tower. Rising just above the tree tops, it was not so tall as to be seen from Cobbleside. But despite its unimposing size, something about its construction, and perhaps its positioning in the woodland,

119

was eerily commanding. Various paths wound through the trees, all of them in the end leading towards the tower.

"I wonder what's inside."

Felix yawned. "Maybe gold," he replied. "Or jewels? Weapons? Or dead bodies!"

"Keep your voice down!" said Bear. The watchman may not have ended the search just yet.

"Dead bodies? Do you think?" Bear asked. The thought unsettled him.

"Yeah, maybe the Overlord's wife is in there."

Bear stared up at the sinister-looking tower as he recalled what had happened to her. The poor woman had fallen from the roof during a rainstorm. At the time, the typical rumours had filled the taverns in Cobbleside, but Bear could see after their climb just how dangerous a rooftop walk could be, and how dazzling.

They stared out of their hiding place for a while, until Bear cleared his voice and spoke quietly.

"That was a witch in the market ... wasn't it?"

Felix sighed deeply. "Undeniably."

Bear felt his heart sinking as he gazed into the sky.

Witches in Calleston. He hated that phrase.

Witches had been whispered about in Calleston since he'd been old enough to hear such things. But when he was still a young boy, he'd learned how *witches in Calleston* could ruin lives, could end them. Bear had lost his mother and Aber had never been the same.

Now, years later, they'd discovered a real witch loose in

Cobbleside with their own eyes. Bear didn't know how to feel. He only knew how he'd felt about this mother. He'd loved her. And now she was gone.

"The Stone shone a torch at us. How come they didn't see me hanging off the railing? Or you stood on top?" Bear asked.

"I don't know exactly," said Felix, " but he saw the owl and he didn't see us."

"It's like the owl was … watching out for us?" Bear continued, "And there was that black bird flapping around on practice day. Do you get the feeling that there's something going on? Something not natural?"

Felix looked as if he agreed, but he didn't say so. "I don't know what exactly is going on, nor do I want to. It gives me the creeps. Let's mind our own business first before worrying about anything else."

They were both quiet for a moment. Then another picture came into Bear's head.

"And that girl in the key room…"

"What about the girl?"

"She saw us."

"She saw two shapes in the dark before screaming and running."

"She looked at us like … like she *knew* us."

"That's impossible. We've never been up here, and she didn't look like she's spent much time splashing around in Cobbleside canals. She just thought we were thieves."

"Maybe," Bear replied. He thought about her startled

face, framed by her long fair hair, the way she'd looked at them ... at him.

He wondered what it would be like to be her, to live up here, not down there.

They sat quietly in their bushy hideout. The dark sky would be getting lighter soon.

"We need to find a way down before dawn," sighed Felix.

Bear's stomach sank. He didn't want to leave just yet. He wanted to get something out, while they had some time.

"Felix," he said, "do you ever feel that ... everything is ... bad? Wrong. Twisted. Like Uncle Jim said. The blots are... There are more and more every day. The harvest gets smaller every year. We're expected to make that better, but how? We've pulled speedweed out of the ground for months. It's already coming back."

Bear pulled at the grass. Felix was absolutely silent. The garden was absolutely silent. There was space to talk, and it felt good. So Bear carried on.

"Everyone's hungry all the time, and we act like things will change once the crop comes in, but what if it doesn't? What if the speedweed and the blots ... win? Sometimes I think everyone must be thinking the same thing, that the town's doomed. But it's so much to sort out, isn't it? Where do you even start? So everyone puffs their pipes and sips their ruby brew. What if we ran out of that? We'll have to abandon it all before we even had a chance of making it to Roofside..." Bear trailed off into silence.

For a moment, Felix said nothing, just put a hand on his friend's shoulder. Then with a grin he said, "But, Bear..."

Bear looked across at him.

Felix spread his arms wide. "We already made it..."

Bear laughed and punched him on the arm. "Look, I know what you mean, of course I do. But there's no point in—"

In the distance, an iron gate squeaked loudly. The two friends froze like frightened squirrels. Someone was in the woods. The gate whined sorrowfully again before clanging shut, and two voices headed towards them. It sounded as if they were trying very hard not to have an argument.

Felix signed at him: *Be quiet.*

Bear nodded. They listened to the voices approach. At first, they were just an indistinguishable rumble, then a deep voice became clearer.

"... but, Noka, the window was smashed from the outside – the Keep has been breached. There's no telling who might have slipped through our home unchecked – and the watchmen do nothing but arrogant posturing! They are failing us on every front."

The deep voice sounded exasperated.

"I understand your distress," said the second voice, soothing. "But try not to let two petty thieves who fled empty-handed upset you. Trust me. I will ensure that the watchmen are up to task."

The voices grew clearer as they walked down a path that led right past the bushes where the boys were hiding.

"You're running out of time, Noka. If our men

remain ineffective and disobedient, what do you think the outcome will be? The royals think little of us, and we must not prove them right. Remember, we are not leaving Calleston to its fate, and the Queen must see that if she is to help."

The boys looked at each other. *The royals? The Queen?*

"You know I support that aim entirely, Overlord Goodman."

Felix gasped audibly. It was the Overlord. Walking towards where they hid. Bear pressed a finger to his lips. Felix nodded, eyes wide.

"But, if the Queen is to think well of us, there are more urgent matters to which we must attend," went on the other voice. "It is imperative that we renew some of the more dilapidated parts of Cobbleside before her arrival. The Queen's eyes will not only scan our faces in judgement, they will also sweep the floor."

Bear couldn't believe his ears. *The Queen. In Calleston?* There hadn't been a royal visit in decades. And never during Queen Meléna's imperious reign. Her late mother, the then Queen Ulúla, had been put on trial for participating in witchwork. And, in the biggest scandal to rock the Queendom in living memory, Princess Meléna had had her own mother put to death. In the following years, the young queen ruled the Free City with an iron fist, determined to eradicate all witchwork from the land, but she had never left the comfort of the Free City Palace to do so, until now.

"You confuse me, Noka. To what end?" The Overlord sounded wary. "Why suddenly waste our time prettying the town for the people who, up until now, have left it to rot? Do we not want her to see the true conditions of Calleston?"

The Overlord and his aide strolled closer. The boys eyed each other tensely as they listened to feet scuffing the flagstones beside them.

It seemed that Noka was not to be deterred.

"It is a delicate balance, my lord. Be mindful that Queen Meléna is renowned for her quick temper. As she draws closer, I fear that she may be so angered by the conditions in Cobbleside that she will refuse to help us at all. She will be looking for someone to blame for Calleston's misfortune, my lord… Is there a risk she would punish the workers, do you think?"

Bear looked at Felix. The idea that Queen Meléna would crack down on Cobblesiders made his blood run cold. Felix looked fixedly at the ground, listening as the men swept past the shrubbery and headed towards the tower. There was a weighty silence until the Overlord sighed. "I see your point, Noka, and I fear you may be right. I can't say I like it, but let the necessary improvements be made. Where are the watchmen now?"

"Sent back to their beds. They will join us here in the tower at Morning Bell."

There was the sound of a key turning in a lock, the door in the tower presumably being opened, then a soft boom as it closed, and the two voices faded.

Felix wiggled his head through the bushes and scanned the gardens. Bear followed suit.

Everything was still.

"The Queen in Calleston," Bear whispered. "When are they going to tell everyone?"

"*We're* going to tell everyone," said Felix, "but we need to get down there first."

Bear nodded.

"Is your ankle all right?"

Bear nodded again.

"Right. Back to the Keep while it's still dark. We won't have a chance of making it down without being seen if the sun comes up. Keep your eye on the tower door. I'll keep mine on the gate—"

As though in response, the gate wailed loudly. They spun round, but there was nothing there.

"Wind," whispered Felix after a moment. "Let's go."

As they slipped out of the walled garden and headed for the Keep, Bear couldn't shake the feeling that somebody was watching them.

In the darkness, an owl hooted.

CHAPTER

12

Meya pulled the dark cloak around her and drooped her head down so that she disappeared among the barrels and burlap sacks between which she was hiding. The cloak was lined with rabbit fur, but the outside was a dull brown leather. It must have been some sort of travelling cloak, not that Meya was ever allowed to travel.

After years of watching the women on the cobbles rush around in their drab brown or grey garments, she was pretty sure she'd selected the most inconspicuous costume she had.

The brown cloak had been her best find; the leather was well-worn, there were dark stains and even a genuine burn mark. She'd been elated when she'd discovered it in the cloakroom during the merchants' dinner and had raced to hide it above the canopy of her bed.

The dress she was less sure of. On first inspection, it was a simple kirtle. The skirts were not too full, which she was happy about, but there was rather a lot of embroidery on the bodice. The decoration was minimal, though, all coppers and golds, which complemented the brown. The delicate threads were woven into agricultural designs: corn, wheat and sinsenn vines wound round her neckline and waist. There was a particularly hideous pumpkin, which was the main reason Meya had never worn the dress, but it would work perfectly for Cobbleside.

She huddled down among the equipment. Early that morning, in a much-needed effort to repair Cobbleside, her father had asked for materials to be sent down below the gates. With the Queen's visit imminent, Noka had been uncharacteristically urgent, and so the workers had loaded the descender haphazardly without inspection or documentation. Meya had jumped at the chance to stow herself away.

The descender rumbled as it began to travel downwards. She was ecstatic. She'd never been to Cobbleside. Occasionally, the highborn would be escorted through Upper Cobbleside to explore the market, but never without a watchman as escort. Now Meya was finally heading to the bedrock bottom, on her own. Well, not entirely on her own; she clutched her dog, Percy, close, nestled securely in a brown satchel. She pictured the boy. She wondered if she would see him today. She'd never imagined she would really see him up close. His face had been unremarkable, but it was exactly as she'd pictured it, pale skin, dark hair and eyes, and a sad, weary look to him. She couldn't believe he'd had the nerve to sneak up to Roofside. It had immediately convinced her of her ability to find a way down.

They must be getting close to the bottom now. The ropes and pulleys groaned as the colossal wheels of the great descender turned, until, with a great thud, the descender came to a jolting stop. There were alarming squeaks as mice ran from the clanging machine. Meya shuddered, but she kept still. She needed to be smart. She'd concealed herself well, and the next step was smuggling herself out without being seen. The great doors swung open. She peeked through the hood of her cloak.

Outside a collection of rag-tag men and women began unloading the goods. From what she could see, the warehouse was cavernous, with an open floor and high ceilings. The giant loading gates leading outside were flung wide open.

The workers began unloading the barrels, packs and burlap sacks from the descender floor. They heaved them on to handcarts to be carried away. From her hiding place, Meya peeked out at their faces as they unloaded the equipment. It was like a missing-tooth competition down here.

"You were right!" said one young man. "The Overlord wants us to tart up Cobbleside. Absolute doylum!"

"There's piss-all scran, either! He's just sent down a bunch of equipment! Useless blotson!"

They all laughed. Meya was outraged. She didn't know what a doylum was, but her father was not a blotson. He was a good man who did his best to make ends meet, but without assistance, or a miracle, he was simply stretched too thin. Yes, they needed a good harvest – even Roofsiders had been tightening their belts. The bad-mouthing of her father sickened her, it infuriated her and something about it scared her too. The floorborn were looking for someone to blame.

Their mocking laughter drifted away as they carted their goods off. Now was her opportunity. Meya rose from her hiding spot and, carrying Percy tightly, slipped out of the descender and into the warehouse.

She hadn't wanted to bring Percy with her, but he really would not stop barking if she left him alone in her bedchamber, which would alert people to her absence. There was no way she could disappear for hours if she didn't take him along; plus, he might offer her some protection. Cobbleside was notoriously dangerous.

She took stock of the warehouse floor. The air down here was heavy with dust and shadows, and it was hard to make head or tail of what she was seeing. Beyond jumbled rows of barrels, she saw bent figures surrounding a large pile of burnt and blackened vines. It was all so ominous. She was absolutely thrilled.

She soon spotted the exit, an enormous entryway where workers tracked in and out. She moved quickly, ignoring an unsettlingly skinny old man who'd stopped working and stared open-mouthed when he caught sight of her. She drew her hood further over her face and stroked Percy discreetly inside his leather carry satchel, more to settle herself than him.

The gates opened out on to one of Calleston's larger docks. Meya forced herself to walk calmly. Men and women lugged sacks on their shoulders, heaving crates and carts across the warehouse. A giant cart with more half-burnt speedweed rolled by. Everyone seemed to be cursing loudly and sweating horribly.

Percy's little tongue found Meya's fingers and began licking. Meya reminded herself that she had been waiting for this moment all her life and strode on to the dock.

Outside, it was a sunny afternoon, though it was much darker down here than up on the rooftops. Much of the daylight was blocked by the towering buildings that surrounded the dock. Wooden pontoons stretched out along it over the water and groupings of longboats were moored in place. Meya baulked as a large figure stepped in her path.

It was a dock woman of enormous proportions. Her dark hair, held back by a strip of dirty linen, was damp with sweat. She put her hands on her hips.

"Are you lost?" she asked Meya gruffly.

Meya shook her head and tried to walk on, but the woman put out a meaty hand to stop her. She looked Meya up and down. Meya felt like a mouse in the paws of a cat. No, not a cat, a lumbering bear. The woman whistled loudly.

"Burna! Come and 'ave a look, would ya!"

Percy poked his head out of Meya's cloak, tongue lolling and panting excitedly. The dock woman frowned.

"Is that a dog?" she said.

"Whadyou say, Petal?"

Meya yanked Percy inside her cloak just as a skinny lady with short white hair skidded to a stop next to them. She hooked herself on to the bicep of the woman blocking Meya's path. Meya's breath caught in her chest as she stared at the woman. The skin on her twiggy arms was inked all over with spidery black designs. There were two great beasts with their mouths open, revealing large fangs. Meya had only ever seen such dreadful illustrations in books.

"What's wrong, Petal?" she said. "I've got enough on my plate right now. I'm just about ready to knock out one of these useless blot'oles…"

The large dock woman swung her head towards Meya. "She shouldn't be here."

Meya gulped, but she wasn't about to be sent back up. Before the women could think twice, Meya tried to dash past them. A shockingly strong grip caught her by the elbow.

"Hold up, darlin'!"

The woman with inked arms clutched Meya, peering into her hood. She had sharp, bright eyes, the kind of eyes that you don't lie to. Meya twisted painfully in her vice-grip and let out a frightened whimper. Percy growled from within the fur of Meya's cloak.

"Get off her, Burna!"

At the dock woman's word, Burna let go. Meya stumbled back out of their reach, grasping her arm. Before either of them could speak, Meya decided to take charge.

She pointed at the woman.

"You. Bertha."

The inked woman blinked. "My name is *Burna*."

At first glance, Burna was as intimidating as her friend: her face crowded with scars, her white hair spiky and her arms begrimed with black ink. But after the initial shock, Meya saw that she was just a raw-boned old woman with a garish exterior. Meya drew herself as tall as she could and used the stony, unbending voice that her father used when he had to put his foot down.

"Burna, I will overlook your ... your *audacious* mishandling of my person, only because I require assistance."

Burna squinted in the sun.

"You require assis—"

"I *demand* assistance."

Burna rubbed her white hair and spluttered.

"L-l-look here. I mean, I don't know who you think you—"

She'd flustered her. *Good*, thought Meya. She was her father's daughter; she knew when to seize the initiative. She flipped off her battered leather hood with a flourish.

"I am Lady Meya Omega, Jewel of the Rooftops. The only child of Lord Greyson Goodman, Steward and Overlord of all Calleston, as appointed by the Queen of the Free City. And I demand your assistance."

She held their gaze in dignified silence. The women looked at each other in what Meya was certain was awe.

"I'm Petal," said the dock woman at last. She didn't

sound awed, Meya thought, but then she was probably too rough to let such emotions colour her voice. "I'm gonna finish unloading the descender. Leave this with you, Burna."

Petal faced Meya and bowed deeply, more elegantly than Meya had thought the great lump capable of, and then she strode into the warehouse.

Burna's sharp eyes took in Meya. They reminded her of a falcon's.

"Well, Meya Omega, sparkling diamond from Roofside, I am Burna Odeffa. The oldest, saltiest and busiest hag in Cobbleside, and if you don't disappear from my dock right now, I will dunk you by that pretty hair of yours into the canal water, and I use the term 'water' very, very loosely."

Burna took a menacing step towards her. Meya gasped.

"But I ... I-I-I'm—"

"I don't give two flying fox farts if you're Queen Mum Ulúla herself back from the dead."

Burna closed the gap between them. One step at a time. Meya couldn't believe she was being threatened.

"Get. Off. My. Dock."

Meya spun on her heel and sprinted down the wooden deck. The boats on either side bustled with activity. She dodged looming Cobblesiders as she fled, Burna's scathing laugh ringing in the air behind her.

Meya had no idea where she was going, she just ran, clutching Percy close in his bag, until she saw an open gate to her left. She shot down it. At last she felt her feet hit cobbles and slowed down. She'd made it. She was Cobbleside! She looked back at the name above the gate. GRUB DOCK, it read. *How vile.*

Now that Meya was safe from those dreadful women, her anger set in. The arrogance of a pair of dock workers to talk to her in such a way! They were uneducated, overbold Cobblesiders … from Cobbleside! Still, she had to remind herself, she was finally here. After years spent peering over the wall, wondering what it was like down here, here she was.

She drank in the chaotic mishmash of homes. The long, creaking wooden balconies were fascinating up close; everything seemed to be falling apart. There were potted plants everywhere, old furniture, a man hanging out washing, a mother nursing her child, neighbours gossiping with each other. More than one person eyeballed her as she wandered through the town. They seemed so … severe. But then they were living a real, authentic, dangerous life. She started to recognize a similar look in them, the same wariness that the boy carried, but, despite looking so thin and gaunt, there was a kind of solidness to them that she couldn't put her finger on.

A group of young children played a game with a linen ball. They were dirty, but their smiles were wide. They flew around Meya like a flock of starlings, screaming with laughter, and none of them wore any shoes. It was all so different.

The only thing it had in common with Roofside was that wherever people were – gathered on bridges, balconies and stairwells, in doorways, down by the docks – everyone was enjoying sinsenn. Red clouds wafted from windows, from haggard women repairing shoes in the street, from a small man selling potatoes and from a quiet group sitting along a crumbling brick wall. They all smoked and drank sinsenn. That felt like home.

But the whole place was a confusing maze. It felt like being a mouse under a floorboard, a strange mixture of comforting and claustrophobic. She entered a street named Ship Street, more jumbled than any she had seen, and was horrified to see real mice fleeing her steps. One floor up, a wooden mermaid jutted from a crooked timber stairwell. A tiny, runny-nosed Cobblesider boy sat on the mermaid's shoulders, clinging to her like a monkey. He stared down at Meya as she drifted past, his eyes wide.

Adorable, she thought. Then, as she passed underneath, she heard a hacking sound and felt a glob of something wet hit the back of her neck.

"Ugh!" shrieked Meya, and she rubbed at the slimy patch as she ran out from under the disgusting little gremlin.

Before she could admonish him, a low rumbling sound began and a shout came from behind.

"Eyes up!"

A woman appeared high above her, suspended in the air, hurtling overhead. She flew over Meya's head, landing twenty feet in front of her, planting her feet firmly on the cobbles. A postal carrier. Giving a mighty push, she soared three storeys high towards a small wooden platform where a man waited for her, blowing plumes of red smoke into the air.

As she headed their way, Meya studied the harness and ropes that allowed her to fly up and down the streets. She began chatting with a scary-looking man on the balcony. He had a shaved head, a thick moustache and appeared to be carrying a large metal hook. The postal carrier handed over the letter, then grabbed the man's hook and shook it, before leaping off the platform and zooming on down the street, wheels rumbling on the track high above.

As Meya drew closer to the shaven-headed man, he sliced open the package with the hook, glancing down at Meya, pipe in mouth. She hurried past into the next street.

Her eyes drifted upwards. From this angle, you could see nothing of the Rooftops at all. She wondered what areas she was passing below: maybe the orchards, or perhaps the games court. From up there, Cobbleside was a miniature world; from down here, the Rooftop was basically invisible.

Meya loved people-watching. Sometimes she people-watched all day. She'd pick an interesting Cobblesider and follow them until they disappeared from view. She would race across the roof, trying to work out what alleyway or bridge they might re-emerge from. The thrill of finding them again was addictive.

Occasionally, Meya recognized people months later, by

their walk, their hair, or a raucous laugh that drifted up to her ears. Sometimes she recognized them for other reasons.

She hadn't been able to stop thinking about the boy. She thought about the other night – him crouched in the key room, his face turned to her, dark eyes shining in the lamplight. She'd recognized him immediately. She felt a surprising rush of fear and excitement at the thought that she could actually bump into him. She wondered if he knew who she was? Or her name? What would she say to him? What *could* she say?

A girl about Meya's age rolled a large barrel through the narrow street, puffing happily on her pipe. She saw Meya and smiled a broad smile. Meya smiled back. They passed, the sound of the barrel rattling over the cobbles cheerfully. Meya looked back at the girl; she kept on puffing and kept on rolling the barrel down the street. Meya wondered what her life was like.

"I like your dress," the girl called suddenly over her shoulder.

"Thank you! I like yours!" Meya called back.

A Cobbleside girl liked what she was wearing! Embarrassingly, her heart actually skipped a beat at the thought. She couldn't help but smile. Meya looked at the girl's dress. It was in fact a simple shirt and a dirty pair of trousers. Meya hurried on.

She stepped through an archway to her right and found herself at the beginning of a long, empty street. It was narrow and winding, with a small canal running down its middle. It was the forgotten backside of the houses she'd passed, she realized. The continuous dark brick ran on endlessly, on both sides, no doors, and just the odd, small window. She tried to peek into one as she walked, but it was too filthy to see anything on the other side.

Percy began to growl. At first she thought it was the unpleasant smell in the area, and then she realized there was a boy up ahead, on the other side of the thin canal. He was sitting on a low window sill, puffing red smoke. The boy smiled as she approached and hopped down on to the street, tossing his pipe back through the window.

"Oi. Girl. Where you goin'?"

She didn't particularly like the smile he gave her. It was overly confident. He was smaller than she was, but there was something about him that made her uneasy. He was very thin, almost bird-like, and had dark circles under his eyes. Meya didn't respond to his call. She kept walking along the canal.

"I'm talkin' t' you! Hello? Can you speak?"

She began striding faster down the cobbles, hoping to escape the stench, and the boy, a little quicker. His face darkened. He began following her along the opposite side of the water. She was grateful that the canal was between them. Hopefully, there were no bridges ahead. He waved and called over again.

"Can you talk?"

He pointed to his mouth as he did so, to make sure she knew what he was saying. He looked angry. She kept walking and shook her head. Partly because she didn't want to talk to him and partly because she was becoming aware of a disgusting smell. She gagged and held her breath, scanning the area for a dead animal.

The canal curved slightly, so she couldn't see very far ahead. She'd have to keep walking until she found an alleyway or street to exit into.

"Are you sure you're goin' the right way?"

He skipped confidently along the path. She peered upwards – floors and floors of brick all the way up to Roofside, but no stairs. There were footbridges above them. Thankfully, they were too high to connect Meya and the floorborn boy.

"Can you hear me?" his voice called again.

His hands made funny shapes in the air around his face as if he were drawing. She decided to trot a little faster. She wanted to be somewhere else; she didn't want to have to draw another breath of the filthy air. She felt a wave of nausea. She covered her mouth with one hand and let out a miserable groan.

"Oh, you're not foolin' no one! I've heard you now!"

The boy danced along beside her. Meya's mouth filled with saliva and she felt her face drain of blood. She waved her hand in the air.

"What's that smell?" she gasped.

"Oh. It's the water," said the boy matter-of-factly. "It's the beginnin' of the Runs, so ... well ... people use it like, you know, a cesspit."

Meya couldn't hold it any longer. She launched a perfect javelin of vomit into the air, which soared impressively, before plunging into the slimy water of the canal.

The boy looked stunned, then blinked. "Yeah, that sort of thing."

Meya placed her hand on a wooden post and heaved. She would not be telling her attendants about this. She felt air cooling her sweaty forehead. Percy whined and wiggled his head out of the fur-lined cloak to see what was wrong.

The boy gasped. "Is that a dog?" he whispered.

"Y-yes," Meya replied shakily.

Percy barked at the boy. The boy smiled at Percy in open-mouthed astonishment.

"Dawdy," the boy said wistfully, drawing out the word slowly like a long whistle.

Meya didn't know what dawdy was, but it sounded positive. The menacing quality in the boy completely melted away. He took off his little brown hat and held it at his heart, dark eyes opened wide.

"Where did you find a dog?"

"Where can I escape this smell?"

"Not the way you're goin'. You're headin' towards Slime Bend."

The boy replaced his cap. "Follow me."

He ran towards a timber framework that climbed partway up the brick walls. Repairs were being made, though everything looked equally dilapidated to Meya.

The boy pulled a ladder from among the scaffolding and let it fall over the canal, forming a bridge. He stepped deftly across it until they were on the same side. Meya didn't move.

"Girl! Dog! Follow me!" he said, walking on ahead.

Meya decided to trust her gut, and swept after the boy, holding her nose. Up ahead, the canal got dingier as the water entered a shadowy tunnel, but before they reached it the boy dodged to the left and disappeared into the wall.

When Meya got closer, she discovered the passageway he'd slid into. The gap was tall but very slim, and worryingly cramped. But there was light at the end of the tunnel, and the boy had almost made his way to the other side.

"Try not to touch the wall," he called back.

Meya turned sideways to pass through and held Percy at her hip. Still, in places the walls pressed against her body.

"Does your dog have a name?" the boy asked as Meya slipped out of the passageway behind him.

Thankfully, the smell was greatly reduced on this side.

"Of course. His name is Percy."

The boy's face lit up like the sun. He was younger than she'd first guessed.

"Can I touch him?"

Meya pursed her lips. Percy was unpredictable, but the boy looked so excited.

"If you go carefully," she said. "He won't hesitate to bite."

The boy nodded, and once again removed his hat. That was rather respectful, she thought. He crouched close to Percy making cooing sounds. Surprisingly, Percy didn't growl at all. He allowed the boy to come close. The boy held out his cap and let Percy sniff that thoroughly, giving him time to make up his mind, then he put out a hand.

"He's a lovely boy." The boy smiled as Percy started snuffling his fingers.

"Yes. He is," said Meya.

After a minute of enjoying Percy nuzzling at his face and distributing a few well-placed licks, the boy stood back up. Meya was surprised to see tears half forming in his eyes. He looked all at once happy and heartbroken. Meya thought he might cry and so she put a hand on his shoulder, then discreetly removed it, and wiped her hand on her skirt.

"Are you all right?" she asked.

"I'm fine … just miss my dog."

He sighed heavily, large eyes wet with tears.

"Oh no, what happened?"

He shook his head. He didn't want to talk about it.

"When the time is right, maybe you'll get another one?"

The boy looked at her like she was mad. "No animals in town unless they're for eating… Witches put animals up to witchwork. Though this one doesn't look too dangerous."

He petted Percy again, then backed off and cleared his throat. "Thank you for lettin' me meet Percy. But you best get him out of here, for his own good."

He popped his hat back on, nodded and began sliding back down the passageway.

"Wait! Where are you going?" Meya yelped.

"Home."

"Back that way? Towards the smell?"

He looked embarrassed. "You don't really smell it after a while." He shrugged. "It's worse when it gets hot. We call it blot-rot hot."

Meya couldn't keep wandering the streets aimlessly. She needed a guide and this local boy, who loved Percy, was perfect.

"I was hoping you'd show me around."

The boy looked confused. He spoke flatly.

"Around what? The Runs? If you couldn't handle the smell on my street, I wouldn't recommend goin' any further."

"No, I mean around Cobbleside."

The boy looked at Percy, then took in Meya anew.

"So you're from out of town? Heard we've had some visitors lately … or … wait. Are you from…?"

His dark eyes flickered to the roof, then back to Meya. She slowly put her finger to her lips.

"Blot-in-a-pot," the boy whispered. "What a day."

Meya smiled. She'd imagined that the floorborn might be excited to meet a girl from the rooftops, but she had to stay discreet. Only tell those who she could trust. She considered the scruffy boy standing before her; he seemed sweet.

He had friendly brown eyes, now she looked at him more closely, and though his eye bags made him look decidedly Cobbleside, she rather liked it. She wondered how he'd appeared so menacing before.

"And what is your name, young man?" she asked him.

He stood up proudly, suddenly speaking with a theatrical gusto.

"Dorloc Odittany. Nice to meet ya. Friends call me Doc. It'd be my pleasure to escort someone from … like you…"

Meya beamed. Doc lowered his voice suddenly. "You should put Percy back in his bag, though. To be safe."

"If that would be prudent, absolutely."

Meya pulled the cloak back over her satchel and Percy wriggled down into the bag.

"Now. Is there anything in particular you'd like to see?" asked Doc.

Meya wondered where she might find the boy. She wondered where he lived. Or would he be out in the field? She didn't want to be so brazen as to ask outright.

"Somewhere a little more lively? Where would you go if you wanted to bump into someone?"

She winced at the indiscreet wording.

"Who?"

"Anyone!"

"That'll be Main Market. All Cobbleside roads lead there in the end. But then I bet you see the market proper good from … where you live. The square's a bit less rough

145

than round here too. If we go much further down my street, smell's the least of your worries."

"That sounds perfect, Dorloc. Do lead the way."

He patted his hat down on his head and strode on. High above them, the buildings jettied towards each other. They walked down the narrow streets towards distant voices.

"What was your friend called?" Meya asked. "Your pup?"

"Orange," said Doc.

"How charming. Why did you call him that?"

"You 'member oranges?"

Meya frowned.

"I loved oranges. So…" he shrugged. "I called her Orange."

Doc's dark eyes crinkled as he smiled, remembering.

"I used to make her fly. She loved it. I mean, I used to throw Orange in the Main Market canal and she'd swim back to my hands. She wun't stop comin' back till she was exhausted, and still her tail would spin and spin like a falling maple seed. She loved to fly."

Meya felt her heart breaking for him.

"'Ere, through this way."

He pointed towards a noisy courtyard where a large group of women were busying themselves with ceramic pots and metal basins of hot water. Clouds of steam rose up into the shafts of sunlight. A girl wearing a linen skirt scrubbed an empty pot vigorously. The girl's skirt was embroidered with sinsenn flowers. She eyed Meya and Doc suspiciously as they walked by. Meya was glad of her hood, though they didn't seem to pay her much notice.

"Watch out, ladies," the girl sang. "Dorloc's about."

A woman in a head wrap stirred a pot forcefully as others dumped various powders into the water, all eyes following them until they'd reached the other side of the courtyard.

They turned down a dark passageway with wooden beams along the ceiling. From the windows above, Meya heard voices hollering. As they walked, she could also hear the feet of the people above them stomping around.

"What's up there?" Meya asked D.

"A hot house. They'll be brewin' or cookin'. Or cleanin' clothes. Or killin' time." He looked back at her and rolled his eyes. "At the end of this tunnel is Corey Canal. We can follow that to Main Market. Erm, 'member, keep Percy hidden ... and quiet."

"Is he really so eye-catching?"

"For us down here, yes. He attracts attention. You're not much better, either. Maybe keep that hood up. You're askin' for your pockets picked."

Meya glanced nervously around and raised her leather hood. "Am I really an obvious target for that sort of thing?"

"I'd say so. I was gonna have a go myself."

"Doc!"

"Quiet!"

They'd emerged on to a street where a group of dishevelled-looking boys were sprawled along the bank of a wide canal. Doc bristled like a cat for a brief moment, then instructed Meya under his breath. "Keep walkin'. Head under the bridge."

The bridge was just beyond where the gang were sitting. They'd have to walk by them to reach it.

"Dorloc!" shouted a curly-haired boy.

"Cassius!" Doc's voice sounded friendly, if a little tense.

"What have you been gettin' on with?" said Cassius, standing and heading towards them. Despite being undernourished, and no older than Meya, his voice and his walk were those of someone who considered themselves superior.

"Nothin' much," said Doc. "Just headin' to Main Market. What you lot up to down here?"

"Nothin' much, either. Just killin' time."

Cassius's gaze landed on Meya, and he looked very interested in what he saw. She focused on the bridge up ahead.

"Come on, Dorloc. Don't be sneakin' about. Introduce us to your new friend."

The gang laughed as Cassius strode towards Meya, blocking her path. Doc tried to lightly push him to one side, but Cassius yanked his arm away in anger. Everyone fell quiet.

"Did Dorloc Odittany just put his hands on me?"

Giddy laughter erupted from the riverbank and Cassius smiled a mocking smile. He smacked Doc's hat off his head and into the water. Doc grimaced.

"Sorry, Cassius."

"Might we just—" Meya began.

Doc held a hand behind him, signalling to Meya to stay quiet. Cassius's eyes narrowed as he got a closer look at her. She wished she hadn't said anything. Something about the way she looked, or perhaps the way she spoke, angered Cassius. The mood shifted from playful to something more dangerous.

"We just need to get to the market," Doc said.

"Let's see what's in the bag, shall we?"

Doc began trying to gently escort Meya round Cassius towards the bridge, but Cassius rammed into them. Doc pushed Cassius back towards his ragtag crew. Cassius staggered backwards before finding his footing, his curly hair covering his face. The boys jeered as he flipped his hair back and set furious eyes on Doc.

"Have you lost your mind?"

Meya wanted to run.

"Pathetic. Cobbleside. Scumbag!" Cassius flew at Doc, his lips pulled back into a snarl. He slapped Doc's hands out of the way and beat him hard across the face. Doc recoiled and inhaled sharply, but still he moved them towards the bridge, bringing his hands back up, holding them out.

"Ca-Cassius … stop, please. We just have to get—"

Cassius struck him again, harder. The sound made Meya flinch and Doc collapsed to the floor.

"Stop it!" Meya yelled.

Cassius turned. He looked at her carefully. So did the

149

others. For a moment, she had their attention. She had to think. She had to move them through this moment.

Meya ignored her heart hammering in her chest and let a playful smile spread across her face. "Stop wasting time on this nobody!" she said to Cassius. "I've finally run into somebody more assertive and he's playing watchman with the floorborn!" she laughed. "You're absolutely right, though. He's truly pathetic."

Doc kept his head down. Meya hoped he understood. She looked over at the gaggle of boys and cocked her head to one side.

"He was trying to pick my pocket … and failing."

"You were walking with him," said Cassius, narrowing his eyes.

"I needed an escort to Main Market."

"Why, where you from?"

"Out of town," said Meya, keeping her voice even. "My coin purse is here for anyone who can give me the time."

Cassius stared at her fixedly. "Where in Main Market?"

Meya wracked her brain… She surely knew one building.

"Oh! Um … near the corner of … erm, I forget the name."

"You think we're stupid, don't you?" Cassius said.

"Not at all! I think—"

"I know what you are." He held her gaze in his, and she saw hatred. He walked slowly towards her.

"She's not from out of town, boys. She's from up there."

With that, he whipped her cloak down roughly over her shoulders, snapping the fastening at her neck. The leather and fur dropped to the floor, revealing the intricate golden patterns on Meya's sleeves and embroidered bodice. But it was Percy popping his head out of his satchel that stopped everybody in their tracks.

The boys squealed, gasped or stood with their mouths open in astonished silence.

Meya placed a shaky hand over the bag. Nobody had ever laid hands on her in Roofside. It was frightening.

"What are you doing down here?" Cassius asked quietly.

Meya tried to compose herself.

"Why shouldn't I come down here? I simply wanted to—"

"Is she a princess?" shouted a large boy with an ambitious moustache.

"A princess?" She forced a laugh. "How preposterous! Although I appreciate the flattery."

Cassius shook his head. "Shut up. You really think we're all stupid down here, don't you? We're not."

Meya glanced at Dorloc. His mouth was bloody and one of his eyes was already swollen shut.

Cassius didn't take his eyes off Meya as he spoke. "You didn't tell me you found a Roofsider down here, Doc. A Roofsider with a dog."

Dorloc rose to his feet and stood with a hand on his ribs. "You're right, Cassius. Sorry I didn't tell you. I-I-I just didn't want all the commotion. I thought—"

Cassius turned and shoved Doc violently into the canal. Doc flew backwards, splashing into the murky water. The pack of boys cackled over Meya's cries of protest. She couldn't decide if she was scared witless, or furious, or both.

Doc splashed wildly in the water. "Help!" he shouted.

A bearded man up on the bridge shouted at the chaotic scene below.

"'Ere, you lot! Knock it off!"

The boys ignored him. "Give me the dog." Cassius wasn't laughing.

Meya blinked, and decided she was furious.

"How dare you?" she shrieked.

Percy began barking. The boys cheered with wild excitement. Blood pumped through her veins. Cassius stalked towards her, reaching out to grab her bag. As quick as lightning, Percy closed his sharp teeth round his outstretched hand. Cassius yowled in pain and yanked his bloodied fingers out of the tiny pup's mouth.

"*Feyatung!*" he hissed.

"What did you call me?" seethed Meya. She had never been called that disgusting word in her life. She slapped Cassius hard across the face. It connected well. He held a shocked hand to his ear. She hoped it was ringing, loud. She spoke quietly, and as contemptuously as she ever had. "You impetuous, floorborn, good-for-nothing coward. *You* are the Cobbleside scum. Not Doc."

She saw the words do something to him.

Cassius roared like a banshee and he ran at her, pushing her back and back to the water's edge, until with a furious shove, he sent her flying into the water.

Her outer skirts engulfed her as she tumbled into the canal, and everything went black.

CHAPTER 13

Unclipping herself from her harness, Olenta frowned down at Main Market.

"More strangers."

They were wearing veils. Not the woollen face coverings that Cobblesiders wore in winter, but the delicate, sheer veils that freemen and women wore in the city. Olenta plonked herself down on the bench outside her window. Rose and her husband were smoking a pipe on theirs.

"Don't get yourself worked up, Olenta," said Rose.

"It's not just all these new folk," she replied. "Those nightly screams are putting me on edge."

Rose's husband leaned over and handed Olenta a tin of dried sinsenn leaves.

"Try that before bed. It's good and red."

She thanked him.

Rose swung her legs over her husband's lap and curled an arm round his neck. Olenta would head in early tonight. Rose's husband gazed across the square wistfully. "If harvest goes well this year, the Overlord better invite us up to the roof. It's long past time, Rose. You've more than done your share."

Olenta grunted her agreement and began unstrapping her legs.

*"I think any chance of that happening has passed, my love,"
said Rose. "And I think these strangers are here to see Field Day.
Poppy can hardly sleep from excitement."*

*She rested her head on her husband's shoulder. He stared
down at Main Market where a man in a net-like veil wandered
aimlessly.*

*"He's definitely from the Free City," he said. "See that fancy
white cloth? Nothing like that round here."*

Olenta frowned. "I'm heading in. Night, all," she said.

*And she went inside, towards the fancy white cloth hidden in
her junk trunk.*

Meya was drowning.

No matter how she pushed the folds of her clothing,
the heavy material would not part where she thought it
should. There was muffled shouting. She tried to find an
opening in the tangled material somewhere. She kicked
off her shoes. She wondered if Doc were nearby. If only
she'd worn trousers. It occurred to her that none of this
would be happening if she were wearing trousers. Skirts.
Such a silly reason to die.

Running low on breath, and trying to fight panic, she
let herself sink downwards; maybe she could part her skirts
if she stopped floundering at the top of the water. She
hoped Percy had escaped. Then, in the gloom, she saw a
flash of golden threads, a band of shimmering embroidery,
the hem of her skirt swirling above her head.

Suddenly she could orientate the direction of the folds. She yanked them open and saw the surface of the water above. She kicked and kicked as hard as she could until she felt cold air, and emerged gasping, spluttering.

There was a crowd on the bridge, a bright sky, rundown houses and some sort of ruckus happening at the bank. Despite her physical exhaustion, her mind raced through random observations and dispassionate thoughts.

And then suddenly in the water beside her was the boy.

The boy from the key room.

It felt like a dream. She'd watched him from the rooftops for so long. He had appeared like a ghost in her home. And now he was right here in front of her.

He paddled towards her, spitting water as he did, worry on his face. "Are you caught?" he asked.

His voice. She could hear the colours of Cobbleside in there, but it was clear, and it sounded concerned.

"No," replied Meya at last. "I mean yes I was. My skirts were tangled. But I'm free now."

"My old man! The girl's alive!" shouted a bearded man on the bridge. "Drag her up, lad! She looks like a drowned rat!"

Meya realized a crowd had gathered on the bridge over the canal. She suddenly felt humiliated. "I'm fine," she said, wriggling free from the boy's grip and swimming off towards the bank.

"Ladder's over here," said the boy, leading the way.

He got there first, climbed up the ladder, then turned

back down to offer her his hand.

She grasped the metal rungs. "I said I'm fine."

The boy retreated a few steps. "Sorry," is all he said.

The ladder was slimy under her hands, and she struggled to heave herself up. The weight of her skirts was exhausting. She did her best to hide the struggle. Straightening up on the bank, she wiped the pond scum from her face and scowled at him.

"You shouldn't do that, you know," she said.

"Do what?" he asked.

She'd started to feel more like herself again.

"Jump in the water to help people. You're supposed to throw a rope."

"There wasn't a rope," he said.

"You could have died."

"No, I'm a strong swimmer."

"You're a fool."

He stared back at her, but didn't respond.

That's when she saw the small wet body on the floor beside them. It was Doc, lying flat on his back. He wasn't moving.

Meya felt her heart stop.

She pushed the dread away and strode purposefully over to him, wiping her dirty hands on her wet skirt.

His skin was waxy. Meya held his nose and formed a seal over his mouth with her own. She blew hard. His little chest rose. *Good.* She placed the heel of one hand on his chest and interlocked her other hand over the top. She began pulsing vigorously down, pumping at Doc's heart.

Almost immediately he coughed and spluttered.

"Blot in a chamber pot!" shouted someone from the bridge. "He's alive!"

The man with the black beard hooted and hollered to a woman next to him. "That's Dittany's boy. She'll be made up. Well done, young lass!"

Meya rolled Doc on to his side. He groaned as water poured from his mouth. She gently brushed the wet hair from his forehead.

"You're going to be fine, Doc. Take your time."

She could feel the boy standing there, his dark eyes watching her with interest.

Doc retched against the cobbles but nodded and gave a weak smile. He opened his mouth. He was struggling to say something...

"What is it?"

"... Percy," he gasped at last.

Oh no. Meya saw her empty satchel, and sat back on her heels.

"Where's Percy?" she asked.

"Who's Percy?" asked the boy, who was still standing there, watching.

"My dog. He was in the satchel around my neck."

She scanned the water, both hopeful and frightened to see him. His bag was inside out and he was nowhere to be seen. She should never have brought him.

"Cassius," said Doc. "He was chasin' him. Tryin' to catch him."

Meya stood. "Which direction?"

"No!" Doc and the boy said as one.

The boy continued. "You should head home. We'll look for your dog, but you should go home. You probably shouldn't come down here alone again."

Meya studied his face. She was tempted to curl her lip at his tone, but she stopped herself. The way he presumed to tell her what to do was so absurd that she couldn't interpret it. He was so straight-faced that she couldn't tell if he was stupid or arrogant.

"I don't know the way back," she said.

Doc sat up.

"Bear, I can find Percy. Would you take her back to … the roof?"

Bear. So that was his name.

He didn't look like a Bear. He looked like a misused street dog, wild and raggedy, but there was something compelling about him. His wet hair was plastered to his pale face, and those large dark eyes, with dark circles below to match, were watching her cautiously.

"Bear?"

The three of them turned round. A girl was standing a little way off, watching them. It was the third one, Meya realized, the one him and the Fennex were always with. She was short, and her big brown eyes were furrowed in concern. For some reason, something in Meya's heart sank. She was pretty, if a bit too skinny, with her long, dark, curly hair falling about her shoulders. She was looking at

Bear, a question on her face.

Meya broke the tension. "I need my bag before we go." She gestured towards the satchel, floating in the water.

"I'm all right, Megg," the boy said quickly. "Don't worry. I just need to do something. Can you tell my dad I'll be home soon? Or, better, tell Jim."

The girl made an odd shape with her hand. She pinched her finger and thumb by her eye, then backed away. The boy nodded as if the girl had spoken. Her large eyes flickered over Meya for a second before she disappeared beyond the crowd.

Bear grabbed the bag and tossed it at Meya without looking at her. It slapped against her torso in a way that she did not find comical. The smallest hint of a smile hovered at the corner of his lips.

"And this is yours, I believe?" he said, popping Doc's flat cap straight on to his head.

"Ta, Bear," said Doc, sitting up. "Owe ya. Not just for the hat."

They grasped hands.

"Maybe me," said Bear.

"Maybe me," said Doc.

"Thank you, Dorloc, for escorting me, and protecting me," said Meya.

"Maybe me." He held out his hand.

She hesitated, before clasping it in hers. "Maybe me to you too," she said haltingly, hoping she'd got the expression right.

She grabbed her cloak from the floor and wrapped it round Doc's shoulders.

"There. That should help with the cold."

"Is this fur?" he asked, pulling the hood up over his head.

"Fox fur and lamb leather, I believe." She smiled at him warmly. "It's yours."

"It's so soft! Thank you." He grinned to himself. "This'll go for an absolute fortune! And don't worry. I'll find Percy if it's the last thing I do!"

Meya's smile crumpled at the thought of Percy. She did her best to pin it back up. She didn't want the boy – Bear – to see her cry.

She looked at him and nodded, and he lead her away.

"Megg?"

She spun round.

"Oh, hello, Felix!" she said as brightly as she could.

"Are you feeling all right?" he said, narrowing his eyes at her. She had been holding on to the wall as if she were about to pass out.

"I'm fine. You just caught me eavesdropping on some watchmen. They weren't at all happy about this royal visit."

Felix looked up towards Roofside, but couldn't see who she was talking about.

"Have you seen Bear?"

"Erm … no."

He got the distinct impression she wasn't being truthful with him, but she looked too miserable for him to press her any further.

"C'mon, Nutmeg. Let's get you home."

He offered her a hand and she smiled and took it. They were heading down a set of stone steps towards the town when something small and furry whizzed across their path. It was followed immediately by Dorloc Odittany, pumping his skinny legs.

"Was that a…?"

"Rats are gettin bigger, aren't they?" Doc shouted over his shoulder as he ran on after it.

Felix sighed. "Things are getting bad round here."

Megg agreed.

CHAPTER

14

Meya could sense the boy – Bear – was uncomfortable walking with her. She tried to make conversation, but he didn't make it easy.

"This way," he said, walking on ahead again. He pointed to a gloomy walkway under the bridge. The path was wide enough for them to walk side by side, but still he chose to walk in front. It was chilly here, and dark, traipsing along in damp clothes without the sun's warmth filtering down. They'd been undercover for a while now. She wondered what was directly above them at roof height – was it her home? The baths? The tower and its gardens?

She remained silent for a while. There was so much that Meya wanted to ask, but she didn't know where to begin.

"What does 'maybe me' mean?" she said at last.

Bear thought about it. "I guess it means that, one day, it may be me."

Meya frowned. "What may be me?"

"Well, think about it. Today Dorloc got jumped and almost drowned. But tomorrow it may be me. So, if a person thanks someone for helping them, we say 'maybe me'. It means ... today you were in need, but tomorrow it may be me."

"So it's like a deal?" said Meya briskly, hurrying to walk alongside him now. "You help me, I help you?"

"Not really," said Bear, looking confused. "It means... It means that things are hard for everybody. You say it to show that you aren't above the person you're helping."

"But Dorloc isn't above me?"

Bear stared dumbly at her. She clearly wasn't getting it.

"Well, maybe me ... for taking me home," she tried.

Bear's face creased into a big smile, and his laughter rang out down the tunnel. He looks good when he smiles, she thought, but she didn't like being laughed at. She certainly didn't appreciate being patronized by someone from Cobbleside.

"What's so funny exactly?" She scowled. "We clearly don't have any of those stupid expressions on the Rooftops, and why should we? They're idiotic! I've had enough of it down here. Just get me home."

Bear went silent, his face an unreadable mask. For a while, the only sound was their footsteps echoing down the tunnel, displacing the echoes of his laugh. She began to feel a little embarrassed at her outburst.

She changed the subject. "What were you doing in the key room the other night?" she asked. She turned to study his face, to see if he would lie.

His expression didn't change. "What were you doing in the key room?"

Meya opened her mouth, then shut it again. The nerve!

"Why were you even on the Rooftops?"

"Why are you down here?"

They stopped walking and turned to face each other.

His arrogance was maddening.

"How dare you? I have every right to go where I please, when I please! Though, quite frankly, I wish I'd never descended to a place where the people are so uneducated, thieving, violent…"

He started walking again.

"… and disgusting!" she added for good measure. "Who do you think you are to ask me what I'm doing down here?"

"I'm Bear," he said with that infuriating blank look on his face. "Bear Aberson."

"Well, *I* am Lady Meya Omega, Jewel of the Rooftops. The only child of Overlord Greyson Goodman, Steward and Overlord of Calleston, as appointed by Queen Meléna of the Free City."

"Were you following us?"

Meya almost choked. "What are you talking about?"

"That night, when we were all in the key room. Had you been following us?"

Meya was lost for words.

From somewhere above, a raven cawed. "Is that your raven?" he asked. "I keep seeing it around. And there's an owl too…"

"No it is *not* my raven! How dare you ask me such

things?" Meya walked faster. "I am no animal whisperer. What do you take me for?"

"Sorry. I mean, you do have a dog…"

"That is not the same!" she shouted. "And I do *not* have a dog. Percy's gone now, isn't he?"

"I'm sorry," he said. "I didn't mean to upset you."

They marched on, the end of the tunnel drawing nearer.

"We didn't take anything, from the key room I mean," said Bear suddenly, glancing across at her. "Just so you know. I'm not a thief."

"I didn't think you were."

She knew he was telling the truth about that; Noka had reviewed every hook in the key room and nothing had been missing. But why did Bear care what she thought?

"Are you going to tell your… Are you going to tell the Overlord? That we were there?"

Meya stopped and studied his face. He was simply worried about getting into trouble.

"No. I won't say anything. But let me give you the best advice I can give. Don't do anything like that again. Just stay down here. Stay in Cobbleside and stop whatever it is you were doing, otherwise I'll tell him without a second thought."

He looked across at her again, for a long moment this time. His dark eyes were so full of questions. Questions and … something else. They looked sad, she thought. Or maybe they were just tired.

She was tired too.

The raven cawed again, this time close and loud.

Meya let out a gasp.

Ahead of them, moored just inside the tunnel, was a boat. A long, black narrowboat.

A lamp was hanging from an iron perch, creaking slightly as it swung.

On the perch sat the raven and the owl, side by side. The owl gazed at Meya intensely. The raven cocked its head to the side, its glassy black eyes glittering in the gloom.

Below the birds sat three women, huddled closely together. One's head was bowed and covered by a veil. A second, who was whispering in her ear, had the golden skin and pointed ears of a Fennex.

But it was the third who made Meya gasp. She stood as she saw Meya and Bear approaching. She had deep wrinkles, ice-white hair pulled back in a tight bun and jet-black eyebrows that were raised in an expression of curiosity. But it was her eyes that stunned her. Pale blue eyes that bored into Meya's like two hot coals.

Meya knew immediately what she was. What they all were. *Witches*.

In Calleston.

Her worst nightmares come true.

Meya's mind raced, but her feet felt as if they were melded to the floor. Everything was still.

Bear placed a firm hand on Meya's back and marched her onwards, away from the boat. She heard his breath rattle as he guided her out of the tunnel. She let herself be steered up some stone steps and out into the comforting bustle of a market square.

"Bear, do you … do you recognize those … women?"

Bear looked at her. He was as white as a sheet. He took his hand from her back.

"I don't know. Maybe. I mean, no…I don't think so." He chewed his lip. "But I've seen that raven, and the owl… The night you found us in the key room. We saw it then, and when we were climbing up … we saw … a witch."

"How do you know?" she whispered.

"It was there. It spoke to us, then … it wasn't. There was a noise like thunder and then it disappeared into black smoke."

Witches in Calleston. Nightmares made real.

"Are you mad? You should have reported it to the Overlord!"

"But how could we? We were out past curfew. If we—"

"I hardly think that matters under the circumstances! I'll tell him somehow this evening."

"Don't!" said Bear. "You can't just put out an alert for women with white hair or in a dark hood. You'd start a witch hunt. You'll put half the women of Cobbleside in danger."

Meya looked at him. "But they *are* in danger now! Real danger! I don't see why you're so—"

"Your Highness!"

Meya groaned as a familiar woman came into view. "Oh, *rats.*"

It was the bony woman from the dock, Burna, with her big burly friend. They were walking through the square, each holding a tin cup of ruby brew. The bigger one, Petal, waggled her cup at Meya and smiled. Her cheeks were flushed pink.

"You're all wet!" sang Burna mockingly. "Did you find the local bathhouses, milady?"

The pair cackled as they walked by. It was all too much for her.

Bear pulled Meya gently onwards. "They were just teasing," he said. "Ignore them."

Meya took a moment to look around and was shocked to see they were in an enormous square.

"Where are we? Is this…?"

"Main Market," said the boy. "Come this way."

Bear lead her on, weaving between the multi-storey market streets that were unique to Calleston, past rows and rows of businesses, all stacked on top of each other with wooden walkways, bridges and staircases linking them.

There was a great buzz about the place, but on closer inspection Meya saw that there was far less trading actually happening than first met the eyes.

"A horsewhip's better than a parsnip!" called a woman, trying and failing to sell whips to a disinterested mob.

"Boots! For snoots, brutes or prostitutes! Get your boots!" called one particularly poetic street peddler, who sat sipping a flask among their large shoe collection.

"Is there any actual food in this market?" asked Meya,

but when she looked around she realized Bear wasn't by her side any more. A jolt of fear passed through her.

"Up here!"

Bear waved at Meya from the floor above and she wound her way up a spiral staircase to join him on the next tier. He led her down a long terrace, past windows and shopfronts, people inside peering out, or huddled in doorways, smoking.

Right at the end, in front of the last window, a woman was sitting on a wooden bench, resting an arm on the window sill behind her.

"Olenta…"

The woman looked up.

"If it isn't Bear Aberson. Heard you had quite the climb recently."

Meya shot Bear daggers. Did everybody know about his little midnight climb to the key room? They were all in on it.

"Olenta," said Bear. He gestured at Meya. "This is, er … This is … Percy."

Percy? Meya shot Bear another look. She could feel him wince beside her.

Olenta flicked a pair of readers down from her head. The glass made her eyes abnormally large.

"Percy, is it? Well! We are honoured. And what brings you up to my neck of the woods?" Olenta's enormous eyes flickered down and then back up to Meya's face. "Or should I say *down*, Lady Meya Omega?"

Meya flushed. Even filthy and damp, her disguise was a total failure. "I-i-it's Percy!" she spluttered.

Olenta placed her hands on her lower back and arched it. It crunched loudly.

"Meya, you've appeared at that balcony" – she gestured to the Overlord's great viewing platform by the bell tower – "by your father's side for years. If you thought wet hair and a plain dress would dupe people, you must be thick."

"I-I-I had an old cloak too."

"Wow. Truly a master of disguise."

Olenta reached below her bench and pulled out a leg, sculpted from leather and metal. It was then that Meya saw.

"You haven't got any legs."

"Master of observation too," said Olenta. "Thank the Overlord you're pretty... Actually, no, you should thank your mother for that."

"My mother said she used to walk through Main Market, before they put the gates up."

Olenta nodded. "She did."

"Did you ever meet her?"

"No," said Olenta. "From what I hear, though, she was a good woman. Cared about the people of Calleston, even us Cobblesiders, which is more than can be said for most of you up there."

Meya flushed with shame.

"Shame about what happened to her," said Olenta. "I'm sorry."

Meya nodded. "What happened to your legs?"

"Blots relieved me of my first legs when I was about your age." She grunted as she fished out another leg from under the bench and pulled it on. "But I'm rather fond of this pair."

She began strapping them on tightly. The metal was exquisitely sculpted, and the leather detailing was both robust and elegant in its placement. They were clearly valuable tools; they were also, undeniably,. works of art.

"They're beautiful," said Meya.

Olenta continued fastening the straps. "Thank you."

"Olenta, Meya's here by accident," explained Bear. "She needs to get back. I was hoping maybe you could take her, along the track?"

Olenta shook her head. "I'm sorry, Bear. I'm gonna have to alert a watchman. She needs collecting and I'm not getting caught up in the—"

"She'll get in trouble," blurted Bear. "Please."

Olenta looked at Meya for a long moment. She sighed. "Well, you'd better come in, then. If I'm sneaking you back up to the roof, we'll need a better disguise. But don't you make me regret it, Lady Meya."

"Thank you," said Meya, breathing a sigh of relief.

Olenta nodded. "You can leave us here, Bear."

"Right," said Bear. He looked at Meya. "You'll be OK?"

Meya nodded. "I'll be fine."

"Right," he said again. "Well … see you."

"See you at Field Day."

"See you at Field Day."

"Good luck," Meya called after him, but he'd already disappeared.

Overlord Greyson Goodman walked through Tower Gardens.

He hadn't been able to sleep so he decided to take advantage of the alone time. The air was cold and his ankles creaked like an old ship. He wandered towards the tower and was shocked to discover an owl perched on the statue of his beloved late wife. Right on her head, looking at him.

His wife had loved owls. He stared for a long moment at the beautiful bird.

"Hello, dear," he whispered.

He wondered if it were a message from her.

When he peered into the owl's round eyes, Greyson felt a chill roll up his arms. Something was off. It didn't feel like his wife. Worse, it didn't even feel like an owl.

A sudden loud motion by the gate startled him.

"Father?"

He turned to see his daughter slipping into the garden through the gate.

"You frightened me, Meya! What are you doing up so late?"

"I've been having bad dreams."

The girl looked absolutely exhausted.

"What about you?"

Overlord Goodman smiled at his daughter. "I was just chatting to your mother. Look…"

He pointed to the statue, but the owl was gone.

CHAPTER
15

The Dawn Bell rang and Bear rolled on to his back. The air was cold, but his bunk felt so cosy he wished he could stay in it all day. He stared up at the ceiling and thought about the day before, about the three women in the black boat. About the Roofside girl. She had pale eyes, a honey colour. They were striking, but the pale blue eyes of the old woman on the boat were burned into his mind like nothing else.

A squeak from above pulled him from his morning daydream.

He sat upright. The mouse that lived above his father's bed scuttled across the ironwood beam.

Yes, yes, I know. Time to get going.

Bear folded his bed up against the wall and latched it, careful to lift the frame so that the hinges didn't whine and creak. He blinked in the flat morning light. Father rustled in his blanket and then was still. It didn't sound like Caber was awake yet. Bear would try to get a warm cup of ruby brew in his uncle before he started the morning chitchat.

It was still chilly, so Bear stoked the fire. He placed the copper kettle into the fireplace and stoked the embers until a small flame danced in the hearth.

A soothing wave of heat radiated over Bear's skin. He shivered happily. If the noises of the kettle didn't wake everybody first, he'd rouse them with a steaming cup of tea. He tossed dried leaves in cups: red in his uncle's, green in his father's. As he waited for the water to boil, he wondered if he'd ever see the Overlord's daughter again.

She'd said, "See you at Field Day," but would he see her? Would they ever talk again? Or would she just be watching from a platform in Roofside, if she even watched at all.

Uncle Caber rolled over in his sleep.

If he could get a cup of sinsenn into his uncle quickly, he'd irritate Father less.

The water began to bubble.

His mind drifted back to Meya. He remembered her marching over to Doc's limp body. Bending over him, pressing her lips to his...

It stuck in his mind. A moment of compassion, but it hadn't just been compassionate – it had been masterful. She'd saved his life, and Doc was about as lowly as someone could get, one of the most incompetent pickpockets in Calleston. His mother, Dittany, was renowned for stealing gold fillings out of the mouths of Roofsiders – back when Cobblesiders were allowed on the roof, before the golden gates were installed.

Despite Dorloc's attempts to follow in his mother's footsteps, he'd never quite caught up with her fingers. Bear wondered if he'd found Meya's dog.

"Big day, Bear! Big day!" whispered Uncle Caber from the bed below the window. "The Queen in Calleston!"

Uncle Caber pushed himself out of bed and huddled by the orange firelight. He winked at Bear. His eyes looked as sprightly as ever, but he was looking especially thin today. Not only were his ribs on full display, but Bear could see his heartbeat hammering in his chest, like a baby bird.

"Bin a long time since we had a royal visit!" he said. "I just hope the Overlord's prepared. Meléna is an unbending Queen, and Calleston's about as crooked as a dog's back leg."

He raked his hands through his long white hair and began weaving it back into a braid. He tried his very best to whisper, but his voice grew steadily louder as he spoke.

"That explains all the restorations they 'ad us doin' in the market, dun't it? Everything spick-and-span new. The eyes of the Free City are on Calleston, make no mistake."

Father groaned again. Uncle Caber quietened for a moment.

He tipped his head towards Aber and then signed to Bear, *He's tired*.

Bear tapped his thumb to his temple and flashed a closed smile. *I know.* Then motioned back: *How are you today?*

Uncle Caber shrugged. *Hungry...* he signed, then, *Excited!*

Bear felt an inner trouble in his belly that he tried to keep from his face. *Me too*, he signed. *Harvest soon! Big one.*

Uncle Caber nodded and smiled. Bear saw something more than the smile.

"There'll be a lot to see in town today, Bear." Caber spoke softly. "Lots of new folk wandering about. I seen some already."

Bear shrugged his indifference.

"Ay, a royal visit's good for Calleston," Caber said, eyebrows raised. "We've been needin' something like this, and not just for the harvest." He put a rough hand on Bear's shoulder and gave it a squeeze. "Just remember, these city folk are a different breed. They look at Calleston the same way the Roofsiders look at us." Caber turned quietly serious. "And be careful, sonny. When those sort of people begin castin' their eyes about, better not to be seen at all."

The kettle hissed. Bear took it off the heat before it started whistling; he didn't want to further irritate his dad, and it was already warm enough to satisfy Uncle Caber's shivering bones. Steam rose as Bear filled his cup with hot water. Father's tinted green; Caber's sinsenn brew flushed ruby red.

Aber sat up and assessed the room. The bags under his eyes were swollen and the lines in his face were deep.

"We had the Dawn Bell, yes?"

Bear fished green leaves out of his tea and carried it over. "Just."

He handed it to his father. Caber winked at Bear and then blew on his ruby brew happily. Bear stretched his shoulders and bent down to touch his toes. He wasn't as stiff as usual, but he was ravenously hungry.

"Is there morning meal today?" Bear asked.

"How would I know?" Father took a swig of his cup.

"Won't hurt to look," said Uncle Caber.

The bed creaked as Caber rolled over and pushed himself from his bed.

Yesterday had been another day of hard manual labour. They'd finally finished re-cobbling Main Market, just in time for the Queen's arrival. The accelerated pace was hard on everyone, especially the older men and women. Caber pressed his eyes hard.

"There'll be moans and groans all across the Cobbleside this morning," he said as he swung himself to standing. He clearly didn't enjoy the feeling and leaned against the wall, breathing heavily.

Aber sighed and lifted himself out of his bunk, folding it noisily against the wall. He made his way over to the fireplace and tossed the last of his tea into the hearth. It hissed as it evaporated. He put his cup on the mantle.

"Let's go." But Caber didn't move.

"Are you feeling all right, brother?" Aber asked.

Caber muttered something incoherent. What little colour he'd had in his face had drained away. His eyes looked unfocused and glassy.

"Sit down, Caber," Aber ordered.

Caber looked up at Aber as if in a daze, then he stumbled sideways, and a moment later collapsed completely, striking his head sickeningly on the mantle before hitting the floor.

"Caber!" Bear wailed, and leapt to his uncle's side. He rolled him over and shook him. The sight of blood on his face made Bear recoil. "Wake up!"

Aber was there in a moment, dipping a washrag in the pewter jug, kneeling and dousing Caber's face, wiping away the blood. There was a deep gash over his eyebrow and his lip was split badly.

Aber pressed a hand to Caber's chest.

"His heart's going like the clapper of a bell. Give him time to settle."

Bear crouched, holding his uncle, frozen in horror. But Aber remained calm.

"Hold the cloth there. His lip'll need stitching up if it doesn't stop bleeding on its own."

Bear held the rag awkwardly over his uncle's forehead and lip.

His heart hammered in his chest, but there was something about Aber's indifference that made the situation feel manageable. Bear did what his father said, even as his heart pounded. He pulled Caber close, not just keeping pressure on the wet rag. He held Caber's skeletal figure close to his, as if his own strength might transfer to his uncle's skinny frame.

As he huddled down, he felt an anger emerge in his heart, a bitterness that Aber was so cold. Caber had become so much of the warmth in their life. Bear found himself cursing his father in his head.

And then Aber began singing a song, an old Calleston song that Bear hadn't heard his father sing in years. Bear looked down at Caber's ashen face, so he didn't break the spell that had fallen over his father. Caber's eyes fluttered, but stayed shut.

"Is he not feeling well?" Felix's head popped through the window. Bear snapped out of his trance.

"He just stood up too quickly," said Aber, "and he needs to eat."

And suddenly Caber's eyes were open. He giggled madly. One of his teeth was missing. A wave of relief passed over Bear.

"Has he eaten his own tooth?" said Felix. "That seems a bit short-sighted, Caber."

"Caber Garrason, you mad old bat!" cried Aber in furious relief. "You scared the life out of us!"

Aber walked over to his brother and pushed Bear aside. The two old men held each other on the floor, and began giggling like little boys. It was the first time Bear had ever seen them behave as the brothers they might have been as children. Caber tried to sit up, but Aber was having none of it.

"You just about cracked your skull open. Stay put."

Caber nodded and lay back in his brother's arms.

"Bit of salt water for you and bedrest until dinner." Aber regained his curt, practical demeanour.

"You boys, get to the cookhouse. And, Bear, you

183

make sure you stand there and make them fill your bowl, all right?"

"Cookhouse is shut today..." said Felix with a teasing grin. He looked at each of them and made the most of a dramatic pause that no one was prepared for.

"Out with it!"

"The royal fleet's been sighted!" Felix hopped in through the open window as he spilled the beans with a smile. "They're sailing through Calleston's outer fields now! The Overlord's lot are gathering in the square on the balcony so there's bound to be a speech."

Caber whistled. "Royal visit... You hurry up, boys!"

Aber flicked his chin to the door, sending them on their way. Without hesitation, Felix yanked the door open and Bear pulled on his boots, following Felix out into the street.

Bear could barely believe his eyes. Cobbleside had transformed overnight.

He gawped as they passed the Dodgy Gut, the largest tavern in Cobbleside. The building's once tatty timber frame was now painted a glossy black, and the yellowed, crumbling walls were newly smoothed and crisp white. The grass they were standing on was a vibrant green, a colour that hadn't been seen in Cobbleside for many a year. It was *too* vibrant, in fact, Bear thought. He crouched to inspect it.

The loud crack of a whip snapped Bear's head upwards. It was the very last watchman that Bear wanted to see.

"Off the grass, blotson!" the Whip shrieked.

Passers-by averted their eyes and continued their business. Bear sprinted up the bank and back on to the cobbles. The Whip held his whip in his hand.

Bear picked up his foot to inspect it. His pale leather boots were stained a deep green.

"They dyed it," he whispered.

"They've bloody dyed it!" Felix laughed. "Come on, have a look at what else they've done." As the boys ran closer to Main Market, everything became steadily cleaner and more colourful. The buildings were patched up, run-down railings were replaced, and window upon window had blossomed overnight, the rickety hanging baskets and old window boxes where Cobblesiders grew cabbages and potatoes suddenly bursting with marigolds, tulips and daffodils.

"Cobbleside looks good!" Bear called out to Felix as they ran onwards.

"Just wait for this!" he called back as they turned the corner into Main Market.

Bear gasped. It was completely transformed.

Every stall had a new brightly coloured cover. The multi-tiered balconies surrounding the square were repaired and repainted. Each shop sign gleamed in its bracket. Bunting hung across the square, draped from the proudly standing oak trees all the way over to the freshly varnished handrails. Cobbleside looked far more capable of supporting its heavy crown.

The smaller drawbridges along the canal had been lifted and merchant's boats were exiting down the various canals, making way for the royal vessels. Olenta whizzed overhead, flinging letters through open windows as she headed back to her balcony in the corner of the square. Watchmen were dotted all across Roofside, watching the square below. It was already beginning to fill up, everyone gathering to hear the Overlord's speech, and Cobblesiders lined both sides of Main Market canal. Dotted among the locals was a smattering of the city folk, conspicuous with their strange veils covering their faces.

The boys headed straight for the cookhouse. Bear looked upwards. The Rooftops were crowded too, apart from the Overlord's viewing terrace, which was still empty. No sign of Meya yet. He wondered if she would join her father. He craned his neck as they crossed the square.

"You took your time," Megg said warmly as they approached. She looked especially pale, Bear thought. But Megg waved them cheerily towards the end of a bench where she had two steaming bowls of stew waiting.

"Bear had a little run-in with the Whip," said Felix.

He plonked himself down and began spooning porridge into his mouth.

"Oh no, what happened?" said Megg, turning to Bear with a worried look on her face.

"Nothing, really. I just walked on some grass. But the grass had … green on it."

As he sat down, Megg clasped her hand over his wrist

so he knew she was listening. "They've painted the grass green."

Bear stared at Megg.

A wicked cackle escaped her mouth and she clamped a hand over it. Felix laughed too – Megg's laugh was infectious. It was nice not to see her worried for once.

"What?" asked Bear with a confused grin.

"He's not wrong," said Felix to Megg. "He's just describing it … in a Bear way."

"No, I know what you're talking about!" She squeezed Bear's arm and smiled. "I'm just glad you're all right." Megg looked down at his feet and grimaced. "Although your boots … aren't."

Bear looked down. The pale leather had absorbed the pigment in the most violent way. They were a bright and breathtaking green.

"Will it come off?" he wondered out loud.

"In all honesty, you could probably sell them to someone on Roofside," Megg said. "They like that kind of thing up there."

Megg and Felix grabbed each other's hands and cackled wildly at him.

Bear frowned. "Are they really that bad?"

"Not at all!" said Megg. "They're just very … Roofside. And that's not a bad thing. Speaking of which … did your friend from the roof get home all right?"

She kept her tone light, but her voice was too emotionless to sound natural.

"What friend?" said Felix. Bear told him the story. Felix's eye grew wide.

"No!" he said. "Is she our friend too now? Could be your ticket to the roof, if the whole growing thing doesn't work out."

Bear felt embarrassed and tried to change the subject. "As I was walking her back, we saw this strange boat and on it was –" he lowered his voice – "a witch. Maybe more than one."

"No!" said Felix.

"Yup. That owl was with them, and the raven too. There's definitely something funny going on in this town."

Bear noticed Megg had a strange look on her face.

"I think everyone needs to stop worrying about witches. We need to focus on Field Day," she said. Her eyes looked tired and worried again. "And no more messing about, climbing around at night, or talking to Roofsiders. Felix, please keep an eye on him."

"What do you mean?" Felix protested. "I'm not his mum!"

There was a silence. Felix winced when he realized what he'd said, and tried to cover his mistake.

"I just mean … he's capable of looking after himself."

"What was she doing down here anyway?" Megg said. "The Overlord's daughter, I mean?"

"I've no idea," said Bear. "She snuck down here, with a dog."

"What for?"

"Not sure. Sounds like she doesn't really like it up there."

Bear looked up to the Overlord's balcony where the watchmen were stationed, keeping an eye on the crowd. "But then, not sure she liked it down here much, either."

Megg placed a small hand over his. "Bear, be careful. I've spent my life looking at the same rooftops as you. But we need to be patient and just put all our energy into Field Day. Growing sinsenn is our one ticket out of here."

"What if you can't grow sinsenn?" said Felix in a soft voice.

"Felix, stop it!" Megg insisted quietly. "Everyone has an off day. Tomorrow you'll—"

Just then a bowl came sailing over Bear's shoulder and crashed on the table between them, sending a spray of cold stew in every direction.

Cassius and his crew laughed mockingly from their table.

"Oi!" Felix grabbed the bowl and sprang up on to his seat.

"Just ignore them," pleaded Megg.

Felix smiled apologetically at Megg before calling out to the boys.

"Did that do it for you, Cassius? You missed, love! You must be as blind as your old man! You couldn't hit water if you fell out a boat, you useless blotson!"

Bear couldn't help but grin. Megg covered her face with her hands. Felix had gone entirely too far.

"Fennex rat!" shouted Bacco, one of Cassius's cronies. He pulled the tips of his ears, mimicking Felix's pointedness.

It was almost too stupid for Felix to react, but Bacco's expression and the hysterical laughs from the table were too much for Felix to resist.

"Felix, sit down," begged Megg. "If we just—"

Felix tossed the bowl casually into the air. He spun lightning fast on the spot, kicking it with enough force to send it hurtling like an arrow over to Cassius's table. It cracked against the wall loud enough for the entire cookhouse to fall quiet. The bowl clattered on the floor and wobbled to a stop. The table of laughing boys was stunned into momentary silence.

Then Cassius got up from the table, fury in his eyes. Bacco and the others followed suit.

"We should probably go," Felix said.

They didn't need telling twice. Megg, Bear and Felix hurtled out of the doors and zigzagged through the people gathering in the square. Bear slowed as he fled through the crowds, weaving as best he could in and out of a cluster of handcarts, heaped with woven baskets, rugs and blankets.

"All your weaved wares!" called a stallholder. "Woven not stolen! Weaved not thieved!"

"Over here!" Bear heard Megg's voice. She was kneeling behind the solid wooden wheel of a poky wagon with Felix.

"Shouldn't we be running?" Bear asked as he squeezed in between them. "We're not fifty paces away from the cookhouse."

"No. Just keep still," said Felix.

"Felix is right," whispered Megg. "They won't expect

us right under their noses, as long as we keep quiet—"

"Can I help you?"

Megg shrieked and then jammed a hand over her mouth.

The stallholder, a pretty woman with greying hair, crouched low behind them.

"Are you looking for a basket? A broom?"

"We're hiding," said Bear.

The woman took in the sight, the three of them huddled under her cart. Her eyes were the same grey colour as her hair.

"Say no more," she said, chuckling.

Hopping back on to her feet, she continued selling her wares. "Baskets! Brooms! Rushwork, dush work! Come for all your weaved wares!"

Megg shifted. She put her arms round Felix and Bear's necks and peeked out from under the wagon, keeping her face tucked behind the large wheel, her cheek close to Bear's.

"Here they come," whispered Felix. "Keep still."

The three of them froze, and the boys appeared from the crowd one by one. They congregated in front of the disarranged row of carts and wagons, eyes scanning the stalls.

"I don't believe it," breathed Felix.

"What?" whispered Megg.

A raven beat its black wings as it landed nearby on a wicker box. It hopped in a circle until it had turned to face them. Bear looked into its eyes. There was an intelligence in there that unsettled him. It seemed to know they were hidden there, and to be interested in that fact. It turned its head, considering them with its glossy black eyes. Bear gulped. There was something chilling in that look.

"It's the same one, Felix," he said softly.

Megg tensed up at his words.

"Stop it," she whimpered quietly. She squeezed the boys close.

"Shh," Felix breathed.

The bird cawed and took a large hop towards them, landing on the handle of a basket only paces away.

Cassius was right by them now. He looked down at the bird and frowned. He took a halting step towards them.

"What in the—"

A sudden racket stopped him in his tracks. From out of the crowd came hurtling a tiny form. An extremely filthy ball of rags come to life.

Bear almost gasped.

Percy! The Roofside dog. Meya's dog was alive and, more than kicking, it looked as if he'd been used to clean a chimney. He streaked through the market like a piglet on hot coals, barking and yelping as he went. The raven squawked in indignant fury and flapped into the air.

"Is that a dog?" shouted the weaver woman.

A small audience grew at the unexpected re-emergence of a dog down in Cobbleside. There was a sharp whistle.

"Percy!" shouted a voice from within the crowd.

"Here, Percy!"

Dorloc Odittany came scrambling through the growing audience, holding on to his brown cap as he raced through the town. He spotted Bear hiding and nodded politely to him as he shot down an alleyway after Percy, calling out to him as he went.

Bear grinned. "Poor Doc. He's just not quick enough to catch a dog."

"It's not the dog I'm worried about," said Felix. "It's the bird."

"That bird was definitely watching us," Megg said in a dreamy voice.

"We should kill it," said Felix.

"No!" shouted Megg.

"Why not?"

She bit her lip. "If the bird is … a companion—"

"Of a witch?"

"Felix, please," she said quietly. "If it does belong to a witch, and we hurt it, we're putting ourselves in danger."

The weaver woman's head reappeared under the wagon and they all jumped.

"Just checking on my three hideaways." She smiled conspiratorially at them.

"We're coming out now," said Bear. "Sorry about that. Thanks for letting us hide out."

"Maybe me," she said with a smile. "You three stay out of trouble now. The Overlord has enough on his plate without you lot causing bother."

"Hey, look. Is that your girlfriend up there?" said Felix with a grin.

Bear looked up to the Overlord's platform where the watchmen were stationed. The Overlord was there now, waving kindly to the crowd. A girl stood stiffly at his side in a bilberry blue dress. It was Meya.

It was odd after yesterday, seeing her up there nestled among the rooftops, while Bear was down in Cobbleside, chasing meals and hiding from trouble.

She looked quite different to yesterday. She looked beautiful – regal, in her bright blue dress. Her long fair hair flowed around her shoulders. It was lighter than it had looked yesterday – it had looked brown. In today's light it was honey-coloured, but then it'd been soaking wet when he'd met her.

"Enjoy the day off, my loves!" Rose called down from a balcony. "I'll see you on Field Day!"

Rose looked so happy she could burst; she'd clearly shared in some of Olenta's ruby brew. A man with red hair emerged from her door, Rose's husband. He passed cups to anyone with a spare hand. The walkways and balconies were packed with people.

There were calls of *hush* across the square. Bear was excited. The Overlord had not addressed them for some time. Overlord Goodman had a way with words and could convey more than one message, if you listened carefully.

He raised his hands for silence. He wore a simple woollen coat, which he still filled quite well at the belly, despite having lost much of the weight from his face in recent years. His voice, however, remained strong as it boomed across the square.

"Thank you, Calleston." The square settled. "It has been many a year since our town was last favoured with a royal visit."

There was scattered applause from the crowd.

"I expect, as can be the case when friends haven't met for some time, that the Free City will hardly recognize Calleston the way that we appear now… And what a wonderful job you have all done in presenting our town at its best. I extend my warm thanks to everyone who has worked so hard to get the town ready for this auspicious visit."

The square filled with applause again, then grew quiet as the tone changed.

"We have persevered in the face of much suffering in recent years…"

The Overlord's aide cleared his throat discreetly. Bear saw now that it was the same aide that had been walking with him to the tower, Noka, he had called him. He was a sleek figure, and wore the same woollen coat as the Overlord, though Noka fastened his at the neck with a silver clasp. He let a small grin stretch his mouth slightly and Overlord Goodman continued with a similar smile. Bear wondered how many people in the crowd had noticed the subtle interaction.

"It is my deepest wish that our suffering is about to end." Overlord Goodman seemed to ignore Lord Noka's frown. "While our town proudly grows sinsenn for the entire Queendom, we have come to rely heavily on the Queen's generosity, and I have remained grateful for the food that she has seen fit to send so far."

There was a disgruntled murmuring around Bear, Felix and Megg. The Overlord's positivity did not seem to be reaching all the way down to Cobbleside. Lord Noka licked his lips and smiled widely. Bear watched Meya's eyes. She studied her father's expression intently, but her face did not move.

"Well, at last the Queen has come to bestow her bounty on us personally and I'm sure once she sees all our town has to offer – including the joy of Calleston's renowned Field Day, and the harvest that follows – she will extend her warmth to us gratefully. In return, I know we will all strive to make Queen Meléna as comfortable as is possible while she remains here within our walls. The Queendom faces challenges untold. And we support her good work, and we welcome the young queen with the generosity for which Calleston is renowned."

There was heartfelt applause, from both the townspeople and the city folk in the crowd.

"Did it sound like he was choosing his words very carefully to you?" Megg asked.

"Yes," Felix replied. "They're terrified."

"Why terrified?" asked Bear.

"Wouldn't you be?" said Felix. "I mean, she had her own mother killed. Imagine chopping your mum's head all the way off."

Bear looked at his feet. Megg gave his hand a little squeeze.

"I still can't believe we're going to see a queen in the flesh," said Megg. "I wonder what she looks like."

"I heard she looks like her mother, except a bit younger, and not dead," said Felix loudly.

Megg's hand flew to her mouth again as she, Bear and a group of people standing around them tried to stifle their laughs.

There was a joyful cheer in the square as the Overlord closed his address. He gave a hearty wave and then took a seat. A hush swept over the crowd.

In the distance, drumbeats began and horns blared.

"That's them!" someone shouted from a level above. "The royal fleet!"

"They'll be opening Main Gate for them!" Felix began bouncing on the spot. "Come on! Let's get a good seat."

The rabble of people around them buzzed with excitement as the crowd surged as one towards Main Gate, sharing cups of ruby brew and blowing giant puffs of red smoke along the way.

The Queen watched the town approaching.

She had long been educated on Calleston's unique history, these people who made the sinsenn flowers bloom. She was curious to finally see with her own eyes how the dingy little town operated.

She was tempted to leave them to rot, but she knew that without Calleston, without sinsenn, the Free City would eventually be thrown into chaos, and the entire Queendom would be at risk. A risk she would not tolerate.

The chaotic heap of a town ahead looked exactly as she'd imagined. Though small, it clearly fancied itself a little city with its stone walls and its towers. Laughable, really.

Multitudes of grubby faces were gathered on the town walls.

"Protect me," she whispered as they approached the entry gate. She was reassured by the presence of the great black cage.

CHAPTER
16

"Oi!"

Felix hopped excitedly as the royal procession made its way towards them.

"Bear, quick, help him up," said Megg.

"Here," said Bear, reaching down a hand and pulling him up on to the wooden rail with him and Megg.

"Now we're talking!" Felix whooped.

Bear and Megg looked at each other and grinned excitedly.

The air echoed with the sound of drumbeats and cheers, as Queen Meléna's boats cruised up the canal towards the town walls.

The growing noise intensified, and so did the crowd's excitement. Every inch of the wall, every balcony and walkway on Roofside that faced the canal was packed. The people in front of them chatted happily, gazing down the waterway and sharing a pipe.

Bear could feel Megg jigging her knee next to him, buzzing with the thrill of it all. He'd never seen the town so festive; he laughed for no real reason. Megg looked at him and laughed suddenly at his laughing. His cheeks almost hurt.

He wondered what the Queen would think of their town. He gazed along the wall, and up and down the many tiers of balconies, hundreds of faces piled on top of each other, crammed together, all curious to witness the arrival of these fancy foreign visitors.

Bear felt a flutter of nerves at the thought of city folk seeing his home, but also a swelling of pride, being a Callestonian boy. They were the town that grew sinsenn, after all. They filled every cup in the Queendom with ruby brew. And now they were about to be scrutinized by these outsiders. As he looked around the faces in the crowd, he suddenly realized how entwined with Calleston he really was, and how deeply protective of her walls he felt.

A strange sonorous wailing began to echo across the water, joining the drumbeats.

The discordant music made Bear feel funny, as if he could sense that something unnatural hung in the air.

The fleet was getting closer now. Bear could see the flag of the Free City billowing proudly from the boat in front, and a bevy of red sails behind it, like great folded bird wings extending up towards the sky.

The first boat was the smallest: the flag-bearing vessel. A man dressed in soft brown leather stood proudly at the bow. Behind him, the Queensguard manned the oars, while others beat large leather-skinned drums. The men of the Queensguard were rumoured to be as strong as three men, and the speed of the ship indicated as much. (But then they were also rumoured to be twelve feet tall, and the height of their heads indicated otherwise.)

Finally, Bear saw the source of the strange music. At the back of the flag boat, a group of musicians stood in a ring, each playing a large instrument. Bear had never seen such an instrument before. It was some sort of giant horn, but the tubes were as long as Bear was tall and extended high into the air. The bell of each horn was shaped like the head of a dragon and from each head hung a long red banner, with the fabric draped all the way to the deck. Facing inwards as they were, they formed a column of deep red, crowned by a horde of dragon heads.

The sound that poured from their jaws sounded like something Bear could've only imagined in his dreams, mournful and beautiful, but chilling.

The city's flag was black and bore a white ring. Inside the ring was the twelve-pointed star of the royal family. Between the twelve points of the star were the twelve jewels of the Free City, each one in the shape of an eye.

"Bin a long time since I saw that flag," said an old, red-faced man on the other side of Felix, "must be ten years."

"Who's that?" Bear asked, pointing to the figure at the ship's bow.

"Tsilas Violet. The Queen's Voice. He makes addresses to the common people on behalf of the Queen."

The oars dipped in and out of the water, drawing the

boats closer, and the Cobblesiders fell quiet. Children waved to the boat, but the man standing at the front kept his eyes facing firmly forward. As he drew closer, Bear saw that he wasn't wearing brown at all, but some kind of textured leather, mottled red and black. He wore gloves made of the same dappled leather, and stood with his hands held firmly on his hips. Curving round his neck was a gold chain, dotted with beetle-sized rubies and pitch-black obsidian. Bear had never seen gems so large. He wondered if they were the jewels of the Free City.

The next boat contained the Queensguard. Thirty soldiers rowed in perfect unison, and poised across the bow of the boat was a company of archers. They wore a thick stripe of black paint across their eyes and had a foot pressed on the guardrail. Each kept an arrow nocked in their bows, an active warning.

In the centre of the ship's deck was an ornate pavilion. Brightly coloured and intricately carved, it was completely surrounded by hooded soldiers, standing in perfect formation. They held a hand on the hilt of their swords, and from the depths of their hoods Bear sensed eyes passing over the crowd.

Felix patted Bear's head madly again. "Megg! Bear! Look!"

Crouched on the roof of the pavilion was a motionless ring of ten warriors.

"The Queen's Claws," said the red-faced man.

"What are the Queen's Claws?" Bear asked.

"The most deadly of the Free City's armies," the red-faced man said. "Far stronger even than the Queensguard. Experts with a blade and born with a natural bloodlust. Thankfully, they are under the Queen's control." He eyed Felix. "Fennex, all of them."

And indeed, as they drew closer, Bear saw that each of the warriors, man and woman, had the golden skin and pointed ears of the Fennex.

Felix was excited beyond imagining and waved enthusiastically. Multiple amber eyes flickered over to where they stood, but their bodies didn't move an inch. Felix stopped waving.

The Queen's Claws wore dark brown leather. The pieces that covered their chests resembled fish scales. Like the archers, they had a black stripe painted across their faces, which made their amber eyes all the more striking. They wore metal cuffs on their wrists, a dull golden colour, and held mean-looking daggers in each hand.

And then it suddenly clicked. Underneath the pavilion where the Fennex blade masters crouched…

"That must be where she is," said Felix, and next to him Megg muttered, "Yes, of course."

Bear tried to spot her. The ornate framework was draped with sheer curtains, pulled apart in some areas to allow those inside to see and be seen.

He could only make out one girl, sitting on a green divan placed just inside the drapes, wearing a lustrous black gown that followed her form closely.

"Is that her?" said Bear quietly.

"No," said Felix. "No crown, no queen."

The girl's hair was long, red and thick. It tumbled down towards her feet, which were pulled up beside her. She had rosy apple cheeks and was more voluptuous than any woman from Calleston. She appeared relaxed and unbothered as she beheld the faces of Cobbleside staring down at her. Her eyes drifted languidly across the people's faces – until they found where Bear stood.

She sat bolt upright and stared, her demeanour suddenly alert and interested. She tossed her long hair over her shoulder and stood, heading deeper inside the pavilion's curtains.

"What was that?" asked Felix.

"Probably nothing," Megg said, a little spooked.

A small bell began to chime, joining the sound of the drums and the mournful dragon horns. The Queen's ship drew closer, and then stopped, and the curtains of the pavilion were pulled fully open.

Inside the ornate structure was an assembly of young noblewomen, some standing, some sitting on plush furnishings of green velvet. They wore gowns and other garments of deep, lustrous black, except for one woman.

It was immediately apparent they were looking at the Queen.

Queen Meléna was resplendent in red, seated on a throne of white in the very centre of the ship's deck. The gold crown of the Free City sat snug on the red veil that hung over her face.

The effect was both mesmerizing and somewhat terrifying. Bear was fascinated, and at the same time he wanted to run away from the drums, the endless wailing of the horns, the piercing ring of the bell.

The Queen stood. She swept to the edge of the pavilion, and stepped gracefully down on to the deck, making her way to the bow of the boat. From there she surveyed the crowd. As she looked in their direction, Megg made a small noise of terror. People standing around them became uncomfortable. Felix, for once, was silent.

From behind the Queen, the party of noblewomen walked out on to the ship's deck to join her. Together the women observed the townspeople like a shadowy committee of vultures.

As the ship drew closer, Bear felt increasingly uncomfortable that the women were looking at him in the same way he was looking at them.

"I don't like this," whispered Megg. "I want to get down."

But she didn't. No one did. No one dared move.

The women were definitely looking in their direction.

A small girl standing near the Queen regarded them in astonishment. She had amber-coloured eyes and her poker-straight hair was jaw length. From it emerged two pointed ears.

The girl gazed at Felix as if he were a ghost, and then sped away. For a moment, she disappeared within the drapes of the pavilion, then reappeared between the girls at the edge of the boat. She raised herself to sit lightly on the handrail.

Like the others, her dress was black, though hers had a high collar, and on her waist she had a belt with two knives attached, one gold, one black.

The Fennex girl produced a silver coin and then kissed it. "A blessing, for a Fennex," she called out in a strange accent.

The girl held it out for a second, and then snapped her fingers. The coin shot like an arrow. Cobblesiders gasped as, quick as a flash, Felix snatched it out of the air.

The crowd cheered uproariously.

"He's a good lad, our Fennex boy!" shouted the red-faced man proudly.

Bear grinned as the applauding and cheering around them grew louder and louder. Megg sighed in relief and held the boys close. The notorious Queen had not only arrived, but she had revealed herself to the townsfolk, and one of the Queen's noblewomen had given a Cobblesider her favour. The taverns would be awash with the retelling tonight.

Bear nudged Megg and smiled. "Wasn't too bad, was it? We did all right, Megg. Don't worry too much."

She gave him a weak smile, but said nothing.

The royal boats stopped as they reached Main Gate. Inside the gate, Main Street Canal was packed all the way into the centre of town, leading eventually to Main Market. Looking back over his shoulder, Bear could see that the canal was lined with people, from the cobbles to the roof, all the way back to the square.

As the last boats approached the large gate that fortified the town's entrance, the musicians ceased the banging of the drums and the blowing of the horns, and a hush fell over everyone.

"Here he is," said Felix.

The Overlord appeared on a balcony high above them. He stood with his daughter beside him, and looked down on the royal fleet, smiling warmly, an excited twinkle in his eye. Meya's eyes were lowered, her face unreadable, as the Overlord began his address.

"On behalf of Calleston, the Cup of the Free City, the North Rose, I extend my deepest welcome to Queen Meléna and to her royal party. Drink of our cup, partake of our table – our door is open, and our lives are humbly yours."

He bowed deeply. The crowd on the wall, along the canal and in the upper tiers all followed suit.

For a moment there was silence.

Then the Queen's Voice addressed the balcony. "On behalf of Her Majesty the Queen Meléna, Crowned Head of the Free City, and Empress of this Realm, I offer greetings from the city of sovereignty."

His voice bore the same strange accent of the Fennex girl, his words slipping over one another in a melody Bear had never heard before.

"And I extend to you the warm hand of the royal family."

His voice rang across the fields.

207

"Also … a warning."

A flash of alarm crossed the Overlord's face and a hum spread through the crowd.

"A warning to you that the Queen will not be insulted."

The Overlord was visibly flustered. He blinked as the Queen's Voice began pulling his gloves off, finger by finger. Slowly. Threateningly.

"Calleston." He sounded the word out as if he had never heard it before. "Ca-lle-ston, 'the Cup of the Free City', correct?"

He stopped pulling off his gloves and looked back up at the Overlord's terrace.

The Overlord nodded, his expression wary.

The Queen's Voice continued: "You are the *Cup* of the Free City because you *belong* to the Free City. You are *ruled* by the Crown. You are *owned* by the Crown. Those who carry the Crown, carry the Cup."

He put his hands back on his hips and addressed his question to the Overlord.

"Who carries the Crown of the Free City?"

The Overlord cleared his throat nervously. When he spoke, though, his voice was steady. "Her Majesty Queen Meléna."

"Then reconsider your greeting. We cannot drink of *your* cup, because the cup is ours. We will not partake in *your* table, because the table is ours."

The crowd was silent. Bear peeked over at the royal ships waiting to enter the enormous metal gate.

The Overlord tugged at the collar of his coat. His hand shook slightly. "We apologize for the insult and ask your pardon. Name anything in my power and it shall be done, Your Grace."

"And yet the impertinence endures…"

The Queen's Voice spread open his hands as he spoke three words. "Open. Your. Gates."

The Overlord looked flabbergasted. He leaned down over the stone parapet and gawped at the water below. The great iron portcullis was still down. He blinked a number of times as if to confirm what he was seeing. The great gate, which should have been opened to allow the boats through, was still closed.

"Open the gate!" he bellowed, a note of panic in his voice. "Watchmen! Open the gate and let the Queen pass!"

Calls of "Open the gate!" echoed through various pockets of the town walls.

"What is happening," said Megg. "Why aren't they opening it?"

"Do you think the Overlord's doing it on purpose?" whispered Felix conspiratorially. "Trying to show the Queen who's in charge around here?"

"I very much doubt that," Megg said. "That would be monumentally stupid and extremely dangerous."

Bear agreed. The Overlord seemed to be living a waking nightmare. There was a sheen of sweat on his brow and Meya edged closer to him, protectively.

But the giant portcullis remained in the water. Noka

reappeared on the balcony and whispered something in the Overlord's ear. The Overlord visibly paled.

"My deepest apologies to Her Majesty," he said. "It appears the chains are corroded through underuse – Main Gate has not been opened since the last royal visit. We gladly welcome your smaller vessels through the wicket gate. We also invite you to enter by way of our ground gates, if you are happy to disembark? I regret that it is not possible to enter this way. We reiterate our most sincere apologies."

"It is not possible." The Queen's Voice rubbed his chin dramatically as he considered the words. "Not possible."

Overlord Goodman looked like he was ready to pass out. Despite any trace of blood in his face being gone, he faced the fleet before him head on.

"It is not possible? We shall see…"

The Queen's Voice looked over to the back of the boat where the musicians held their glittering copper dragon heads high in the air. The long red banners that hung from their horns swayed. All was quiet. He raised his voice so that it carried.

"I was hoping that we could demonstrate the weapon we carry in your private halls. But perhaps it is more important that the people of Calleston are reminded of the power of the Free City."

He gave a gesture of command. The horn players turned and laid their instruments down. As they did so, the magnificent crimson drapery that hung from the towering instruments parted like a sinsenn flower blooming.

"What is that?" Felix asked.

The red silks concealed a giant cage with a domed ceiling, its bars wrought in twisted iron.

At first glance, the cage looked empty. But there was a shifting mist that hung and swirled in the air within it. Shadows flickered and sputtered as dark clouds formed from nowhere and then diffused back into the smoke.

Bear felt his stomach twist into a knot, then tighten.

"Bear," Felix whispered, his eyes not leaving the smoke, "doesn't that look quite a lot like—"

"Witch!" someone shouted, and the rest of crowd gasped.

The Queen's Voice held a staff in his hands. The shaft was long, straight and bone white. At its end was a vast black jewel – an orb, the size of an apple, and perfectly round.

He ran his fingers over the polished black orb as he addressed the people on the wall.

"The power of the Free City is indomitable. For generations, we have destroyed every enemy, every saboteur, and every poisonous disease that has scourged this realm."

He held the staff out towards the crowd.

"No blade shall cut, no arrow strike, no sickness corrupt the rule of the Free City. Not even the power of the –" he pointed the white staff towards the cage and pressed the dark orb on to the black metal – "*Feyatung*."

A roaring fireball burst into life within the centre of the cage, hurtling outwards towards the cage's bars, but when it reached them the flames rolled back on themselves.

"Worry not!" called the Queen's Voice. "Fear not! There is nothing *to* fear. For nothing – not even a *Feyatung* – can threaten the might of the Free City. We hold its power in our grasp."

The crowd stared in horrified silence.

"No…" gasped Felix. "They've actually *caught* a witch."

Bear felt sick.

Megg gripped Bear's arm and held it close. She knew how shocked he must be. He squeezed her back, as reassuringly as he could. He couldn't take his eyes off the wretched figure in the cage.

"How…?" Felix said.

As the dense mass of smoke in the cage subsided, inside, the figure of the witch emerged, hazy and indistinct. Terrifying. Blot-like. Waiting to come into Calleston. Bear looked up at the Overlord's balcony. Father and daughter wore identical expressions of pale horror.

"What's he doing?" said Felix.

The Queen's Voice was holding something aloft in a gloved hand. He held it towards the witch like a lure. Bear couldn't make it out. It wriggled like a little—

"Mouse," said Megg in horror.

She made a nauseated sound. Bear didn't understand why. The Queen's Voice smiled widely as he dangled the mouse through the bars of the cage. The hazy figure of the witch shifted and a gnarled hand emerged from the shadows, extending eagerly towards the tiny creature.

"No…" muttered Felix in disbelief. "It's not—"

The crowd gasped in horror as the filthy claw snatched the mouse from Tsilas Violet's hand and stuffed it into its mouth.

Megg groaned weakly, her eyes rolling backwards as she collapsed.

"Megg!" Bear held her as she sank heavily to the ground. She was covered in sweat, her face ashen.

"I've got you," said Bear, sitting her up and brushing her hair from her face. "It's all right, Megg. Breathe."

"She all right, love?" a woman asked as she puffed on her pipe.

"She will be if she can get some air!" said Felix, wafting away the red smoke.

Bear studied Megg's face, the rapid pulsing of a vein in her neck. She needed more than just air. She needed to eat properly.

Felix crouched beside them, but his gaze lingered on the black cage.

"Disgusting…"

Bear couldn't help but look. Afterwards, he wished he hadn't. The witch's mouth worked horribly fast, crunching away on the little bones until it was all gone.

Apart from a few nauseated groans, the crowd was silent. Tsilas Violet held aloft his staff and spoke.

"The Queen will eradicate the filth of the *Feyatung* from every corner of the realm, for that power is hers alone, as the ruler of the Free City. Now —" Tsilas Violet breathed three words over the orb and then pressed it between the twisted bars of the cage – "raise the gate."

The witch reached out a shadowy hand. It paused, charred fingers outstretched, and clutched the orb. Bear heard a rushing sound streaming through the air, like wind and water crashing.

And then, the giant iron portcullis began to slowly rise up out of the water. The gears snapped and crunched as metal, wood and stone were ground against each other.

"Advance!"

Calleston watched in stunned silence as the great oars of the ships dipped back into the water as one, then emerged again, shining like blades.

And the Queen's fleet entered the city.

The Queen had tolerated the miserable town for less than a day and already she wished to leave. But she would endure it nonetheless. She was here with a purpose. Tomorrow was the first day of the harvest, and she would judge the decline with her own eyes. And decide what to do about it. She would do that with pleasure.

The Overlord's great hall was a testament to their family's arrogance; they still imagined themselves royalty of the squalid little town.

"And, finally, may I present my daughter, Lady Meya Omega."

A touch of a smile almost reached the Queen's lips.

These Calleston exiles, parading their children as lords and ladies, it was as laughable as her mother had described.

"Her Majesty, the Queen Meléna, Crowned Head of the Free City."

The Queen didn't acknowledge the girl's curtsey. Doing so was beneath her.

The man who called himself the Overlord stuttered. He was nervous.

He should be nervous.

If Calleston didn't double its harvest, he would be dealt with. Of course, the girl would have to be dealt with too. Dead fathers so often yielded vengeful daughters. The smile reached her lips.

CHAPTER 17

Field Day had arrived. But with none of its usual fanfare.

The new bloomers gathered in silence along the north edge of Top Field.

Bear, Megg and Felix stood at the back. It was cool and windy, and so Rose wore her thick cloak, embroidered all over with black blooms. Everyone else shivered in their cotton work clothes.

"Just give it everything you've got and it'll be over before you know it," said Rose as she walked along the lines, maintaining an encouraging smile. But the mood was sombre.

"Don't hold back, Megg! Show us what you've got!" Megg's little sister Freya bellowed suddenly from across the water.

All of Cobbleside was gathered behind the town's moat or up on the wall, with watchmen posted evenly throughout the crowd. A good many had dyed their everyday clothes new shades of red and pink. Freya's uplifting outcry triggered a cacophony of yells and whoops from the crowd, and then the chanting and the pipes began.

Megg's mum, Elma, stood at the edge of the water with her daughters surrounding her. Young Ophelia sat proudly on her shoulders. Elma joggled her about to keep her entertained, and to calm her own visible nerves.

Bear looked for his father and uncles in the crowd, but couldn't see them.

"Have you seen what your girlfriend's wearing?" said Felix, gazing up at the rooftop.

Bear squinted up at the marble parapet where the Roofsiders and the royals were seated. His mouth fell open at the sight of Meya. She was wearing a blood red gown, her fair hair braided and piled atop her head and dotted with jewels. The jewels woven into her hair made her look, Bear thought, rather conspicuously regal. To finish it all off, on top of her interwoven creation, she'd pinned a bright red veil. Though red was the colour of Field Day, Meya had never dressed so dramatically. The veil was almost identical to the one worn by Queen Meléna the previous day.

Bear felt Megg watching him and let his eyes wander over the lower crowds.

"She looks beautiful," she said.

Felix tutted. "She looks nuts. Why is she dressing like one of *them*? It's embarrassing."

Bear took it all in. The Queen and her cluster of noblewomen all wore heavy velvet cloaks and black furs, their faces veiled with black lace. Queen Meléna rested on her white throne and wore the gold crown of the Free City. The Queen's Voice spoke in her ear.

Overlord Goodman gave Rose the nod.

Bear's stomach turned flips at the simple gesture. Field Day was about to begin.

He felt sick now the moment had arrived. There was nothing to be done now. It was simply down to them and their training. He felt woefully underprepared. What was going to happen to Calleston if they did badly? What future would any of them have?"

"All right, my loves!" Rose called brightly. "Time to take your places! And please don't be shy! Give yourselves plenty of room."

It was time.

They filed past the platform where the drummers assembled around Rose. The red drummers were led by Grace, her silver-auburn hair flowing wild and loose. She tossed her tipper into the air. Bear stared as the red baton twirled high in a blue sky. Then she caught it smoothly and thwacked her drum with an encouraging grin.

Lutch stood in front of the black drummers, wearing the eye patch he'd taken to wearing since the Whip had half-blinded him. He held his drumskin out for the new bloomers to see. There was an eyepatch painted on the snarling face.

"Looking good, Lutch love," called Rose.

Lutch waved happily and beat out a little drum roll.

"Spread right to the bottom of the field, my loves! No dilly-dallying! Find your ground and then you bloody well stand it!" Rose called.

Felix, Megg and Bear were the last to find their place. They stood in the back row behind everyone else, as far from the town as they could be.

"This is it, then, my darlin's! Field Day is upon us! A day of new beginnings, for each and every one of you..."

Bear glanced up at Meya. Had she seen him? It was hard to tell. He stopped himself staring at the balcony where she sat and studied the rest of Calleston from afar. From the back of the field it looked like a giant castle on a crumbling rock. He followed all the crooked beams, bridges and balconies of Cobbleside, all the way up to the elegant terraces and towers of the roof, and found himself gazing at where Meya sat in red.

Rose's voice drifted through the air.

"Remember, stay relaxed, stay focused. All you need to do is direct the power of the plant..."

He wondered what they all looked like from Roofside. Probably quite small. Meya probably couldn't even tell which one was him.

He looked across at Megg, who signed quickly, *Good luck*. And at Felix, who gave a terse nod. He looked small suddenly, and lost.

"Grace! Lutch! Everyone ready, my loves?" Rose called out.

The drummers raised their arms.

Bear gestured to him: *Whatever happens, I'm with you.*

Felix flashed a small, sad smile. *Do your best, Bear. Don't worry about me.*

Bear looked up at the white flag. He scowled when he saw the large raven that was perched on top of the golden flagpole. That wasn't a good omen. A bell began chiming, and the crowd settled, until the only other sound was the snapping back and forth of the white fabric.

The Queen was motionless.

Meya leaned forward tensely.

Grace and Lutch held their drumsticks at the ready.

A shiver ran through Bear.

Without warning, and in the blink of an eye, the white flag turned a deep and unmistakable red.

In the distance, the town erupted into cheers. The raven launched itself from the flagpole into the air. Grace and Lutch began pounding their drums, joined by the company of drummers behind them.

Bear's heart clamoured in his chest.

This was it.

This was Field Day.

Bear looked down at the earth and saw bright green boots.

They had to go.

He kicked them off and buried his feet in the loamy black soil.

All right, Bear, no distractions.

The red drums were low and steady. He aligned his breathing with them.

Six beats in.

DUM, dum DUM, dum DUM, dum.

Six beats out,

DUM, dum DUM, dum DUM, dum.

He concentrated on the steady pulse. He felt his feet in the cool earth and the sun warming his skin. He waited. He wouldn't force it. The drums beat slow and loud; they resonated in his mind.

DUM, dum DUM, dum DUM, dum.

Bear's heart boomed in his chest. He swayed in circles. His breath was a river.

And then, from somewhere inside, he felt it. The familiar rushing feeling began, a flowing, a folding into himself and back out again and into the ground beneath him.

He was beginning to enlace.

He felt a smile spread over his face, and he got to work.

Bear directed a pool of energy outwards. The drums resounded in his head. He let the pool flood out into the soil, washing over the little souls of the seeds.

A thought bloomed in his mind.

No seed allotments today. No boundaries.

He could spread as far as he was able to.

He took in a deep breath and let the pool of energy flood wide. As he washed over countless seeds, he extended an invitation in his head, an invitation to connect and grow. He held the offer in his mind's eye. The seeds said "yes".

His heart pumped blood through his veins.

He dug his feet deeper into the wet earth and an army of ruby-red seeds sent their roots darting deep into the ground, racing down excitedly. Then his mind recoiled suddenly in shock – speedweed. It was a small outbreak, but it was as onerous as a rotten tooth, silently infecting its neighbours. The thorny growth consumed everything it touched.

Bear ran his mind over the contaminated patch. He extended a feeler and discovered something abhorrent in their touch; the black vines wanted to use him. They extended an invitation to Bear, to help the rot spread faster.

The pounding drums quickened.

He jerked his mind away from the speedweed patch. Above ground, he shuddered and moved on.

Bear directed his roots to link together. They began exchanging what they needed, growing thicker and thicker, becoming a central web of roads and arteries that worked together as one. Wondering how many seeds he'd connect with was meaningless. They'd become an underground cloud of energy, of thought, working together, growing together. He was ecstatic.

Bear heard his own muffled laugh from somewhere above, while his mind raced through the soothing dark soil. He was ready. The seeds were ready. It was time to reach towards the sun.

The drums pulsated, growing louder and faster, roaring in his ears.

He clenched his fists, bringing them together. He drew them slowly upwards and felt hundreds of tiny shoots emerge from the earth, breaking the surface and rising into the sunlight.

Joy. Tiny shoots, no taller than his fingers, hummed and vibrated as they were charged by rays of light.

Power built inside him as he held his palms out flat, absorbing sunbeams, then sent that power back down through the earth and outwards, further and further and further—

And then it stopped. While the plants recharged in the light, he felt a hard boundary limit to his growth. The limit of his ability.

He wrestled with the feeling. He found he didn't like it at all.

As if in answer to his disappointment, Bear felt something else. A presence. It was alive. It brushed against him quickly, and then drew back, as though it were afraid.

Bear gasped. That was strange. Sinsenn had never enlaced in this way before. Had he awakened it somehow? This *felt* like sinsenn, but with a personality. He liked it, whatever it was.

He decided to see for himself. Bear imagined reaching out slowly.

Don't be afraid, he thought. *I won't hurt you.*

And there the skittish presence was again.

Bear extended an invitation, and after just a brief moment of hesitation he felt a warm, shy soul flooding through the system he'd built, exploring his design, tenderly testing flexibility and strength. He gasped at the feeling. The plant, whatever it was, was alive.

Like sunlight rushing through his veins, he felt the presence alongside him. He was not alone any more.

They decided as one to proceed together. And so, working with this presence in the soil, their vines erupted across the earth, countless leaves unfurling eagerly in the sun. They hummed with excitement together.

The drums were a distant throbbing.

They permeated through the earth, racing alongside each other in excitement, tumbling over and through each other as they expanded across the land … and after a while they came to a natural pause. When they did, before Bear even had time to reflect, something new happened. The presence gently reached inside Bear's mind and took a look around.

Visions flooded his mind.

A girl on a high balcony dressed in blue.

Bear and Felix in a Roofside garden, staring at the sky.

Bear swinging from his uncle's hook, giggling, begging to be swung higher.

Megg by the canal on a summer's evening, dark hair blown across her sunlit face.

And then there was his mother.

His mother with a bird on her finger: a red siskin, chirping.

His mother stroking Bear's hair and whispering secrets as he fell asleep.

His mother smiling at Bear as the field behind her turned red.

Hot tears rolled down his cheeks.

Hurt and pain and love.

Two blots, their wet mouths glistening, advancing on Bear and Felix.

A crack as the Whip furiously blinded Lutch.

Blood gushing down Uncle Caber's face.

Flames exploding in a cage—

Their visions went deeper.

Megg's parents singing together as they restitched a pile of clothes.

Megg's sisters laughing as their mother ran screaming from a tiny mouse.

Bear and Felix at the far end of a shadowy field, signing.

Bear holding Megg in his arms, whispering to her "breathe".

Bear looking up at the parapet, at someone else, his mouth open...

These aren't my memories, he thought.

These are mine, she thought.

The drums raced faster and faster until they both felt dizzy.

Their eyes fluttered and then opened.

They saw in double.

They turned to each other, heart pounding.

The drums stopped.

The town erupted into deafening cheers.

And as he stared at her, he felt their minds untangle. He felt *her* feel their minds untangle.

And then he was alone again.

They had been ... together.

He'd been enlaced ... somehow ... with Megg.

The wind blew and Bear shuddered. He was covered in sweat. He collapsed to his knees.

The drums stopped, but the cheers reached a deafening pitch. He gazed up at Cobblesiders dancing around the town's walls.

He looked over the field and gasped.

Top Field was completely red. Sinsenn covered the ground all the way from where they stood to the moat. That hadn't happened for years. Almost everyone had cultivated something. There was only one perfect ring of bare, black earth… Felix.

Felix didn't even seem to notice. He stood, immobile. The sun blinded Bear. His field hat hung at his back. He replaced it and got back to his feet.

He hesitated to look at Megg, but he needed to see her face. When he did, she was already looking at him.

She had enlaced with him – he was sure of it. But how was that possible?

Megg was looking past him, behind him, with wide, frightened eyes. She raised her finger. *Look.*

He turned round.

Bear gasped at the vision.

They hadn't just flooded Top Field.

They'd flooded the next field too.

And the next.

And the next.

And the next.

CHAPTER
18

Noka scurried behind the Queen. "We are overjoyed to share with you Calleston's most fruitful bloom in a decade. The eye of the Queen brings good fortune to our town."

Tsilas Violet raised a hand so that the grovelling fool didn't get too close.

"Your workforce is half what it was ten years ago. Why?"

The Queen eyed the man as he walked. Lord Noka didn't hesitate.

"A myriad of reasons, my lord. We are a diminished town, there has been sickness, and much predation from the blots. They draw ever closer to our walls."

The Queen had seen the reports, and the countless pleading letters from the Overlord. But now she had seen the sinsenn yield for herself, it seemed she would have to remind Calleston that the Free City was not to be deceived.

"Our field workers have struggled in recent years..."

The queen ignored him.

An execution would serve as a convincing reminder. The only question was who it would be.

*

"Remove this rag. *Immediately*," Meya ordered.

Meya was livid. She hadn't wanted to wear the stupid veil anyway, and it pinched painfully as they teased it out.

"Be careful!" she snapped.

Meya looked at herself in the mirror and tried to avoid shooting death stares at her attendants. They had once again allowed Noka to dictate her wardrobe. She huffed her displeasure but held her tongue while they untangled her. She was absolutely certain that if she could see the clasp herself, she would already be free of it.

"Would you like us to change your gown before you join the celebrations, Lady Meya?" Finea asked quietly.

Meya nodded. She knew she should be happy. When she'd seen those fields of red, rippling outwards like a wave, her father had looked completely dumbstruck, like an overwhelmed little boy. He beamed at the Queen and all at once had buried his face in Noka's shirt. Meya knew he was hiding a quick joyful tear. Even Noka had seemed astonished.

"That young pair were just amazing, weren't they? The girl and the boy? Really, my lady, I'm stunned," said Sara.

"Yes, very promising," Meya said stiffly.

She couldn't get the image out of her mind. The way they had just stood looking at each other afterwards…

"They might actually get an invite up here after a few years of hard work."

"Luca! Concentrate! You're pulling my hair!"

"Sorry, my lady."

Finea bundled back into the chamber with gowns hung over her arm. Luca carefully resumed picking at the tangled veil on Meya's head. The girls presented the dresses one by one.

"What do we think of this green?" Finea stirred the skirt a little so Meya could see the movement. "It complements olive skin, no?"

Meya curled her lip in disgust. "Too busy, old-fashioned."

"What about this silk one in royal blue?"

Meya made another face.

Finea held up another. Meya shook her head and sniffed. She felt miserable. Luca saw something in her face. He pulled a handkerchief from up his sleeve and discreetly held it out to her.

She burst into tears.

Sara took the handkerchief from Luca and began dabbing at Meya's cheeks tenderly.

"Don't worry, my lady. We'll find something."

"I don't care about the dress."

"Then what is it, my lady?"

Meya didn't know if she was angry, upset or something else, but she let the tears run their course. They didn't stop coming for a while, but she did not let herself make a sound.

After a while she began to feel more like herself.

"Luca. All of you. Forgive me, I haven't been sleeping. It's ... it's been a hideous week, and without Percy... I miss him so much it hurts. I just want things to go back to how they were."

It wasn't a lie.

"Of course. We understand, my lady."

Luca squeezed her shoulder. "I'm sure Percy will turn up soon. He's indestructible."

Meya nodded once and gave him a tight smile. Finea held up a black gown with a high collar. Meya grimaced.

"No, Fi, nothing black! I'm not dressing like the Queen again, like some fanatical floorborn nobody. That was Noka's brilliant idea. I should have known better than to listen to him."

Finea nodded mutely and placed the dress on top of the growing pile.

As if on cue, there was a rap on the door and Noka swept in. "Oh, my darling Meya, you really looked exquisite up there."

She felt the fire in her belly return. Since she was a child, Noka always made Meya feel as if she were some hot-headed, hysterical fool.

"Noka, don't you dare come creeping into my quarters with your tail between your legs now. You saw how ridiculous I looked with that veil flapping about like a dying fish! You've no right to tell me what to wear!"

"Meya, I merely made a suggestion – you, of course, can wear whatever you choose."

"I'm not wearing red to the feast," she insisted.

"As you wish, my lady," said Noka. "Perhaps the gold?"

"No. I want something simple."

Noka's expression stayed open and understanding, despite Meya's abruptness, but she would not be placated. After the embarrassment she'd just endured, she wouldn't let him talk her round. Time and time again, Meya found herself pacified by him until the moment he left the room, only to realize she hadn't got what she wanted.

"Something simple? My Lady—"

"I looked a fool up there, Noka. I was uncomfortable and overdressed and there was nothing I could do about it."

Noka tilted his head, concerned.

"My intention was never to make you uncomfortable. I apologize."

Meya yelped as Sara accidentally caught the pin and yanked at her hair. Sara held up her hands and a pair of scissors in fear. Meya blinked rapidly, but didn't comment.

"Almost free, Lady Meya," Sara whispered before carrying on snipping.

"If your intention was not to make me uncomfortable," Meya said, eyes shining, "then you catastrophically failed."

Noka laid a comforting hand on her arm. "My dear, I shan't make you wear anything you object to. I only want you to ingratiate yourself with the Queen. It is important she see you as the lady of Calleston that you are, no?"

There was a subtle click. Meya felt the gold clasp on her head come loose as the veil slid to the floor. Sara held out a scrap of knotted red cloth triumphantly.

"There we go! All done!" She beamed at Meya in the mirror.

"Anyway," Noka murmured in her ear, "I come with other news. Might we have a moment?"

Meya nodded. Now she'd calmed down, he'd share whatever bad news he'd come to deliver.

Noka ushered Sara and the others out of the room, though as the door shut, Meya heard the inconspicuous thud that was ears being pressed to it. He stood behind Meya and adjusted the jewels in her hair as he spoke, fixing loose pieces back in place.

"I am sorry to say the Overlord will not be presenting the lord's gift at the festival this year."

Meya frowned. It was traditional for the Overlord to present something to the people during the harvest celebrations. Surely the Queen hadn't claimed the role for herself?

"But that is his right! Father is—"

"He will not be presenting the lord's gift during the festival," Noka cut in, "because you will."

Meya gasped. "Really?"

He continued tweaking her hair with a slightly amused smirk.

"Meya, you serve as a symbol of Calleston, and the family that has ruled here for generations."

He looked over his shoulder and then crouched down so his face was level with hers. He spoke to her as if his life depended on it, or hers. Meya wondered what the play was. With Noka, there was usually a play. But something in his demeanour left her absolutely mesmerized.

"My dear, it is my very last wish on this earth that in the coming days you feel hurt or anger. You wonder why I suggested the red gown? I did so not to embarrass you, but to elevate you. Now is the moment for you to step forward, Meya, into the role you were born for. Through great effort, Calleston is entering a new era. The fields flourish anew! And now the people need hope. Cobbleside sees you as a symbol of their new beginning. But your part is not just a symbolic one." He held her hand in his. "Meya, if you foster a sisterly relationship with Queen Meléna, it will be for the good of everyone who shelters here in Calleston." He looked deeply into her eyes. "Even the floorborn. Do you understand, Meya? If we win the Queen's favour, we protect everyone, from the most privileged to the lowliest ... pickpocket."

He didn't blink. Meya swallowed, but didn't let her expression change. She had a feeling her secret trip to Cobbleside had not gone unnoticed.

"The Queen is unpredictable, and ill-tempered," Noka whispered. "Our people need you now, more than ever."

Meya looked into his wide, earnest eyes and felt an unsettling sense of duty, but also a sense of pride – pride in who she was. Perhaps, with the blooming, the tides really would turn. A new era of prosperity and hope, if Meya could avoid provoking the Queen's temper ... or her own. She would like to see Dorloc Odittany with a twinkle of hope in his eye, or maybe even a new dog in his lap.

"Of course, Noka," she said quietly. "I understand. I'll

present the Overlord's gift. And I'll do it … graciously."

Noka smiled. He reached out and gently tucked a strand of hair behind her ear.

"Sweet girl. Queen Meléna and our people will grow to love you, as they once did your mother…" Meya felt a lump rise in her throat. "How could they not? Now, why don't you change into that gold dress and meet me in the hall? And do not even think about cutting through the gardens. We've had enough garment destruction for one day."

He winked, straightened up and then swept out of the room, leaving her alone with her thoughts.

She smiled at herself in the mirror; she looked a lot like her mother with her hair braided up. She dabbed at the corners of her eyes.

Meya had spent a long time wondering where she fitted into Calleston, and suddenly it seemed so obvious. She could become a champion of her people. Her mother had always been an advocate for the floorborn; she had walked among them happily. The postal lady had confirmed what she'd always imagined – her mother had been loved. And maybe, in time, Meya would be too. She frowned at the memory of the exhausted Cobbleside faces below.

She remembered her mother's objections when the golden gates were first erected. She had cried bitterly on that day. And now Meya understood why, in some ways, Cobbleside had been abandoned.

Meya stood up. She would wear the gold. She would be every inch the lady that her father and her people deserved.

After her secret visit among the floorborn, she saw why she'd been sheltered from such things. But she didn't want to be protected any more. She wanted to help. She knew that there must be some way for Calleston to survive if Roofside and Cobbleside were united.

And perhaps she was the woman to do it.

"Uncover the cage."

Tsilas Violet pulled down the sheet.

From her throne, Queen Meléna peered at the vile creature hiding in the corner. It tried to disguise itself in smoke, forming odd shifting stripes that mimicked the bars of the cage. It was clever, always trying to escape, always trying to go against her will.

She would be glad to find another one, an easier one to control. Of all the witches the Free City had captured, the most vicious one had survived the longest.

"Give it water."

Tsilas Violet held out a bowl on the end of a large handle. The creature dragged itself forward and drank. Without its smokescreen, she saw how thin it had become.

"I need it strong."

"That's dangerous, my Queen. When she gains strength, she is more difficult to—"

"I need it strong," she repeated. "Feed it. We will catch another one before we leave. I can smell it."

CHAPTER 19

Down in the Main Market square, spirits were high. The Overlord had distributed sugar apples and barrels of ruby brew in celebration. Outside the Dodgy Gut, Megg's mother and the girls were chattering happily to Bear's uncles. Even Aber had a smile on his face.

"Bear lad!" Jim proclaimed. "Not just a field – you and Megg went and filled half the land! You take after your mother! You've done us proud!"

"She would have been delighted," Caber sang, whistling through his missing tooth. "She always had the knack for growing."

"And your dad too, Megg," said Elma, beaming down at her daughter, and giving her arm a squeeze.

Megg and Bear smiled awkwardly and avoided eye contact. They hadn't yet discussed what had happened out in the field. Bear had no idea where to start, if there was any precedent for such things. He felt suddenly awkward around her. Had something … unnatural happened?

Megg kept her focus on her apple.

Felix offered Bear another one.

"No, thanks, Felix. You have it."

"I've had enough, I think. Take it."

Bear shook his head.

"Megg?"

"No, thank you."

Felix looked at Megg and Bear and then sighed loudly. He kept his voice low, and the noise of the crowd gave him the privacy to say what he wanted to say.

"Come on, this is supposed to be a celebration. Don't feel bad on my account, both of you. I meant what I said – I wanted you both to do your best. And you were amazing. Better than amazing. You might have turned things around for Calleston."

Megg swallowed a piece of apple and spoke quickly. "I've been thinking. You should ask Rose to continue your training and try again next year. Some people just take longer to learn. Some people…"

Felix held up his hand. "That's just it, though, isn't it? I'm not *people*, not a human person at any rate. I'm Fennex. Whoever heard of a Fennex that could grow sinsenn? I just … have to accept it. I'll find something else to do. Don't worry about me. Let's enjoy the music, and the food! I'll be all right!"

Felix sounded as if he meant it. But Bear couldn't tell if he was putting on a brave face so that he and Megg could relax.

"I never really cared about growing sinsenn anyway. I just wanted to get rich and move to Roofside."

Megg laughed and Bear felt some of his tension lessen. Nothing had really changed. The sun was out, they had sugar apples, they were celebrating a bloom Bear couldn't have imagined and Cobbleside was rejoicing after a hard year. The morning began to feel like a dream. Maybe what had happened in the fields was just part of enlacing, maybe Rose hadn't got around to explaining that yet, maybe it just … happened sometimes.

"Felix, lad!" Uncle Jim waved his hook and pointed towards the busiest part of the crowd, below the Overlord's viewing terrace. "Get over here!"

The human tower was beginning. Every year, once Field Day was done, Cobblesiders formed a giant tower by clambering up on top of each other and standing on each other's shoulders. If the tower reached the Overlord's balcony, he would bestow on them the lord's gift.

The strongest men and women were already establishing the base levels: feet planted and shoulders forming the footholds for those above. The surrounding crowd supported those on the bottom, grasping, pressing their shoulders and buttressing the weight of the tower as it formed.

Felix grinned.

"Do you fancy it?" he asked them.

"Why not," Megg said with a smile. "Bear?"

Bear felt a jolt of something as she raised her eyes to his.

Felix sprinted off through the crowd. Megg and Bear looked at each other for a long moment.

"Megg," Bear said hesitantly, "out there in the field ... did you feel something happen? Something..." He wasn't sure how much he dared admit. "Something...? Did we...?"

Bear couldn't bring himself to say it. He was too scared to even find the words. He was terrified that a look of horror would cross her face.

Megg slipped her hand into his and gave it a little squeeze. "It's all right, Bear," she said. "I know why you're worried, but it's... I don't exactly know what happened out there, but we can figure it out later, all right? What matters is we created the best harvest in Calleston for years. Focus on that. Come on, let's go find Felix before he breaks his neck?"

She held his hand and led him through the crowd. As her warm fingers closed round his, Bear's mind flooded again with the visions he saw in the field – Megg's laughing, sunlit face; his face looking back across the field at her; his face looking up at the parapet...

She pulled her hand away as they approached the tower. It would be their first time joining the human tower – only those who had completed Field Day could take part.

Bear could hear Cusht calling for volunteers. "We're getting there! We need strong, skinny and brave!" Red sinsenn smoke swirled up from Cusht's pipe as he shouted directions to the participants and yanked new ones in from the crowd.

"Here, boys!" he called. "I want the lot of you! Is that Cassius? That's a bit o' luck! Get that mop-top up there where it belongs. You're not skulking away that easy!"

Bear watched as the rag-tag boys who'd ganged up on Doc began pulling themselves up the trunk of the tower. Cassius climbed with strength and certainty, stepping his bare foot on the head of a bald man, who seemed not to mind.

Felix pointed out Bear and Megg to Cusht.

"Perfect! Come on, young'uns! First bloomers, you haven't finished your day's work yet!"

Megg kicked off her shoes, tossed her long hair over her shoulder and, placing her bare foot against a man's hip, pulled herself up on top of his shoulders and began her climb.

She looked back at Bear and smiled. "Come on!" she said, and carried on up the tower.

Bear slipped off his boots and placed them gently on the floor where the other shoes were piled.

"Don't worry, lad," said a voice. "Nobody's stealing boots that colour," and everyone laughed.

Bear was quickly lifted up on to a burly man's shoulders, then he followed the swish of Megg's skirts as she scaled up the tower of bodies. They clambered past Petal, the dock worker, bracing hard on one of the lower levels of the tower. She gave a sly grin when she caught sight of Megg.

"Megg Ovelma! Brilliant bloom, girl. Now would you please get to the top and put us out of our misery!"

The lower levels laughed again as Megg and Bear climbed higher. The atmosphere was one of excited focus.

"Not on my arm – on my shoulder!"

"That's it, love! Get up there."

"Climbing again, Bear?"

Bear searched for the owner of the voice. It hadn't come from the tower, Bear was pretty sure. He looked over the crowd, and eventually spotted Rose and her family sitting with Olenta on their balcony. Olenta gave him a wink. Bear smiled when he saw Rose's youngest daughter.

"Hi, Mister Bear!" shouted Poppy's high-pitched voice.

"Hi, Poppy!" he shouted.

"Hurry it up, Aberson!" Cassius shouted from somewhere above.

Bear climbed a little faster. He was almost at the top level now. Megg was up there, smiling at him. She reached a hand down and pulled him up till he was level with her and then, without warning, she kissed him – just quickly on the cheek – as easy as a summer breeze, but Bear felt his whole face go red and he saw that hers had too. She looked at him with a smile that was somehow so mischievous and yet so bashful that he laughed out loud.

"Watch out, you two – I'm coming!" shouted Felix.

He darted up the tower like a squirrel. He sprang up lightly beside them, then jerked his head towards the balcony. "Your girlfriend isn't exactly a shrinking violet, is she?"

The smile fell from Megg's face. Bear looked up.

Stood there on the balcony was Meya. She wore a dress that was stitched with threads of gold. The material shimmered in the sunlight. Standing just behind her on the balcony was the Overlord's advisor.

Bear hadn't imagined she'd be there, or that they might be so close. She looked straight ahead, not down at the gathering crowd, or the tower. Or him. He couldn't tell if she hadn't seen him yet, or if she were avoiding looking.

He stared at her. She looked so different somehow. She was close enough so that if he spoke her name, even quietly, she would hear it. But, at the same time, she seemed a world away.

He felt Megg's arm slip out from his.

A foot pressed down on his shoulder as Felix vaulted past them both to balance proudly on their shoulders, top of the tower. He stretched out his hand to the balcony.

Market Square erupted into cheers.

Meya waited for the crowd to quieten. Then she spoke. "It is a great honour, on behalf of the Overlord..." She paused and seemed to reconsider her words. "On behalf of my father, the man who has served Calleston for a lifetime, to present to you this token of recognition."

She leaned down towards Felix. Bear watched transfixed, the jewels in her fair hair flashing and her long golden sleeves shimmering and wafting in the breeze as she reached down delicately for Felix's outstretched hand and placed something in it.

Felix took the small parcel and held it overhead in joyful triumph. The crowd cheered in celebration again until Meya held up her hand for quiet.

"It is widely known that Calleston's sinsenn yield has been left … wanting … in recent years. But considering the abundance of this year's Field Day, we are hopeful that the bounty of the righteous and generous Queen Meléna will go some way to soothe these shortages."

There was an almost imperceptible tension in her voice, Bear thought. The thoughtful words seemed unnatural in her mouth, as if she had been coached to say them. But then maybe she had.

"I want to thank Queen Meléna, on behalf of you all, and personally, for everything she has done for our town."

There was faint, scattered applause. Bear saw the Overlord's aide, Noka, give Meya a small reassuring nod.

"What's in the package, Fennex?" a voice shouted from the crowd.

Felix didn't need asking twice. He unravelled the stumpy little package in a flash. He gave it a big sniff.

"Cheese!" he shouted. "The lord's gift is cheese!"

There were cheers from around the square, but also a great deal of laughing. It was a fine gift, but comically small. It seemed like the Queen's bounty had yet to make its way down to the Cobblesiders.

"Grand speech for a poxy wheel of cheese," said a voice from below.

Bear glanced down. It was Cassius.

Among the cheers and the laughter, Bear heard something else now. A few people were booing. That was unusual, partly because the watchmen were usually quick

246

to stamp it out, and partly because when the red smoke blew and the ruby brew flowed freely, nobody seemed to mind too much. Cobblesiders were many things, but rarely angry.

Until today.

There was a sudden wobble of the human tower and shrieks of panic rippled up and down before they regained their balance.

"Quite the drop," said Cassius, looking up at Bear. "Reckon we get down now?"

Bear nodded. Cassius was right – it was a long way to fall. Bear longed to get his feet back on the cobbles.

The boos and jeers grew. The people of Cobblestone had triumphed at Field Day, for the first time in years, and the lump of cheese had been taken as an insult. Bear looked up to the Overlord's balcony and saw Meya's face flush, her expression shifting from confusion, to hurt, to anger. She looked as if she were about to speak.

But before she could say a word, she was ushered away from the balcony by the Overlord's advisor.

"Bear…?"

It was Megg. "We need to get down, Bear," she said in a soft voice.

Bear nodded. "Felix!" he called. "Let's get down – this might turn ugly…"

The crowd suddenly fell silent. Bear looked up, expecting to see the Overlord, but someone else had stepped forward on to the balcony. His nostrils flared in indignation; his eyes were two calm pools of black. Intelligent and cold.

"Well, it seems that a heartfelt congratulations is in order then, Calleston."

It was the Queen's Voice. He wore dark blue leather like a second skin and was using the white stick as a cane.

Bear felt Megg shift nervously next to him. There was no telling what this man could do with that ivory stick. If people started panicking, the whole tower could come down.

"The Queen is delighted with a yield that will surely be the beginning of a superb harvest. Truly, Calleston is the Cup of the Free City. And it seems, for the first time in a generation, that the cup is overflowing."

His voice was surprisingly warm and friendly, but up close Bear saw that it was an affectation, a play for the people. His cold eyes gave him away.

The Queen's Voice rested his staff against the marble balustrade and began clapping, an odd muffled clap, muted by his leather gloves. Cobbleside, and the people gathered on the rooftops, clapped along uneasily.

"When the people are left wanting, Queen Meléna is left wanting. When the people are gratified, Queen Meléna is gratified in turn. That is the way of the Free City."

Tsilas Violet reached into a leather purse hanging from his hip. He brought out a shiny gold coin and held it up to the light. Bear heard Felix whistle from above. Megg shushed him.

Tsilas Violet looked at Felix, and a wicked smile spread slowly across his face. He raised his voice triumphantly to the crowd.

"One gold coin, minted by the Free City, for each of the younglings who participated in the sinsenn bloom today!"

Cheers and whistles rang out across the square. That was more money than Cobbleside had seen in years. The Queen's Voice held up a finger for quiet, and then pointed that finger at Felix, with a sweet smile on his face.

"Except for you, little Fennex pup. The land that you tended to today was fruitless and barren. As dead and as lifeless as the scorched deserts of your ancestors... You may keep the cheese."

Bear's heart dropped down into his stomach. His body flooded with anguish for Felix. The crowd was mostly silent, but Bear was crushed to hear some laughter and jeering from the square. The fact that Felix was stuck at the top of the human tower for everyone to see made it even more heartbreaking.

The Queen's Voice wasn't finished yet. He spoke with the excitement and pride of a father congratulating his children. "And bring me this pair who flooded our fields! The girl and the boy! These champions of Calleston shall be Queen Meléna's honoured guests at the feast tonight!"

Bear's ears were ringing. He and Megg were invited to visit the roof, while Felix stood humiliated in front of the whole community? He could felt Megg shaking beside him. He took her hand in his.

The Queen's Voice scanned the crowd with his hard unfeeling eyes. Bear felt like a mouse sitting in the coils of a snake.

"This talented pair will serve to remind your Overlord of the abundance he already has under his very feet. Now, where are they?"

"There."

Bear looked up. It was Meya's voice that had spoken. She was leaning over the balcony, pointing down to where Megg and Bear stood. Her face was hard and cold.

"Someone fetch them and bring them up here," said the Queen's Voice. "The Queen is waiting."

The Raven was alone. He swept freely over the town, over the market square, up and over the rooftop gardens and the black tower, then round and back down towards the fields.

He'd made some good finds in the fields recently, and, better yet, there were no people to shoot arrows at him out there. He knew exactly where he was flying.

When the night men fed on flesh in the dark, there were always leavings in the light. That was if Cora hadn't got to them first. He flew over the fields, and among the red flowers he saw great scratches in the ground.

He began rooting through the earth. The smell of blood led him to a little prize. A ropy piece of man-flesh. He laughed inside his head as he swallowed it down.

The meat was tender; it was from a youngling. He would share this knowledge with the women later.

But, for now, he enjoyed having no one in his business, and no one in his mind.

20

The descender rattled and rumbled as it rose upwards.

"No need to be alarmed," said the man, flashing them a reassuring smile. "It's perfectly safe. We transport huge wagons on this thing so it's very strong."

Bear wasn't nervous about being in a room hoisted up on great big wheels; he was nervous about the watchmen that were in the room with them. He peeked from under his field hat at their faces. They ignored him.

The Overlord's aide kept talking. "This descender was designed to assist the Overlord in the transporting of large goods between levels." He smiled at Bear and Megg. "Or, in your case, valuable goods."

He laughed at his own joke. "The Overlord can't wait to meet you. It appears the glory days of Calleston have returned!"

The descender ground to a halt and the rumbling stopped.

"I will escort you through the accession hall and straight to his private quarters. Do you have any questions?"

Bear shook his head.

"Your name, sir?" asked Megg.

"Forgive me! I am Noka, privy counsel and aide of the Overlord, and if you will accept me as such, aide to the both of you too."

The great doors parted and Noka stepped into the accession hall.

The hall was cavernous. It had the same high ceilings and open floorplan as the warehouse, but instead of machines and tools it was covered in carpets and tapestries and paintings.

"Follow me!" said Noka as he strode towards a towering golden gate. A young watchman stepped forward, scowling.

Noka put a hand out. "What do you think you're doing?" he said.

"We need to search them," the watchman muttered sourly.

"Bear and Megg are our honoured guests, Malka, not intruders."

"Honoured guests," Malka sneered. "Floor scum."

Bear noticed that his tongue and lips were stained with sinsenn. *Strange*, he thought. It clearly had not taken effect yet. The watchman looked murderous.

"Malka. This behaviour is unacceptable. Stand down," said Noka quietly.

Malka dropped his hand and stood stiffly back, scowling as Bear and Megg walked past him through the great golden gate.

But, as they passed, he curled his hand into a fist and

pulled it back. Both Bear and Megg flinched, but instead of turning on them the watchman pounded his fist as hard as he could into the stone wall. To their horror, it crunched into the stone, leaving a crumbling hole where his fist had struck.

Malka himself looked a little shocked at his own strength.

Noka broke the silence. His voice was strained as he said, "Malka, you are relieved of your duties tonight. Head to your quarters and wait for me. Drink a ruby brew, and do not leave your room until I arrive. Do you understand?"

"Yes, Lord Noka."

Malka scurried away. Noka addressed the other watchmen. "Anyone who feels unable to treat our guests appropriately can do the same."

The watchmen looked at each other, but no one moved.

"Good," said Noka. He gave an apologetic smile to Bear and Megg, and led them on down the corridor.

"My deepest apologies. Perhaps they have been training too hard recently."

Megg shot Bear a worried look. She held her hand in a claw and tapped her heart twice. *I'm nervous.*

Bear pressed his index fingers next to each other. *Me too.*

They entered a vast circular room through a great white archway. Three other archways led away in different directions. Hanging down from the ceiling was a monstrously large golden wheel, covered in candles. Their flames flickered and glowed, casting an eerie light around the room. Bear gaped at the sheer size of the thing.

"The main feast hall is that way." Noka pointed to the archway to the left, which was draped with a thick red curtain. "If you get lost, you can always go there."

They passed through the archway to the right instead and down a wide stone corridor. Soft end–of–day light poured in through high circular windows. Bear ran his hands along the cool yellow stone wall as they walked. Everything was clean and uniform and perfectly kept. He wondered what was on the other side of the high windows, and if they were anywhere near the rooftop garden in which he and Felix had hidden. Noka rapped on an unassuming wooden door, and a moment later it opened.

"Noka."

Bear was surprised to see the door was opened by the Overlord himself. He ushered them into a tiny circular room filled with books.

"Bear, Megg, I have been longing to meet you! I wanted to be the first to welcome you into our home," the Overlord said with a smile that appeared genuine. "I hope that Noka has made you comfortable."

"Yes, my lord," said Megg.

"Yes, my lord," said Bear.

"Please, call me Gordon," he said as he sat down on a circular wooden table.

Bear was struck by how different he looked up close. He seemed less imposing, and older than Bear had imagined.

He had deep blue eyes, and soft grey hair, though his goatee beard and eyebrows were still quite dark. They were perhaps what made him seem striking from a distance – that and his unmistakable voice. Deep and booming when he spoke from the terrace, it was warm and gentle in person.

"Gordon Greyson Goodman. And, tell me, what are your names?"

"Megg Ovelma."

"Bear Aberson."

"Ovelma? I can't say I know an Elma. What does your mother do, young lady?"

"Field and needlework mostly, but after the harvest she works in the drying houses."

"I see. And what does your father do, young man?"

"General labouring, my lord."

"Good honest work. Do remember to call me Gordon. I've only ever made my wife call me my lord … and sometimes Noka."

Noka laughed and placed a hand on both Bear and Megg's shoulders. "I shall leave you in the Overlord's remarkable hands. No doubt I will see you again shortly."

"Might you keep the corridor clear, Noka?" said the Overlord.

"Of course."

He slipped out of the door and closed it behind him.

"Please, Megg Ovelma, and Bear … Aberson! Do sit down."

The Overlord pulled chairs out from the big round table and slid on to one himself. He clasped his hands together. Megg and Bear sat. On the table was a bowl filled with black seeds. The Overlord noticed Bear looking.

"Speedweed seeds," he said, and a worried look coloured his face for a moment, before he covered it up with a smile. "Just another problem I need to deal with... Anyway! I do apologize – now is not the time for my worries. Would you like a ruby brew?" he asked warmly, gesturing to a jug beside him.

"Yes, please," said Megg.

"Bear?"

"No, thank you."

"Well," said the Overlord. "What a spectacular Field Day this has turned out to be. Not merely one field of sinsenn but many. And all thanks to you two! My watchmen didn't report anything so extraordinary in the practice session. You must both have been sitting on this talent for a long time. We had long expected, no, *feared*, that the harvest would be poor." The Overlord slid Megg her cup and looked at them both with an expression of great intensity. "You ought to be proud. And your families too."

"Yes, my lor— Gordon," said Megg.

The Overlord leaned back and smiled.

"Well, we are simply overjoyed, not just for you, but for the entire town. I'm sure you know that Calleston has struggled, in years past, to fill sinsenn quotas for the Queen."

Megg and Bear nodded. "Well, I no longer fear that that will be a problem. It seems you were sent to us in the nick of time. And if you continue to bloom sinsenn with such success, I believe you may be the first in many a year to be invited to the roof ... permanently."

Bear's stomach rumbled loudly and the Overlord frowned. Bear felt his face flush.

"And of course we must have you fed! But, first, a word of friendly advice while you are here." The Overlord pressed his fingertips together as he considered his words. He cleared his throat and folded his arms. "Queen Meléna is a very wise woman. A wise woman, and a gifted queen, who I admire greatly. However, the young Queen has left the Free City for the first time in her short life. She is finally travelling the land and meeting her people. But we in Calleston are still strangers to her. She knows our history, but she doesn't know our ways, or our struggles." His deep blue eyes passed between Megg and Bear as he conveyed his message. "In her attempts to understand our town better, she has taken to giving some of my staff ... truthwine."

Bear felt a tingle go up his spine. Truthwine was the most concentrated form of sinsenn. Traditional ruby brew simply made a person feel open and agreeable; drink too much and they might reveal an embarrassing thought. But truthwine was something else. It rendered the person unable to lie, or even twist the truth.

"Now, the royal family, that is to say, Queen Meléna,

has taken a long-standing oath. An agreement that my family can never be subjected to such procedures. But I am afraid I cannot extend that protection to you."

Megg put a calming hand on Bear's leg. She must know what he was thinking. What if the Queen asked them what had happened in the field? He couldn't even explain it to himself. He fought down a rising panic.

"Don't worry, child," said the Overlord. "The Queen has no reason to give you truthwine. And, if she did, there is nothing that could come out of your mouth that would be wrong. She is a strong Queen, but I believe she is a fair one."

Bear thought that seemed rather generous.

The Overlord lowered his voice. "I fear that Queen Meléna is concerned about … and I'm sorry to say this … witches. Here in Calleston."

Megg took a big sip of her ruby brew; Bear almost wished he had one.

The Overlord held up his hand. "Panic not. The Queen has always been wary of such things. It is understandable considering her own mother, no? But, despite the rumours that have been circulating in Calleston taverns, there's no reason to presume that there is witchery in Calleston, just because we suffer. We've been suffering perfectly well without witches for years now."

The Overlord smiled a weak smile.

Bear nodded. He thought of the hooded woman disappearing in a cloud of smoke. The three figures on the black boat. The raven and the owl. He knew he should tell the Overlord about it all, but something told him not to.

There was a rustling from above and Bear glanced upwards. He was surprised to discover they were actually in a small tower. Behind a bookshelf was a staircase that wound up the tower.

"My private library," the Overlord said. "Languages, medicine, poetry and some of the most accurate records of our land's history are kept here. I taught my daughter to read at this very table."

"Mother taught me to read," a voice rang down from above.

Bear froze, and he felt Megg stiffen beside him.

"*You* taught me to swear."

The Overlord laughed as Meya walked down the spiral stairs, taking her time not to trip on the hem of her long, gold dress.

"Here she is. Megg, Bear, this is my daughter, Meya."

"You've had quite a day," said Meya, eyeing Bear coolly, before turning her gaze to Megg. "Congratulations. Your sinsenn blooms were astonishing."

"Thank you," said Megg, meeting her eyes. "Your dress is beautiful."

Meya's hazel eyes looked Megg up and down slowly, appraisingly. "Thank you," she said with a smile that needed a little longer in the oven.

"It must almost be time for the feast," said the Overlord.

"Meya, would you take them to the banquet hall? I have a matter to attend to."

"Of course," Meya said. "It's easy to get lost, if you haven't been here before." She fixed her eyes on Bear for a second, before brushing past him and opening the door. "Follow me."

Bear and Megg walked a few paces behind Meya. Nobody spoke a word, the only sound their footsteps echoing down the corridor. Bear flicked an anxious look at Megg and gestured silently, *Are you all right?* but she didn't seem to notice, her gaze fixed ahead.

Soon they were back in the large white room. Meya swept through the red curtain, leading them down a corridor and out into a vast bustling hall.

There were hundreds of people gathered there, standing around gossiping, sipping from goblets of ruby brew and laughing enthusiastically.

It's like the Rusty Compass in a way, thought Bear, only everyone was wearing gowns and suits. He began to feel very underdressed in his cotton work clothes.

The influence of Queen Meléna and her companions was obvious. Roofside was awash with black or deep red gowns, and everyone was wearing the cumbersome veils that seemed to be the style of the Free City.

One very old man stood proudly with a red scarf gathered at his neck. He had unnaturally dark hair, as if it had been dipped in black ink. Bear was stunned. Surely it was painted on?

262

Stop staring, Megg warned Bear in Field-Speak.

"He's the last successful field worker to move up here," Lady Meya said, noticing where Bear was looking. "Hopefully not the *very* last."

Bear coughed and looked at the ground.

Meya signalled for an attendant to bring over drinks. Megg and Meya took one, but Bear shook his head.

"Everyone is going to try and talk to you," Meya said, taking a sip. "But they'll all be saying the same thing. *Congratulations, you must be so proud, so on.* It will grow tiresome fast. You can just nod if you like, and I'll move them on."

"What's out there?" asked Megg, looking through some glass doors.

"The roof gardens. Do you want to see?"

"Yes, please," said Megg, and they followed Meya out and down some yellow stone steps that led to an attractive walled garden full of blossoming trees. Megg gasped in shock, gawping at the rows of uniform trees that covered the manicured green, which stretched out before them.

In the distance, Bear could see an iron gate that looked like one he had seen before.

"What's that way?" he asked.

"Tower Gardens," replied Meya. "There are more trees in there, and, of course, a tower. The watchmen train below it in the tower clearing. It's nice, and the trees feel a little wilder than here in the orchard."

"So many trees!" Megg's face was flushed with excitement.

"It's a shame you won't be here when they fruit," said Meya.

"They fruit?" asked Bear. "What fruit?"

"I'm not sure. We have apple trees, pear trees, cherry trees ... lots of stone fruits. We have so many. I'm sorry, I forget which these ones are. When they're fruiting, you can just reach up, pick one and eat it."

"How wonderful ... for Roofside," said Megg.

Meya picked up on something in Megg's tone. "Don't worry. You'll eat before you go back down."

Megg's nostrils flared slightly, but she didn't respond.

A group of boys approached them. They wore robes of black silk and had opted for head wraps as opposed to veils.

"Hello," said a boy who looked as if he could be Meya's brother.

He swallowed a big chunk of the apple that he was chomping on and then wiped his hand on his shirt. He was olive-skinned and had brown hair, lightened somewhat by the sun.

"Are you two really from Cobbleside?" he asked.

"Yes," said Megg.

"I see." He took another bite of his apple. "Are you scared being up high?"

"Do shut up, Zazie," said Meya.

The boy grinned. "Meya's afraid of heights. Understandable, really, after what happened to her mother. But don't worry, you wouldn't even know you're

Roofside in these gardens; the walls are too high to even look over."

"Why?" asked Bear.

"For our privacy." Zazie paused for a second. "From you, actually!" He laughed again, loudly.

Bear managed a smile. Zazie took a last bite of his apple and then tossed the core over his shoulder, sending it flying over the balustrade down to Cobbleside.

"Anyway, splendid performance with the Field Day thing. Well done both of you."

Meya patted down her hair. "Zazie, boys, would you excuse me. It's high time I escorted our guests to the feast hall."

"An excellent idea!" Zazie turned to the other boys. "Come on, you miscreants and rascals! Why don't we all go and see how it's shaping up?"

Before Meya could protest, he winked at Bear and Megg and began leading the way. "Are you two as starving as I am?"

Bear nodded and glanced at Megg. "You have no idea."

The Raven hopped from window to window, hoping to see inside. But the glass made it impossible; it was all fragmented and pieced together. So he leapt from the window ledge and was carried upwards by a great gust into the evening air.

The sky was getting dark, and it was about time to head back to the boat. It was Cora's turn now.

As he flew back past the tower, another gust sent him upwards, and he saw that the roof of the tower was occupied. There were two people up there. One of them stood looking out over the garden, and the other lay convulsing on the floor.

Dying.

The Raven decided to circle back and watch.

There was a strange device on the roof. The Raven knew enough about humans for him to recognize it as a death bringer.

Once the convulsions stopped, the other brought out a large knife.

The Raven decided to circle back again.

CHAPTER
21

Bear had never eaten so much in his life. There was an enormous spit-roasted pig being turned over a flame. He sucked his fingers clean of the fat and juices that covered them, and raised his hand for another portion when the attendants passed by the long table again.

There were so many Roofsiders that Bear gave up trying to remember names. Everyone they were introduced to congratulated them on their bloom, and each one of them sized Megg and Bear up as they did so. Without fail, they seemed to study the effect of their words before turning back to talk to other Roofsiders. It put him slightly on edge, but Bear enjoyed listening to the high-spirited conversation almost as much as he enjoyed the food.

"If we focused on clearing the forest of blots, we could reclaim a lot of the land we've lost," said the old man with the pitch-black hair.

"And who would be doing the clearing? Don't talk nonsense," said Meya. "One bite from a blot and you're dead. We'd lose untold workers attempting any such thing."

"But their grandchildren might live in a Calleston that wasn't shuttered within its walls every night."

"Then why don't you strap on a sword and see how many blots you can take before you are overwhelmed? I'll be sure to tell your children how brave you were."

The man bristled.

"I only had one child," he said, and plopped a grape into his mouth. "Plenty of children down in Cobbleside, though, aren't there?" He glanced at Megg. "How many siblings do you have?"

"I have five sisters," Megg replied.

He choked on a grape.

"Five? There you go. That's what I was talking about. They tend to have large families down there."

"Angallo, do shut up," said Meya. "Your daughter has five children."

Bear let his attention wander around the banqueting hall. It had high, vaulted ceilings, with criss-crossing beams and tall windows. There were long tables arranged in a half circle around a group of musicians, who were playing viola, flute and harp. Watchmen were posted at regular intervals around the room. Though they stood sternly at their stations, the overt disdain that people faced from them in Cobbleside was curiously absent. Maybe it was because Queen Meléna was in the room.

The watchmen stole glances at her throughout the meal, along with everyone else. Including Bear.

She was seated in the middle of the head table. Her head

was bowed, and she still wore the black veil she'd been wearing since she'd arrived. On her head was the gold crown of the Free City.

Behind the centre table was something else that Bear couldn't stop glancing at. The iron cage that contained the witch. It was covered with a red cloth and neither movement nor sound could be detected from it.

The Queen had yet to raise her veil to eat, though she did seem to be conversing freely with the noblewomen who shadowed her. The girl with the thick red curls, who was seated to the Queen's right, lifted her veil and peered around the room, then whispered something in the Queen's ear.

"Do you know…" Zazie's voice was loud and insistent. "Do you know you're actually a very pretty girl?"

Zazie stared at Megg with his head to one side. His lips were stained red and curled into a confident smile.

Megg's face didn't move an inch.

Bear felt a defensiveness rise in him. Despite the playful tone, there was something that was simply too forward. He felt suddenly like he and Megg were on show, playthings for the Roofsiders' amusement. He looked at Megg and wished in that moment she could hear his thoughts, or he hers. Something about seeing her surrounded by all the pomp and bluster, the velvet and the lace, made her simple beauty – her dark curls, her white cotton shirt – stand out. There was a raw, wild beauty in her that felt powerful among all the Roofside pageantry. It was as if Bear was looking at her for the first time. But he wasn't just seeing her, he was seeing her value in the room in some odd game they were in.

Zazie reached out and grabbed Megg's hand. "It's just so incredible to have you here. Very pretty girl…"

Megg pulled her hand back with a decidedly unimpressed expression and everyone laughed. Zazie, full of ruby brew, tried for her hand again.

Bear stood up angrily.

"Leave her alone, Zazie!" snapped Meya. "Bear, if you aren't leaving, then do sit down. There are enough bad manners on the roof as it is."

Bear took his seat slowly, ignoring the quiet sniggering along the table. Zazie picked up a rib and bit into it happily, unbothered.

"You *are* very pretty," said Meya, drawing Megg away, "and do you like it up here, so far?"

"Yes, I do … like it," said Megg, taking a sip of her ruby brew. "It's … different, as I'm sure you know. But, yes, it's beautiful."

"What are the main differences?" asked Meya pointedly.

"Roofsiders know how to dress," said Zazie, tearing the meat from a large rib with his teeth, and again everyone laughed.

"Yes, and you really know how to eat," said Megg.

Zazie swallowed as the table giggled on. They were clearly full of ruby brew themselves.

"But one of the main ones is not worrying about blots," said Megg.

The other guests at their table fell silent. Bear sensed "blot" was an unwelcome word, even up here.

"Every time we walk out into the fields, they're there, waiting just inside the trees, waiting for an opportunity to take one of us... I think about them all the time. I never realized how much. I even dream about them. But here ... you just don't have to worry about them at all. It's amazing."

The table sat quietly for a long moment.

"I mean, really, how much do you actually come across blots, though? Honestly?" Zazie said. "It's not like you see them every day, is it?"

Megg stared back at him. "How many times do you think you'd need? If there was a person in this banquet hall who wanted to kill you, someone who had already killed someone you love, would you be able to forget they were there? Even if they never struck?"

"Who says there *isn't* someone who wants to kill Zazie in the banquet hall?" said Meya, and again the table laughed.

Bear, though, felt an irritation rising inside.

"I saw a blot," he said. "Two actually. Not long before Field Day."

"No way!" cried Zazie.

"It's true. They nearly got me."

"What happened?"

"Me and my friend Felix, we were out weeding later than everyone else. The sinsenn field was full of speedweed and we had to clear the rot before Field Day. Before we knew it, a pair of blots caught sight of us. Chased us to the town wall."

"How terrifying," breathed a young girl, her eyes round.

"Terrifying, yes." Zazie refilled his glass. "But you said it yourself. You stayed out too late. We have rules for a reason, dear boy."

"Zazie, stop being insensitive," snapped Meya.

"It's not insensitive. It's the truth."

"My father didn't stay out too late," said Megg as she looked in her cup.

The table quietened again. "He was clearing the brush line at the edge of the forest. The forest itself creeps towards us, you know, over time. One winter, we were cutting back a lot of the growth, getting a head start before spring. It's necessary, but it's hard work."

The jaunty music paused for just a moment, and Bear sensed how closely they were all listening to her. Bear's heart was heavy as he listened.

"It was patchy weather," said Megg. "Just bad luck that killed him. The blots had been emerging earlier and earlier, and during winter it gets dark so early. Clouds covered the evening sun. And he was..." Megg took a deep breath and looked up at the table. "They got him."

They sat and listened to the music in silence for a while.

"Well, this is why the forest should be cleared," came Zazie's loud voice.

"Enough!" Meya said acidly as she slammed her hand down. Eyes up and down the table glanced in their direction. "Enough of this nonsense! We could never clear the forests without the assistance of the Free City, and since they refuse to help us we are stuck with it. Everybody here has suffered losses. *Everybody.* I don't wish to discuss this any further. No more talk of this nature!"

Everyone within earshot held their tongue. Megg and Bear exchanged a fleeting glance. There were Roofside tensions of which they had been unaware. Clearly, the Overlord had been asking for assistance from the Queen for some time.

"Your father is a patient man," Zazie replied, lifting his cup. "And he's had to be to—"

Suddenly, there was a resounding *crack* and a blinding flash of red light burst from where Queen Meléna was sitting. Screams rang out across the banquet hall and the music stopped. A watchman was standing over the Queen, a knife in his hand.

CHAPTER

22

There were screams and cries of alarm. The Queen's Voice launched himself to his feet.

"Treason!" he screamed.

But something was wrong. Bear was confused. The watchman with the knife wasn't moving. He was completely frozen where he stood, like a statue. The Queen sat passively, as if the knife at her throat wasn't there.

Through the large doors, the Queensguard streaked into the banquet hall. There was a clashing of metal as, to Bear's shock, the watchmen posted around the room all flew to meet the Queensguard's swords.

"What is this?" cried the Overlord, on his feet. "Men! Have you lost your minds? Stand down! She is your Queen!"

Roofsiders shrieked and hid under their tables. Bear had never seen Calleston's watchmen fight with such fury, or strength; it didn't seem possible that they could challenge the strongest men in the land, but it looked as if the watchmen and the Queensguard were well matched – until, from high up on the rafters, the Queen's Claws leapt down from the shadows to the floor below. Bear had not even seen them up there.

They hit the ground and spun through the fight, blades flashing as they went. There were shrieks and groans as every watchman who dared fight was brought down. In moments, each one of them was pinned into submission with a Fennex blade at his throat, including the one that had dared wield the first knife.

"Treason!" screamed the Queen's Voice again.

"Compose yourself, Tsilas."

It was the voice of Queen Meléna.

It was the first time Bear had heard her speak.

She spoke softly, and she sounded younger than Bear had imagined, but with the tone of someone who was never refused.

The Queen looked down at the watchman who had held the knife. He was pinned to the floor, face down, by her guard, a small Fennex girl.

The Queen said one word. "Truthwine."

The girl with the red hair stood up from the table and glided out of the room. The Roofsiders sat back in their seats in terrified silence.

The Fennex girl held the watchman fast. It was then that Bear saw her face. She was the Fennex who'd given Felix the coin. She took the knife from the watchman and handed it to her Queen.

"An assassination attempt," said Queen Meléna. "I will know who sent this blade."

Bear heard the subtle accent of the Free City in her voice. She walked round the long table at the head of the room. She held the knife momentarily in front of the Overlord's eyes as she passed him. He stood, but said nothing, looking baffled and terrified all at once. Bear peeked over at Meya – her gaze was fixed on her father.

The girl with the red hair strode back into the room, carrying a goblet.

"Afena, lift his head. We will hear from him."

The Fennex girl yanked the watchman's head up. Bear recognized the man immediately.

It was the Stone.

The Stone had tried to kill Queen Meléna.

Bear's eyes met Megg's across the table. She looked as confused as him.

Afena walked to The Stone and placed the cup to his lips.

"Drink," she said.

His eyes rolled wildly left and right. The Fennex girl tightened her grip on his arm, pushing him into the floor. He yowled in pain.

"Drink," she hissed.

The Stone drank from the cup until it was removed from his lips. Afena released him from her grip.

Queen Meléna walked slowly to the centre of the room and stood before the Stone. She observed him as he lay there, waiting.

"You may sit up."

He raised himself on to his knees. His face had relaxed somewhat.

"What is your name?" she asked.

The Stone looked up at her and smiled. Bear had never seen him smile.

"Jakka, Your Majesty," he said.

"Do you have children, Jakka?"

"Yes, Your Majesty."

"How many?"

"Three."

"What are their names?"

"Sascha, Gordy and Tom."

"Who is your favourite child, Jakka?"

"Sascha."

"Why?"

"Partly because she's very strong, like me, partly because she's a sensitive girl, like her mother."

The truthwine's effects were evident.

One of the attendants sobbed loudly. She put her head down and her shoulders shook. She was shushed and held by the woman who stood next to her.

"Is that the mother of your children, Jakka?"

"Yes."

"Take her away from here," Queen Meléna ordered. The weeping woman and her workmate were escorted out of the hall by one of the Queensguard.

"Bye-bye, Clover," said the Stone Jakka over his shoulder.

The woman wailed loudly as she was led away. Queen Meléna waited until the echoes of her sobs had faded to nothing. She leaned down to Jakka. Her face was distorted by the veil she wore, but he held her gaze without a trace of fear. She spoke without emotion.

"Do you remember trying to kill me with this knife, Jakka?"

"Yes," said Jakka.

"And who ordered you to kill me?"

"Nobody."

The Queen stood up straight.

"Who suggested that I should be killed?"

"Nobody, Your Majesty."

The Queen laughed, a wild laugh that burst from nowhere and then abruptly subsided. She stood perfectly poised once again. Bear felt the hairs on his arms rise.

"Why did you try to kill me?"

"The knife had your name on it, and I hate your guts."

Jakka didn't hesitate. But the effects of the truthwine coloured his speech with a friendly indifference that made his words all the more cutting.

"Why?"

"You made a prison of this town and left it to rot. Where you go, magic defiles the land. You murdered your own mother. Your mother—"

The Queen pressed a gloved hand over his mouth.

"Lies!"

Her young voice rang across the feast hall. Jakka fell silent.

"Lies," she hissed.

She let go of his mouth and held out the blade.

"Do you know what this is, Jakka?"

"A knife."

"Do you know what kind of knife it is?"

He shook his head. Queen Meléna walked round Jakka. She spoke to the tables around the hall.

"This is an assassin's knife. It is marked with my name."

She turned the knife and Bear saw the engraving on its blade. *Meléna.*

"A formidable weapon. The power within this blade grants the wielder an unnatural strength. It was crafted by witches of old. A rare weapon... There are maybe fewer than twenty of these knives still in existence. Now there will be one fewer."

The Queen held the knife aloft and looked back at Jakka.

"Either you have forgotten the past, or you are ignorant of history. Jakka, your mission was in vain. No knife, not even one imbued with this power, can break my skin. This is not the first assassin's blade proven worthless at my neck."

She turned to the Overlord. He was deathly pale.

"My family made an oath to yours, Overlord Goodman. We will protect you and your heirs until our own house falls."

Meya's eyes widened.

"I had not anticipated such an ambush in your halls."

"This was not our doing! Y-Your Majes—"

She held up a finger for silence and turned away. "Lord Tsilas."

The Queen's Voice stood. "Yes, Your Majesty?"

"The blood oath that our people made in return, when the royal family took the seat of power and vowed to safeguard this land, and to irradicate it of such unnatural powers?"

The Queen's Voice smiled and he opened his hands, as if he were welcoming the room to join in with his words. He spoke proudly. "No blade shall cut, no arrow strike, no sickness corrupt the rule of the Free City."

"That is correct. The power of such an oath is unbreakable, even by an assassin's knife," replied Queen Meléna. "Overlord Goodman, sit down. For you, unfortunate Jakka, there are questions yet."

Jakka waited, smiling the friendly smile that the truthwine had gifted him.

"Where did you get the assassin's blade?"

"I found it laid on my pillow," he replied. "Plain. Uncovered. Waiting."

"And who put it there?"

Jakka blinked and frowned. "I don't know."

Queen Meléna rolled down her long glove and revealed a small piece of skin. The entire room watched as she held the dark blade against her exposed flesh, and then sliced smoothly.

As a bead of red bloomed on the knife, the blade began

to glow orange as if it had been left burning on hot coals. It continued getting brighter and brighter until it shone a hot white. There was a ringing sound and the knife disappeared entirely, leaving the Queen holding a small golden coin. The cut resealed itself, as if it had never happened.

There was a gasp, and scandalized chatter passed along the tables. Bear was deeply troubled, for someone who had spent years eradicating magic from the land, Queen Meléna seemed to have more than a passing connection with it.

The shaken Overlord gathered himself. "Your Majesty, I must apologize profusely. I had no idea one of my men could do such a thing. I-I have no idea what's got into the rest of them. I will question each one of them personally until—"

"No need, Overlord Goodman," Queen Meléna said. "Each of your watchmen will drink truthwine immediately and be questioned before the evening is concluded, by me."

The Queen placed the golden coin against the cut on her arm and then rolled her tight sleeve down over it.

"Until each watchman has revealed his truth, we will continue our merrymaking. We must celebrate this new prosperous era in Calleston. Should we not?"

"O-of course, Your Majesty." Uneasily, the Overlord sat. He signalled for the festivities to resume.

Immediately, attendants brought out steaming apple

pies and large jugs of sinsenn. The music began anew and the long tables burst into exhilarated gossip that seemed entirely too enthusiastic for Bear.

Bear couldn't take his eyes off Jakka, on his knees on the floor, his eyes glazed over.

"Assassins at dinner," said Meya in a fake, light-hearted tone. "Who'd have thought it!"

"Better than blots at breakfast," said the old man with the dyed hair.

The table chuckled.

"I think you'd better watch out either way," a bespectacled man shouted back to him. "Assassins kill the wealthy, and blots kill the slow – you're rich *and* stupid."

Bear looked at the man, food in his mouth, surrounded by others laughing raucously. He thought about Megg's father, her mum and the girls. He thought about Uncle Jim's hook, and Olenta's legs, his own mother … and he looked at the half-eaten food bouncing around the man's mouth as he laughed. Suddenly there was such a horrid tightness in Bear's chest that he couldn't breathe.

"Are you feeling all right?" whispered Megg.

"Just thirsty."

He reached for his water, but spilled the cup. His hand was shaking. Meya snapped her fingers for an attendant to come and mop up the mess.

Meya frowned at Bear. "Is he all right?"

"Look at me," Megg said, ignoring Meya and fixing her brown eyes on his. "I'm right here. Take a breath."

Bear breathed in through his nose and tried to calm something … an anger … a panic that was rising in him.

"Do you think this might help?" said Megg quietly. "It's just ruby brew, Bear, nothing as strong as truthwine."

She held out her cup of sinsenn. Bear hesitated. He knew to drink it would go against his father's wishes, but he felt such a terrible rising dread in his body. He steeled himself, grasped the cup and finished what was there.

It tasted mild, like any other herb or fruit tea. He let out a slow breath and smiled his gratitude, a warming calmness immediately pouring through him.

"Now…" Queen Meléna's voice drifted down the table.

"Queen Meléna is coming this way," warned Meya through her teeth. "Nobody embarrass my father or I'll have you thrown from the rooftop."

"Where are my guests of honour?" the Queen continued. "The young bloomers?"

The Queen's Voice scanned the room, then pointed a finger down the table at them. Bear was glad of the ruby brew steadying his nerves as the Queen said, "Lead the way," and the pair glided towards them.

Tsilas Violet fixed Bear and Megg with a mirthless smile. "Queen Meléna is delighted with your performance in the field today. You are the finest flowers of this town. And … you have made a filthy liar of your Overlord. He warned us that the harvest would be poor."

Meya disguised her surprised choking with a polite chuckle.

"In the Queen's eyes, you two can do no wrong," went on the Voice. "Such is the gratitude we feel now that the sinsenn region is thriving, thanks to honest people such as yourselves. But now, forgive me, I must ask a question of the most beautiful young woman in the room."

The Queen's Voice smiled at Meya. Meya smiled and lowered her eyes graciously. She *was* beautiful, Bear thought. The same cold, unfeeling beauty of a Roofside statue. Tsilas Violet turned and spoke to Megg.

"The bloom you made in the fields today. Has there been bigger in all of your history?"

Megg swallowed, but she responded calmly. "I'm not sure, sir."

The Queen's Voice walked towards Megg and lifted her cup from the table. "Take a sip, my dear, and think again."

Megg did so. Tsilas Violet looked at Bear.

"You, boy. Do you remember a red bloom like the one we witnessed today? Or was this truly an exceptional day?"

Bear smiled wide. An image had slipped into his mind and, before he could stop himself, he found himself saying, "I do have a memory of a big bloom, but I don't remember if it was a dream or not. I remember my mother was smiling at me, and then the whole field turned red, in an instant."

The Queen's Voice stared at Bear. "The whole field turned red, in an instant? And your mother can't fill a whole field any more?"

"No," said Bear, and again, before he could stop himself: "She's dead."

Tsilas Violet took Megg's cup and handed it to Bear. He gestured for Bear to take another sip. His smile was cold and empty. His eyes were two dark pools. He fixed them on Megg.

"You never saw anyone make the field bloom like it did today?"

"No, Lord Tsilas," she said. "I've never seen more than Top Field filled in a day."

The Voice turned back to Bear. "You must be glad of a decent meal. Tell me, what do Cobbleside inhabitants normally eat?"

"If the cookhouse is open, usually stew. But at the minute, just what we can find. Greens. But not fruit like in the trees out there. Dandelions and things. Rat if we can find it!" Bear found he couldn't seem to stop talking, even while Zazie made retching sounds. Bear didn't want to embarrass the Overlord. He wracked his brain for something more impressive. "Oranges! Do you remember oranges?" continued Bear.

Meya and the Roofsiders were all laughing; he didn't understand why. Megg was looking at him, a sad smile on her face. Why was she sad? It was a happy memory, and he was having fun talking about it.

"We had oranges once. The Overlord gave them to everyone one winter. The winter before my mother died. They were my favourite."

"I remember," said the Overlord, smiling at him. "They were blood oranges. Very difficult to come by out here, but such a wonderful colour. I'm glad you remember them fondly."

Bear smiled. "My mother soaked our oranges in ruby brew to put my father in a better mood."

The table laughed heartily. Queen Meléna raised a gloved hand and lightly touched the shoulder of the Queen's Voice. He slid backwards. She grasped the hem of her black veil and pulled it up over her head, showing her young face for the first time.

Bear looked up at her. She was young, much younger than he was expecting, but her expression was as regal and as self-assured as any he had seen.

"How did your mother die?"

The question was a shock.

"She was killed," he said. The sinsenn made it easier to say. "She was killed for being a witch."

A breath caught in the Queen's throat.

"You are the son of a *Feyatung*?"

Bear wanted to say no. He also wanted to say yes. Instead, he said the truth. "I don't know."

He looked at Megg for reassurance. Her eyes were glistening with tears, but it was all right. It was simply what it was. It felt good to finally say it.

"How can you not know?" The Queen spoke without emotion. "Was there not a truthwine confession? To be certain of her guilt?"

"Yes," said Bear. "She drank the truthwine and then denied the accusation."

"Then why was she executed?"

He was numb. And for the first time he felt able to speak the truth. The everything truth. "I always thought that she was a witch. A good witch. I'd thought that since I was a little boy. I saw her turn the fields red, not a lick of speedweed in sight, and it seemed like magic. I thought it was my mum's power, and not the flowers... I knew about witches and their animals. I saw her sing to the birds. I saw them sing back."

He smiled at the memory of his mother singing to a little red bird.

"When they chained her up, she drank truthwine. She told them she wasn't a *Feyatung*. Father was so happy. But they didn't believe her. They made us drink it too. When they asked me, I told them what I thought was the truth... I'd seen her talking with the birds... I thought it was beautiful. I thought she must be a witch – a good one."

"Bear ... no..." Megg whispered.

Bear hung his head. But he would finally say it out loud.

"It was me. I'm the reason she died." He took a deep breath. "I named my mother a witch. And she was executed."

Tsilas Violet snapped his fingers and immediately the white staff was brought to him. He rubbed his hand over the smooth black sphere on the handle.

"Did no one ask you about your own abilities?" he asked.

"No," replied Bear.

"No?" said the Voice, looking accusingly at the Overlord.

Bear turned to Megg. Her face was drained of colour.

"Calleston has a long history with the blood of the *Feyatung* ... yet it seems to want to forget it. Before Queen Meléna returns to the Free City, the rot will be rooted out and destroyed." He fixed the Overlord with a look of disgust. "Whether this 'Overlord' Goodman has ever been driven to do so or not. Tonight, we interrogate the watchmen. Tomorrow, the rest of the town."

Chatter burst across the feast hall as the Queen's Voice escorted her back to her table.

Megg put a hand on Bear's shoulder.

"I talked too much," he said. "I know. I–I'm not used to ruby brew."

"You told the truth," said Megg. "And I'm proud of you for that, Bear."

She laid her hand against his cheek, and he closed his eyes. When he opened them, he found hers looking back at him, smiling this time, shining. For a moment, they made everything feel better.

The chatter in the room ceased and a tense silence fell. Bear turned and saw that Tsilas Violet was approaching the great dark cage. He held out his white staff and passed it inside the bars.

"Awaken."

The witch stirred and raised itself up to its feet. Red ribbons of light crackled all over its body.

"Death. For the watchman," Tsilas Violet said. "For the watchman on his knees." He sounded out the words clearly and carefully to the witch. "And then sleep."

The witch reached out a gnarled and blackened hand. It grasped the polished orb and the crackling red ribbons of light were drawn into the dark stone.

The Queen's Voice carried the white staff over to Jakka. He was still smiling.

The Queen's Voice stood above Jakka and held his white staff towards him, red lights flickering in the depths of the black jewel. Jakka stared at the orb as if he were in a trance.

"For the glory of the Free City."

As the black jewel touched Jakka's forehead, blood erupted from his nose and his ears in great streams and he fell backwards.

In the cage, the witch collapsed to the floor and returned to its sleep, landing in the same position as Jakka. A Queensguard covered the cage with the cloth.

Shrieks rang across the hall.

Jakka's eyes were open and his face still carried the hint of a smile.

He was dead.

CHAPTER 23

"Hold still," said Olenta.

Her eyes were magnified into giant eyeballs by her readers. She plopped the field hat on Bear's head and then smeared it in mud and leaves, appraising her work before moving on to Megg. Rose's and Uncle Jim's and Aber's were already done.

"We all ready, then?" said Uncle Jim.

Bear nodded. He'd only been back in Cobbleside a few hours, but as soon as he'd told Uncle Jim what had happened up there Uncle Jim decided they had to act now. While most of the watchmen were being interrogated, it was their best chance to sneak out of the town.

Bear and Megg had described the feast, the many courses – meat, cheese and, most importantly for their purposes, fish.

Crowded together in Bear's damp home, Olenta had worked to camouflage field hats for Rose, Megg, Bear, Uncle Jim and his father so they would be invisible from above. Caber watched from his bed. Uncle Jim was holding aloft the copy of the key from the Keep when a face popped in through the window. "What's going on here, then?" said Felix.

"Not tonight," growled Aber. "Someone get rid of the Fennex."

"I will try not to take that personally," said Felix. He looked them over. "What are you all up to?"

"It's a secret mission," said Bear.

"Bear!" snapped Aber, eyeing his son. "Did you drink something while you were up on Roofside?"

Bear felt his stomach drop. "Yes, Father. A little ruby brew."

"Of all the foolish things—"

"Brother," said Uncle Jim, interrupting Aber quietly. "We used to do this after a keg of sinsenn and never had a problem. He'll be fine."

"Can somebody please tell me what's going on?" Felix complained loudly as he slid in through the window.

"Shh!"

The entire room hushed him, including Caber, who lay on his bunk. Everyone had agreed he was too weak to come, despite his protestations.

"We're going to the Overlord's lake," said Uncle Jim, talking quietly. "Megg and Bear returned with news from Roofside that suggests tonight will be our best chance to … relieve the Overlord of some of his fish reserve."

Felix's mouth dropped open. "We're *stealing*?"

"Shhhh!"

Bear knew exactly how Felix felt; he had been as

292

stunned when Uncle Jim and his father had told him the plan. Upright Aber and discerning Jim, common thieves! Rose and Olenta too, or "the old gang" as they had been calling themselves.

"We're stealing?" Felix said again in a whisper this time.

"Just enough to fill some bellies," said Jim. "People aren't well in Calleston. Mothers can't nurse. More and more people are getting sick and struggling to shake it…" His eyes flickered over to Caber. "Wounds aren't healing the way they should. People can't wait another day for the sinsenn money to come rolling in, if it ever does. We've given them a fine harvest; we deserve this much."

Felix nodded firmly.

"We've done this before," said Uncle Jim. "Aber, myself, Rose, others … but not for many years. Some things will have changed. So we'll have to take our time and be careful."

"Say no more," said Felix. "So what's the plan?"

"The plan is to be invisible," said Rose. "Olenta, is there another hat in that chest?"

Olenta stood and lifted the lid of the trunk she'd been sitting on. She began muddying another hat as Rose continued.

"We wade through a quiet section of the canal system towards the town walls, and out through an old disused gate."

Jim held up the copied key from the Keep. "Thank you for this, boys. Now, once we're outside, we head upriver, into the forest and straight on to the lake. We take what we can, and head right back."

"But what about the blots?" said Felix.

"We stay low in the water, and we don't make a sound. Slow and quiet. No reason for the blots, or anyone, to ever know we were there."

Felix whistled and looked over at Bear. Bear grinned. He was scared too. But people were starving. And Uncle Jim was right – with the watchmen being interrogated, they'd never get a better chance than this.

Felix made a face, but he accepted the hat that Olenta handed him, and nodded.

"We'll be glad of those Fennex eyes, my love," said Rose, putting a hand on his shoulder. "Especially in this low light. You just keep focused on the shadows. We'll be back safe in no time."

Bear gave Caber a hug and a kiss before leaving.

"Back soon," Bear whispered into his ear.

Caber saved his voice, and just held on to Bear extra long.

Bear, Felix and Megg followed Rose out of the door and into the cold night air.

"Not done this in years, my loves…" she said, throwing an arm round Aber and Uncle Jim excitedly.

Bear walked in silence, listening to Rose chat happily about their younger years. It was funny to think of them all the age he was now – his father and Rose and Uncle Jim. And his mother too, he supposed.

The group wound their way through the streets,

avoiding Main Market. They carried no lights, and stuck to the shadows, guided by the light of the moon. Only a handful of windows still carried their flickering lights.

"Hurry in, then!" said Old Fern as they arrived at the Rusty Compass. Old Fern held the heavy door open, and they filed inside. The main room was lit only by candles, dotted here and there. "Quick drink to settle you all before you go? No food I'm afraid."

"We plan to fix that," said Jim as they all took a seat around a table. "Over to you, Aber."

Bear felt a flush of pride as his father stood and turned to the table.

"So," said Aber, and he planted his hands down on the table. "Jim'll lead us. Felix, you keep in step with Jim. Let's have those Fennex eyes up front."

Felix nodded.

"I'll go at the rear," he went on. "I can slow down anything in pursuit, give you all a chance to get away if need be."

Bear noted that he'd said "anything" and not "anyone". He shuddered at the thought of being outside the town at night.

He looked around the group that circled the table. Covered in mud and leaves, they were an unsettling sight, but their eyes shone excitedly in the candlelight. Fern came out of the kitchen with a tray of drinks, followed by Burna and Petal, a pair of muddied hats on their heads. Petal squeezed Megg's arm and nodded towards Bear.

"Not seen a Field Day like it since I was a little girl. You're the talk of the taverns."

"Were you ever a little girl?" asked Felix as he looked up at her with a cheeky grin. Fern poured drinks and everyone sipped, except Aber.

Petal laughed heartily. "Believe it or not, I was your size once."

"She grew sinsenn like you as well," said Burna with a grin. "That's why she works on the docks."

Felix's face fell.

Uncle Jim took a sip from Aber's cup, shooting him a wink as he put the cup down again. Then, to Bear's surprise, Aber raised the cup and drained what was left. "Right, enough gossip," he said, standing. "What are we still doin' here?"

CHAPTER
24

"Follow me," said Old Fern, and she led them through the back of the Rusty Compass, beyond the main room, with its corners and cubbyholes, past the crooked stairways and low arches, to a small private room with a fireplace.

There were long wooden benches built into the walls, and a small lamp rested on the mantle, casting a warm orange glow.

On the wall above the fireplace was an iron sculpture – a giant compass, rusted dark brown. The silver needle in the centre was shaped like a fish with a knife-like nose, and the letters mounted at the four points of the compass were forged in yellow metal.

"The Rusty Compass," breathed Bear, suddenly understanding the tavern's name.

"Not opened her up in some time," said Old Fern. "Let's see how she's doing."

She grabbed the compass firmly with both hands and, with some effort, twisted it ninety degrees, as if it were a doorknob. From inside the fireplace, there was a metallic crunching and grinding.

"Takes me back," murmured Rose, her eyes gleaming as Old Fern pushed the sooty brickwork inside the fireplace, and, like a door, the dark bricks swung inwards.

"A hidden doorway!" said Felix incredulously. "The only secret this tavern has ever kept!"

"Not by a long shot." Uncle Jim smiled.

Bear couldn't believe this was happening. He looked at Megg and they both grinned. "When you're inside, keep to the left. Put your hand on the wall to be sure," said Old Fern. "Put your hats on, and be careful!" she said, giving them each an affectionate squeeze as, one by one, they lowered their heads and slipped through the secret fireplace door.

On the other side, the homely atmosphere of the Rusty Compass was gone. They faced a stone wall in a dark tunnel that went in both directions, the only light coming from Uncle Jim's lamp. There was the sound of water slopping about and a chill air washed over Bear's exposed neck. He pressed a hand to the brick wall; it was damp.

"I forgot how cold it was in here," Uncle Jim said.

Running down the tunnel was some sort of deep gutter, filled with dark water.

"Let's go!" said Felix. He set off straight ahead down the walkway. Bear heard Petal and Burna laughing in the dark.

After a moment, Felix realized that no one was following him.

"Wrong way, my love," said Rose with a chuckle.

"Follow me," said Uncle Jim. He turned and stepped down into the gutter. Bear saw now that there were stone steps leading into the murky water, and the gutter was far deeper than he had first thought. Jim continued, sinking deeper and deeper into the dark water as he went.

"Are you serious?" said Felix. He hesitated at the top of the steps.

"Get it done with, lad," said Jim, beckoning with his silver hook.

Felix gritted his teeth as he slid into the water.

"It's freezing!" he yelped.

Petal and Burna went next, followed by Rose, gasping as she lowered herself into it. "It'll put hairs on your chest, my loves."

"Yuck!" Felix called from the front.

Bear looked at Megg, and she gave him a small nod. They followed the others down the steps. The water was icy cold. Bear heard his breath rattling as the waterline rose up over his thighs, and then his chest. The bottom was covered in a smooth layer of mud, and the clay squeezed around his foot and sucked it deeper.

"Yuck," Bear muttered, and he heard his father chuckle behind him.

"Told you!" said Felix.

The steps kept going down, until they were all up to their necks.

"This is the deepest bit now," said Uncle Jim.

Up ahead in a brick wall was a low arch through which

the water flowed. One by one, Bear saw the heads in front of him disappear under it, wide-brimmed hats and all.

On the other side, the submerged steps climbed again until they all stood in waist-high water under a stone bridge. It was tall enough for the boats that were moored underneath it. Bear scanned the decks nervously.

"Don't worry. This tunnel is unused nowadays, even in the daytime," said Uncle Jim. "We can talk quietly here."

Megg emerged from the hole, her teeth chattering, then Aber. Bear smiled. It was like watching water voles come out from their holes.

Jim waited for everyone to emerge, then waded on. They followed in single file.

"Everyone, eyes up for any watchmen," Uncle Jim said softly. "Stay low in the water and move slow."

The chill of the water was tolerable. Bear had got used to the feel of the mud and slime squelching around his feet. As they emerged from under the bridge, Bear looked upwards. He could see the back side of a sky-high row of buildings, dark windows dotted all the way up to Roofside. Above, the night sky was a heavy ceiling, a network of stars sprawled across the deep blue, glittering like distant candles. The moon looked like a ghostly fruit, with a big bite taken from it. An owl glided silently above their parade of muddy field hats. Bear lowered his head.

"Stick to shadows best you can," Uncle Jim whispered as he waded out into the moonlight. Aside from the gentle sloshing of water and the hint of a breeze, Bear didn't hear a sound.

They walked quietly behind him, alongside the row of sleeping houses, hugging the shady side of the canal. After a while, Felix signalled for them to stop.

Crossing the canal ahead of them was a footbridge. A man was walking across it, turning his head left and right as he went. He approached a crooked-looking building with no windows. Golden light washed over him as he drew open a creaky wooden door and slipped inside.

"Bear! That was the Whip!" hissed Felix.

Bear frowned. *What was the Whip doing in Cobbleside?*

"Listen up." Jim waved everyone into a low huddle. "No talking from now on. This is Smuggler's Way, and they occasionally have rooftop guests. We're going under the floorboards, under their very feet, so be quiet."

Jim turned and observed the door through which the Whip had disappeared. Once he was satisfied nobody was coming out any time soon, he waded quietly towards the muddy bank under the footbridge, the rest of them following like ducklings.

One by one, they emerged from the water and trudged up the squelchy bank. The night air on Bear's wet clothes was bone-chilling. Uncle Jim approached an old metal gate in the wall beneath the footbridge. It squeaked as he swung it open and they all winced. He hurried inside and they whisked in after him. There was another mournful squeal as Aber pulled the gate closed.

The walls of the passageway beyond the gatewere made of slime-covered bricks. Above them, candlelight seeped through cracks in the floorboards. Uncle Jim paused again and put his finger to his lips. They listened in silence a moment, floorboards creaking as feet passed overhead, and then they carried on down the pathway, as quietly as they could.

"... telling you, I heard a noise! Let me look," snapped the acidic voice of the Whip.

The sound of the door opening was followed by a cold silence. Everyone in the tunnel held their breath.

"There are always odd noises down here, Ashka," came another voice, a woman's. "You know that. Now close the door. It's freezing. What happened up there?"

The door squeaked shut and the group began creeping silently through the passageway. The Whip's footsteps creaked overhead.

Bear slid the leather bag off his back and turned sideways so he could better shimmy along the narrow passage, listening all the while.

"Tell me," said the woman's voice. "What happened? You're scaring me."

"Jakka," came the Whip's hoarse reply. "They killed Jakka. He tried to assassinate the Queen."

"No!" she breathed.

"And now we're all paying the price."

At that moment, Bear passed under the table where the two of them sat. He glimpsed the side of the Whip's

302

sunken face through the gap in the floorboard.

"Poor Jakka!" the woman breathed.

Bear shivered as he trudged along. The tunnel began to descend slightly and the slimy passageway floor gained an inch or two of water.

"Another watchman has gone missing too."

"Who now?"

"Young Malka. They couldn't find him for the questioning."

"I'm scared, Ashka. There's something at play … something unnatural."

"I won't lie – I feel it in my bones too," said the Whip, "and Queen Meléna seems to think so as well. I guess we'll find out tomorrow… There's to be a witch hunt. Every adult in Cobbleside will be gathered in the market square and given truthwine."

Bear felt his blood run cold at the reminder. He didn't know if what he'd done in the fields with Megg would be considered natural or not. He was scared to find out.

The voices grew faint as the group moved through the tunnel. Uncle Jim found the exit door and pulled it open. The metal hinges squeaked loudly.

"What was that noise?" asked the Whip.

"I've got mice under the floorboards," replied the woman.

As Bear slid back into the cold water, he was grateful to be out of the even-colder air. They emerged into a backstreet canal with no pavements or street access. These dark alleys of the town were only navigable by the waterways.

"Careful here." Uncle Jim's voice was low.

The water was choked with reeds. They weaved under rundown jetties and long-forgotten wooden docks.

"Wait!" Felix breathed out a short, sharp warning and Uncle Jim raised his hand.

High above them was a Roofside bridge, where Bear saw the moving torchlights of watchmen strolling along. The group crouched low in the water. Felix's yellow eyes were like a cat's in the dark, fixed high above on the stone bridges. Bear stayed completely still, hunched down so the brim of his hat almost touched the water.

"Did you see something?" a watchman's voice echoed from above.

A stone plopped in the water between Petal and Burna, perhaps disturbed by the watchmen's feet. Another stone, larger this time, plunged into the water next to Megg. Then a third. The watchmen were dropping them.

"Should I shoot an arrow?" the voice said.

Uncle Jim kept his hand up, directing them to stay still. There was no sound. Suddenly a barrage of pebbles fell all around them, streaking into the water or bouncing off their hats.

Bear held his breath and prayed that the moon stayed behind the cloud.

There was a screech from somewhere in the distance. It sounded human, or something like it. It also sounded as if it were coming from outside the town's walls.

"Another one, then," the watchman said from somewhere up above.

"Sounds like it."

"Witches?"

"Sounds like it."

The watchmen passed on. After a few minutes, Uncle Jim gave them the nod to continue. They moved through the waterways until, finally, Calleston's town walls loomed ahead and the canal became little more than a wet ditch. Bear felt a wave of relief. They'd sneaked through the belly of Calleston undetected, though he knew the real challenge lay on the other side of the town's walls.

And then Bear saw the culvert – a low, round tunnel nestled in the shadows under a set of steps. It led all the way through the wall to the other side.

Uncle Jim pulled open his bag and took out the key.

"At the end of this culvert is a locked gate. The gate allows water through as needed, but not people. Not for many years, anyway. Let's see if she still works."

And, with that, he disappeared head first inside. Bear let Felix, Rose and Megg follow Uncle Jim through the gate. There was the sound of metal scraping in the tunnel and then a satisfying *clunk*. Burna gave Bear's shoulder a good slap as she squeezed past. Petal almost filled the width of the culvert as she made her way inside.

"After you, son," said Aber, and Bear crawled through on his knees. The tunnel was cramped and wet, he heard their puffs and pants as the group made their way through, but it was short at least, and soon he stepped out on the other side.

Once Aber was through, Jim went to lock the iron gate, then stopped, and put the key back in his pocket.

"Best not lock it. Just in case we need to get back in quickly," he said.

They headed upstream, through the North Field, towards the woods. The water flowed against them now, but it wasn't too strenuous in the shallow waters. Unlike the systematic canals that linked Calleston to the Free City, the North River was left to meander where it liked. The fields either side were traditionally used as vegetable gardens, but they'd recently been cleared for sinsenn production. Red flowers waved at them from either side as they passed through.

Here, enormous rocks dotted the river, its banks and the fields too. The water started to become choppy as the river divided and re-emerged around the boulders. Many of the large rocks had been chipped at over the years, and much of Calleston was built of this stone.

As they drew closer to the trees, the sounds of rushing water disguised the sounds of wading and allowed them to move more quickly. After a while, Jim stopped and surveyed the edge of the woods.

"All right, everyone, stay quiet and keep watch for blots. They won't cross the river, nor the lake – but it's shallower here than I'd like. If we see one, head for deep water."

"What if we aren't near deep water?" asked Megg.

"Run," said Jim.

"As fast as your legs can carry you," Rose added.

"Don't even look back," said Petal.

"Understood," said Megg.

"Then let's get going."

Bear kept his breath steady as they entered into the trees. Jim and Felix took the lead again. The water was navel high, but they hunkered lower in the water.

There was a sudden rustling and everybody froze, eyeing the direction of the noise. Bear squinted at the shapes moving around. Rabbits, hopping in and around a large warren. Bear smiled. He'd thought the blots had stripped the forest of all life. It was wonderful to see such vulnerable creatures surviving at the forest's edge, even at night. He doubted they would see more than a moth when they slid deeper into the shadows.

They pressed on, everyone keeping their eyes on the gaps between trees. The air began to smell of earth and damp moss and the sound of rushing water grew louder and louder, and then, up ahead, Bear saw the shimmer of moonlight on water.

Megg turned back to him, her eyes wide with wonder. They had reached the Overlord's lake – with water crashing into it from a waterfall on the opposite shore.

Bear had never seen anything so beautiful. He imagined what it would be like to be there on a summer's day, to strip off and dive into the deep, cool water.

"The quicker we fill the bags and get out, the better," said Uncle Jim, breaking the spell. He pulled a long net from his bag and waded into the lake. One by one, they grabbed a piece of the net, took out their knives and followed him in. They spread out across the shallows until they'd sectioned off an entire corner of the dark water.

"Keep your feet wide, Bear," Petal grunted.

They shuffled through the water, dragging the net closer and closer to the shore. Bear felt something yank the net, but saw nothing. Then, as they made their way back to the shore, driving the fish before them as they went, Bear saw that the lake was teeming with life. There were hundreds and hundreds of trout all clustered together, leaping and diving.

As one, they all pounced. Bear watched Aber and Rose as their knives cut expertly through the water. Uncle Jim used his hook with great enthusiasm, lifting big fish from the water and dumping them in his bag.

Bear struggled at first. He was too slow to impale the fish on the end of the knife. Instead, he held the knife between his teeth, and any fish unlucky enough to glide below his hands, he slammed down into the lake bed and pinned them to the floor. After impaling the fish between its eyes, he'd yank it from the water and toss it into the bag on his back.

In what seemed like no time, everyone's bags were full.

"That's enough, I think," said Uncle Jim, rolling up the net again. "Let's not push our luck."

Jim and Bear took the lead this time. Felix brought up the rear with Aber, keeping his eyes on the trees. It was easier going back. Bear felt relaxed enough to let his mind drift for a moment. As he did so, he felt a troublesome weight settle on him despite their success. It wasn't just the return of the quiet, as they left the rumbling waterfall behind, nor was it the weight of the fish strapped to his back. Tomorrow, they would all be subject to interrogation. He glanced behind him at Megg. As he did, her eyes met his. Her face looked worried in the moonlight. What had they done?

Uncle Jim held up his hand. He stopped and sniffed the air. Everybody stopped. Bear sniffed too. *Oh no*, he thought.

The group crouched down in the water immediately. The smell of rot was faint, but once you'd smelled it up close there was no mistaking it. As they walked past the mounds of earth where the rabbits had made their warrens, Bear's heart dropped to his stomach. Blots had been here. Deep scratches were gouged out of the rabbit holes and blood glistened on patches of grass.

They emerged from the trees and followed the river back through North Field. They were so close now. Just up ahead, Calleston sat in the darkness, encircled by the glistening moat. It looked like a refuge and a prison all at once.

A sudden piercing scream cut through the silence. Bear's blood ran cold. It had come from the town, from the rooftops. A moment later, there was a whistling sound in the air. Bear looked upwards and saw something dark whizzing across the sky. It was too big to be a bird.

There was a low *thump* as it landed heavily somewhere ahead of them. It didn't move. It stayed hidden down among the sinsenn.

"Caution!" whispered Uncle Jim. "Felix, what can you see?"

Bear looked at Felix. He was frozen in horror.

There was a commotion from the forest behind them, leaves crunching and twigs snapping.

Then a dark shape burst from the trees.

Then another, then another, then another.

25

There was no time to think.

Everybody ran – as fast as they could – towards the culvert.

Blots were exploding from the edge of the forest and didn't break stride as their feet struck soil. There must have been at least ten.

There was a horrible tearing sound as the blots began feasting. Bear felt his blood run cold. Already? *Who had they got to?* He looked over his shoulder and saw a blot jerk its head up from the ground, its glistening black eyes staring straight at Bear.

"Keep going!"

A hand yanked him along. Petal grabbed his elbow in a death-grip. She dragged him and Megg along as fast as she could, one in each arm. They scrabbled over the uneven ground but didn't slow. She guided them up on to the bank where they could run faster.

The stench of festering flesh filled Bear's nose. Felix whizzed past them, lightning fast. The large bag on his back didn't slow him at all.

"Cross up there!" he panted.

Up ahead, the river spread into a wide, shallow network of streams. They could put a little water between them and the blots.

Bear could hear footsteps behind them now, misshapen feet striking the ground. So close. They were almost at the moat, when Bear heard a cry. He knew that voice. He shouted in horror.

"Father!"

"No!" He tried to stop and turn, but Petal yanked them on. "Don't look back!" she called, and she pushed him into the tunnel after Rose.

"Crawl," she barked.

"Keep going!" Rose urged from a little way ahead.

Bear, Megg and Felix followed through the damp tunnel on their hands and knees.

There were calls sounding from inside the town walls. As he joined Rose at the end of the tunnel, he peeked out and saw torchlight among Roofside. Rose cursed quietly.

"Watchmen – there are already some back on duty. This is going to be trickier than we'd hoped."

"Blots at the wall!" shouted one from somewhere above.

Rose cursed again. Burna and Petal appeared behind them.

"Make room," said Burna. "Gate's shut, but the blots are piled up against it, reaching through."

They crawled out and lingered in the shadows under the stone staircase. Felix tugged Bear to his feet.

Megg turned to Bear, concern in her eyes. "Were you bitten?" she asked quietly.

Bear shook his head. "I'm fine. Where's Father, and Uncle Jim?"

"Be quiet," Rose whispered.

They huddled under the stairs, but they couldn't stay there all night. Bear gazed at the tunnel anxiously, waiting for Jim and his father. High above, torches bobbed along the rooftops. Watchmen had begun making their way down stairways to Cobbleside. If they didn't move, they wouldn't have long before they would be discovered.

"I see 'em!"

A watchman leaned over a parapet high above them. He had a bow and arrow in his hands. Thankfully, he didn't look directly down. He pointed out to the field where the blots were gathered against the wall.

"Twenty of them at least, right against the base of the wall. I can't shoot any more from here."

"Don't worry. I see 'em too."

A beefy watchman carrying a torch walked along the top of the wall, heading in their direction. They needed to move before they were discovered. Bear heard scraping from inside the culvert.

At last, Uncle Jim emerged. He heaved himself out, then turned to help Aber. Once they were out, Uncle Jim threw Aber's arm round his shoulder, and nodded.

Bear breathed a sigh of relief. His father had made it.

He looked shaken, but very much alive. He scanned him for anything like a bite.

"Are you all right?" asked Burna.

Aber nodded.

"Really?"

"Really. Just pulled something. I'm gonna struggle to run, but keep going. You lead the way."

Burna crouched low and made her way through the ditch water, the others following behind. The watchman on the wall stared out at the blots in the fields, allowing them to sneak further into the town, but as they turned into a wide street a pair of watchmen appeared and began striding towards them, holding their torches aloft.

"Blotson," muttered Burna. Their escape route was blocked. They pulled out of the street and pressed their backs to the wall, looking for an escape.

"Here! Down here! Quick!" shouted the beefy watchman up on the wall.

Bear didn't dare breathe.

"Blots have made it through the gate! The gate's been breached!" he shrieked. He ran off in the other direction.

"He thinks we're blots!" hissed Burna. "Come on, quick. This way!"

She raced along the shadows and they fell in line behind her. One watchman would never challenge a blot, but they wouldn't have long before the full force of the watchmen descended on them. Sure enough, from all around them, they heard more voices.

"They're heading towards Moonshine Street!" a watch-man shouted.

Burna screeched to a stop outside an old set of wooden doors, almost ten feet high. Petal struck the rusted lock hard with the hilt of her knife. The wood crunched and the entire lock separated from its fixing. She pulled open the door and dashed inside.

"It's the old shipyard," Burna whispered. "Come on, inside quickly!"

"More watchmen coming down from the wall," Jim grunted, catching up and pulling Aber inside.

Aber groaned on his brother's shoulder.

"There's an old slipway on the other side," said Burna. "Head for the ramp. Should take us back down into the waterways."

They scurried through the warehouse, racing under wooden catwalks and sliding between the old forgotten ships. Bear heard calls coming from outside, from every direction. He saw torches flickering through the gaps in the wooden walls. The building was being surrounded.

"I can't," panted Aber.

"You can," growled Jim.

A door burst open high on their left, and a cluster of guards swept along the wooden catwalk above, bows and arrows at hand. They split up and spread along the walkways.

"Where are they?"

"They came in here!"

"How did they get through the gate? What are they chasing?"

The light of the watchmen's torches cast long shadows that danced and leapt on the walls. Petal grabbed a small wooden barrel and tossed it clear over to the other side of the warehouse.

"Over here!" On the footbridge above, feet raced after the noise in the wrong direction.

Quickly, the group made it to the ramp. Bear and the others followed Burna and Petal as they slipped down the ramp and into the water.

They half swam, half waded between the moored boats until they were back under the open sky. The tall buildings that encircled the dark harbour left them with only one option. There was a dusty, tumbledown passage, flooded shoulder-high with water and the rest filled with cobwebs. The support beam over the door had cracked in the middle, and the entire channel looked as if it were ready to cave in.

"That looks too dangerous, Burna," said Petal.

"We've got no other choice, babe. Don't forget, we've got enough fish on our backs to feed half of Cobbleside. They won't need truthwine to find out what we've been up to."

Burna pressed on through the collapsed entrance, Petal following after her. As they did, the crossbeam suddenly cracked loudly and a shower of dust poured into the water below.

Bear gazed upwards. There were crooked buildings piled on top of each other above the passage. He didn't like the idea of being inside it when they came tumbling down.

"Are you sure this is a good idea?" he said.

"I think it's the only idea," said Felix. "Come on," and he launched himself into the crumbling underpass. More dust tumbled from the ceiling, hiding him from view.

"Over there!" a watchman called. "I see them moving!"

Bear and Rose pushed his father and uncle into the hazardous passage. Aber was clinging on to Jim as they half swam, half waded under the cracked beam.

Stones tumbled from the ceiling and dust fell in an endless stream.

"Don't stop! Keep going, Bear!" he heard Burna shout from somewhere inside; it sounded as if she were impossibly far away. Dust continued raining down from the ceiling. The walls lurched and rumbled horribly. There was a violent cracking sound.

Rose squeaked and nosedived through the dust.

Bear and Megg looked at each other in terror. "Take my hand?" she said.

"It's not a blot! They're in the water! It's people!"

An arrow whizzed through the air and struck the crumbling beam over the door.

Hand in hand, Megg and Bear charged inside. And in a second they were through. They emerged from the dust into a giant underground cavern.

The rumbling stopped immediately. *Strange*, thought Bear as he looked around.

The others were already huddled together on a giant wooden platform in the middle of an underground lake. The walls were lit by multiple torches, casting a bright light that Bear was sure he hadn't seen from the outside.

"But … how?" he said.

Felix held out a hand and pulled Bear from the water as Petal helped Megg and Rose.

Bear looked around in wonder at the vast space.

"What is this place?" asked Bear.

"It's a bloody death trap," said Aber.

"Possibly," replied Uncle Jim. "But it's a port in a storm."

The cavern was perfectly round. There were several tunnels carved into the rock, with underground rivers leading off in various directions, easily large enough for a barge to pass through.

"Look," Megg said.

She pointed at the little collapsed entryway through which they had all come in.

Only it wasn't little at all. It was just as big as all the other exits, with no collapsed beam, no falling dust. Beyond the tunnel was a perfectly clear view of the harbour and the shipyard, and the watchmen's torches moving back and forth in the night, gathering by the entrance. But then – why couldn't they see them?

"It's a trick," said Megg quietly.

Bear looked at her. "What sort of trick?"

Megg didn't look at him. "It seems like ... magic, doesn't it?"

"How do you know?" said Aber gruffly, narrowing his eyes at her.

"She's right," said Burna with a touch of panic in her voice. "I watched you come in behind us, coughing and waving your hands in front of your face. But there was no dust, no sound ... in a tunnel wide enough to fit a wagon. It's a trick – trying to keep people out."

They gazed at the tunnel, at the watchmen, some gathered close to the entrance, others beginning to search the area.

"Will they follow us in?" Bear asked.

"Would you have come in here? If your life hadn't depended on it?" Megg replied.

Bear looked around the odd underground lake. Cobbleside really was full of secrets.

"How on earth did you get away, Aber?" Rose asked, her voice anxious. "I thought I heard them behind us ... eating."

Aber laughed a bitter laugh. "I dropped my bag. Fish everywhere."

"Well, that might have saved us all," she replied.

"Oh, yes, quite the *trick*," he said. And then he collapsed on to the floor heavily.

"Dad!" said Bear rushing to him.

He was convulsing, making awful strained sounds.

"Aber, no," breathed Jim.

"He's been bitten," said a woman's voice from behind them.

They all turned. Bear inhaled sharply at what he saw. A long black narrowboat was drifting into the cavern from one of the passageways behind them.

"Who are you?" Uncle Jim barked.

But Bear already knew. He'd seen the boat before.

The three women stood on the bow of the boat: the veiled woman, the Fennex and the woman with the white hair.

It was the white-haired woman who spoke.

"Check for yourselves," she said.

Uncle Jim ripped open Aber's shirt.

Megg gasped. Bear's heart sank.

Blot-rot.

Rose wailed as Petal pressed a hand to her forehead in anguish. The veins that spiderwebbed across Aber's chest were already dark and bulging. Bear couldn't turn his eyes away. His skin looked putrefied.

The woman hopped off the boat on to the pontoon. She held out a lantern as she approached.

"Cora, would you lead the guards away from this area, please? I don't want to take any chances."

Neither of the other two women on the boat responded. Instead, the owl launched itself from a large perch on the boat. The raven that was seated next to it squawked its displeasure at the sudden flapping.

The owl sailed towards the woman and grasped the lantern in its claws. It flew towards the archway. Outside, the watchmen were still searching the area. As the owl flew past them, the watchmen raced after it, following the light of the lamp.

On the wooden platform in the middle of the lake, Jim traced the network of discoloured veins to a central point on his brother's shoulder. Aber's body stiffened and he grimaced in pain.

Jim looked at Bear. "I'm so sorry, boy," he whispered. "I tried."

Aber twitched as black rot spread through his body.

"I can feel it," he whimpered. He groaned when Jim pulled him up to a sitting position, and his eyes seemed to turn black as they landed on Bear's face.

"B-boy," he said, and he waved for Bear to come closer.

Bear took a halting step towards the shuddering form in front of him.

"Your mother … was no … *Feyatung*," he spat the word in anger. "Killed her … for nothing… Clueless … blotson."

"Ignore him," said Rose sternly. "It's the rot talking."

Bear's ears rang with high-pitched pressure. It was as if a huge wave were waiting to crash in on him, and yet it didn't. It just hung there, suspended, leaving him with nothing inside but an awful, empty silence.

The white-haired woman strode across the wooden boards towards the huddled group. As she got closer, she pulled her cloak open, revealing a green leather sack at her waist.

"A strong dose of sinsenn would lessen the rage, but it's the infection that you should worry about. It's quite deadly." The woman spoke as if she were discussing ingredients to bake a pie.

"Who are you?" asked Burna.

"Who am I?" she scoffed. "Who are *you*?" She reached into her green bag and pulled something from it.

"Stay back," said Petal. She pulled her knife. "Burna asked you a question. Who are you?"

"Put that knife away, girl," said the white-haired woman as if she were talking to a child, "before someone gets hurt."

She pulled a glass vial out of the green bag. It glowed with the light of a candle. She held it up. The orange glow illuminated her face.

"What's that?" said Petal suspiciously.

"That's a better question, though the answer won't mean anything to you. The important thing is that it may reverse the rot, but you're running out of time if you want to save him."

Petal didn't budge.

The hooded woman from the boat spoke.

"Don't waste it on them, Maggie."

Aber's head lolled backwards.

"How do we know you're telling the truth?" snapped Burna.

"You don't. But what are your options? If he doesn't drink it, he dies. If I'm lying, he still dies."

"There are worse things than death," said Burna.

The woman nodded. "That's true enough. Well, suit yourself."

She shrugged matter-of-factly, and headed back towards the boat.

"Wait," Bear heard himself say. "Please. Let her try."

The woman turned back. Burna and Petal shared a look and stood back to let her pass. She swept forward and leaned over Aber, emptying the little vial of liquid directly into his open mouth. The fluid that wet his lips shone as if it were lit from within.

"We may have been too late," the woman whispered.

Aber's veins still looked angry and infected. The woman held her hand on his forehead, then on the side of his neck, then on his heart.

"It's working," Felix said. "I can see it."

Bear watched. He couldn't believe his eyes. With every beat of Aber's heart, his blackened veins flushed clear, each pump dissolving the rot further. His body broke out in a sweat and he sighed heavily.

"That's what I was hoping for," the woman said. "He'll be all right."

"Impossible!" gasped Burna. "There's never been nothin' that could reverse the rot, nothin'! Nothin' but cutting off the limbs has ever worked."

"What was that stuff?" Petal asked, turning to the woman.

"Was it ... witchcraft?" There was a tremble in Megg's voice as she looked up at the woman.

The old woman stared at Megg for a long moment, her head on one side, but said nothing. She placed the empty bottle back in her bag and walked back to the boat.

"Hey, she asked you a question!" shouted Petal, following after her. "*Was* it witchcraft?" She put a hand on the woman's shoulder.

There was a blinding flash, then everything went black. No torchlight, no moonlight, nothing. It was a pressing, solid black that silenced everything.

The woman's voice permeated the darkness. She no longer sounded like a disgruntled grandmother. The authority in her voice was unmistakeable.

"We mean no harm. We only take precautions to keep ourselves safe."

Her voice was everywhere all at once, but also quiet and close. "There are evil forces in this realm, and so your uneasiness is understandable."

"If a little ungrateful," a second voice added.

"And at the same time extremely stupid," came another voice, interrupting in the same booming fashion.

"Oh, do shut up!" the white-haired woman's voice snapped.

There was a pop and the darkness vanished. The light of the moon and the torches returned in an instant, and the black boat was already drifting towards the exit with the three women perched on the roof.

The owl swept back into the cavern and flew silently overhead; it landed softly on its perch alongside the raven.

A moment later, the black boat had disappeared through the archway, and the cavern was still and quiet once more.

Rose crouched by Uncle Jim and helped him close Aber's shirt. Aber gazed around the cavern.

"What just happened?" he asked.

"Witches in Calleston!" moaned Burna. She was trembling.

"They weren't witches," said Petal grumpily. "Flashing lights and silly voices. It's all trickery."

"A bleedin' magic tunnel? Healing blot-rot? That's no trick, Petal ... How do you explain that?"

"We don't explain it, my love," said Rose. "For now, we just accept it, and thank our lucky stars."

"Let's thank them on the way to the Rusty Compass," said Uncle Jim, helping Aber to his feet. "I think we could all do with a brew."

CHAPTER
26

Meya gasped as Bear stepped closer towards the edge of the cliff.

It was a starry night. They were high above the desert valley. Jagged rocks littered with bones lay far below.

"Please... Don't..." she begged.

He looked at her gravely with those dark, unyielding eyes. And then he stepped over the edge.

She screamed and ran to the edge. Her breath came out in ragged gasps. It was done. Bear's broken body lay among the skeletons in the valley.

A whine escaped Meya's throat as she woke, heart hammering madly in her chest.

"Shh, Percy, it was just a bad dream."

But Percy wasn't there. She was alone.

Back at the Rusty Compass, the mood was sombre, despite their dry clothes and wet cups.

Old Fern gathered her long grey hair over one shoulder and eyed the worried faces round the table. As she refilled their drinks, she spoke in the same brisk, no-nonsense tone that Bear was used to.

"Well," she said. "I can't say I'm happy about the witch hunt tomorrow. I'm sure none of us are. We know what happens at these things, witches or no witches. But at least we'll be going into it with full stomachs, thanks to you all."

They nodded their agreement.

"Speaking of which, we'd better get these delivered before dawn," said Uncle Jim. "Is everyone ready? Know where they're going?"

"Yup," said Megg. She slung her bag over her shoulder and waited for Felix and Bear to do the same. The three of them were delivering the fish to families around the market area.

Bear looked at his father. "Are you—"

"Right as rain," said Aber, though the dark circles under his eyes said otherwise. It was agreed he would take fish back to Caber, then rest. Rose and Jim would cover the dark streets around the outer walls, Petal and Burna the docks.

"Keep your head down out there," said Aber as they walked out. "No fooling around!"

The three friends stepped out of the Rusty Compass into the cold night air. They walked for a while in silence. There was so much to talk about that no one knew where to start, so for a while they walked quietly into town.

Bear's head was bursting with thoughts and images – of the Queen Meléna and the knife, of Jakka lying bleeding on the floor, of the witch in the cage, the blots, the white-haired women and his mother. He didn't know what to do with it. He didn't know how to organize it all in his head; what was right and what was wrong.

There was a chance the women on the boat were just illusionists with a good herb bag. There was certainly a clear difference between their talents and the evil talents of the witch that had been captured by Queen Meléna. Maybe the thing in the cage was a *Feyatung*, and the women on the boat were … something else?

When Bear thought about his mother, he knew which one she had been.

Bear felt a little hand slip into his and give it a quick squeeze.

He turned to see Megg looking at him. She looked worried, and more tired than he'd ever seen her, as if she'd aged ten years in one night.

Would she be all right tomorrow? Would he?

Felix cleared his throat.

"I'll take the first street here," he said, slipping down an alleyway to the left. "You two take Gearers Way and then we can head to Treat Street?"

Bear nodded and he and Megg walked on a while. She hooked her arm through his. After a while, she stopped and turned to him.

"Bear…" Her voice was so quiet he had to strain to hear her.

He felt himself tense as he turned to her.

"I…" She avoided his gaze, her eyes darting around the dark street. Bear realized she was trembling. "What's wrong? Are you cold?" He rubbed his hands up and down her arms.

She raised her eyes to his. Tears were spilling down her cheeks.

"Megg, what is it?"

"I just want you to know … whatever happens…"

Bear felt his stomach twist and tighten. "What do you mean? What's going to happen?"

"Nothing," said Megg. "I don't know. I think I'm just tired."

Bear gave her some time to find her words. But they didn't come. She just stood close to him, looking into his eyes, waiting for him to say something.

He did the best that he could do.

"Megg. Whatever happens. I'm here. You need some rest. Go home. Let me and Felix handle the deliveries."

He lifted her chin.

She nodded and smiled. Before he could study it, she put a hand to his cheek. Her eyes seemed to be searching his face.

"Megg…" His voice came out in a whisper.

She closed her eyes. A dizzy feeling swirled within him.

"Are you still here?" came Felix's voice from the end of the alley.

Bear jumped and Megg's eyes sprung open. They stared at each other. Bear smiled at the sudden shock. Then quick as a flash, before Bear could fill the moment with some foolish comment, she kissed him – her soft lips pressing firmly against his for just a second. She meant it.

Then she ran off into the night.

Bear stood in the street, staring after her, stunned.

"Where's she going so fast?" asked Felix, appearing next to Bear.

"I told her to go home," said Bear, watching her until she disappeared round the corner. "She was tired."

Bear should have walked her home.

"Right," said Felix, eyeing him for a second. "Well, I guess it's just you and me, then."

Bear nodded. They had a job to do. He would think about it later.

They wandered down Gearers Way, until they came to a door with a fish scratched on the wood in chalk.

"That's the sign," said Felix. "When you see it, they get a fish."

Bear pulled out a wet trout and carried it to the window. As Uncle Jim had said, it had been left open. Bear lifted the fish through the window and placed it inside a basket that had been left on the windowsill.

"Thank you," somebody whispered from the dark.

Bear jumped at the voice. He hadn't expected anyone to be awake.

"Maybe me," he replied to the darkness.

The next door was unmarked, and so they carried on. Felix slipped up a rickety staircase to check the doors up on the level above. Below, Bear found another door with a fish scrawled on the wood. He pulled out a fish and placed it gently inside a metal bucket.

"Thank you, Aberson," whispered a man's voice he didn't recognize.

"Maybe me," said Bear quietly, and he pulled his hood further over his face.

Felix slid down a drainpipe and landed lightly on the ground.

"Everyone's awake," he whispered.

Bear nodded. The next house had three fish chalked on the wooden door. Felix unloaded three and slipped them through the window into a large basket. There were excited gasps from inside.

"Thank you!"

"Thanks very much!"

"Thank you, Mister Fennex!"

There was an adult voice, and two very young ones whispering from the dark.

"Maybe me," Felix whispered back.

"Pull your hood up," said Bear. "We don't want people to recognize us."

Felix shrugged. "I don't mind if they do."

"Felix!"

"What if people see a Fennex helping?"

Bear frowned. Felix knew how dangerous that was, but something was clearly on his mind. Bear didn't want to push him.

"Just be careful," he said.

"What if I'm tired of being careful…" Felix muttered.

Bear decided not to say anything more for a while, and

they kept making their deliveries until their bags were almost empty.

There was a light rumbling sound from above. They looked up and saw dark purple clouds had covered the moon and half the sky, and sure enough a moment later rain began to fall, lightly at first, then heavily.

Felix grinned and ran down the street, looking for cover. "Over there!"

"What?"

"We're here!"

It was the wooden door with the faded engraving on it – the red beaver smoking a pipe. Felix opened the door and squealed as something rushed out, pushing past his legs, barking.

It was Percy. The little dog tore off down the street, followed a moment later by a very scruffy Dorloc Odittany, running as fast as he could after him.

"Doc!" Bear shouted. "Here, catch!"

Dorloc stopped mid-run, turned and deftly caught the fish in one hand, before setting off again. "Lovely! Thanks for the scran!" he shouted, then set off chasing after Percy's distant yapping again.

"Maybe me!" called Felix and Bear together, then they laughed.

The boys headed through the door and down the red tunnel until they came out on to Treat Street. They looked up and down the timber-framed buildings, checking each door for the mark of the fish. It was getting late or, rather, early, even for the nocturnal residents of Treat Street. No music played and only a few windows were still aglow. Following a collapsing set of balconies, Bear placed one of his last fish into an open window. A calloused hand grabbed his wrist.

"Thank you, darlin'," a raspy voice said from the dark. It pressed a copper coin into his hand.

"Th-thank you," Bear replied. "M-maybe me."

"I hope not," said the rough voice, and it laughed a croaking laugh.

Bear rejoined Felix in the street. His bag was empty, but Felix had one hefty package left.

"Final delivery," Felix said as he walked them to a familiar space, tucked away under a red-tiled roof.

"The Daisy Beds Well," said Bear, remembering the last time they were there.

The room was still lit by a scattering of candles, and in the middle was the statue of the woman, kneeling in the centre of the flower. The rushing sound of the water and the flickering light from the candle was comforting.

"It's nice here," said Bear simply.

Behind the well was the little golden gate they had crawled through all those nights ago, the portal to Roofside. He thought about Meya, then about Megg, then he sighed.

He suddenly felt exhausted. He sat on the floor, his back against the well. Felix sat down next to him.

"Bear," said Felix in the low light. "What do you think

your life is going to be like?"

"Erm…"

Felix sighed. "I mean, what do you *want* your life to be like?"

Bear thought about this. "I just want to be free," he said.

Felix smiled. He waited for him to elaborate.

"I want to do well in the fields," said Bear simply, "and, if I can, I want to live above Cobbleside some day."

Felix's smile had faded a little. Bear noticed, and realized what he'd said.

"Does it have to be *above*?" said Felix.

"What do you mean?"

"I mean, does it have to be in Calleston at all?"

Bear frowned, not really understanding. He went on. "Listen, I know it will be … harder … for you to change things if you can't work the fields, but you can still try, and maybe—"

"Stop, Bear! Stop!" Felix groaned and rolled his eyes. "We all know only field workers have a chance of moving to Roofside – that's just the way it is. You're safe here. You can fill the fields with red flowers, year in, year out, and some day you'll find yourself sat on top of the houses we grew up in."

The rain grew heavier, pinging loudly off the red tiles of the roof above their heads.

"There isn't anything for me in Calleston," said Felix. He sat there for a long while.

"So I need to leave."

Bear frowned. "You can't leave."

Felix cocked his head to one side. "Says who?"

"You can't leave Calleston without papers. This isn't the Free City. You need permission."

Felix laughed. "What do you care about permission? We've been out stealing fish all night." He looked at Bear seriously. "Merchant boats have been coming and going since the Queen got here. That's how I'll get out. If that Fennex woman on that boat can come and go freely…"

"Is that what this is about?" Bear looked at him. "That woman? You'll never pass the checks."

"I'll be stowed away."

"They'll catch you."

"Just let me worry about that. Remember, you've never seen any other parts of the Queendom. I have."

"But you're a Callestonian."

"Partly. I walk like a Callestonian, I talk like a Callestonian, but I'm a Fennex too, aren't I?"

A cold feeling settled in Bear's chest. Bear could tell these were things that Felix had been feeling for a long time, things he'd never told him. They were supposed to be friends.

"Please don't go," Bear said in a hoarse whisper.

Felix turned to him, his face glowing in the candlelight. His amber eyes took in Bear's without judgement, the same way they had looked at him since they were young.

"Come with me, Bear."

They sat looking at each other for a long while.

Bear broke the silence. "I can't."

"Why not?"

"Felix! I don't know ... everything. My dad, my uncles ..."

"Megg," said Felix.

Bear looked at him. "And you too, living right here with me, like you should be."

Felix sighed and crossed his hands over his legs. The rain was lighter now, tapping lightly on the roof. The only other sound in the little room was the rushing of the well.

Felix pushed himself up on to his feet. "We'd better go back."

"Wait," said Bear, following him out into the street. He put a hand on his shoulder.

Felix turned. He took Bear's face in his hands and stared into his eyes. Then he leaned back and seemed to take in all that he could see, his amber eyes darting back and forth.

Bear realized what Felix was doing. He was memorizing Bear's face. He was looking at him for the last time.

"No, Felix. Don't. It's not—"

"Look, I've got my tricks, Bear. You've got yours. You just do your best here and don't worry about me."

And then he leaned into Bear and kissed him on the cheek softly. He rested his head against Bear's shoulder. Bear put his arms round him. He had never thought of Felix as vulnerable before, and now he suddenly felt afraid that Felix was about to take on more than he could chew,

337

and Bear wouldn't be there to help him.

With a heavy sigh, Felix lifted his head and, shooting Bear a smile and a wink, he set off down the street.

"Wait," said Bear.

Felix turned. "What?"

Bear dug around in his pocket and found the little copper coin he'd been handed earlier. It seemed such a silly thing to give him, but it was all that he had. He flipped the coin up into the air.

Felix caught it and grinned. "If you ever get tired of Calleston, come find me."

Bear nodded and did his best to smile. He was glad it was raining. "I'll miss you," he said.

Felix nodded back.

Then he fixed his bag tight to his shoulders, flipped up his hood and dashed off into the rain.

The Queen watched the Feyatung *crouching in the corner of its cage.*

The witch sensed her gaze. It slid to the edge of the cage and held the bars in its claws as it peered through.

Those eyes made Queen Meléna want to shudder, but she refrained. She wouldn't give it the satisfaction. That's what it wanted. It wanted to kill her. It wanted to snap her neck and watch her hit the floor. It was hard to believe this had once been a woman just like her. Just like her mother.

The witch slowly drew a dark claw down its face. It was an unusual gesture. Queen Meléna pressed a hand to her cheek and was horrified to find a tear running down it.

"Are you ready, Your Majesty?" said Afena from the doorway.

The Queen stood, relieved at the interruption.

She smiled. "I'm ready."

CHAPTER 27

"Welcome, my darling," Noka said sweetly as she emerged on to the marble balcony.

"Morning, Noka," said Meya.

"You look beautiful."

She ignored him. She had dressed as plainly as she could. The idea of some poor floorborn being dragged forward and executed while she looked on, playing princess, did not fill her with excitement.

She took a seat next to her father. He looked exhausted, dark circles under his eyes. She smiled encouragingly. Meya knew he didn't want this witch hunt any more than she did. He cared for the people of Cobbleside, but, like her, he had no choice but to go along with the Queen's wishes. She hoped the people knew it too.

Meya peered anxiously over the parapet at the crowd below. The Cobblesiders had been rounded up that morning and were gathered in the square, but where normally there would be the warm hubbub of gossip and chatter, today there was a frightened silence. She looked for Bear, but so many of the floorborn were wearing their straw hats that she didn't stand much chance.

The Queen's Claws marched out on to the balcony and placed themselves among the watchmen at regular intervals. The watchmen shuffled their feet – Meya sensed a fear in the air. They were tired too, no doubt. They'd spent half the night enduring the Queen's interrogations. Still, they stood with their heads held high among the Fennex fighters.

Meya cast her eyes on either side of her. There, and all around the market square, the Roofside balconies heaved with bodies. More had turned up to watch the witch hunt than had for Field Day. This was much more exciting to them: the scandal, the danger, the death. She glared at the faces occupying the Overlord's balcony – revellers from last night rubbing their eyes or yawning nonchalantly. Meanwhile, every adult in Cobbleside awaited a dark cup of truthwine. Meya was disgusted.

Her father stood and stepped forward. In his deep, authoritative voice, he addressed the crowd.

"As we attempt to root out the dark forces that have sullied our good town in recent years, we are honoured to welcome the Good Queen Meléna to help us in this fight!"

The Queen's Claws struck their metal cuffs together as one, and everyone on the balcony rose for the entrance of the Queen.

Queen Meléna appeared in a mahogany gown that clung tightly. Her wrists were edged with a fur of the same deep brown, and she held a wrap of the same fur around her body. Her veil today was close to her face, and sheer. The same colour as her dress, it was almost invisible against her skin, but the gold of her crown shone brightly for all to see.

Meya curtseyed as she passed, but Queen Meléna's eyes didn't leave the packed market square below. The Queen's entourage followed her out. They wore woollen coats that draped to the floor, and, like the Queen, they clutched furs of brown or grey.

Noka stepped forward and spoke quietly in the Overlord's ear.

"They're ready. He can begin."

Meya took a deep breath as her father cleared his throat. She could tell he was nervous, though nobody else would know. He was trying to stay strong, as usual, for the people in Cobbleside.

"We look to the Honourable Tsilas Violet, Voice of the Queen."

Every head turned to the man in the middle of the square. He stood on a raised platform. There were two barrels beside him, one dark and wooden, the other a brilliant shining gold. Meya recognized that gold barrel from somewhere…

Finally, covered by the large black cloth, was the witch in her cage. Meya shuddered as she thought about the creature lurking beneath.

The town square was as full of people as it had been on

Field Day, though today there was no human tower, no music, no dancing.

"Calleston!" The Queen's Voice spoke loudly and clearly, as though he were about to tell them a story. "The Queen is delighted with the harvest. However, along with your virtue, we have also discovered your vice. After an ill-advised attempt was made on the Queen's life, no doubt prompted by the evil forces that lurk here, the Queen now must rid you of the shadow that has passed over this town." He waved to a Queensguard. "Wherever we find wickedness, we find, without fail, witchwork."

Meya shifted uncomfortably in her seat.

The first boy brought to stand before the two barrels had a cheeky face and a wild mane of curly hair. Meya leaned forward over the marble guardrail. She squinted. It was Cassius. That was it. The boy who had pushed her in the canal. The boy who had hit Doc and driven Percy away.

Even so, Meya hoped he would remain unharmed. She looked at the faces of the people of Cobbleside and could see they were hoping the same thing. She wondered how it felt, spending so much time hoping, waiting, for instructions, for food, or like today – just waiting to see who would die.

Cassius was handed a large golden cup. From up on the balcony, the deep red liquid inside looked black. The Queensguard watched carefully while Cassius drank from it.

"No blade shall cut, no arrow strike, no sickness

corrupt the rule of the Free City!" the Queen's Voice shouted. "Not even the power of the ... *Feyatung*!"

He's enjoying himself, thought Meya.

Cassius looked up from the cup and laughed, a wild, shameless laugh. Truthwine worked fast.

"And so we begin..." spat the Queen's Voice. He stood in front of Cassius, eyeing him with undisguised distaste. "Listen to me carefully, boy."

Cassius smiled and gazed at the Queen's Voice. "Hello, handsome." His voice rang out across the square.

Surprised laughter rippled along Roofside balconies. The Queen's Voice scowled.

"Just answer the questions. Have you ever, in any capacity whatsoever, heard of a plot to harm the Queen?"

"Yes."

Roofside gasped, as did some on the cobbles.

"When?"

"When watchmen dragged us from our beds this morning. They told us someone tried to kill her last night."

There was a sigh of relief, and then a smattering of applause from the roof.

"And before then?"

"No, never."

Tsilas Violet continued pacing the stage. He slapped the dark orb into his hand repeatedly as he circled Cassius.

"And do you possess any powers, unnatural or wicked, forceful or corrupt, ones that could be considered witchery, or deriving from the powers of the *Feyatung*?"

"No," said Cassius.

There was a timid applause from Cobbleside. People were too scared to be relieved.

The Queen's Voice plucked a red flower from inside the wooden barrel and pinned it to Cassius's shirt.

"Is there anything else you think Queen Meléna, or I, or the Overlord should be made aware of?" he asked.

Cassius looked up at the balcony. To Meya's surprise, he was looking straight at her. "I want to eat your dog!" he shouted.

There was raucous laughter from Roofside. Meya gripped the arms of her chair in a combination of embarrassment and fury.

"Bring the next one!"

A slim girl with long thick hair drank next. She shivered after her drink and stared at her feet. Tsilas Violet lowered his chin and looked her in the eye.

"Outside of this morning, have you in any capacity whatsoever, heard of a plot to harm the Queen?"

"No," said the girl, and she beamed wide.

"Very good."

He looked up to the balcony briefly as he circled the girl.

"And do you possess any powers, unnatural or wicked, forceful or corrupt, ones that could be considered deriving from the powers of the *Feyatung*?"

"No!"

The Cobblesiders clapped again, their faces blank, their claps short.

"Is there anything else the people should know?"

"The watchmen beat up my granddad!" she said. "We haven't seen him for a week!"

The Queen's Voice raised his eyebrows and spun to look at the Overlord, then pushed a red flower behind the girl's ear and sent her on her way. Meya glanced at her father. His expression was grim.

"Bring the next!"

They continued painstakingly in the same fashion, on and on, one floorborn after another. For every new person that stepped up on to the stage, Meya was terrified it would be him. She still hadn't spotted him in the crowd. She didn't want to. She couldn't take it any more. She leaned over and spoke into her father's ear. "Father, may I be excused?"

"Why, my dear?"

"I don't wish to watch."

"Darling, nobody wishes to watch. We are here at the Queen's behest. How would it look if you showed your disinterest in this moment? If the people we rule must endure this, then so must we."

"I refuse," Meya said.

His deep blue eyes grew steely at the tone of her voice. "Meya Omega, these sort of foolish power plays are beneath you."

"Father, don't make me cause a scene. I will not be forced to watch this torment."

He sighed. "You are so like your mother."

Meya's breath caught in her throat. He never talked about her mother. He smiled wistfully for a second.

"She was a very beautiful woman, a very caring woman. But she was stubborn, and prone to outbursts of anger, just like you."

Meya stood up as if to go, but her father grabbed her arm roughly and pulled her back down into her seat, speaking into her ear in a low, urgent whisper.

"I loved her desperately, Meya. And because I love you also, I am going to tell you what I told her."

Meya waited, her cheeks flushing. She pressed the backs of her fingers on to her neck to cool it down. He looked deeply into her eyes as he spoke.

"Your emotions do *not* dictate my actions. *I* dictate *yours*. Tread carefully, Meya. I am your father. I am also your Overlord, and you will obey me. Do I make myself clear?"

Meya stiffened at his words, leaning back into her seat as her father loosened his grip on her, then turned to face the crowd again as if nothing had happened.

Meya sat frozen in her chair, blinking back tears.

"Bring the next one!" shouted Tsilas Violet below.

Meya tried to watch, but she couldn't focus on anything. She felt as if she had just been dropped into the bottom of a well. Her father had never spoken to her like that before. He had admonished her many times over the years, but always he had treated her with a tenderness that made her feel safe. What had happened to him?

She heard a voice along the balcony say, "Isn't that the boy who came to the feast?"

Her heart lurched as she looked down at the platform, and Bear stepped up on to it.

For once, he wasn't wearing his silly straw field hat. He pushed his messy hair back from his face, and Meya caught a glimpse of his eyes – dark and sad and ringed with worry and sleepness nights – as he crossed the stage to meet his fate.

Please let him pass, she thought.

Tsilas stepped forward, a smug smile on his face.

"And, now, a luminary in our midst!" he called. "Was this not the boy who ran your fields red, Calleston? Welcome! Welcome to the stage, young man! Why not have a drink?"

There was laughter across Roofside.

Meya felt miserable. Bear looked miserable too – so skinny and sad and lost up there on that stage. How must he be feeling, Meya wondered, knowing the entire town was watching him. And then another thought sickened her further.

His mother died in these very circumstances.

After his confession at the feast, she had wanted to tell him it wasn't his fault. He was so young. How could he have known that growing sinsenn wasn't magic? It was easy to see how a child would see it as such. But he had been so absorbed in the girl that Noka had swept them away and back down to Cobbleside before she'd got the chance.

As Bear reached for the cup, Meya saw that his hands were trembling. Not just trembling but shaking violently. Others had noticed too. She heard muttering from all along the balcony. Meya's heart raced as she gripped the parapet. All of Cobbleside knew his history.

"This young man was a witness to last night's malevolent attack on our Queen," said the Voice. "It must have been quite the shock."

Bear finished his drink and stood perfectly still. His hands were steady now. Meya waited for him to laugh or smile. But he didn't. He just stood there and waited for his questions.

"Outside of your witnessing of the assassination attempt on Queen Meléna, and the innocent discussions that have occurred since then, have you ever, in any capacity, heard of a plot to harm the Queen?"

Bear shook his head.

"Oh, no, no, no. We can do better than that I think, young man. Say it loud!"

Bear lifted his chin. "No," he said.

"Very good!" shouted Tsilas Violet. He strode over to the golden barrel and dunked the cup in again. He walked back to Bear and handed him the cup. Then, using the black orb on the end of his staff, the Queen's Voice tipped the base of the cup upwards until Bear had drained it.

"Next question," said the Queen's Voice. "Do you possess any powers, unnatural or wicked, forceful or corrupt, ones that could be considered deriving from the powers of the *Feyatung*?"

Bear blinked up at the man standing in front of him. "No," he said, his voice ringing out loud and strong across the square.

Meya let go of a breath she hadn't known she was holding.

For the first time that morning, there was a ripple of talk among the Cobblesiders. Meya struggled to see their facial expressions underneath their stupid straw hats, but all the energy in the town was focused on the tall, skinny boy with the dark eyes, the one who had named his mother a witch all those years ago – but wasn't one himself.

The Queen's Voice sensed a shift in the air, and he took a long look at Bear.

"Is there anything … unsavoury that you know of, that we should be made aware?"

Bear spoke loud and clear, truthwine colouring his voice. "Yes. My Uncle Caber died in bed last night. He hadn't eaten properly in weeks. Nobody has."

There were speculative whispers across the rooftop, but Meya understood better than most Roofsiders the hardships that the floorborn faced. Tsilas Violet leaned over and said something inaudible to Bear. Bear spoke loudly.

"I don't blame Queen Meléna. I blame the Overlord. He pretends there's no food, but I was at… I was at…" He shook his head and then carried on. "I was at the feast and I saw with my own two eyes. They've more than enough

351

to go around. So why are we all left to starve?"

There was a collective gasp. Meya stole a glance at her father. His expression remained calm, though she could see his knuckles were white as he gripped the arms of his chair.

The Queen's Voice's cackled loudly. "The truth according to your champion! Bring the next one. You can go."

Now it was the girl's turn. Megg. Tsilas Violet welcomed her up as if they were old friends.

"A greater grower we do not know. Come forward, come forward. Can I get you anything in particular to drink, my dear?"

He drew a drink from the golden barrel. Megg held the cup in her hand and studied it. She seemed perfectly calm.

There was a woman just a few rows from the stage, a toddler on her shoulders, and a gaggle of identical girls surrounding her. They had the same skin and the same hair as Megg – her mother and her sisters no doubt, thought Meya. When Megg had finished the truthwine, the Queen's Voice began.

"Outside of your witnessing of the assassination attempt on Queen Meléna," said Tsilas Violet, "and the innocent discussions that have occurred since then, have you, in any capacity, heard of a plot to harm the Queen?"

"No, sir," said Megg.

The littlest girl shrieked happily and was shushed by her mother. Meya smiled. *How adorable*, she thought.

"And do you possess any powers, unnatural or wicked, forceful or corrupt, ones that could be considered deriving from the powers of the *Feyatung*?"

Megg looked Tsilas Violet in the eyes and sighed happily.

"Yes," she said. "I do."

The raven hopped down on to a low branch and got a good look at the witchling on the platform. Even he could sense her gift. Strong little thing, they could have used a power like hers. Shame she was going to die.

"She may survive yet," *said a voice in his head.*

Hmph, *thought the raven.* We'll see.

But the raven had seen events like these before. He knew how the man with the white staff worked. The chain would go on, and then…

"What about the other one?" *said the voice again.*

They don't even know it themselves yet, *thought the raven.*

"They will soon enough."

CHAPTER
28

Bear couldn't speak, couldn't breathe. It felt as if all the air had been knocked out of him.

A solitary voice began wailing in the crowd. It was soon joined by others.

Megg's mum, Megg's sisters, thought Bear helplessly.

The Queensguard on the platform pulled their swords. Bear expected Tsilas Violet to be angry. But he wasn't. He smiled.

"It appears we have ratted out the problem quicker than anticipated. But let us first make absolutely sure."

A Queensguard presented a chain and handed it to the Queen's Voice. Tsilas Violet held the chain in two hands. He spoke to Megg cautiously, though the effects of the truthwine made her calm and unafraid.

"May I put this about your neck?"

Megg nodded and smiled. He walked towards her, slow, as if she were a wild animal. She watched him, untroubled.

He closed the black chain round her throat and then pressed the end of his staff against it. As the dark orb touched the chain, the metal glowed bright white, before returning to a sooty black.

Bear recognized the chain. It was the same as the one they had put on his mother, right before they'd killed her.

"Tell me," said the Queen's Voice, "what vile witchwork have you performed?"

Megg blinked. "I haven't done anything *vile*, sir."

"So you say. What unnatural acts are you capable of?"

Megg put her hand over her mouth, hiding an embarrassed smile. "Can I whisper it?"

"No," he sneered. "Out loud."

"Well, I can enlace with mice. With lots of things, actually, but I'm best with mice."

A flurry of gasps and wails came from the Rooftops. The Roofsiders raced to the railings to get a closer look, peering down with a kind of invigorated shock.

Bear knew he should feel revulsion – he could see it on the face of the Queen's Voice as he recoiled from her, in the uncomfortable stiffness in the people around him.

But all he could think was – *Megg, his Megg … a witch?*

That explained what had happened when they were out in the fields …

And yet it had felt so innocent. When Megg enlaced with him, it hadn't felt evil. Cobbleside was heavy with quiet, apart from the sobbing of Megg's family.

"I was enlaced with the mouse you fed to the witch, actually." The words came tumbling out of Megg's mouth, and once she started she didn't stop. "I'd been wondering for a while, you see, if I might be a witch. I knew that nobody else could enlace with animals. When I saw the witch coming right into town, it seemed like my chance to find out more. I thought if I got a bit closer, I could check. So I reached out and enlaced with the mouse on your boat. It was the oddest feeling being picked up, but when you fed us to her ... I've had nightmares about being eaten ever since that day."

"Silence, *Feyatung*!"

Megg's mouth snapped shut. She grasped the chain at her neck in confusion.

Tsilas Violet strutted towards the balcony and called up to the Queen.

"Do you hear that? The witch is barely fledged, and it already uses the vermin beneath our feet for purposes of espionage."

Gasps and concerned chatter erupted from the roof, but not a soul in Cobbleside said a word. Megg tried to speak again, but not a sound came out of her mouth. The Queen watched silently.

Elma edged forward so she could see her oldest daughter. The people in the crowd made way as she drew closer.

She held Ophelia on her shoulder. Ophelia didn't understand what was happening. Freya wailed in misery and the other girls clung to each other and their mother's trousers in stunned silence. Elma's eyes glistened, but she stood tall. She stroked Andy's hair over and over.

Megg saw her mother and her breathing appeared to

quicken. She signed clearly in Field-Speak, rubbing a closed hand on her chest and tapping three fingers on her palm. *I'm sorry, Mum.*

Elma shook her head angrily and signed back clearly. *Never be sorry!* A tear rolled down Elma's face. *I love you, Megg. I'm proud of you.*

Megg smiled, eyes shining. She pointed to herself, pressed her hands tight to her heart, and pointed at her family. *I love you.*

The Queen's Voice returned; he held his stick aloft. "You must leave us with no doubt as to your … abilities."

Megg nodded.

"Show me how you enlace your mind with the vermin."

Megg nodded again.

And the people on the roof leaned in for a better look.

She clasped her hands together, closed her eyes, focused on her breathing. Bear recognized it immediately. She was enlacing.

Nothing happened. The entire town stood watching Megg with her hands clasped and her eyes closed, but nothing else happened.

And then a mouse ran past Bear's feet towards the stage.

Followed by a second. Then a third, darting between the feet of the crowd. Soon, a steady stream of mice in varying shades poured towards the wooden platform. The mice found the wooden steps and clambered up, their little tails swinging as they clumsily made their way to the top.

Tsilas Violet backed away as the creatures formed a perfect ring round Megg, and sat, as if waiting for instructions.

"There we have it!" Tsilas Violet thundered. "The rot has been found! Calleston is not dying, and the fields will flood red anew. You simply need to remember to pull out the bad weeds."

The Queen's Voice bowed deeply, bending down so far that his head almost touched the floor. Roofside erupted into rapturous applause. The Queen herself stood and clapped.

"Bring it out!" Tsilas Violet shouted to the Queensguard.

The guards headed to the giant cage and began untying the cloth that was draped over it.

Bear suddenly felt an odd tugging and looked down.

A small brown mouse was trying to crawl up his trouser leg. It was tiny, and its honey-coloured fur was glossy and sleek. It struggled to climb as it swung in the folds of the fabric. Bear reached down and lifted it gently into his hand. It nuzzled against his fingers happily, curling into a ball in the palm of his hand and closing its eyes.

Bear looked up at Megg. Her eyes were shut too and she had a serene smile on her face. He looked back down at the mouse. Something dawned on him.

"It was you, wasn't it? You visited me sometimes in the morning?" Bear asked quietly.

On the stage, Megg nodded her head and smiled.

"Megg, I'm so sorry," he whispered to the mouse. A lump was forming in his throat. "I-I wish I'd known. I wish..."

On the stage, Megg gently shook her head.

"Awaken!" shrieked Tsilas Violet, as behind Megg the cover was ripped from the cage and the witch was revealed. It crouched on the floor like a spider, half concealed within unnatural fluid shadows.

Bear felt a great sob rip through him as the Queen's Voice slammed his staff against the metal, causing torrents of flame and smoke to erupt behind the bars. The mice that circled Megg didn't flinch. They sat patiently, watching her.

The mouse in Bear's hand sat up too.

"There is only one punishment fit for the *Feyatung*!" the Voice called. "Their doctrine poisons the minds of the vulnerable, their unnatural practices defile the purity of the Queendom! And their power infects the land wherever they go!"

The smoke in the cage cleared and Bear saw the wretched form of the witch emerge behind Megg. It staggered forward drunkenly, and as it reached the bars of the cage it extended a clawed hand towards her.

Megg's eyes remained closed.

She raised her hands and began to move them in the air.

Clearly and deftly in Field-Speak she addressed the crowd.

I never meant any harm. It's just a piece of me.

She paused, considering her next words.

… I'm sorry.

Bear looked over the faces in the crowd, and saw Dorloc remove his little flat cap. He didn't take his eyes off Megg.

"Maybe me!" his voice squeaked.

Bear was stunned. But behind him, Rose removed her field hat and held it in her hand.

"Maybe me," she called softly.

Bear was surprised to hear his father's voice, firmer than the others, take up the call beside him.

"Maybe me."

There was a quiet rustling as the various field hats and flat caps in Cobbleside were removed. And men, women and children murmured the same two words quietly.

Elma and the girls wept openly. A tear rolled down Megg's cheek and she closed her eyes. Bear looked down at the little honey-coloured mouse in his hand.

She was sitting up now, gazing back at him. He brought her close to his face and kissed her softly on her head.

The Queen's Voice extended his staff to the outstretched claw. "Kill this witch," he said, "and then sleep."

Bear couldn't bring himself to lift his eyes.

There was a loud crack and a blinding flash on the stage. A raven cawed loudly from the rooftops.

Distantly, Bear heard the Queen's Voice say, "Collect the body."

Bear stared down into his cupped hands.

The mouse lay perfectly still. Her heart wasn't beating. She was dead.

29

The knock at the door came only a few days later.

When Bear opened it, the Whip was standing there. Bear blinked dimly at him through a ruby-brew haze.

"Pack your things," said the Whip without ceremony.

"Um, why?" Bear asked.

"You are being repositioned. The Overlord has prepared new quarters for you and your father Roofside."

In the room behind him, Rose gasped. She had come round with a keg of particularly strong ruby brew to give Bear. He hadn't left the house since the witch hunt. Even Aber had no objections. He let Bear sit and stare up at the ironwood beam above his bed all day long.

"I suspected as much, after that harvest," breathed Rose. "That's just the boost you need, Bear. I *promise* you, the sun will shine again. Now let me get out yer way... Congratulations, my loves!"

Rose gave Bear's shoulder a squeeze and hugged Aber, then hurried out of the door; the whole town would know by sunset.

Aber was in a daze. "What do we bring?"

"Just bring what you need for today," said the Whip. "You'll get all new things Roofside."

Bear looked around the dark room that had been his home. He didn't want to leave, but then he didn't care to stay. The ghosts of Caber and a little mouse haunted the place. Bear and Aber hadn't touched his bunk since his body had been carted away. It still looked as if he would return home to tidy the blankets in a moment.

But that was impossible. Caber would never return home. Megg would never make it to Roofside. And Bear would never see Megg again.

It was a concept he couldn't make head nor tail of. His mind wandered through endless scenes, memories and fantasies, and always led back to one simple yet incomprehensible thought: she was dead. He didn't know a word or a collection of words that encompassed such an unshakable and monstrous idea. It was wrong. She should still be here. And now there was a hole, in the air, in Calleston, in Bear.

No mouse had tiptoed along the beam since she'd been gone. If Bear had just paid more attention, maybe she would have told him. Maybe he could have helped her. Maybe he could have helped her hide it.

Even that thought sickened him. She didn't deserve to be hidden.

Megg had had a gift. She'd been made rare, and uncommonly good, and entirely special. And the world hated her for it.

Bear felt an insistent ache threatening to rise in his chest. He walked towards the keg of ruby brew.

"Leave it, Bear," said Aber quietly. "There'll be time enough for that later. Pack your things and let's be gone. Unless you don't want to go?"

Bear obeyed his father silently and began gathering items. Aside from a small chest with a few clothes in it and the pot in the unlit fireplace, there wasn't much to pack. Certainly nothing worth staying for.

He grabbed the few things that were in the chest, and his field hat. Then they followed the Whip out of the door into the street.

"Can you believe it, boy?" whispered Aber as they walked. "Repositioned."

"Yes, Father."

"Repositioned," Aber repeated.

The Whip stopped and looked around, confused. "Blast it!" he said. "Everything looks the same down here."

"Where are we heading?" asked Bear.

"The big marina."

"Grub Dock," replied Aber. "It's this way."

Soon they arrived at the docks and the big warehouse where the descender transported things and people between the rooftops and the cobbles.

Bear felt a sudden reluctance to go any further. He didn't care about Roofside. He could stay here, work in the docks. It looked like a hard day's work, and everyone looked weather-beaten and weary, but it somehow seemed like the only thing that made any sense. He didn't want to go out in the fields. He didn't want to enlace any more. He didn't want to enlace ever again. He just wanted something that would take his mind off everything … permanently.

"Heard the news! Wasn't sure if it was true," Burna called out.

She jumped off a small transport ship and walked their way. She must have been working a lot recently. The contrast between her sun-kissed skin versus her shock of short white hair was even more dramatic than usual. She grasped Aber's hand firmly and shook it, then started packing sinsenn leaves into a pipe.

"I'm glad someone made it out of Cobbleside alive."

"Not the best choice of words, Burna," said Petal, walking over to join them, and giving Bear and his dad a hug.

"Want a puff, lad?" Burna offered Bear the pipe.

Bear reached out a hand but Aber pushed the pipe away. He glowered at Burna. She shrugged, gave Bear a friendly wink, and stood back, allowing Petal to lead them into the warehouse.

The giant descender gates were thrust wide open. Inside, the Overlord's assistant, Noka, waited, flanked by watchmen.

"Aber Garrason! And Bear Aberson, dear boy! Welcome home!"

Noka had a twinkle in his eye as he greeted them. He seemed genuinely pleased to receive them. He'd grown a small moustache and goatee. Bear thought he looked like a younger, slimmer version of the Overlord.

"Now, let me show you both to your new living quarters."

As the great descender rumbled upwards, carrying Bear and his father up to the rooftops, Bear's spirits sank lower and lower. The morning ruby brew was wearing off. He felt sick to the stomach. He tried to picture where they might be going and found himself wishing he was slumming through Cobbleside with Felix, or chatting with Caber in their bunks, or doing anything anywhere with Megg ... but they were all gone now.

A strange noise escaped him. Noka looked alarmed.

"Is he all right?"

Aber nodded. "Might need a brew. Been a rough week."

Noka placed an affectionate hand on Bear's arm. "Well, for people like yourselves, Bear, who live on Roof Proper, there is as much high-quality ruby brew as you can stomach. Does wonders."

Noka smiled at him. Bear nodded. He needed something to slow his heart, and stop the strange tightness that was rising in his chest.

The doors parted and Noka walked into the enormous accession hall. Bear wondered why they needed all that space when so few people worked up here.

Noka's shoes struck the floor as he marched on ahead. "Of course, you'll still work the fields, Bear. We know it may take some time before you find your flow again.

You've been through a lot, so no need to worry yourself. But once the day's work is done you will be escorted through any of the golden gates and you'll find a nice clean bed and a ruby brew waiting for you on the other side."

They strode towards the towering gate where a watchman waited. He swung the gate open for them, and they swept through without comment. After winding their way down countless halls, Bear and Aber were shown to their living quarters.

It was a simple yet beautiful room. There were polished wooden floors, vast arched windows with fragmented glass and a carpet so thick that Bear could sleep on it.

"We didn't bring any bedding or anything," said Aber.

"I'm sure there's more than enough of that here," Noka said with a smile.

He pushed open a door and revealed an entirely separate room with a giant bed.

"This chamber has been prepared for you, Master Aberson. Do go on through. You'll find a welcome gift has been left by one of your neighbours. I'll leave you to settle in. Aber, allow me to show you to your room. Someone will be back to collect you before dusk for dinner."

Noka closed the wood-panelled door and then Bear was alone. He listened to the heavy silence that he was left with. It weighed down on him. He fell on to the big bed in the centre of the room. He felt a plush featherbed mattress supporting him from beneath the linen sheets. He lay for a while, letting himself sink into the bed. He felt exhausted, and yet so wide awake he would never sleep. He rolled on to his back and stared up at the ceiling. He wondered where the ruby brew was stored.

He looked around the room. There, shining in the corner, was a golden jug. He walked towards it and dipped his finger in. It was ruby brew. He poured himself a cup and downed it, then filled a second and lay on his back on the bed. He rolled over on to his side. There was a red leather bag on the bedside table. He peeked inside. Oranges. He began peeling one, and then gave up. He sipped from his cup while his mind absently wandered.

He considered where Felix might be. And he thought of Megg, her wild laughter that seemed to come from nowhere, her shy gaze. Her secretive smile. He had been so focused on making it to the roof that he'd been blind to what was right in front of him. And now it was gone.

There was a knock at the door.

"Come in," said Bear, pushing himself up from the bed. When nobody entered, he went to the door and opened it.

There in the doorway was Meya.

"I ... I just came to see how you were settling in," she said.

"Very well, thank you," said Bear. His voice sounded colder than he felt.

They stared at each other for a moment, then Meya busied herself with her sleeve.

"I'm sorry about your friend."

"Yes. Thank you."

He didn't know what else to say, and neither did she. It was horribly quiet, and it didn't seem to be stopping. When the silence had gone on for too long, she said in a muted voice, "Let me know if you need anything."

"Thank you," he said again.

"Maybe me," she said as she closed the door behind her.

As soon as she was gone, Bear went back to the golden jug, glinting on its tray, and topped up his brew. He found himself thinking about Megg, and remembering the golden barrel in the square. He suddenly remembered where he'd seen it before.

He looked down at the glass he'd poured himself, then he put it down, untouched.

He grabbed his bag of oranges and headed out of the door.

CHAPTER
30

Bear jogged up the spiral staircase and along the corridor. Then hopping out of the large wooden door he landed squarely on the path, and back into the sunlight.

With a quick glance behind him, he began walking towards the roof gardens, heading for the orchard, where the apple trees grew. A raven stared at him as he passed by. Otherwise all was still.

He soon found the orchard, and wandered around it a few times.

"There you are, young man!" Noka's voice called pleasantly. He was strolling in among the trees, his arms crossed behind his back. "It's lovely to see you enjoy a stroll around the gardens. Why don't we take a moment to walk together?"

"I would like that," was Bear's truthful reply.

They walked side by side, for a while just listening to the sound of the trees rustling in the afternoon wind. Bear decided to start the conversation.

"Noka, why was I moved here? I haven't grown nearly enough sinsenn."

Noka dipped his head from side to side, as if weighing up the best answer. He seemed to settle on one. "After the interrogations of the witch hunt, the Overlord couldn't stop thinking about some of the things he'd heard. And saw..." Noka looked at Bear; he seemed to be trying to word things in a delicate way. "Not only was Megg taken from us that day, one of our most talented growers, and a promising young woman ... turned over to evil, but he heard the others speak of how hard life was, how they had lost loved ones. Hearing the struggles of those people out loud, it just broke our hearts. We knew we had to act."

Bear nodded. That was what he had expected Noka to say.

Again they walked in silence for a while. There were nice views of Cobbleside in these gardens. It was relaxing.

"We've had our troubles here, yes. Why do you think the Queen came to visit, after all these years?" asked Bear.

"Hmm, another good one." Noka didn't look at Bear as they walked; he looked down and seemed to chew over the questions before answering them, but his voice when he spoke was honest and clear. "She was worried about the terrible harvests and the news of the rot spreading over the land. Sinsenn doesn't grow anywhere but here, Bear, and the entire Queendom enjoys a ruby brew." He smiled. "We all know the fields have been failing, speedweed growing stronger, the number of deaths by blot increasing... The Queen was worried, and quite rightly too."

Bear nodded his understanding. He reached up for an apple, then stopped himself, looking at Noka.

"Go ahead." He smiled. "There are plenty more."

He plucked a small green apple and bit into it. It was tart. He made a face.

"Here," said Noka. "I'll find you a sweeter one."

Noka took the sour apple from him and tossed it down to Cobbleside. Then he reached for a pinkish one on an outermost branch. "Here," he said to Bear. "Try this one."

Bear took a large bite. The juices made his mouth flood with water.

"Better?" Noka asked.

"Better." Bear nodded. "Thank you, Noka. Try one of these. They're my favourite."

He reached into his bag and pulled out an orange. Noka's eyes crinkled. He peeled it and popped a segment in his mouth.

"Ooh, blood oranges! I didn't know we had any left." Noka nudged Bear fondly. "You know, I walk most days with the Overlord. But it's rather nice to talk with somebody new."

Bear let him talk.

"I know things may seem uncertain right now. I've heard Overlord Goodman talk himself into and out of many a situation on this very path." Noka laughed to himself. "But you will find your feet here, Bear. We all do."

"I wonder why we were moved up here at all," he said casually, focusing on his apple. He wondered if Noka realized Bear had already asked him this question. He wondered whether he would get a different answer this time.

"The Queen insisted we bring you up, my dear boy. After the girl's death, she said we had to do something to ease the tensions of the floorborn, oh, excuse me, the Cobblesiders."

Bear laughed. "Don't worry, I've heard worse. From my own father, actually."

Noka gave Bear a sympathetic look. "Yes. At some point, we all realize our parents are flawed." He glanced around the pretty apple trees. "Just remember, the Queen of the realm had her *Feyatung* mother executed, so you could always have it worse."

Bear almost choked on his apple. Noka's thoughtlessness was a good sign. The truthwine that Bear had soaked the oranges in had clearly taken effect. Bear took another bite of his apple.

"Also, of course," Noka went on, "we had to protect our best remaining sinsenn-growing asset – that being you!" He smiled broadly at Bear.

"That makes sense," said Bear evenly. "And … why did the Queen want to come to Calleston?"

Noka popped another bite of orange in his mouth. "Well, it was the reports we were sending her. Every report we sent to the Free City got steadily worse," he said. "Mostly lies at first. I mean, sinsenn numbers had declined slightly – but the past decade of harvests have been truly awful – that is, until you came along." Noka poked Bear affectionately. "But it was us who had engineered that steep decline, purposefully encouraging the speedweed and the blots, starving the workers, false scarcity, anxious hearsay, that sort of thing."

"I see," said Bear. He swallowed, trying to keep his voice steady and calm. "And why would you want to do that?"

"Well, it's the Overlord, dear boy. He is quite frankly desperate to leave. The kind of desperation that turns sane men into something else. He was born here and knew he would die here growing sinsenn for the Queendom if he didn't do something. The only way he could be granted freedom would be if Calleston itself collapses. The royal family of the Free City has a duty to protect the Overlord and his people. If the town falls to ruin, we must be brought to safety."

Bear nodded thoughtfully even as his heart hammered in his chest. He bit into his apple again. Noka popped another orange segment in his mouth.

"But wouldn't Overlord Goodman get blamed?"

"Yes, dear boy! You've hit the nail on the head. This was one of our biggest problems." Noka put a friendly hand on Bear's shoulder. "How to get the Overlord out of Calleston without also getting him executed? All the misfortune had to seem beyond his control. The plan started simply. Launching speedweed seeds into the fields, for instance. We use an ingenious machine called a catapult to launch them over the walls at night."

The whistling noises overhead. The endless onslaught of speedweed that always grew back, however much they pulled…

"Sinsenn yields immediately diminished. That drew the Queen's attention. But that wasn't enough. You field workers were just too good! However much we planted, you just yanked it all out! We needed something more extreme. The blots have been Calleston's curse for centuries, but we needed them clamouring at our gates. That's why we started launching dead bodies off the walls. To attract more blots."

The object flying through the night air. The thud as it landed. The blot hunched over it, ripping it to shreds.

"You were feeding the blots," said Bear, trying to keep the shake out of his voice. "Feeding them … dead bodies?"

"Yes, I know. Not pleasant. But you soon find a great many number of things can be launched from a catapult. First, it was people who died naturally, but then there are only so many of those. We turned to criminals and, more recently, watchmen, especially the ones who knew too much. The blots come running like a dog at dinner time. I find the whole thing disgusting."

Bear felt sick. All the screams that soared above Cobbleside… How stupid to assume they were witchwork, to let that fear him from asking questions.

"The watchmen are different," he said. "More violent. Why?"

"Oh, you noticed?" said Noka. "How fun! Well, the Overlord has been trying to convince Queen Meléna to resettle the Roofside families in the Free City. But the Free City is a dangerous place, Bear. Witchwork, assassinations and treachery are a daily occurrence. Our watchmen weren't fit to protect us against the powerful families that hold sway there."

They walked through a gate into a wooded area; rabbits ran ahead of their feet.

"The Overlord has a testing room in the tower. In there, he's worked tirelessly on a new brew, a brew that builds physical strength in our watchmen, but, more importantly, a brew that counters the effects of truthwine."

Noka looked at Bear with a proud smile. Bear was stunned. If there was a counter to truthwine ... Megg could have been saved.

"A protection from it? How?"

"After much trial and error, he has created a new elixir using the very thing that counters sinsenn in the fields... Speedweed."

Bear gasped. It was so simple: speedweed destroyed sinsenn. He remembered the bowl of speedweed seeds on the Overlord's desk. It changed everything.

"So the Overlord was behind the attempted assassination of Queen Meléna? And the watchman lied?"

Noka smiled.

"No, dear boy. No. The watchman didn't lie. The speedweed brew does not block the truth-telling effects of truthwine. The new brew only reverses the calming nature of sinsenn – all that joyous undirected cheerfulness?

It turns it to rage. I believe that is part of what gives the watchmen their unnatural strength. But even if Overlord Goodman succeeds in finding a defence against truthwine, he would not dare order her assassination. We have no idea who left the knife on the watchman's pillow, though we have a good idea where the aggression came from…"

Bear nodded in fascinated horror. He didn't bother smiling any more. Noka wouldn't have even noticed.

"Very clever."

"Not clever enough, so we moved to Plan B."

"Which was?"

"Bargain with the Queen. Make our escape, and leave Calleston to rot … I mean, ha-ha, to Meya."

Bear felt ill. "I can't believe it," he said. "He's leaving Calleston to the blots, just so he can escape?"

Noka held Bear's hand affectionately. "Yes, well, he and I together. But there you go. We realized the Queen would never let us leave unless Calleston had a ruler capable of protecting the sinsenn harvest, so we encouraged Meya to befriend the Queen and present herself as a suitable ruler."

"So he's abandoning his own daughter?"

"As far as I can tell, yes." Noka laughed.

"What's so funny?"

Bear looked up. Meya had appeared at the orchard entrance gate. She looked at them warily.

"Your father!" replied Noka. "I was just getting to know this one better. I very much recommend it." He patted Bear on the arm affectionately. "Right, I'd better get packing. Those bags aren't going to pack themselves."

Noka drifted dreamily out of the garden and back towards his quarters.

Meya watched him go. "Bags? What's he talking about? What's got into him?" She narrowed her hazel eyes at Bear suspiciously.

"Truthwine," said Bear.

"Right." Meya stared at him. "So what did you learn? And tell me the truth."

"All right," said Bear. "I will."

CHAPTER 31

"You're lying," Meya said sharply. "You're a liar."

Bear opened the bag and pulled out an orange. He squeezed it and the dark juices that flowed out made her eyes go wide.

"Truthwine. From the golden barrel in the key room. I soaked the oranges myself."

Meya's eyes widened. Then she shook her head.

"Lies!" Meya's face was contorted in fury as she screamed at him. "My father fought for you all down in Cobbleside – and this is how you repay him? With these lies? He would never let his people suffer and starve needlessly … and he would never just abandon me."

"Meya, Noka drank truthwine. They weren't my words, they were his. I'm so sorry," he said. He felt truly sorry for her as he watched her pace back and forth along the path, ringing her hands. He knew what she was feeling, how her world was crumbling. His world had crumbled too. He reached out, put a hand on her arm.

"Get off me!" she screamed, slapping his hand away. "It's not true! None of it! Not the blots, or the stupid potion in the tower, none of it! This is all just lies!" said Meya bitterly.

"Then why is Noka packing his bags?"

Meya kept pacing, ignoring what he'd said completely. "You hate us up here, and you dream up these stupid fictions so you don't have to feel so bad about the squalor you live in! You'll find any way you can to tear us down and claim Roofside for your own!"

Bear took a few steps back. He tried not to take her words personally. He held out an orange to her.

"Give one to him, Meya. Just give him one and ask him."

She slapped the orange out of his hand. It fell to the ground and rolled away.

"How dare you," she hissed. "I got you those oranges as a present! To make you feel more at home, because ... because I cared about you. And I thought for a second that maybe you cared about me. But obviously ... you're just ... you're floorborn!" She laughed suddenly, wildly. "And you're a *Feyatung*'s son!"

Bear recoiled as if he'd been slapped.

Immediately, the part of him that had been trying to reach out to her withdrew. It transformed, hardened into rock. And from behind that wall he could speak without passion.

Meya saw the change. Bear didn't care.

"I don't care what you believe, Meya. Being on Roofside means you get to believe whatever makes you happy. And if calling me ... *that* ... makes you feel better, then go ahead. But make no mistake: you live up here on the backs of the people below you. It's us that are keeping your world afloat. And, once you've squeezed us too hard, it'll be you who has further to fall."

Meya's eyes flashed with a mix of fury and disbelief. They flitted between his eyes, from one to the other, back and forth. She looked as if something inside her was breaking.

But he couldn't be the one to fix her.

He walked away.

The Queen sighed with relief as her boat entered Cut Mountain Passage.

Her visit to the wretched town was over at last. She hoped not to have to come back for another ten years at least.

Still, she'd got what she came for – a bountiful harvest, another witch rooted out and sinsenn production returned to acceptable levels. She smiled at the bow of the boat weighed down by sacks and sacks of the dried red leaves.

"Morning brew, Your Majesty?" said Afena, placing a cup of ruby liquid beside her.

Queen Meléna waved her away and began pulling at a loose thread on her sleeve.

There was just one thing bothering her – the Fennex boy, living freely in Calleston. How had a Fennex freed itself? She'd make sure the pup was captured long before winter came anew.

She snapped the thread off and threw it overboard, watching as it floated down into the dark waters.

32

Bear floated aimlessly through Cobbleside. He felt lightheaded, unmoored.

It was a busy night, people rushing around here and there, and he had no idea where he was going. The Overlord had seemed so kind, so warm; now the very thought of him made Bear angry, angry at how selfish and how weak a man could be. How stupid Bear was not to have seen it. He hadn't seen anything.

He didn't know what to do. The truth was so overwhelming and so unbelievable. Who should he tell? Who could do anything about it?

He drifted through the crowds like a ghost. The town looked exactly the same as it always had; the beautiful Calleston sunset beginning, labourers returning home to their families, posties whizzing overhead on their last jobs of the day.

Bear watched men and women stand at their doors, smoking their pipes happily, chasing their squealing children into dark little houses. He wondered how happy they would be without their cups and their pipes.

He walked past Megg's house and stopped at the window. The girls sat on the floor quietly while Elma fixed their hair. Her hands moved steadily. Her eyes stared at the wall.

Bear headed for Main Gate. He wanted to see the sky and the fields. Maybe there he'd be able to think.

He strolled along the canal, past the entrance to the docks. And then, emerging from a tunnel, he saw a black boat nestled under a stone bridge up ahead.

He slowed as he approached. The white-haired woman was standing on the deck.

"I think it's time you came inside, young man. Don't you?"

She disappeared through the small double doors, leaving them ajar.

Bear moved as if in a dream, stepping up uneasily on to the creaking ship. Sitting on the guardrail were the owl and the raven. They regarded him with curiosity. He ducked his head below the boat's wooden doors, passed through a heavy curtain and found himself in one of the most cluttered little living spaces he had ever seen.

He stood at the top of the steps and peered down. Inside was a smattering of cushioned chairs and rickety tables. Haphazard shelves covered the wooden walls, packed with books, bowls, lamps and knick-knacks. In the middle of the cabin was a single stool, below a glittering glass dome through which he could see the sky.

The warm light of sunset streamed through the

multicoloured glass. The effect on the chair below was beautiful, magical even.

"Why don't you take a seat, young man? We can get started without the other two."

"Get started?"

The woman began rattling around in the back of the room. She opened a shabby wardrobe that was full of fur coats. She pulled them aside and produced a shiny copper kettle.

"Yes, dear boy. We have plenty to discuss, but we must set sail tonight, with or without you. So you have a decision to make."

Bear took a step down the stairs into the chaotic room. The narrow passageway creaked as he made his way down.

"Mind your head on the—"

Bear's head smacked painfully into the sharp edge of an overhead beam.

"Ouch!"

The woman hadn't even turned round. He rubbed his forehead vigorously.

"How did you know I was about to—?"

"Low beam. Tall boy. Creaky floor."

She plonked the kettle on to a stove in the corner.

"Is that ruby brew?" Bear asked hopefully. It had been a tiring day.

She frowned at him.

"Better that you stay sharp, young man. You'll need all

your faculties tonight. Time is of the essence. Why don't you sit on that stool over there and we can come to an understanding?"

There was a spark of light and a flame flickered to life on the stove. Bear sat on the stool and looked up at the little domed ceiling, marvelling at the beautiful curiosity. The slivers of glass were impossibly small and glittered like jewels. They formed the shape of a beautiful twelve-pointed star.

"First let's decide if we need you. Then, we'll see if you need us." The woman held her hand out. "Maggie's the name, by the way, among others."

"Bear," said Bear, and he shook her hand.

"Do you have any questions, Bear, before we begin?"

He looked around the room. He looked at Maggie. He had a thousand questions. He began with the simplest.

"Are you a … are you some sort of…"

"Out with it, Bear – we don't have all night."

"Witch?"

She cocked her head to one side. "Some people would name me as such, yes. I think if you came to know me well, you would too. Though I hope recent events have opened your mind in some ways … to people like me?"

Bear nodded. He'd asked a question he already knew the answer to. Maggie waited for him to carry on. She had a strong nose and an even stronger brow, but she looked at him with a softness that helped him to open up.

"And was Megg … my friend Megg, was she…?" He

felt his nose tingle and stopped talking before tears came to his eyes.

"Had you never suspected?" Maggie asked. "There are subtle ways to tell, some not so subtle once you know what to look out for."

"Is that why you came here? Did you want to make Megg join your … witch gang?"

Maggie laughed loudly. There was a thumping from the floor below. She stomped back down in return.

"We're here for many reasons, my dear boy. But we did take a particular interest in your friend Megg, yes."

Bear frowned. "You followed me and Felix that night, when the two of us climbed up to Roofside, didn't you? You made that noise like thunder and lit up the tunnel."

Maggie fixed Bear with an inquisitive look. The kettle began to hiss quietly on the stove. "We did follow you, yes, but only through the eyes of an owl. The witch you saw in the dark was … not one of my sisters. She is a figure of some interest to us, and some concern."

"But why follow us?"

She removed her cloak, and hung it on a hook.

"We followed you that night because of the actions of your Fennex friend. He's quite the little illusionist that one."

"What?" gasped Bear. "Felix has powers too?"

Maggie wiped her hands on her skirt and tutted in disapproval.

"Everyone has powers, Bear. Fish breathe underwater. Birds fly. It's all a matter of degrees. Fennex have their own."

Bear was confused.

"There is great power in many an unsuspecting corner of this Queendom. Now, are we touching on a connection that you are ready to make? What am I getting at, Bear?"

Bear racked his brain.

"Oh dear," said Maggie. "So, you're one of those. Needs to take their time. Never mind! The slower path is better taken, I hear!"

Maggie dragged aside a large plant pot placed in front of a bookshelf. On the floor where the pot had rested was a handle. Maggie yanked it and a second stool rose up out of a hole in the floor identical to the one that Bear sat on. She placed her stool next to his, then kicked the plant pot into the hole where it fitted snugly.

As Maggie sat down, she found herself a good foot shorter than Bear. She clicked her fingers and the seat of her stool began spinning. She held on tight as her short legs spun round and round, spiralling upwards until she was eye to eye with him.

She looked a bit pale when the stool came to a stop.

"I need to start adjusting this thing before I sit on it."

Bear smiled.

"Cora, my dear!" Maggie shouted. "Get ready!"

A screech sounded from outside. The quiet rushing of the kettle grew louder.

"Bear, I want you to know that while you are here, I will never force you to do anything you don't want to do. You are free to leave at any time. I only ask that you keep an open mind. Do you understand?"

"Yes."

"Good. Now, you have lived in Cobbleside your whole life, correct?"

"Yes."

"I imagine you've spent much of your life wondering how different, how strange, maybe how scary things might be in other places, no?"

He nodded.

"Well, let me reassure you that you are absolutely correct in one sense – those sorts of places do exist. However! You must hold one thing clear in your mind. There are many people, across the other towns and cities of the realm, who would be amazed and terrified of *your* world."

She poked him in the chest.

"Your world. Where the people flee behind a wall at dusk to escape the predators of the night. Where the houses are stacked higher and tighter than any palace in the Queendom. Where, by day, the fields burst with blood red flowers, in the blink of an eye."

Bear suddenly felt a sense of wonder about Calleston he had never felt before.

"And how do you grow those flowers so fast, Bear?"

Bear looked deep into her eyes; her question was simple.

"How do you grow those flowers so fast, Bear?"

She peered at him, willing him on.

"By ... enlacing with them." he offered.

"And what is enlacing?"

She didn't blink.

"Magic," he said.

She smiled wide.

"There it is."

She placed an affectionate hand on his cheek and gave him a look that Bear couldn't decipher.

"I was much older than you when I made the connection, boy. But magic springs up from every corner of this land, in all kinds of ways."

"So … my mother *was* a witch."

Maggie looked at Bear with sympathy. "Yes, child, and all you sinsenn growers have some talent. Whether you know it for what it is or not… I must confess I knew your mother, long before she came here…"

Bear gawped at the small woman before him.

"We had no idea how sinsenn was made. She discovered Calleston in a time when we thought magic would be eliminated. I see now the very notion is impossible, no matter how Queen Meléna and the Free City try to stamp it out, or, rather, twist it, and use it for their own purposes." Maggie's brow furrowed. "Don't get me started on that girl."

She shook her head. "Here in Calleston, you have channelled your powers into your fields. From a scorched earth, still a hundred flowers will blossom."

"So … I'm a witch?" Bear said, looking up at her.

She nodded.

"So Felix has a little bit of magic in him? He grew a

little bloom at practice."

Maggie tutted again.

"You young men really need to learn how to talk to each other... The Fennex boy can't enlace a lick – no Fennex can. That boy has never grown a flower in his life, and he never will."

Bear frowned. Maggie sighed.

"Fennex have a great illusionary magic, Bear. Never a magic that you can touch, but one that you can see. That little red flower you saw was one of his conjurings! A rather good one. The poor boy has spent days on end camouflaging you and your friends from watchmen!"

Bear's jaw dropped wide open.

Maggie laughed loudly again. There was another thump on the floor below. Maggie's feet dangled from her stool.

"My sisters are nothing if not impatient. Would you stamp on the floor, please, my dear? And make it a good one."

Bear stomped on the floor until Maggie signalled that he had done enough.

The rumble of the kettle grew louder.

"Some would call you a witch, Bear, yes. Some a *Feyatung*, some a wise man, others a do-iller. None of those changes who you are, only how they see you."

Bear nodded. So he was a witch. Like his mother, like Megg. One thing was still troubling him.

"But how did I lie to the Queen's Voice? I swore under truthwine that I'm not."

"You told him exactly what you believed to be true, Bear. You would have a different result now. Now, you – what do you call it? – *enlaced* with your friend, Megg, on the Field Day, no?"

Bear nodded.

"Excellent. Now I would like to guide you, if you like, and we can see how well you do with Cora."

The owl screeched from up on the roof.

"She does sound rather scary, but once you understand her you'll find she's a total sweetheart."

"Wait – what do you mean, with the bird? Will I be … enlaced with her?"

"Something like that. If you succeeded with Megg, an owl should be a piece of cake. Are you ready? I'm going to pop you right in with no messing about."

"I'm ready," said Bear, and he gripped his stool with both hands.

The rush of the bubbling kettle was the last thing Bear heard before he was yanked unceremoniously out of his body.

He felt a presence completely engulf him. It could only be Maggie. It was nothing like the tentative touch of Megg during Field Day. She had hesitatingly occupied a shared space with him. This felt as if he'd been dragged into a lake.

The lake became a waterfall. It carried him through a rushing passageway inside himself that he didn't know existed until he slipped through it. He was upside down and inside out and there was no boundary between where he ended and anything else began.

And then all the odd sensations became solid, and he found himself able to name things again. To see things again. His ears felt incredibly sensitive. As he turned his head from one side to the other, the sounds around him clarified.

No, the sounds around *them* clarified.

Hello? Bear said from inside their head.

There were three of them there. Bear, Maggie and the owl.

Her name is Cora, said Maggie. *She doesn't use many words.*

Hello, Cora.

Cora sent a welcome.

This is weird.

Cora and Maggie laughed. It made Bear laugh. They laughed silently together.

Cora left an empty space for Bear to fill. It was an invitation.

Why don't you show Cora your town, Bear? She knows Calleston well. But tonight she can see it with your eyes, while you see it through hers.

He tentatively entered the empty space Cora made. He turned their head from side to side. Cora flapped their wings; Bear felt her encouraging him to be assertive.

Bear screeched loudly. A bizarre, meaningless screech that was a mixture of different calls. Bear felt Cora's merriment flooding through their body and everyone laughed again.

Fly.

I'll leave you to it, said Maggie.

And then her presence was gone. Bear and Cora stretched out their wings to get a sense of things. The air was still. They shook out their feathers and then launched themself into the sky.

They rose above the boat, the water and the area called Cobbleside. Cora liked this town a lot; there were mice everywhere, and the desirable nesting spots were higher. They were excited to find an updraft.

The feeling of tension in their wings was magnificent. Bear marvelled at how the slightest movement directed them sideways, up or down. And everything looked crystal clear, even at dusk. Owl eyes were so much sharper than his own.

They scanned sections of the territory below, the forest, the fields. They couldn't help but look for targets. They found the breeze and soared up and up.

And Cora felt the joy of a first flight. It was her favourite.

They soared above roofside orchards, completely silent and unnoticed by the humans who wandered below them. They circled around the black tower that rose sharply above the rooftop grounds. They sailed under a bridge and shrieked joyfully in the cavernous space below. As they emerged, they saw the stars in their timeless arrangement. Bear had never known how endless the night sky truly was.

They swooped down among the twinkling nooks and crannies of Cobbleside and glided silently between the buildings. The town wall loomed ahead. It was dark now. Something caught their eye at the gate: someone was standing there. There was something familiar about them.

It was a moment before Bear realized: it was Meya. She stood on the walkway above the West Gate, gazing over the wall. The drawbridge was up at this hour. She was completely alone. Why? Why had she come down to Cobbleside?

Meya was looking down at the fields below, frozen.

They soared above her head and saw what she was looking at.

Blots.

More blots than Bear had ever seen. A crowd of writhing shadows, leaping on top of each other and clawing at a carcass.

Meya stood transfixed, watching them from the top of the gate. They flew closer, being careful to stay unnoticed. It didn't matter. Meya was mesmerized by the horrific picture below.

Tears ran down her cheeks. She stepped closer to the edge of the wall and watched the blots with a dead-eyed stare. One foot closer. And then the other.

A wave of fear pulsed through Bear and Cora.

Stop her, they thought.

They swooped down, screeching loudly. The noise and the violent battering of wings startled her and she stumbled back, tumbling away from the wall.

"*Feyatung!*" Meya screamed at the owl in fury.

Bear had never heard her use that word, or that tone. When they saw her face up close, they saw madness in her eyes, and blackness on her lips. A horrid realization hit them. She'd got inside the tower, she'd found the dark drink and she'd drunk it.

Meya leapt towards the winch lock by the gate. Whimpering, she yanked it. It was stiff. With an almighty scream, she got it moving. Bear and Cora watched in horror as the drawbridge started to fall.

Meya Omega opened the town gates.

The blots' heads snapped up from the carcass as one.

33

Bear was falling, falling back through the waterfall in their head until he found himself sitting on the stool in the little black boat.

Maggie held a steaming cup of tea. "When you're ready, have a sip of this. It'll help you readjust."

"B-blots," Bear stammered. "Meya opened the gates and let blots into the town."

Maggie stared at him. Then she grabbed him by the scruff of the neck and dragged him through the narrowboat, out through the red curtain and into the cold night air.

There was no panic in the street. Everything was calm and ordinary.

"How many?" she asked as she whipped the red curtain closed behind her.

"I ... uh, thirty? Maybe forty. A swarm."

A group of boys were wandering along the canal.

"Get inside, lads!" Bear shouted. "The West Gate is open! Blots heading for the town."

They stopped in their tracks and frowned at him. But they didn't run. Bear realized they didn't believe him.

"Run, Bear!" Maggie urged. "Lead me to the gate."

Bear leapt off the boat and ran as fast as he could across the cobbles into the town.

"Lock your doors!" he shouted as he ran. "Blots! Blots in the street!"

"Liar!" shouted one of the boys in the group.

It was Cassius. Bear ignored him and continued screaming. The boys watched Bear and Maggie sprinting away in stunned silence. An owl screeched overhead.

"Follow Cora!" shouted Maggie.

They followed her towards West Gate, Bear still shouting warnings at anyone who would listen. Cobblesiders leapt from their doorways and slammed them shut, or ran upstairs to the safer levels, shouting "Blots!" as they went. A wave of sickening rot hit Bear's nose as they turned a corner, and Bear saw a nightmare.

Blots were racing down Main Street.

"Send for watchmen!" a man screamed as he fled past.

In the distance, Bear saw a group of blots squatted over a body, eating their fill.

"Bear!" cried a voice.

It was Dorloc Odittany. He ran up the street alongside an older woman, dodging under bedsheets that hung from a washing line. Blots darted through the shadows behind them. Bear sprinted towards them and was horrified to see a blot emerge at Doc's back.

Maggie held out her hands and grunted heavily. Suddenly a large empty handcart rose into the air. It flew towards the blots, smashing into them and knocking them over like skittles. The old woman hobbled to safety.

The streets were slick with blood and Bear almost slipped and fell when he found himself pulled to his feet by strong hands. It was Petal.

"Head to Main Market!" she said. "We need to get to higher ground, and a golden gate!"

There were bodies everywhere, blot and human alike, as they ran through the street. Cobblesiders raced up the stairwells, slamming doors as blots crawled upwards after them.

Bear heard a loud whooshing noise from behind and looked over his shoulder. Maggie was swirling her hands over her head and was suddenly surrounded by a ferocious wind just as a snarling blot dived from an upper balcony. Mid jump, a blanket from a washing line engulfed it, wrapping it into a tight bundle as it hit the cobbles. Maggie squeezed her fists until they shook. The bed sheet tightened and tightened until there was a sickening crunch and the blot lay still. They passed the Dodgy Gut tavern just as a window broke and blots poured into the candlelit building. Screams burst from inside.

They ran on towards Main Market.

"Get up here!" shouted a voice Bear knew.

It was the drummers, Grace and Lutch. Equipped with bows, they stood together on a footbridge and fired arrows down at the shadows crawling the streets. Over and over they fired at the putrid creatures.

"We need watchmen, Bear!" shouted Lutch. "Where are they?"

And then, from the shadows, a blot tore across the bridge and launched itself on to Grace. She gasped as it sank its teeth into her neck and began eating before she'd even hit the floor.

Lutch screamed and drew a large knife; he drove it into the blot over and over.

"Burna!" cried Petal, as Burna came skidding around the corner, a giant cleaver in one hand, a dark severed claw in the other.

"Main market! Come on!"

They sprinted round the corner and burst into the square, not daring to look behind them. It was a battle scene. The market was littered with bodies, while blots hunted in the shadows. They crawled through broken windows, and scrabbled through holes in the rotten wooden doors on the lower levels. They chased anything that moved.

The town bell was ringing, and screams rang out across the market. Bear heard the postal track whirring and saw Olenta and the other posties grabbing people from the street and transporting them to the upper levels.

A crowd had gathered outside the golden gate.

"Open the gates!" Olenta screamed, scooping a young girl out of harm's way.

But Roofside remained locked. A watchman stood back, bow and arrow in hand, ignoring the mass of Cobblesiders outside.

Cusht bellowed at the resolute watchmen, but he ignored them.

"Uncle Jim!" shouted Bear. Uncle Jim was outside the gates. He held a small barrel over his arm as a makeshift shield. His hook dripped black with blood. A blot was hurtling towards him. It jerked back suddenly as a whip swung tight round its neck. Bear looked up. From a footbridge above, the Whip was yanking the blot into the air. Its neck crunched loudly and it hung, twitching.

"Get back into your houses!" screamed the Whip.

"They're not safe!" shouted Bear

"Open the gates!" Olenta screamed again.

"Burna!"

Bear spun and saw Petal. She was standing over Burna, who was hacking at a dead blot with her knife. Her arms were bleeding. She was covered in bites.

"Burna, love," Petal said again, quieter this time.

Burna looked at Petal, then down at her arms and chest; black veins snaked across her skin.

"Blotson," she cursed. "I got him, though, didn't I?"

She flashed Petal a weak smile just as a giant shadow reared up behind her and pounced. Too late, Maggie sent a sharp piece of wood into the blot's skull. Petal flew to Burna's side, gathering her in her arms.

"Somebody open the gates!" screamed Cassius over the sound of the tolling bell as he and his gang raced up the steps to Roofside.

There was the sound of smashing glass from higher

up the tiers and new screams joined the night. The gates didn't open but watchmen's arrows rained down on Main Market.

There was the sound of barking and a creature whizzed by. It was Meya's dog, Percy. He streaked past, barking in terror as a pair of blots chased after him, blood dripping from their jaws. More blots began to join the first two, attracted by his frenzied bounding across the square and his furious barking.

A blot collapsed at Bear's feet, its head full of arrows.

As the growing pack of blots pursued the speedy little dog, the watchmen had better success picking them off. More and more blots fell.

"Percy!"

Bear heard the cry from the roof. He looked up and his blood turned cold. There was Meya, on the Overlord's balcony. Her father and Noka and a group of other Roofsiders were collected there, looking down at the nightmare unfolding in the square.

"They're up there!" shouted Bear.

"Have mercy! Open the damn gates!"

"Open the gates! Open the gates!"

The cries grew louder and louder as the crowd gathered.

Watchmen fired arrows from every vantage point they could, picking the last of the blots off, little by little. But they would not open the gates.

Eventually, the last blot fell in a heap in the middle of the square, and Percy darted up a set of stairs.

The town bell stopped ringing and Calleston was quiet. Petal held Burna's lifeless body to her chest and rocked it back and forth. One by one, the remaining doors around Main Market opened, and people emerged from their homes.

And then from their doorway Rose appeared with her husband and young sons. She was carrying little Poppy in her arms. She wore a white dress embroidered by red flowers and stained by the blood that seeped through her clothes. Rose wailed loudly into the night.

A horrible animal wail of despair.

Bear gazed up at the Overlord's platform where Meya stared down in horror.

"Shame on you!" Olenta shouted to the watchmen at the golden gate. "Shame on you!"

The cries around the market got louder and more insistent.

"Shame on you!" Petal shouted from the floor.

"Shame on you!" shouted Doc from a footbridge. He lay on the ground, wounded, stroking Percy.

People began shouting from their windows and doors and the Overlord raced to the edge of the balcony. He raised his hands.

"Please! Let us not turn on each other in these dark times. We must all do better. We must take care of one another—"

"I saw you, Meya!" shouted Bear. "It was Meya who let the blots in! And you −" he turned to the Overlord − "I know what you've been sending out into those fields!"

"Lies!" roared the Overlord. "These are the untruths of a mad man! Watchmen! Bring him to me!"

"You leave him alone!" Cusht bellowed at the gate.

A watchman raced to the golden gate and began unlocking it.

"Bear!" It was Aber's voice.

His father stood at the golden gate, clothes and hair freshly washed. His arms were wrapped through the bars, keeping the gate shut.

"Run!" he shouted.

Watchmen tried to prise Aber's arms from the gate, but he would not be moved.

"She opened the gate," shouted Bear, "and he's been launching bodies over the walls into the fields for years! He's been feeding Cobblesiders to the blots! That's why the blots have got worse!"

There was a ripple of shock that passed through the people gathered at the gate. There was a ripple on Roofside too.

"It's true!" the Whip shouted up from a stairwell. "I have seen the catapult on that tower with my own eyes. With all the bodies you have sent into the fields, I'm surprised the fields aren't red with blood!"

"You wanted the blots to get worse! You want Calleston in ruins so you can bargain for your own freedom!" continued Bear. "But you failed! Me and Megg brought the bloom back." Bear remembered enlacing with Megg and his heart quickened. He suddenly pictured her face, her hair, and he wanted to put his arms around her. He thought it impossible but in that moment he had hope, or was it a premonition, of meeting her again, touching her small shoulders, and telling her how he felt. "Megg Ovelma!" he shouted. "The greatest grower this town ever saw … and you let them kill her!" Bear's voice cracked. "All the people that have suffered! All that death! While you sit up there and pretend to care!"

"These can only be the dark fantasies of the *Feyatung*!" the Overlord boomed. "*Feyatung*, both of them, spewing poisonous lies! Watchmen – kill them!"

"This way!" hissed a voice from the dark.

Old Fern had concealed herself in the lip of an alleyway, a shawl around her head. She beckoned for Bear to follow her.

Bear stared at the madness that surrounded him. The Whip leapt from the stairwell and ran. Rose sobbed loudly, holding Poppy in the blood-soaked white dress. Petal hugged Burna's body like a rag doll. On the roof, Bear's eyes found Meya. Her lips were still stained dark, but her face was drained of colour.

"Bear, run!" Aber shouted from behind the golden gate. "Go!"

"Run, fool!" hissed the Whip and he darted past Old Fern into the alleyway.

And then Bear heard his father scream. He saw a sword burst through Aber's chest, through his fresh white shirt. Uncle Jim roared and raced towards his brother. Aber wailed in agony as the watchmen wrenched him from the golden bars at last, heaved it open and hurtled out of the gate.

"Go!" was the last word Bear heard from his father's mouth before he collapsed into the crowd.

"You heard him, Bear! Follow me!" shouted Maggie as she swooped after Old Fern into the shadowy passage.

The watchmen raced down the stairs towards the square. Bear put one foot in front of the other, stumbling on. His limbs were wooden, as if he were in a dream.

"Faster, boy! Or they'll 'ave you!" a woman called down from a balcony.

"I've got you, Bear," said a voice, and Bear felt himself pulled off his feet. Suddenly, Petal was carrying him through the square. She was strong, and she ran much faster than he would have guessed possible. The first few watchmen poured down the passageway after them, swords in hand.

"Don't let the *Feyatung* escape!" Overlord Goodman screamed.

But his voice was drowned out by something else. Down in the market, Cobblesiders bellowed as they swarmed to meet the bulk of the guards, makeshift weapons in hand. Skirmishes broke out across the square. The townsfolk grouped together and began pushing the watchmen back, jeering.

"You leave him be!"

"Try it, Blotson! This has gone too far!"

"Shame on you all!"

Bear clung on to Petal's shoulders as they flew down the alleyway and escaped into the shadows. He couldn't believe that the townsfolk were protecting him. He closed his eyes as Petal ran, listening to her breathing.

He remembered Meya on the wall, opening the gate to the blots. He heard her voice in his head: *Floorborn scum.*

And then he thought of something. He focused on Petal's tireless breaths.

He listened to her heartbeat.

Dum DUM.

Dum DUM.

Dum DUM.

Magic. It had been there all along.

He let his mind flow inwards and outwards. And soon he was soaring over the cobbles and Calleston's streets, until he found who he was looking for. With gentle insistence, he let his mind sink into theirs until the pair were enlaced.

Bear made a thought clear in their mind, and suddenly Percy was racing as fast as his paws could carry him. He zipped easily across footbridges and up the stairs, dodging the footsteps of people and streaking through the bars of the golden gate. Percy pounded his paws into the ground.

"He's passed out!"

Bear heard Petal's voice from somewhere far away.

Percy raced through the corridor to the Overlord's balcony. He skidded round the corner, and there he saw her. His mother. Meya.

Bear brought a new thought to their mind, an image: Meya opening the gate to the horde of blots, welcoming them to hunt the townsfolk as if they were prey.

Percy growled low in his throat, his teeth bared.

Meya looked confused. "Percy...?"

He barked a furious warning.

"Percy, no!" And then the connection was suddenly severed.

Bear's eyes snapped open and he was being carried by Petal once again.

"Enough of that!" shouted Maggie over her shoulder. "You need to save your strength."

Petal raced on. Bear found himself smiling darkly as he looked over her shoulder.

They were by a dark corner of the canal now. The owl, Cora, hooted as she glided above them.

"Where are we going?" called the Whip.

"Almost there," said Maggie cheerfully.

When they came to the black narrowboat moored in the shadows, Petal lowered Bear to his feet.

"Is this a joke?" said the Whip. "We can't escape in this feckless rust bucket."

"You watch your mouth, watchman," snapped Old Fern.

"You're welcome to walk," Maggie said, and she stepped on to the boat and pulled back the red curtain, revealing a cavernous room below. Bear, Petal and the Whip gasped at the impossible vision, the grand staircase disappearing far beyond the boat's natural proportions.

"Shameless witchwork!" The Whip grinned widely at Maggie. "That's more like it."

He strutted inside without hesitation.

Maggie turned to Bear and Petal. "And what about you two? I'll be frank – things'll be as dangerous with us, as bad or worse than they are here in Calleston." She held her hand out. "Are you ready to leave? Knowing you might never come back?"

Petal didn't have to think. She nodded grimly and took Maggie's hand, stepping on to the boat. The raven cawed loudly from its perch.

"Bear?" said Maggie.

Bear hesitated. "I don't have papers."

"Papers we can handle. Soldiers are a little more difficult…"

Watchmen's shouts started coming closer, reverberating down the alleyway.

It was time to go. Old Fern pulled Bear into a tight hug, then shook Maggie's hand, saying "Go safely."

"And you," Maggie replied.

She stepped onto the narrowboat and disappeared through the red curtain.

"You be careful with this lot," said Old Fern as she ushered Bear on to the black boat.

Almost immediately, it began to glide away from its mooring. Old Fern hurried back the way they'd come. Bear caught sight of Maggie standing on the bow, next to the Fennex woman and the lady in the veil, their eyes fixed ahead. He edged down to join them at the bow, and they all looked out over the water and at the dark shapes of Calleston passing by.

"I'll handle the gates. You make sure we aren't seen," said Maggie.

The Fennex woman nodded. Maggie noticed Bear and beckoned him closer.

"A certain little birdie tells me that your friend is alive and well."

Bear's heart leapt. He felt his ears ringing.

"M–Megg? How? I–I thought she—" His voice cracked. He felt a great lurch in his heart. He couldn't believe it. She was alive. Megg was alive.

"No," said the woman in the veil.

Bear was confused.

Maggie shot the woman an irritated look and turned to Bear, her face softening in sympathy.

"Forgive me, my dear. Not the girl. I'm afraid the girl is gone. The way we all go. And there's no way of changing that. I meant your Fennex friend; he made it through Cut Mountain safely. And he's lucky beyond belief to have done so."

Bear blinked rapidly and lowered his head, nodding. He was an idiot. He felt the great lurch in his heart sink and twist back into something heavy. Felix. He would go and join Felix. Maggie put a hand on his shoulder.

"Dearie, right now we're following Queen Meléna's movements. We mean to rescue that poor creature from that cage of hers. But, once we're done, I'll do everything in my power to see if we can … find him."

The women shared a look. Bear took a deep breath. He avoided their eyes.

"So if I help you with the witch, you'll help me find Felix?"

Maggie nodded. "That sounds like a fair deal to me, Bear. But, until then, there are a few things I think I should be teaching you."

She held out her hand and a large red sinsenn flower appeared, spinning slowly above her palm. Bear smiled. He wondered if there was any ruby brew down on the boat.

Maggie smiled back, and then the flower was suddenly engulfed in a bright orange flame. It curled over the petals, crackling and burning brightly until there was nothing left but ash.

"Lesson one," said Maggie.

34

She walked out on to the balcony where he stood chewing on an orange. Her hands shook with anger. Or was it fear? She couldn't tell any more.

"How do I look, Father?" Meya asked.

He gasped when he saw her.

"You look terrible, my dear! The cuts go far deeper than I expected; I fear your face is quite ruined."

He smiled glassily as he spoke. Meya glowered at him. She knew he was telling her the absolute truth. Red juice stained the corners of his mouth. It almost looked like blood. Bear's version of a blood orange had swept away all of her father's carefully constructed walls.

After Percy had been locked away in a room, Meya's face had been stitched up. All the floorborn had been forced back into their homes. Only then had she learned of Bear's escape. He'd made it out of Calleston – and in more ways than one, he had ruined her life. She suddenly recalled the dream she'd had about him: Bear's body lying broken among piles of bleached bones. And then she laughed for the first time that night.

"You laugh, Meya, but it looks frightful." Her father's smile faded and a vague curiosity coloured his face. He took a closer look at her. "There's something else. You look … different, worse, somehow… Is there something wrong?"

She glanced down at her hands and held on to the wave of unrelenting fury. It boiled inside her, begging to be released. She wondered how long her father's dark brew would make her feel like this. She wasn't entirely sure if it repulsed or delighted her. She made sure to keep any trace of it out of her voice, not that it mattered now.

"I think I'm just tired, Father. I've been having nightmares again. Like that one I used to have about Mother falling off a building. I've been having them about lots of people."

The Overlord frowned as though he was trying to remember something, or work something out.

"But … she didn't fall off the balcony, did she, Father?"

"No."

"You pushed her. Didn't you?"

The Overlord's smile was one of dreamy surprise.

"Yes, my dear, I did. She was adamant that we accept our burden. Spend year after year in this midden heap growing sinsenn for a tyrant. She was beautiful, Meya, like you used to be, but she was a stupid woman."

He frowned, then said, "How did you come to know that? I've never told a soul."

Meya sighed. She really had hoped that she had been wrong.

"I didn't know. Not until you told me. In a way, you've confirmed all my nightmares at once. Only … I suppose they're not nightmares."

She placed her hands on his shoulder and pushed him mightily over the railing.

"They're premonitions."

ACKNOWLEDGEMENTS

Thank you, Damien, a million times. Thank you for nudging me down scary new avenues (and always trying to make sure I don't get mugged in these scary new avenues). Succeed or fail, we prevail. Win or lose…

Oscar, I marvel at how satisfyingly the three of us have clicked. Thank you for your expertise, the balance you bring, and the fun. It's been a proper dream.

Yas, thank you for yanking Blood Flowers out of a dream and warmly welcoming me into Scholastic (just before you slipped out of the back door) – the ULTIMATE parting gift, and I won't ever not be grateful. Ever.

Polly, thank you so much. You just get it. Blood Flowers and I are so lucky to have you, and I'm looking forward to continuing what I hope is an extremely long journey. (And if you pull a Yas, I'm calling my manager.)

Harriet, the mental and (let's be honest) physical labour you have endured is beyond thanks! Thank you.

Lauren, you are saved in my contacts as "Big Boss Scholastic". Thank you for making that nickname genius in how misleading it is. You're just effortlessly supportive and I'm really grateful about that.

Gen and Lily, thank you for your keen eye and for keeping me company in the margins. What a magical experience to spend so much time together entirely in our heads.

Katt, thank you for the awesome cover artwork, and Beth for the amazing design. Thank you to Olivia and Wendy for your desk-editing expertise.

Sheila and everyone at Scholastic, for a friendly welcome – thanks, babes.

Without being too self-satisfied, thank you to supporters old, very old and new (through the various chapters of life). I'm a very lucky man, and I feel that strongly – much love to you all.

Mum, you made five quite odd children, all weird in their own way, and we are happy exploring our lives because you think that whatever we choose is OK. We adore you. Thank you.

Dad, reading the fantasy books you shared with me hardwired me to believe this world can be better. I just won't ever believe otherwise. Aside from those grandiose beliefs, I'll always love popping into a tavern and chatting the best nonsense with you. Thank you, Dad.

Kaitlyn, Isaac, Freddie, Jacob, Lois (and whoever is to come) – I can't wait until you know how much I love you. It will hit you one day, and you will know me then in a new way. Thank you for all your time. I won't ever get enough.

© Eva Pentel

Singer/songwriter **Jay McGuiness** is best known as a member of the international chart-topping boyband The Wanted. He won the thirteenth series of BBC's *Strictly Come Dancing*, and in recent years has forged a successful career as an actor, with several leading roles in the West End to his name. Jay is an avid reader and his writing has been influenced by authors such as Philip Pullman, C. S. Lewis and Lauren Beukes. *Blood Flowers* is his first novel.